TIME STOOD
STILL

BETTE PRATT

WESTBOW
PRESS®
A DIVISION OF THOMAS NELSON
& ZONDERVAN

WestBow Press books may be ordered through booksellers or by contacting:

WestBow Press
A Division of Thomas Nelson & Zondervan
1663 Liberty Drive
Bloomington, IN 47403
www.westbowpress.com
844-714-3454

Scripture quotations taken from The Holy Bible, New International Version® NIV® Copyright © 1973 1978 1984 2011 by Biblica, Inc. TM. Used by permission. All rights reserved worldwide.

ISBN: 978-1-6642-2125-3 (sc)
ISBN: 978-1-6642-2127-7 (hc)
ISBN: 978-1-6642-2126-0 (e)

Library of Congress Control Number: 2021901337

Print information available on the last page.

WestBow Press rev. date: 02/02/2021

ONE

"MISTER, HERE, TAKE THIS."

In all the chaos, the rumblings, the gusts of hot, scorching wind, the flying debris, and the constantly shifting rubble under his feet Matt looked down to see where the little voice came from and discovered a small girl. His heart turned over at the sight. With all the dust and flying debris he could hardly make out her features. Her head couldn't possibly come above his waist, yet she stood on top of the rubble holding out a small, brightly colored picture to him. She had nothing covering her dark curls or her face and with all the smoke and debris, he was surprised she wasn't coughing her lungs out. She wore tennis shoes that at one time were probably white, but now were a dull gray. Her jeans and T-shirt may have started the day perky and bright but were now also a dull gray. The wind blew smoke, dust, and debris around her, engulfing her, blocking her from his vision several times, but still she held out that little picture to him.

He, a city fireman, wore a turnout coat, helmet, boots, a mask that was attached to an oxygen tank on his back, and goggles, and he held a long pickaxe. He shook his head, not to say 'no', really, but to clear his fogged brain - perhaps she was a mirage that would go away if he closed his eyes. For a reason he couldn't understand, the child was not intimidated by him at all, even though he towered over her. A great belch of air nearly knocked her over as more debris settled in another place. Instinctively, he reached out a hand to grab her so the wind gust wouldn't knock her over.

"Mister, please, you need this, real bad!" she exclaimed above the racket. She even shook the little paper for emphasis, and took a step closer to Matt, her face turned up to him, so sincere and pleading.

Just then, there was a great rumble and more walls tumbled down some distance away. The child was so intent on her mission that she hardly looked that way. Of course, as a fireman, Matt was well aware of all the sounds around them. His breath hitched a bit, knowing how close the roar was to where he and the child stood.

His heart began beating in double time. He knew the danger they were in and how vulnerable she was. Carefully, Matt placed his axe down on top of the rubble beside him, and squatted in front of the little girl, still very aware of where they were and completely tuned to the rumblings going on around them. He wiped his hand on his turnout coat, not really wiping anything off, just smearing the nasty stuff on his hand.

He yanked down the mask so he could speak to her. He held out his hand, and asked, "What's your name?" as he took the little piece of paper from her. Some how in all the dirt and grime floating around them, the little paper was nearly clean; the colors still vibrant and bold. He didn't take the time to analyze that.

"I'm Brandi. But Mister, you need to read that right now! It'll show you how to get to heaven!" she exclaimed, earnestly, as she put the paper into his large hand. As he took the small tract, he was aware of how tiny her white hand was in his.

His brain nearly laughed at him. *I should care about heaven when this is happening here on earth?* He'd heard somewhere about the sounds of hell; didn't what was around them right now sound just like that? With the rumblings, the earth moving under their feet, and the screams all around, he was sure that's what they were experiencing. He looked up from the tract into the child's trusting eyes; she was waiting for him to say something. "Yeah?" he asked cynically. "What makes you think so?"

Nodding her head, her curls bobbing around her smudged face, Brandi said, "'Cause it tells how Jesus loves us, no matter how big we are or how bad we are, and how Jesus died for us, so we can live with him forever in heaven!"

Heaven? Really? Matt swallowed. He was a big man, a fireman, and he stood over six feet tall. He wasn't afraid of anything; he'd been involved in putting out fires all over the city for several years, but as he watched these towers come crashing to the ground in a matter of minutes, and heard the thundering sounds of hundreds of stories of concrete and steel becoming rubble, and heard too the screams of hundreds, maybe thousands of people who would never take another breath, he had to admit fear was everywhere in his body. His mind was almost numb with it. The smoke and dust were so thick at times he could hardly see, let alone breathe, and some of it even penetrated his oxygen system. Incredulously, he looked at this child, no protection on her face or her body at all, urging him to take a piece of paper? *Heaven? Would he really go there? In this life?*

He looked down from her earnest face to the paper, reached for it, and slipped the little piece of paper, which he realized was folded in half, inside his black slicker to the pocket of his shirt. Maybe he'd read it sometime, or maybe toss it when he got back to his room. As soon as he pulled his hand from his shirt pocket, he reached out to the little girl. "Sweetheart, things are still falling! Who sent you out here to give out these things?"

Seemingly oblivious to all that was happening around them, she exclaimed, "Nobody! Mommy and some other ladies are back there somewhere." She waved her hand behind her, but didn't take her eyes off the fireman. "But Mister, I knew there was lots of people who needed to know about Jesus, so I came and here you are!"

Pointing to Matt's pocket, Brandi pleaded, "Mister, don't put that away! You need to read that paper *now*, really you do, *Right Now!*"

Yeah, here I am, here we are, we could die at any minute!

Scowling, Matt looked at the little girl; her face was smudged with the grime of the fallout. The dust, heavy with humidity, had settled on her lips giving them an un-natural color, and her eyelashes were caked with soot. He saw her rub her eyes twice already. She was a pretty child, but he needed to make sure she knew she was in the wrong place. He stood up and reached for her hand. He took a step, then looked down at her, hoping she would take the hint and take his hand.

He pointed ahead of them and said, "Brandi, there's a yellow tape strung up back there, can't you see it?" She nodded. "That means people aren't supposed to come this far, except people like me who work at putting out fires and rescuing hurt people. You need to go back and find that tape and get on the other side of it!"

Earnestly, she held out her hands, palms up, and said, "I know, but Mister, it's real important that you know you're going to heaven! Just suppose, Mister, that while you work here some building falls on you or some fire comes out at you and you can't get away. Will you go to heaven? You need to *know* that!"

Matt crouched down in front of the child and put his arm around her. "Brandi, you ask a hard question, but I'm not sure I'll go anywhere if some building falls on me." She was tiny, when he picked her up to carry her to the yellow tape, she weighed hardly anything. Really, how could such a small child have such a powerful impact? He started walking but after only taking two steps felt impelled to stop.

"Well, Mister, you need to read that paper! It'll tell you how you can know and be sure right now! I know that's true!" She squirmed in his arms, rocking back and forth, trying to get loose. "Mister, put me down! Give me that paper and I'll show you! You really can know, and you can know right now!"

Looking into the child's earnest eyes, his oxygen mask still around his neck and uselessly blowing oxygen at his neck, he said, "Brandi, I need to get you back to your mommy and behind that tape so you won't get hurt, and I need to get back so I can help rescue more people. If I'm going to heaven…" He didn't finish, as he was pretty sure he wasn't.

Shaking her head, almost in despair, she put her arms around his neck, looked him in the eye, and said, "No! No! Mister, it's much more important that you know you're going to heaven, right now! Really! I know you gotta rescue people, that's your job, but Mister, if you die while you rescue people or try to put out fires, you gotta know that you're gonna go to heaven! It's really, really important. Jesus says it's the most important decision you'll ever, ever make in all your life!"

Deciding to give it up, he moved to a large slab of concrete away from everyone and sat down with the child on his leg. Pulling the little paper from his pocket, he said, "Okay, Brandi, we'll sit right here and you show me."

A smile like he hadn't seen in a very long time, burst across Brandi's face, her teeth were white in her smudged face. "Oh, yes, Mister. I'll show you right now!" She sat on his knee, but she held her hand toward his pocket.

As the smoke and dust swirled around them, Matt pulled the little paper from his pocket. He held it between them and Brandi took it eagerly from him; squirming her bottom on his leg. Holding the paper open with one hand, she pointed the finger from her other hand to the beginning of a paragraph about half way down the page. She held it so he could read and said, "See, read this, Mister!"

Matt scowled through the fog of ash and dust, but had to wipe the dust off his goggles to see the words. After a very loud rumble when more rubble settled; he read to her, "'For God so loved the world, that he gave his one and only Son that whoever believes in him should not perish but have eternal life.'" (John 3:16) He stopped and looked at her.

Brandi was still holding the paper, but she was looking at him. Before he could read anything else on the paper, she asked, "Mister, what's your name?"

"Why should you know that?" He guessed it was okay to tell the child his name, but he couldn't see why it mattered.

"Oh, it's important, really! How can you know you're going to heaven if you don't tell me your name?"

Not quite sure how this reasoning worked, he said, "I'm Matt."

Lifting the tract up again and making sure her finger was again on the paragraph, she said, "Okay, Matt, read that part again, but everywhere it says world or whoever, you say 'Matt'. Come on, you can do that!"

Looking again at the child's earnest face, Matt lowered his eyes and very slowly, he began to read the simple verse again. "'For God so loved,' Matt, 'that he gave his one and only Son, that,' Matt, '(who) believes in him should not perish but have eternal life.'" By the time he finished reading those two lines, he was whispering.

Putting her finger into Matt's chest, she said, "See! That means you! Mister Matt, God gave His one and only Son for you!"

"Me?"

"Yeah!" she said, excitedly, "You can believe right now that God gave his Son, Jesus to die on that ugly cross for your sins so you can have eternal life! Eternal life means you can go to heaven and live with God and Jesus forever and ever! Isn't that super?"

"Yeah, it is, Brandi."

Still holding the tract, but letting her hand fall into her lap, she bowed her head and said, "Bow your head, Matt and tell God you want Jesus to take away all your sins and live in your heart so you can live in heaven with him forever! Really, Matt, that's all you gotta do! God hears you and He does the rest for you, because He loves you! He loves you a whole lot! More'n your mom even."

Feeling very foolish, bowing his head, there on the cement slab with other rescuers shouting and cursing around him, he murmured, "God, I'm a sinner, but Brandi here says if I believe that verse, You can make it so I'll go to heaven when I die. With all of this going on, I think I need to know that." He'd never said it before, but he knew others end a prayer with 'amen', so he said, "Amen."

Matt thought Brandi was going to clap her hands; instead, she brought her hands to his cheeks, and kissed him on the mouth. "You did it! You can go to heaven!"

The little tract fluttered to the ground when Brandi put her hands on Matt's cheeks. As he reached down for it, she scrambled off his knee and began running through the rubble back toward the yellow tape. As he looked for the tract, he pulled his mask up. Only a second later, with the tract in his hand; Matt looked up to find her. A huge cloud of dust swept around him and when it cleared, she was nowhere. She had vanished!

Looking in vain through the dust and debris, Matt shook his head and muttered, "She must have been an angel. Had to be!" He stuffed the tract that was now smudged and dusty, back in his shirt pocket. He adjusted his mask over his mouth and nose and took a deep breath of the clean air coming from his tank. He went back to his axe, picked it up and headed back into the smoke and rubble.

Before he reached his fellow firemen, there was another loud rumble and more debris shifted. He could just make out his commander, so he went to join others from his fire station. He moved up beside his partner and took another breath of clean air. The man nodded, but didn't stop moving debris. Matt started right in another spot close by, because they could hear screams and moans all around them. It was as if that little spot of time had never happened, like he and Brandi had never found each other. However, in his heart of hearts he knew it had happened – Brandi had found him. Something *had* changed!

As he worked beside his fellow firemen, he thought of the child who had confronted him. He put his pickax under another slab and muttered, "She had to be an angel! She had no fear; she didn't care about all the falling stuff around us. She just wanted me to go to heaven! Then she was gone!" He straightened up and exclaimed, "That was unbelievable!"

Some time later, word-of-mouth reached the firemen that some volunteers had a table set up to give cold water to anyone who wanted a drink. Matt had been working for several hours and the dust and smoke had seeped around his mask enough that his nose, mouth and throat felt like he was on the Sahara. When he tried to speak, only a croak came out. He needed a cold drink; it sounded better than anything he heard about in a long time. Mario pointed towards the yellow tape; Matt nodded and hoisted his pickaxe over his shoulder.

Matt and Mario stumbled over rubble, using their pickaxes as a third point of contact with the ground for some stability. With effort they moved away from the hulk of the burning building. They were only about five yards from where they were, when there was a great rumble behind them. They turned just in time to see the wall of the building where they had been working come crashing to the ground, the spot where they stood only moments before was covered instantly with about three feet of debris and rubble, still more continued to fall. Dust billowed out toward them and the force of that gust toppled them backwards.

"My God in heaven!" Mario said, in awe, as he pushed himself up from the rubble, "That's right where we were!"

Matt was on one knee, his pickaxe on the ground and sweat stood on his forehead. It was a hot day, but his sweat was more from the adrenalin rush. He said, "Yeah, I know!" However, goose-bumps skidded up his arms when the realization hit him.

When the smoke and dust cleared enough and they were standing, their heart rates hadn't quite settled, because they saw that the rubble lay about ten feet high over the spot where they had been. Without another word, they again turned to walk to where the refreshment stand was. Others were still working, either they had water with them or they had just come from the stand, they were actively swinging their pickaxes and digging with their bare hands, moving large pieces of rubble and small debris, always searching for someone alive.

As he moved along, Matt looked for Brandi. He had to admit that she could very well be walking on this side of the yellow tape handing out tracts. His heart constricted, suppose she hadn't gone back to her mommy but in that swirl of dust and smoke become disoriented and was now in that heap of rubble behind him. A shuddered went up his back; he knew he'd rather die himself than have that happen!

Finally, they saw the yellow tape. Farther away, at an intersection, people were milling around. Off to one side were two ambulances with their lights swirling, but no sirens. Rescuers loaded victims and as one ambulance was filled and left, another took its place. It was a constant stream of people and vehicles. Police cars and fire trucks sat everywhere, most were empty as firemen worked to rescue buried victims and policemen constantly urged people to cover their mouths and noses, either with cloth or their hands, but directed them to run, and leave the area.

Things were so unstable, a fire could erupt; a building could collapse; rubble could settle. Any of those happenings caused fierce winds which made new fires, or picked up huge chunks of debris. Walls were still collapsing, causing more fires and huge clouds of dust that could disorient a person. Large debris was flying around; someone could be struck by one of those large pieces and either be hurt or killed, or buried.

There was also plenty of noise, not only from the fires, and the constantly shifting rubble. There were also screams coming from many places. They were heart-wrenching cries and everyone knew those people would die if they weren't rescued soon. Every person possible who could be classified as a rescuer, first responder or fireman was trying to do that.

Only a few feet beyond the yellow tape, on the sidewalk of the intersection, was a large patio umbrella dipping and swaying in the gusts of air. It was held in place by a table and around the table on three sides were many people, some holding paper cups that they held to their mouths momentarily then held out to the ladies behind the table for more. Others reached for a cup a lady held out.

Like thirsty men on the desert, Matt and Mario, made their way toward the table, it was hard; the rubble and debris shifted constantly; they had to step aside several times, many people were milling around it. When the dust and smoke cleared enough for them to see, they made out four ladies filling paper cups from large thermos containers that came from a fast food restaurant. Frequently, a lady reached for something on the table and handed the small paper with the cup of water to the person in front of her. Matt couldn't hear any words anyone said but the universal need for water didn't really need any words to be understood.

Matt and Mario walked on. Others were coming from other areas; their one destination was that table and its promised refreshment. Not only were there firemen, but policemen, others in hospital scrubs, some of the EMT's driving the ambulances and even some people not in uniform were coming to the table, all of them with the same intent, getting a drink of much needed water. The heat and the dust swirling around made it imperative.

Anticipating the drink, Matt pulled his mask from his face. Just as they reached the back of the crowd, three people in front of Matt moved so that he had a clear view of the table.

Time stood still.

Matt hauled in a breath, dust, tiny pieces of rubble and all. Before him stood an older version of the girl who had confronted him with the tract that morning. His eyes fastened on the lady, he couldn't look away; she was lovely, what he could see of her, even though there was dust and ashes swirling all around them. At that same instant, the lady stood from filling another cup and with it in her hand, she turned and looked straight into the eyes looking at her.

Faith felt her fingers become like soft pudding. She had to will the strength back into them enough to keep the cup from falling from her hand. In all the madness, destruction, screams, sirens and every noise imaginable around them, those eyes focused on her and wouldn't let her go. Her mouth became parched, but her eyes couldn't move. She had to swallow; even then her mouth was parched.

"Hello," a deep voice said, "were you holding that cup just for me?"

Breathlessly, she answered, holding out the cup to Matt, "Yes, yes! I'm sure you're thirsty, we'll fill it up as often as you need." The man before her stood head and shoulders above her. He was dressed in full fireman's gear, his black turnout coat grimy with dust and his helmet pulled down low on his forehead, but even through his goggles his eyes never left her face. She could see them clearly through the swirling dust. They were a radiant blue. They sparkled, even through the dust, smoke and the plastic of the goggles. She was not immune; her heart nearly took leave of her chest as their eyes held.

"Thank you, Ma'am." He took the cup and swilled down the cold water in only three or four swallows, but he did it in such a way that his eyes never left hers. He stayed right where he was while he drank then held out the cup to the lady again. "Thanks, I'd like some more."

"Of course!"

After two more cupfuls, Matt waited for his next and said to the lady, "Do you have a little girl about eight or ten, perhaps?"

Embarrassed, the lady handed him the cup, then moved her hand away from the table. She shook her head and her curls bobbed. "Yes, she's here, and then she's gone. Just now she's gone, but she was here only moments ago. Why?"

Matt reached into his shirt pocket and pulled out the tract. "She gave me this earlier and told me I needed it to go to heaven."

Faith's smile rivaled that of her daughter. "She did? Are you?"

"Am I, what.... going to heaven?"

"Yes!" Her eyes sparkled.

"Yes, Ma'am, I believe I am!"

"That's terrific! It's all worth it if you are, Sir! Thank you for telling me, I'm glad Brandi found you!"

Matt nodded. "Yeah, me too."

He barely finished his fourth cup of water when others crowded around the table, effectively cutting in between Matt and Faith. With him not front and center, her brain clicked into gear again, so she handed another cup to another firefighter. Others crowded in and soon Matt found himself nearly back to the yellow tape. Mario was beside him.

He sighed; she was an interlude, part of the oasis in the massive desert of destruction that surrounded him. Under his breath, he muttered, "Probably just as well."

"What was that?" Mario asked.

"I guess it was nothing." Matt slung his pickax over his shoulder, replaced his mask and both men turned back the way they had come.

The lady had a little girl, she was obviously a Christian. He didn't know too much about Christians, but Christian ladies with children had husbands; at least that was what he was always led to believe. As others stepped between them and the water, Matt and Mario silently made their way back into the clouds of dust and debris. They both adjusted their masks; then together they headed back to the awful task of rescuing another buried victim. There were too many screams and moans to stand around.

From close beside him, Mario asked, "So... you know that beautiful lady?"

Matt shook his head. "Never saw her before. Just making conversation."

"Mmm, try to convince me."

Matt scowled. "What's that mean?"

"Hey, you couldn't take your eyes off her!"

"So, she's a beautiful woman."

"Oh, yeah, I'll give you that! And you, my friend, are single and not a bad specimen," Mario countered immediately.

Matt sighed, "Give it a rest, Mario. What's the chance of seeing her again? Besides, she's got a daughter...."

"Ah, where was she? How do you know that?"

Me and my big mouth! "I saw her earlier."

Mario scowled. "The child?"

"Yeah."

Matt and Mario were back in their position, there was no more talk. A huge gust of hot wind picked up some large pieces of debris that hurtled at them and dropped close by. When they settled Mario brought his hand up and wiped across his goggles. At that moment they both heard a scream only a few feet away. They both rushed toward the sound and both put the points of their picks under the huge slab of cement and heaved it out of the way.

Matt's shift started yesterday afternoon at three. It was quiet, he and his shift buddies played cards after supper, did a short run and slept. They were on for a twenty-four hour stretch, so he should be off at three this afternoon. However, this tragedy struck in the morning, hours from the end of his shift. In such a huge emergency, shifts meant nothing, so when three o'clock came he was still knee deep in rubble and dust. Smoke and dust from everything that collapsed still covered the sun, billowing around them, making it like a solar eclipse. There were screams coming from different places under the rubble and as they heard the sounds, the rescuers moved to the spot to start their methodical routine to reach the person without hurting them any more. With the dust swirling around them, it was hard work. Fires, that seemed to sprout from nowhere hampered them as they moved huge segments of concrete. Of course, the ever present dust swirled around them making it hard to see.

So far, Matt and Mario had rescued quite a few people. After their drink, they went back to their squad and worked all afternoon. He and Mario pulled three women and two men from the heaps. One man was only slightly injured, his injuries were superficial cuts and abrasions, but he still needed to be examined. The women and the other man needed transport to the nearby hospital. Those they carried over their shoulders to get them to the ambulances.

Never, all afternoon, did the thought of Brandi leave his mind. He looked for her, either to come sailing over the rubble or, heaven forbid, be one of those whom he dug up from the rubble. Her mom's eyes never left him for long either. Even with dirt smudges on her face and gray debris in her hair, she was lovely. Knowing she had a little girl he wondered why her image stayed with him. As Mario said, he was single, after all.

Around three o'clock, Matt and Mario made their way back to the table with the umbrella and water containers. His mouth was dry as the desert again, but he not only wanted some water, he also wanted to see the lovely lady with the auburn curls and her little daughter with the same auburn curls, well, he assumed they were auburn, they looked gray when he saw her before. When he reached the table, another lady offered him a paper cup, he took it, he was too thirsty to refuse, but even though he stood long enough to see all four ladies, the lady who gave him his water that morning was not one of them. His heart sank, he wanted to see her, to talk with her, but he couldn't. Actually, he couldn't talk to any of the others, there were too many people around and they were too busy giving out cupfuls of water to take the time to talk to him.

He sighed. *Maybe they're both angels. Do angels have children?*

That wasn't something he ever inquired into and probably never would. Actually, it was a foolish thought, these ladies were from a church, but their mission made them angels of mercy to him and many other rescue workers. He took several refills, as many as he could get before Mario tugged on his arm and motioned him back toward the tragic scene. Matt sighed, threw the paper cup in the container and followed Mario back across the tape, replacing his air mask as he walked. There were still many screams coming from many places and there was still daylight. After all he was a fireman doing his job.

The smoke and debris hid the sun all day. He couldn't tell the time by the sun at all, but he kept on working, trying to save just one more person from a certain death. It became dusk and Matt was dog tired. He found a large slab of concrete and collapsed onto it. His pickaxe slipped from his hand and rested against his knee. He pulled down his mask, hiked his turnout coat up and reached for his handkerchief to wipe some of the grime clinging to his face with the sweat. He took the cloth from his face and looked up to see his commander coming toward him.

"Matt," the man called, "it's after nine. You're exhausted, go on home."

Stuffing his handkerchief back into his pants pocket, he exclaimed, "But Colin! There's still screaming under the rubble!"

"I know, but you and I are the last of our squad that's still here. As tired as we both are, you know we won't do much to rescue many more. Your muscles have to be screaming just as loudly as mine. We need to get out of here. I'm rounding up our crew and sending them home. The other two shifts are here. We need you fresh when it comes your time again. As soon as you're on your way, I am, too." He bent over and reached for Matt's hand. He pulled him to his feet and gave him a grin, as he started walking he said, "You've done yourself proud, man! All my men have! If you still want to help, come back tomorrow after a good night's sleep. I'm going to do that."

Matt nodded. "Okay, I'll do that." Before he moved, Matt grasped his pickaxe.

The two men moved over the rubble together, heading for the roped off area where the fire engines from their substation were parked. The men were quiet as they stumbled along; the dust and debris still swirled around them. They barely had enough energy to put one foot in front of the other, talking was out.

Nearly to the engine Matt turned his head and saw sticking up from all the rubble, a cross silhouetted against the dim glow in the night sky. It was tilted a bit because of the debris around it, but there it stood, a silent reminder of the decision he made earlier. He sucked in his breath and had to stop to stare at the beautiful sight.

Colin also stopped to look where Matt was staring. "Wow!" he whispered. "Isn't that awesome!" Colin swallowed and in reverent tones, he said, "God is still among us! Awesome!"

"It sure is!" Matt felt a peace come over him as he looked at that cross. Brandi said Jesus had died on such a thing… for him! Matt pulled in a deep breath, he had been dragging his pickaxe, but energized; he slung it over his shoulder.

For a moment peace and quietness engulfed the two men. Moments later, they moved on. One of their trucks was there, the driver had the big truck running and other men sat on the seats, obviously Colin had instructed the driver to wait for him. Matt climbed onto the back and found the last seat; Colin opened the cab door and slid onto the seat. The slamming door was lost as the driver put the truck in gear and started to move. He must do it with all caution; the truck was there so long that many other vehicles had parked very close to it.

No one spoke as the truck moved slowly away from the awful sight. Every fireman was exhausted. This day was a day the firemen would remember for the rest of their lives. It was the most horrendous thing that had ever happened anywhere! Their lives were altered completely for all time. However, for Matt, one little girl had found him and showed him how he could go to heaven! Along with seeing that cross, his heart was at peace. That was amazing! Something he had never experienced before. He heard a saying once – 'a little child shall lead them.'

Faith stayed at the table handing out water until four o'clock, only taking a few minutes breaks once in a while, but the tall fireman never came back while she was there. Brandi came and left many times during the time Faith was at the table, each time, she grabbed more tracts and ran off hardly before her mom knew she was back. The child loved Jesus and she wanted everybody, big or small, man, woman or child, to know about Him.

Faith loved her daughter; she was all she had left of her husband who died three years ago from injuries in service in the Middle East. He never completely recovered from his injuries. The doctors told her after his death it was something internal, that was so subtle no one found it, that had killed him. Except for the Lord's strength, she would be devastated. Actually, she was devastated, but she knew she must go on; Brandi needed her to be strong and courageous. With the help of her church family who stood with her and loved her she made it.

At four o'clock, a lady from her church returned with another huge container of water and set it on the table. A rescue worker followed her with another container and set it beside the other. The empties were on the sidewalk. The lady turned to Faith, and since Brandi was there, she said, "Why don't you go, Faith. You've been here since the beginning, you need to go home and rest. I know you're just getting over that bug you had. You shouldn't be out here any longer, you'll get a setback, I'm afraid."

Picking up a towel someone left on the table and wiping her face, Faith sighed and said, "Amylou, I think I'll take you up on that, since Brandi's here. We'll see you at church."

The other lady smiled. "You sure will! And Faith, thanks again."

"Of course! I'm glad to help wherever I can. You know that."

Faith picked up her purse and slung it on her shoulder, and grabbed

Brandi's hand before she could run off again. Brandi had more tracts in her hand that she waved in Faith's face and looked imploringly at her. "But Mommy," Brandi said, "there's so many more people who need to know about Jesus!" Tears started making tracks down through the grime on Brandi's face.

Wearily, Faith looked at her daughter and said, "I know, Sweetheart, but you've given out lots of tracts, I'm really proud of you! We need to go home, though. You better leave that pile of tracts on the table. Perhaps some of the ladies can give them out along with cups of water after we're gone."

Brandi sighed, "Okay, Mommy."

"Thanks, Sweetheart."

Fires were still burning, they could hear screams everywhere, all around them sirens were wailing as they transported rescued victims to hospitals. Not only were there screaming ambulances, but there were also silent hearses transporting bodies from the scene. Smoke, dust and debris floated in the air, gusts of hot wind, made by the fires, and settling debris carried them relentlessly, swirling them high and low. Fragments of destroyed buildings still crumbled only yards away behind the yellow tape. It was a sight not soon forgotten; maybe even causing nightmares. Life, for many of these people had changed drastically and forever, no one who witnessed the destruction would forget. Everyone knew many families were torn apart, never to be the same again. Faith knew how that was, first hand.

All this at the hands of some fanatical terrorists.

Leaving the awful sight behind, Faith made her way through the smoke and dust to the closest subway station that was open. Actually, it was quite a walk for both her and Brandi, because not only had the collapsing towers caused the rails to buckle under them, but there were trains on them that crashed, making it impossible for any service. The destruction was far behind them when they found an open subway station.

Faith had to get to a certain line that would take them to the Long Island Railroad Station. Max, her late husband, had provided for them well, they had a nice home not too far out on the island. Even though it wasn't far from the huge city, Faith felt fortunate that there were some trees and green grass where Brandi could play safely. She had hoped to have some brothers and sisters for Brandi to play with, but that hadn't happened before Max became so ill that he died and with no single men her age at church, she didn't hold out much hope for that, either. Still, life went on, you coped as best you could and put your life in the Lord's hands. She did that faithfully every morning and evening when she read her Bible and prayed. God was well aware of her needs and desires.

After they settled in a seat on the train headed home, Brandi spent a long time looking out the window. Long after the train left the station Brandi looked at the aerie glow that lay over so many city blocks. The smoke and dust blocked out the sun all day. Finally, she settled back and looked at her hands. They were nearly black; there hadn't been anything to wipe them off with except the filthy towel on the table.

When Faith realized that Brandi wasn't looking out the window, she turned to her and said, "You know, one of the times you were gone today, a fireman came up for a drink and told me you told him how to go to heaven."

Brandi immediately turned toward her mommy, her eyes bright. Nodding, as she said, "Yeah, he sat down and took me on his lap. I showed him there in that tract where to read. He did and then he prayed. Mommy, now if he's killed he'll go to heaven just like Daddy did." She grew quiet and looked up at Faith with clear, innocent eyes. "But you know, I hope he doesn't get killed. I'd kinda like him for a new daddy."

Faith sucked in her breath, her eyes wide with astonishment, as she looked at her daughter. Where did that statement come from? Brandi hadn't asked for a daddy before, always been content to know that her daddy was with Jesus in heaven. Faith grabbed a tissue from her purse and wiped her nose to stall for some time. Shaking her head, she said, "How can that ever happen, Brandi? Really! You only saw him for that little time and he only stayed at the table for a few minutes to get a drink and to tell me he talked with you. He never told me his name and he didn't ask for mine. We have no way of knowing how to reach him." Scowling, Faith said, "Besides, just because he's asked Jesus into his heart doesn't mean we're to get together! Maybe he has a wife and family."

Brandi bounced on the seat, clapping her hands, apparently excited that there was something she knew that her mommy didn't. With a wide grin, she said, "Oh, Mommy, his name is Matt. Fireman Matt. I'm positive he doesn't have anybody. We gotta find him and make him my new daddy. Jesus told me that!"

Knowing that sometimes Brandi included Jesus in things she wished for very much, Faith said, "Now, Brandi, I'm not too sure Jesus told you any such thing."

Nodding emphatically, she said, "'Course He did, Mommy!'"

The train slowed for their stop, and the trainman yelled, "Thomaston!"

Faith pulled her purse strap onto her shoulder, took Brandi's hand and stood up as the brakes hissed. She urged Brandi into the aisle; then walked beside her to the door, while others walked in front and some crowded in behind them. The trainman stood on the platform helping the passengers off. He nodded to the pretty girl and grinned at her mommy as they stepped from the last step to the platform. He noticed how grimy they were and knew they must have been close to the destruction. He was still in shock from hearing the news.

The platform was crowded with those getting off the train. After all, it was rush hour and many people didn't work at the towers, but were coming home after a normal workday. Faith couldn't even thank the man for his help, there were too many people. Faith couldn't hold Brandi once they reached the parking lot, so she followed more slowly to her car.

Brandi was much smaller, she could scoot around people's legs much better than Faith could even imagine. When she finally saw her car, the crowd had thinned out and other car doors were slamming. Brandi was skipping around, waiting for Faith to reach her door. Faith felt her energy draining away and wished her car worked on a remote, Brandi could already be in the car by now. Somehow, the extra hundred or so dollars for a remote didn't seem worth it at the time. As she reached the car and inserted the key in the door lock, she wished not only for a remote for the car door, but also that the car could drive itself home. She was bushed.

Once they were inside, Faith made sure Brandi had her seatbelt fastened. When she heard the click, Faith started the car and Brandi said, "Now, we gotta think our strategy through, how we're gonna get Matt as our new daddy. He'll havta come to church." Faith sighed; her child was persistent, if nothing else.

She glanced over at her and said, "Maybe the best way to do that, Brandi, is when you say your prayers tonight, thank Jesus that you could tell somebody about how he could have his sins taken away. Tell Jesus you want Matt to go to a good church."

Brandi couldn't bounce too much in the seat with the seatbelt fastened, but she tried, as she said excitedly, "I will! What better church is there than ours?"

Knowing she was too tired to argue, Faith said, "Yes, there isn't one."

Several blocks from the train station, Faith turned on the lane that led to their house. Brandi pointed up ahead and exclaimed, "Oh, Mommy! Stop at the big tree, I haven't had a swing on my swing all day, 'cause we were gone. I want one now while you fix supper."

Knowing there were no crowds for Brandi to get lost in and also knowing that she did have to fix their supper, Faith sighed again and stopped under the big tree. "Okay, Sweety, I'll call you when it's ready. Oh, while I'm still sitting here, can you get the mail?"

"Great! Sure!" Brandi exclaimed, her seat belt clicking.

Full of energy, Brandi had her door open and was out hardly before Faith could look at her. Faith sighed, wishing for some of that energy. The child ran down the few feet to the mailbox beside the driveway. She rushed back and nearly threw the mail at her mommy, then rushed up the small grassy bank before she turned and grinned at her mommy.

Quickly, she grabbed one of the ropes and jumped onto the seat. Before Faith even thought to put her foot back on the gas, Brandi had her rhythm and was pumping herself toward the deep blue sky. At least here there was no scorching heat, fires popping up, swirling debris or choking dust that could hit her or hurt her daughter.

Faith knew they must soak in the tub a long time to get rid of the smoke smell and the clinging dust and debris. She might have to run several tubs full of clean water before they both felt clean enough for bed. She didn't even have to look in the mirror to know they each needed a shampoo; maybe it would take two applications to get all the grime and debris out of both hers and Brandi's curls. Then would come the fun job of combing out the rats.

As the car accelerated, Faith looked again in the outside mirror to watch Brandi and mumbled, "Oh, to have that much energy!"

Only a few minutes later, Faith parked in the garage and went into the cool house. It was a comfortable home, large enough to raise a family. There were lovely big trees close by that gave good afternoon shade. Not only did the house have central air conditioning, but this time of year, she turned it off and left windows open to let the breeze in. None of Long Island was far from the ocean and even in the hottest summer, there was always a breeze that came in off the water. The curtains in the living room moved lazily, giving evidence of the delightful breeze. Faith was glad for it, it smelled fresh, there was no hot wind from fires and falling rubble.

She was thankful that Max put a rider on his insurance policy that the house and property were paid for at the time of his death. She often wondered if he had a premonition or if he ignored how he truly felt for him to add that clause. How could he know he'd die so young? Even to her, and she felt she knew him well, he seemed healthy until only months before his death. Of course, she never got an answer.

Since his death she couldn't be a spendthrift with monthly running expenses. He made good money while he worked at the Trade Center. She got a widow's pension from the military, since on autopsy it was determined his death was from war related injuries and the company he worked for had a generous package she was entitled to, but shutting off the air conditioning helped her stretch her budget this time of year.

A tear slid down her cheek. She still missed him, of course, but it had been three years. She wasn't old, could she hope for another chance at happiness? Max told her as he was dying to find someone who would love her. She half-heartedly agreed. At that time it was hard not to agree with anything her dying husband asked.

TWO

FROM WHERE SHE STOOD, SHE LOOKED OUT THE KITCHEN WINDOW TOWARD THE driveway to the crest of the hill to the big tree. Brandi was pumping her legs for all she was worth, at her highest point, both forward and behind, she was lost in the leaves for a second. She loved that child, but she reminded her of herself, not Max. She did have Max's disposition.

Faith's thoughts turned inward. Was she ready to look for a new daddy for Brandi? Was she through grieving Max? Did God have another man who could love her, a widow with a ten year old child? She loved Max with all her heart, could she love another man with as much love as she gave her late husband? In counseling sessions with Pastor, he told her often that Max would always hold a special spot, but she had plenty of room for more love. Could she find that room? For Matt, the fireman? Really? What a preposterous thought! They met because of a tragedy. He was a New York City fireman, she a widow living on Long Island!

She opened a cupboard and pulled down two cans of chunky soup. She was too tired to start anything from scratch and Brandi loved chunky soup with lots of crackers. Whenever she bought chunky soup she always thought about her cracker supply. Instant pudding for dessert sounded perfect, so she grabbed a box when she pulled out the crackers. There was always milk for Brandi and she fixed a pitcher of tea last night. After today they needed lots to drink. They'd both have water as well as milk and tea. What they experienced today left her mouth and throat nearly raw and she hadn't talked very much at all.

Matt sat in his seat on the fire truck, his axe against his thigh and his hands on top. None of the men talked; the truck engine was too loud for conversation. Like himself, the other men were exhausted, their throats were parched. The times he was able to get away and find those ladies with the water were few and far between. All the men on the truck had been on the clock for well over twenty-four hours. Fortunately, they had a quiet night and slept. He hoped with all the places he was in today he could sleep tonight when he was in his own bed.

He sat motionless, thinking about the scene he witnessed right before he and Colin left the rubble and reached the truck. There on top of the huge piles of rubble and debris and with lights strung up to help the rescuers; he saw that cross back-lit by those huge lights. It stood there, tipped just a little with only the rubble to hold it upright. As Colin said, it was awesome! He knew there were three things he would never forget about this horrible day; Brandi sitting on his lap urging him to pray, her mother offering him a drink, and the cross in the rubble.

He couldn't take his eyes from the cross for just a minute. Now that he sat on the truck, the words, "'For God so loved" Matt, "that he gave his one and only Son, that" Matt, who "believes in him should not perish, but have eternal life." came to his mind. Tears clouded his eyes and fell to his cheeks. Silently, more tears slid down his cheeks, making tracts on his dusty, filthy cheeks. Colin said God was there. *God was there!* God sent Brandi to him and He pulled his eyes to that cross. *GOD IS HERE! GOD IS REAL!*

Slowly the truck made its way through all the congestion, toward their substation. At this time of night there was no table with a patio umbrella over it with ladies busily giving out water. He knew there were scores of people very thankful for that little oasis today. His mouth was dry again. He wished the truck could hurry back to the station so he could get a drink. He wasn't surprised that it was church ladies who came. All his life he had great respect for church people. Today, as a fireman, more than ever.

Thinking about the table reminded him of Brandi. He wondered how old she was. Her mother hadn't had time to tell him anything. She could be eight or she could be small for her age at ten. However old she was, she made Matt read the Bible verse. That didn't mean she couldn't read, maybe she knew it'd mean more if he read the verse for himself. It sure had, especially when he did as she said and put his name in those places. In all that rubble, that child found him! He thought about it, in all that rubble, God had found him!

Not only that, God pointed him to that cross, standing upright in the rubble! What an awesome thought!

Time stood still.

For a child to be that enthusiastic about people going to heaven, she had to come from a place that taught her that and believed it. He thought of the lady who had to be the child's mother. They were cut from the same mold; the lady probably saw herself growing up. The auburn curls had to be real, in all the dust, smoke and ashes, her hair still had lovely curls. On both mother and daughter they were matted with debris. He couldn't decide what color her eyes were. He looked into them for several seconds, but with all that was in the air, colors were distorted. He couldn't see how she was dressed, because the table with the huge water jugs hid everything. He guessed he was at least six inches taller than the lady.

Finally, the driver backed the huge truck into the station and cut the engine. Matt sighed, jumped from his seat, and moved as fast as his tired legs would take him to the locker room. He deposited his axe in his locker, pulled his arms out of the sleeves of his turnout coat and hung it on the hook, then slapped his helmet on top of it. His goggles and breathing apparatus found their place. There was another day when he wasn't so exhausted to wash the grime and dust off everything. He climbed out of his boots and put them beside the axe and pulled out his shoes. Before slipping his feet into them, he stood and rolled his shoulders, it had been a long stretch in that coat, nearly twelve hours.

The lady at the water stand was a spot out of time; probably he would never encounter that spot again. Just like her daughter was an angel who floated down from somewhere so she could give him a tract. Still in the lighted locker room, he pulled the tract from his pocket. Being in his pocket for over eight hours, there was no way he could pass it on. It smelled like him, which didn't smell too good.

His leaden feet took him to the break room where he turned on the cold water, letting it get as cold as possible; then filled a huge glass. He stood at the sink and gulped down half the contents, and filled it again. Still holding the glass, he decided to read the entire tract before he went to his sleeping room. His stomach growled reminding him he hadn't eaten since the truck left the firehouse. He chugged more water; he would grab dinner on the way to his room. There certainly wasn't anything to eat there! The landlady didn't supply refrigerators and he wasn't about to buy one for the room.

He slid down onto the worn vinyl couch that had served the station since long before he started working here. He held the glass in one hand and pushed his thumb between the two halves of the tract to read from the beginning. When he came to John 3: 16, he read it slowly, putting his name in the places again. It overwhelmed him that God could really love him. When he finished, he noticed the white space after the last paragraph and in it was the name of a church with an address. The city was on Long Island, but that didn't mean he couldn't go there.

"What's the use," he grumbled, "Brandi's her daughter; she surely has a husband to go along with her. There have to be other churches closer than that." However, it was the church on Long Island who manned the water table not one of those that still stood close by. He decided that had to tell him something.

Below the address the rest of the church stamp gave service times. He noticed that they had what they called Bible Study and Prayer Meeting on Wednesday evening. Colin invited him to come back tomorrow to help again, but it was not his normal time to work. Perhaps he could leave so he could hop out there to that church tomorrow evening. He realized he wanted to see if Brandi really was alive, after he last saw her disappear in the swirl of smoke. What an experience! In all that chaos, a child came to tell him how to go to heaven!

He washed out the glass, put it back where he found it and headed out the door. There was nothing at the fire station he needed. His room wasn't far from the station, he rented it for that reason, but that's all it was, a room. It had a bed, a dresser, a small desk and a miniscule closet. He stopped at the fast food restaurant between the station and the old house and went in for supper. He realized he better eat fast, the fatigue from his thirty plus hour duty was catching up to him. He hoped that after he ate, he had enough energy to make it the last few blocks to his rented room. A sigh escaped, he definitely needed enough energy to take a shower and shampoo his hair. Even with his helmet on his hair felt grimy and his neck gritty.

As he came out of the restaurant to walk the few blocks he looked up at the night sky. Thick clouds of smoke still billowed up downtown, hiding any stars that might be out. There was ash in the air, even though it was many blocks from the terrible happening. He shook his head, how could those pilots, if they were even true pilots, think that by crashing planes full of passengers into those two huge buildings and killing all those innocent people they would receive merit with their god? The notion was preposterous!

When he reached the house, he let himself into his room and stripped. Throwing on his bathrobe and stepping into his flip flops, he grabbed his towel and shampoo and went to the bathroom down the hall. Behind the door, he turned on the shower, waited for the warm water, then stepped in to wash the grime of this awful day off his body. After shampooing his hair several times, he let the water pound on him for several minutes. He was glad for the in-line water heater the landlady had installed, he never ran out of hot water even with a long shower and shampoo. Finally, he stepped out, and brushed his teeth. All the smoke, dust and ashes left a nasty taste in his mouth and his supper hadn't helped. Exhausted, he headed back to his room and his bed. He knew he'd sleep the sleep of the dead from exhaustion.

Faith and Brandi ate their supper, but as Faith's energy lagged, Brandi's eyes started to droop. Faith took advantage and sent her to take her bath. Brandi was in the smoke, dust and ashes all day and even her hair needed a good shampooing before her head ever touched the pillow. The water, when Faith finished scrubbing all the grime off her, was dark gray. She had to use several squirts of shampoo to finally get all the dirt and grime out of Brandi's hair and bring back the true auburn color. Combing it gave another challenge.

"Okay, Sweetie, go in your room and read your book while I take my bath. Did you see that water from your bath? I know I'm just about as bad."

Brandi pulled on her shorty pajamas, then shook her damp curls out of the top and said, "Yes, Mommy, your hair looks awful! You better use lots of shampoo too."

Faith chuckled. "Mmm, thanks, Brandi, I really needed to hear that!"

Brandi grinned mischievously. "I know, but you're such a good mommy!" She patted Faith's cheek affectionately.

Brandi hurried to her room and curled up in the big chair then opened her Bible that she won for having perfect attendance at Sunday school during the contest last year. She loved to read it and look at the wonderful pictures. It was her own special Bible, it had her name written on the front cover and also inside. It made her feel so close to Jesus when she sat in this chair and read about Him. He was her friend, He loved all the children.

She tried to imagine sitting on Jesus' lap so long ago. Would it be like sitting on Fireman Matt's lap today? He was big, he was a man; would Jesus have been like him? She really liked Matt, he was a cool guy. His fireman's coat was slippery and when she sat on his leg, then slid off, where she sat was shiny. She thought that if Mommy could get to know him, she'd like him a whole lot, too. Some how she had to get Matt and Mommy together. She must pray about it; surely Jesus had an idea He was just waiting for her to learn!

As she heard the water gurgle down the drain from her mommy's bath, she slid from the chair to put the Bible back on her shelf. Mommy would be in soon to put her to bed. It was their special time, sometimes Mommy read to her, but they were so tired tonight, maybe they'd just pray together. That's all they did sometimes. Instead of sitting in the chair, she fell to her knees. She would pray her special prayer before Mommy came. She knew Jesus would hear her.

She folded her hands and closed her eyes, then whispered, "Dear Jesus, You know we need a daddy here real bad. I met this really nice fireman today and You know I introduced him to You. I know his name's Matt and You know that, too, 'cause You know everything. You're God and You're supposed to know everything. I know You got his name written in Your book up there for Your special people, 'cause he prayed and asked You to take his sins away. You even know his last name! Jesus, we need him. Mommy needs a husband and I need a daddy. Could You make that happen, please? I know You can if You want. Thank You, Jesus, amen."

As tired as he was, Matt was sure he'd fall instantly asleep, but when he closed his eyes, he saw Brandi begging him to take her little piece of paper. He had. He read the verse and it stayed with him all day, even with his name in it. He prayed; something he couldn't remember ever doing. He realized that he felt differently; maybe there was a change he hadn't realized while he worked in that awful nightmare. Another picture scrolled through his mind, he and Mario were spared from the tumbling building by only a few feet. Had God done that? Even as he lay in bed, he nodded. Yes, God moved them from that spot. There was no other explanation for it than that. "Thank You, God! Thank You from the bottom of my heart."

Vivid pictures of the horrid flames, the crumbling cement and white hot steel that melted into heaps of rubble scrolled through his mind. His efforts seemed so pointless considering how few people he encountered and helped rescue. He felt again the hot smoke and ash the gusts of wind swept along. Dust from the crumbling buildings was everywhere, plastering against his mask and goggles, matting his hair, even inside his helmet, gritting on his teeth, even with the mask in place. As the day wore on when he tried to talk to someone, he couldn't, because of the fine grit lodged in his throat. All of those things he never experienced as a fireman.

All day there were rumblings and what felt like mini-earthquakes, as the huge piles settled first one way; then another, as the fires continued to burn. In many places it was like an inferno, forcing those who tried to enter back, that along with the huge gusts of smoke and dust. The tragedy was so extensive they couldn't get their fire truck anywhere close, it seemed like everything they tried to do was futile. He knew life for him and many others who were there would never be the same.

What drove him from sleep, however, were the screams of those trapped and dying in the huge mounds of debris and rubble he climbed and dug in all day. Those screams would haunt him for a very long time. Many of them were muffled or distorted by the sounds of crumbling debris and the flames that seemed to shoot up anywhere and everywhere. Those screams were different from the screams of people trapped on higher floors of buildings on fire, usually, they could be rescued using a ladder truck, but most of those who were screaming today had no way of escape. Some were buried too deep.

Matt wasn't one of the first firemen to the scene and he was glad, his fire station was some ways away. By the time their squadron arrived, Tower One was on the ground. Those first there, from the closer firehouses were the ones who climbed as many stairs as they could in the hot, enclosed fire escapes, with their turnout coats, boots, air tanks, pickaxes and helmets, full gear. He realized as he lay staring at the ceiling before his mind shut down that many of those screams were fellow firemen who couldn't escape or who fell exhausted inside those death traps.

In those few minutes he was at the fire station before he left for the fast food restaurant, he learned that the New York City Fire Chief was one of those still missing. *What if he's lost? What'll this city do without him? He's a good man, a great leader.* He did a lot for their department and fought many battles at city hall for the career firemen. He shook his head, as he flipped over onto his stomach and punched his pillow, hoping for a better position to rest his mind and his many sore muscles.

Many good people were lost today, innocent people who shouldn't have died, all at the hands of terrorists. There were those in the hijacked planes who first realized the terror. Every one of them had died. There were those in the buildings which the planes hit; unsuspecting victims who died just because they happened to work in those huge towers that reached to the sky and were sometimes hidden when low clouds or fog moved in off the harbor.

The only ones who should have died were those self-centered, self-advancing terrorists who thought that they could gain merit in the next life by snuffing out innocent people. Just a few had piloted those planes, but most of them sat at home, in their own country, gloating on how easy it was to bring America to its knees! These thousands of people they called infidels because they didn't believe in the same religion. When he learned the cause, his blood boiled, it did, even now.

There were still blazes as his truck left the scene. He felt helpless, he was a fireman. It was his job to put out fires and rescue those he could, but he hadn't. He couldn't! He lived and worked in a nightmare all day. The major oasis that he could remember was Brandi giving him a tract and bringing him to Jesus. Another oasis was the table with the ladies giving out cold water. The last oasis was the few minutes when he saw the cross. It stood there on all that rubble and even now, brought tears to his eyes. In all of that awfulness, God was there.

In the quiet room he let that quiet moment with Colin at the scene of the cross quiet his racing mind. As he thought about it, the sight of that cross blocked out every other noise around them for those few minutes. As he thought about his time near the cross his mind relaxed, his heart took up its regular rhythm and he fell asleep.

Time stood still on September 11, 9-1-1, the number for Emergency! How ironic!

It took about a half hour, and the thoughts of the cross to shut down his exhausted body and distraught brain. However, it was a restless sleep; several times scenes from the disaster crowded his dreams. Once he slept, he never woke until the sun shining in his window made it too warm under his cover. He threw it off, but he was too much awake for another nap. An exceptionally vivid dream woke him. Reluctantly, he headed for the bathroom.

Another day had dawned, another day to try to rescue anyone who could possibly be alive. There was a remote possibility there would be someone alive in the rubble. The awful events of yesterday never left his mind during the night. Unfortunately, they were still vivid this morning. Would that horrendous happening ever leave his memory?

Matt dressed in a clean uniform then headed to the diner where he usually ate breakfast. The talk around the tables and at the counter where he ate was only about the disaster. Several people commented about the irony that the date was September eleventh. When you wrote it using only numbers, it was 9-1-1, that stood for Emergency! It was a devastating emergency.

The talk in the diner was one of incredulity. How could anyone do that to innocent people? Since he was in his uniform, he received congratulations for his part in the rescue efforts, something he could do without. He was only doing his job, what he got paid to do. It was around ten o'clock when he reached his fire station. There were three others from his shift who came in and were now suiting up, ready to go to Ground Zero, as it was now being called.

When they arrived, they looked around at the total destruction. Others from their fire station and other shifts were there, some since noon the day before, but their commanders were sending them home as new, fresh reinforcements arrived. Matt and the others pitched in immediately, doing the job they knew how to do – putting fires out and rescuing people.

There were still some faint cries and he joined several others who concentrated on one such place. Most of the dust and debris had settled and the sun shone on the devastation. There were other noises now, the rumble of buildings collapsing infrequent, but at the fringes of the piles of rubble trucks and bulldozers were moving some of the rubble that were declared free of bodies. It was hot, depressing work, there were still many fires and lots of smoke. The day itself was hot, since it was September 12.

Matt lifted one large slab of concrete with his pickaxe, while Mario fell on his knees to peer under it. Moments before they heard a noise right around here and began to dig through the pile until they reached the slab of concrete. It was huge, neither of them could move it with their hands, so Matt stuck his pickaxe under it and lifted it. His muscles strained against his clothes as he tried to push against the huge chunk.

Mario's head only stayed bent a minute. He straightened up, threw his arms out and yelled, "Hey, hold it right there! Anybody come help! I just found a hand and arm under here!"

With all his might, Matt grunted as he heaved the slab the other way, letting his axe fall with it and fell to his knees to help his buddy, digging with his hands to try and find more of the person. They didn't want to use their axe or pick for fear they would hurt the person even more without intending to. As he moved some small pieces of rubble, his hand brushed the hand of the victim, shocked it was still warm. It put a burst of adrenaline into his system and he dug feverishly for several minutes.

Finally, the two firefighters moved enough rubble that a shoulder and some hair were visible. Matt cleared his throat, he realized how dry he was and how much dust was still in the air. Tears were very near falling from the adrenaline rush. Here, even over twenty-four hours later, in all this rubble, they were about to find someone else alive. Both men picked up rocks and steel, flinging them as far away to either side as they could. It took over twenty minutes more to move enough of the debris so they could tell that the person was a young woman.

She was so weak her eyes stayed shut, but her lips formed the word, "Water."

His own throat clogged with emotion, Matt whispered, "Yes."

Not sure if there'd be water available again today, Matt filled a small bottle with water for himself at the fire station, but he grabbed it from his pocket, pulled the top up and moistened her lips. Her tongue snaked out and he squirted a few drops on it. When he knew she was conscious, he slowly let some follow her tongue and she swallowed. Matt let out a long sigh, thankful he had the water with him. He and Mario wasted no time in moving the last of the debris from around her, but even that took nearly a half hour. They lifted her gently from the rubble and carried her to a waiting ambulance.

Both of them let out a long breath as the ambulance zoomed away, its siren wailing. Yet another person saved from certain death. As they went back to work, listening carefully for other sounds of possible victims who could be still alive, they both knew that this was the real reason why they were in this dangerous line of work. Yes, firefighters put out fires all the time, but their mission in life was to save lives, even if the building was totally destroyed.

Rumor was that some of the underground passages and stores were accessible. He guessed, after all hope of rescuing live people was past that they would be directed to those places to see what was salvageable. He took out his handkerchief to wipe his forehead, as hot as it was, that time would be soon. Injured people under all that rubble couldn't live much longer.

Brandi woke up at her usual time, a little after sunrise. She slept well, so she jumped off her bed enthusiastically and went to the window that faced the city. Yesterday, when they came home, as she was swinging, she saw the heavy, black smoke hovering over the city. She looked out the window this morning toward the same direction and realized there wasn't near the smoke there was when she looked yesterday. However, today was another day to pull people from under all that stuff. Maybe they could go back and find Matt or maybe when they went back, she could give out more tracts and tell people about heaven. She was excited. Mommy didn't have a job, maybe Ms Amylou would want them to go back today.

Soon after her daddy died, Brandi started leaving her bed as soon as she woke up to go to her mommy's room. Faith hung a battery clock in Brandi's room and taught her that sunrise was not the time for her or her mommy to get up. Brandi looked at the clock now and sighed, she must read or play quietly for quite a while, Mommy would not be up yet. Why did grownups have to sleep so much?

Some time later, Faith opened her eyes. Amylou was right, Faith had just recovered from some stomach upset that left her below par, it zapped a lot of her strength. As Faith lay in her bed, she realized that lots of smoke, dust and flying debris yesterday had entered her lungs. It hurt to breathe deeply and she had a headache. She hoped her symptoms were only from being exposed to those things yesterday, not a relapse of what she had before.

She sighed and turned her head to look at the clock on her bedside table. Faith knew it was daylight, there was light framing the drapes across the windows. Brandi would be in soon and the day would be off and running, whether she wanted it that way or not. Brandi didn't know any other speed but fast. For just another minute she lay there, putting her arm across her eyes, but all that did was show in graphic color some of the scenes she witnessed yesterday.

They were on a street corner with the closest access for ambulances and hearses to wait for the rescuers to bring either an injured person or a body. She watched many ambulances with sirens screaming streak away full of injured people along with at least one medical professional toward some hospital. It broke her heart to see the silent hearses also leave with their burdens.

She wondered if she would ever forget those sounds they heard all day. The screams of people buried and in pain; of ambulance sirens coming and going; and other people shouting and cursing. She rarely heard sounds like that in her neighborhood, although an ambulance had come to this house three years ago and taken Max to the hospital. He never came home. She was glad she rode with him; his body had shut down very quickly after the first symptoms. Just the thought made her breath hitch.

Slowly, Faith threw off her sheet and comforter and sat on the edge of her bed. She tried to shake off those thoughts by wiggling her toes on the cool floor. She tried to muster some energy. When thoughts of Max crowded into her brain it seemed to zap every ounce of energy she had and today, adding all the thoughts of yesterday's tragedy made it worse. She was glad she could help the rescuers and others working by giving out water, but she realized it had taxed her in many ways, not just physically. It happened so close to where he worked.

She went in her bathroom and splashed water on her face, even before she looked in the mirror. She knew she didn't want to scare herself this early. With her complexion, dark smudges under her eyes stood out like a beacon and she was sure, without looking, that she had some dark ones today. She slept last night, but her dreams were about the awful tragedy.

Brandi heard the water running and that meant that Mommy was up and she had a very important question that needed an answer now. Since her daddy died, Faith never kept Brandi from her room, so the child opened the bedroom door, then came to the bathroom and knocked. Before it opened, she asked, "Mommy, will we go back to hand out water and tracts?"

Faith spit out the foam in her mouth, opened the bathroom door and looked at her child. She was a pretty girl, even though she was rumpled from sleep and had her jammies on. They looked very much alike; her mom often told her she was watching herself grow up. "No, Love, Mommy doesn't feel good today. Besides, Pastor didn't give you two days off, just yesterday."

Brandi hugged her mommy. "I know, I heard him tell us. I'm sorry you don't feel good, Mommy! Where does it hurt?"

"I think I got too much of that smoke and dust inside yesterday. I have a tummy ache and a headache," she said, patting her stomach.

"Well, Mommy, take two aspirin. You'll feel better real soon," Brandi said, just like she heard her doctor say.

Faith swallowed a sigh. "If only it were that easy."

"Oh, yes, Mommy!"

Brandi hopped up on the toilet seat and began swinging her legs. Faith watched her for a few minutes; then she asked, "Do you feel okay? Does your head hurt or is it hard to take a deep breath?" After all, the child was far closer to the fire, ash, smoke and dust more often during the day than she was. Even as she asked the question, she knew the answer, how could the child have so much energy if she felt as bad as she did?

Brandi pulled in a deep breath, still swinging her feet energetically. With a huge smile she shook her head and said, "Oh, no, I'm real good! I don't hurt anywhere, Mommy. Akchally, I'm kinda hungry, but when we have breakfast that'll be good." Her eyes sparkled, as she said, "I been up a while, Mommy, I been workin' on some strategy to find Matt." She swung her legs extra hard and said, "You know we gotta find him!"

Faith swallowed a groan along with some of the toothpaste she was brushing with. "Oh, you have? What is that?"

The smile vanished from Brandi's face as she thought about what her mommy told her. "Well," she sighed, "maybe it's gonna be harder than I thought. If you feel bad after you take those aspirin, maybe we can't go back today. I thought maybe I'd go look for fireman Matt while you give out water cups."

Faith didn't say anything, not with a toothbrush in her mouth. It was just as well, she knew aspirin wouldn't cure her that quickly, if only it would. She could see that nightmare almost as plainly now as when they were there yesterday. She woke up several times during the night hearing the rumble and the screams. Something else she didn't want to acknowledge, she remembered those blue eyes vividly. The man was tall, at least six inches taller than her late husband, but even with the grime, he was a handsome man. He pulled his mask down, but he still wore the goggles, even so, she saw his eyes. Even through the goggles they sparkled.

As Faith spit out the foam, Brandi said, "We gotta find fireman Matt, Mommy. Jesus told me he's supposed to be my new daddy." Faith sighed; fortunately she masked it by putting the glass to her lips for a mouthful of water to rinse out the suds.

Faith shooed Brandi from her room, found some decent clothes and dressed. Brandi was long finished dressing when Faith made it downstairs. She fixed a little pot of coffee, since she was the only one who drank it. She poured a cup, fixed Brandi's lunch and set it on the end of the counter. Brandi found her lunch box and brought it to the kitchen to put her lunch in. Faith poured Brandi's cereal and milk and fixed her own bagel, then poured another cup of coffee.

As they sat in the sunny kitchen eating breakfast, Faith said, "Brandi, you must put Matt out of your mind at school. You missed a day yesterday, because Pastor Harding closed school, after he heard about the disaster. You know how hard it is for you to settle down after the weekend, but you must listen to your teacher today. She'll probably want to catch up."

Brandi sighed and put another spoonful of cereal in her mouth. After she swallowed and took another drink, she said, "Mommy, I *always* listen, it's just that it doesn't always stick. Besides, I bet Miss Lambert'll have us talking about what we did yesterday and I got so much to tell them!" Her happy face turned sad and Faith could feel the breeze of Brandi's feet swinging. "Do you think that some of the daddies from church got hurt yesterday?"

Faith covered her daughter's hand before she said, "Brandi, it's a very good possibility that some of them were hurt; maybe there were some who even went to heaven. You know there are so many of the daddies who go to our church who work in downtown. If your daddy were still alive, he'd have been working down there."

Brandi patted the back of her mommy's. "Mommy, that's awful, but those guys would go to heaven, just like Daddy did!" Brandi looked at the wall that, if it had a window, would show them the New York skyline. "I wonder if Matt's there working yet."

Faith sighed, choosing to ignore the last few words Brandi said, what was the use, anyway. "Yes, Brandi, those daddies would go straight to heaven, but they left mommies and children just like your daddy left us. Now it's time to brush your teeth and get ready so we won't keep Mrs. Olsen waiting for your ride to school."

Brandi scooped up her cereal dish and her milk glass, and put them on the counter by the sink. "Yes, Mommy," she sighed, "I'll hurry."

Faith looked at the little girl, who had dressed herself that morning. "Brandi, your sox don't match, hurry and change one of them."

"Okay, Mommy, I'll hurry." The child scampered from the kitchen, but it sounded like a whole herd of elephants when she reached the stairs. Faith shook her head and wondered how tennis shoes worn by a nine year old girl could make so much noise!

Faith was cleaning up after breakfast when her mom called soon after Brandi left on the minibus for school. They didn't talk every day, but Faith was always glad to talk with her mom. As they talked, the older lady asked, "How did it go yesterday?"

Of course, the older lady went to the same church as Faith and Brandi, so she knew that a group of ladies went to give out water and tracts. "Mom, it was the most awful sight I've ever seen. There is nothing the same in downtown Manhattan, nothing. I think the worst was that we were so close we could hear screams almost all the time. I don't see how those rescuers can stand to work there hour after hour. It has to be devastating to pull out a body instead of a live person. It just has to be! And... and to know so many were killed instantly! There were so many fires! They just belched out! It was awful."

"I'm sure that's so, Dear. Will the church ladies go back today? Was anything said?"

Faith watched out the front door as the minibus pulled away. All she could see of it was the white top, but she knew it was the bus. "No one spoke of it before I left and it was Amylou who told me to go, but even if they were, I wouldn't go; I'm not feeling well again. All that smoke and stuff really got to me, I guess."

"Oh, Dear, perhaps you should call and get a refill on your prescription that you just finished. I worried about you going down there so soon after getting better."

Knowing how much those pills cost and knowing how many other things she needed to use that money for and also remembering Brandi's cheery remedy, she said, "Mom, I'll be okay, really, don't worry." She quickly changed the subject, "Brandi gave out so many tracts! We gave out a few at the table, but we were so busy we hardly had time for anything but drawing water. Even so, the pile of tracts we left with the ladies was half the size after she got done."

"She is something else, isn't she? Really, that child is a wonder! I love her to death and I'm so glad she loves Jesus!"

"Mom, I'm so glad she loves Jesus so much! I know of one person she showed how to become a Christian." She knew some children could become very bitter, losing a parent the way she had. She was glad Brandi hadn't.

"Oh?"

"Yes, a fireman came for water and told me." She was not about to tell her mom what Brandi was insisting would happen with her and Matt!

"A fireman? How did she get to talk to a fireman? Wouldn't they be really close to where the buildings went down?"

Way to go, Faith! Way to go! Spill the whole kettle of fish, why don't you! Faith groaned to herself, she must be an imbecile. "Oh, remember we gave out lots and lots of water yesterday, not just to bystanders."

"Well, yes, of course. Dear, take care of yourself. Take two aspirin, you know, but call down there to the pharmacy and get that prescription refilled. I'm sure that'll cure it right up!"

"I know, Mom." Faith hung up and sighed; grateful she didn't have to give her mom every detail of her day. She was glad that her mom usually was content to listen to the broad overview. Faith, after all, had lived away from her mom for a good many years.

She really didn't lie, he had come and talked with her at the table, she had given him a cup of water. It's just that Brandi hadn't talked to him at the table. However, she knew there'd be a tirade if her mom found out that Brandi was down on all that rubble so close to the fires and falling buildings. It upset her the first time she saw her run off, but they were so busy giving out water cups she couldn't hold her and there was so much noise she couldn't call her back. Besides, now God has another child!

A few minutes after she hung up, Faith took two aspirin with a large glass of orange juice, then lay down and fell asleep in minutes. Much later, when she woke up, she felt much better and was glad she hadn't wasted her money on getting her prescription refilled. Perhaps she'd go shopping later and buy Brandi's favorite for supper. What was that? Oh, mac and cheese, of course, how could she have forgotten! She chuckled, she hadn't really forgotten, Brandi would have mac and cheese every night after school if she could.

Brandi was in third grade in Christian school. As she predicted, Miss Lambert went around her classroom asking what the children did the day that they had off. Brandi wiggled in her seat, waiting her turn. However, her seat was in the third row and Miss Lambert almost always started with the first row. Brandi tried very hard to sit still and listen. However, when she was excited that was almost impossible. The last boy in the second row had lots to say, but it wasn't about what happened downtown. Brandi sighed; it was so hard to wait her turn.

Finally, Miss Lambert reached her row and after the first two girls shook their heads and said they hadn't done anything but go home and play, the teacher said, "Brandi, you're about to jump out of your skin! What did you do yesterday?"

"Oh, Miss Lambert, some of the ladies from our church went downtown and gave out water to all those rescuers! Mommy took me and I gave out tracts to lots and lots of people! I gave one to fireman Matt and he's going to heaven now!"

"Really? How do you know that?"

"'Cause I had him read the tract where it says "'For God so loved the world...'" and he did! He put his name in there, too and then he prayed to Jesus so now he's going to heaven, if he dies!" She pulled in a deep breath. "But I know he's not gonna die!"

"Why do you know that, Brandi?"

"'Cause he's gonna be my new daddy!" she answered, earnestly.

Marcy Lambert knew Faith Lankaster quite well, she often volunteered in the classroom, so she didn't gasp, even though it came up in her throat. She also wondered if Brandi had shared her knowledge with her mother and if so, what Faith thought of it. She knew Faith would never settle for a man who wasn't a Christian, but Brandi just said she showed the fireman how to give his life to Jesus and Marcy was sure Brandi knew how to do that. Still, Brandi's revelation gave Marcy pause; this was something to speak to Faith about.

Marcy covered her mouth and made a face. She saw coverage on the TV of the horrendous happening. Those pictures showed the yellow tape and how far from the actual destruction it was. Had Brandi gotten that far? However, without making any comment about Brandi's revelation, Miss

Lambert asked, "So you gave out tracts while the ladies gave out water? That was really great, Brandi!"

"Oh, yes! Fireman Matt and me sat on this big slab of sidewalk, or maybe it was part of one of the towers and talked about heaven. It was so neat! Later on, he went and got a drink from Mommy and talked to her."

Scowling, the teacher asked, "Were you down in all that rubble and fire?"

Her face shining, she exclaimed, "Oh, yes, Miss Lambert! How could I talk to people who needed to know they'd go to heaven if I didn't go where they were hurting? I just ran under that yellow tape a couple of times!"

Miss Lambert nearly choked. "You mean your mommy let you? She let you go under that tape to talk to people?"

Waving her hands, she dismissed what the teacher asked, "Oh, she was too busy handing out water, she couldn't give out tracts, so I just grabbed some and went back. And fireman Matt's going to heaven because I did!"

Hardly able to say the words, Marcy exclaimed, "Brandi, you could have been one of the ones who went to heaven!"

Brandi waved her hand and said, as if it was nothing important, "Yeah, I know, but it's just like fireman Matt, he's not gonna go now and I'm not either. Daddy's up there, he'll take care of things for a while."

The teacher shook her head and went on to the next child. There was no stopping Brandi when she was on a roll. She found out, even in the few days school was in session this school year that one didn't argue much with Brandi, she always, somehow got the last word. That was pretty bad, when a nine year old could out-talk her teacher. Even the bell didn't stop her sometimes. It made her wonder how Faith worked with that.

Matt kept an eye on his watch, but at about two thirty, Colin came around and asked that he and Mario find one of the entrances below grade and see what they could find. Being a fireman and living so close to his firehouse, Matt never went underground below the Twin Towers. He picked up his pickaxe, shouldered it and followed Mario through the rubble, to a gaping hole and headed down.

It was eerie down below. It felt like being in a mine, except things down here were much more sophisticated than just rock. One level was the subway platform with tracks twisted and unusable, sticking up through piles of rubble. It was amazing that no train was in the station when the towers came down. Some were close by and some had wrecked because others plowed into them. There had been many people hurt, but no one died in the stations.

The catastrophe happened early enough in the morning that some of the shops weren't open for business. However, there were many that were totally demolished when all that cement and steel came crashing through their ceilings. However, there was much more open space than either Matt or Mario could imagine. It was quiet, so quiet, compared to the noise outside. Another thing they noticed, even without their normal power source the area underground was much cooler than above ground. Possibly that was the cave affect. The cooler temperatures were a welcome relief.

They walked around, only having to use their axes occasionally. It was a welcome change from ground level. In other places, the only thing that seemed strange was that everything was covered with a thick layer of dust and soot. However, what they noticed most was how still and quiet it was. Usually, there were hundreds of people down here, now there were none. Usually, there were trains roaring into the station and belching out people onto those platforms, while others swarmed into them to hurry them on to another stop. Usually there was the sound of motors running, escalators rumbling, elevator bells dinging or even an occasional sound from a climate control unit. Today there was no noise at all.

Matt knew if he wanted to get to the church on Long Island for the Bible study and prayer meeting, he must leave Ground Zero by four. That would give time to return to his firehouse, get to his room and clean up, eat supper and get on the Long Island train. Even then, he must find out after he reached Thomaston, how to find the church.

However, when four o'clock came, he and Mario were deep inside the underground catacombs of the Twin Towers, going through one of the shops, seeing if anything could be salvaged. It was tedious work, usually it was climate controlled, but of course, nothing was working now, only the emergency lights that rescuers had stretched to help them find anyone who could still be alive, that was heart-rending work. There was no one, not even a body.

They worked until six; and finished one store, so they decided to head out. Neither of them had eaten since breakfast and their stomachs were complaining quite loudly. They both brought a container of water from the station and emptied it several times, their throats getting so dry from the smoke and dust still swirling around them.

THREE

As they reached ground level, Colin was close by giving out assignments. He saw his two men and came right over, putting his arms around each man's shoulders, then clamping their heads in a vice. "You guys are super! We've called in some subs and put a rush job on some new cadets." He had to swallow, remembering the reason why they needed so many new men. They lost so many good, seasoned, firefighters to this catastrophe. Continuing in a voice not quite steady, he said, "These new guys need experience, so a bunch'll come in tomorrow, it takes a little time to get them here from the school, you know. I want you guys to take tomorrow off. Your regular shift starts at three tomorrow, doesn't it?"

"Yeah," Mario answered.

The man squeezed his men's shoulders and said, "Okay, don't come in until then and expect to stay at the station. We haven't heard any screams in hours and it's way past time for anyone to still be alive."

Nodding, hoping he could sleep better tonight, Matt said, "Gotcha! It'll be a pleasure not to come here tomorrow."

Colin slapped their shoulders and said, "I know that! Go on home and hey, break a leg!"

"Will do, boss," Matt gave him a cocky grin.

After eating his meal, Matt tried to remember if there was anything on that tract that listed something that would happen on Thursday. Maybe what he should do was take the train out to Thomaston and find the church tomorrow. He was off Sunday morning, but on at three o'clock for twenty-four hours. If he knew exactly where the church was he could make it, he was sure. There wasn't a church close to his room or to the station; besides, perhaps he could see Brandi and her mom. *Where had that thought come from?* Well, sure, he wanted to see Brandi, he hadn't seen her since she was down in all the rubble. Just for his own peace of mind he needed to know she hadn't been hurt – yeah, that was it.

After sleeping in the next morning, Matt dressed casually in walking shorts and a polo shirt; it was September, the sun was shining, it was a hot day. He headed to the restaurant for brunch, and then to the Long Island Railroad Station. It was a long time since he went out on the Island, so he knew he must watch for the stop. When the train stopped at the station in Thomaston, he went directly inside and up to the ticket window.

After the last person bought his ticket for the train that was there, Matt stepped up to the window and asked, "Could you tell me how to reach the Bible Church here in town, please?" When Matt had the directions he set out. His long legs took him quickly for those blocks. It was several blocks, but it wasn't stifling, there was a breeze. The air smelled and felt clean, nothing like what he lived through the last two days. It was a chance to remember that there was life away from rubble, debris, fires and screams of the hurt and dying.

It was lunch time for the school children, many of them were on the playground and the huge parking lot that doubled as playground on school days. As he came to the large church, he was astonished to see so much activity; nothing on the tract mentioned that there was a school located at the church. It made him wonder if he should go in. However, he made this trip, regardless if everyone was at lunch, he hoped someone was in the office and could help him. He didn't want to go back to Manhattan without knowing something. This was a good way to take his mind off the devastation.

Brandi finished her lunch and put her box in her cubby, then ran out the door to the playground, since it was such a beautiful September day. She looked out to the sidewalk close to where she was and saw a tall man with broad shoulders. The other day Matt had his helmet covering most of his hair, but today it shown in the sunlight. There was no smoke out here to hide his blond waves and Brandi saw him walking rather slowly by the play area.

Of course, Brandi didn't know any speed but run, especially on the playground, she had so much energy to let out after sitting in class all morning. Her heart started beating fast and a smile formed on her lips, could that be Matt? Had he come, in answer to her prayer? Had Jesus told him she and Mommy needed him? Just before he turned the corner to walk up the sidewalk to the front door of the church, she started waving.

"Mister Matt! Mister Matt! Remember me?"

Matt couldn't believe what he saw! He wondered about Brandi ever since she slipped off his knee on Tuesday. Of course, he knew she was fine, her mother had confirmed that when he went to get a drink, but that was hours before dark and he hadn't seen her again. So to see her now, well and in good shape - did wonders for him. His heart took a little trip when he saw the child with his own eyes. A broad grin spread across his face as he waited for her to run up. As he had decided at Ground Zero, she was a beautiful child.

"Mister Matt!" she said, breathlessly. "You came all the way out here?"

"Yes, I did, Brandi. That tract you gave me had the name of this church on it."

When she came to his side, she grabbed his hand and looked up at him. "Oh, yes, of course! How come you came?"

Closing his hand around the tiny hand, he looked down at her and smiled. "Brandi, I wanted to know where to come for a service. The stamp on the tract gave the times of the services and the address, but didn't tell how to get here. I haven't been out here on the Island in a long time and I've never been to Thomaston, so I wanted to know how long it'd take to get here when I had the time off."

Giving Matt her biggest smile, Brandi started dragging him toward the front doors and asked, "Wow! That's super! So you're not rescuing more people now?"

"Brandi, I was there most of yesterday and by afternoon all those screams had pretty much stopped. Other firemen are there today still trying to find more people, but I have to go back to work later on today."

"Oh. So you gotta go back later and rescue more people?"

Matt shook his head. "No, not unless there's a fire run somewhere in our precinct. My boss said we'll stay at our station today. They're pretty sure they got all the live people out by yesterday, so it's only cleanup today and other guys get to do that."

"Well, come on, I'll take you in and show you where you go. All the big people mostly go in the front door. Are you gonna come to Sunday school?

It's good, you know. Mommy goes in this special class; it's for mommies without daddies and people who never had anybody. We got other classes for mommies and daddies and even one for old people like my gramma, but that's way too old for you." Matt couldn't help but chuckle.

By now Brandi had Matt inside the large church foyer. Unlike the playground, it was quiet and cool. Brandi looked up at him innocently. "What kind of class would you go in?"

Matt looked at the bulletin board inside the big doors and said, "Sunday school begins at nine o'clock?" When she nodded, he said, "Wow! I'd have to get up really early to get here for that. It takes two hours to get from where I live out here."

Her grin was infectious, so much that he had to grin back at her. She said, "That's okay, Mister Matt. You just have to go to bed early on Saturday. It's easier to get up early that way. If you have a good night's sleep you wake up good." That all sounded like somebody's mom had to work hard to convince an active child they needed to go to bed. She began pulling him across the large foyer. Their progress was too slow for her. "So what class would you go in?" The child was persistent; he had to give her that.

Brandi pointed at the names beside several doors that obviously led into classrooms around the large foyer. He cleared his throat, realizing only now what Brandi had said. Her mommy went in a class for mommies without daddies, in other words, a singles class. Somehow, the lovely lady was unattached. That was something he hadn't thought of. "Um, I guess I'd go in the one your mommy goes in."

"Oh, yippee! That's the easiest one to find." Now that the big outside door was closed, it was dark in the foyer; obviously this part of the building wasn't used by the school. Unlike his time at Ground Zero, it was climate controlled.

Straight ahead was an office that was much brighter than where they stood, it looked state of the art, however just to the side was another large room. That one was only lit by daylight coming in two windows. Brandi led him to that one. "My class is downstairs in that other building, but here's where Mommy goes and you'd go, too. See, it says..." she scrunched up her nose and read, "...'Berean Class,' um, that means, singles, so you'd go in there. Come on, I'll show you our principal."

"Your principal?"

"Yeah, he's the guy who preaches most of the time on Sunday, but he's also our school principal. He's a really neat guy, you'll like him."

Matt felt a little strange walking along, being pulled by a little girl, but he went with her through the open doorway into the office. The lady behind the computer terminal looked up, first at Brandi, then at the tall man who came to stand beside her. "Brandi, why are you in here? Aren't you supposed to be on the playground now?"

Brandi flashed her contagious smile. "Oh, yes! Mrs. Fisher, but this is Matt, he's going to heaven because I showed him how the other day. See, he's a fireman and he was down in all that fire and stuff where me and Mommy went the other day – where Mommy gave out water. I gave him a tract and showed him how he could go to heaven. Mommy gave him water."

Matt held out his right hand toward the lady. He smiled and said, "I'm Matt Barns, Ma'am, I work for the FDNY."

The lady gave Matt a very close look, as she reached for his hand. She hadn't seen such a handsome man in a very long time. It was good her husband wasn't there; he might have had a jealous thought. However, Matt didn't seem to notice, he looked at the lady and smiled, then down at the energetic child beside him.

"Mrs. Fisher?" Brandi said, immediately, then looked at the open door of the pastor's office. "Is Pastor Harding in his office now?"

"No, Brandi, he's probably out on the playground wondering where you are!" She took Matt's hand and said, "I'm Marian Fisher, I'm happy you came by. Were you wanting information about the church? We have a booklet of our church activities. Of course, you can tell we have an elementary school here and our pastor is the principal."

Matt smiled down at Brandi. "Well, Ma'am, on Tuesday, Brandi gave me a tract and we read part of it together. Later, I noticed the church stamp and decided to make the trip to find out where you are so I can visit when I'm not on duty. I guess, if you have more information than that, I'll take it. I do plan to come back."

The lady jumped from her seat and exclaimed, "Oh, yes, of course!" She hurried to a file cabinet and pulled open a drawer. "We are happy to give out our booklet. The more people who know about our church, the more will hear the Good News!"

"Yes, I'm sure that's true."

Just as Marian came back with a booklet and several papers in her hand, a man walked in the office. He looked down at Brandi and said, "So here you are! What are you doing here, Brandi? It's play time and you always love that. Play time's almost over. You know the bell's going to ring in only a few minutes."

Still holding Matt's hand tightly, she looked up at him and her grin spread across her face, as she said, "Yes, but you see, Pastor Harding, this is Matt. He's going to heaven because I gave him a tract the other day. He read it and talked to Jesus. He came out to find out about our church so he can come to Sunday school and stuff. Isn't that great?"

The pastor held out his hand and smiled at the younger man. "I'm Pastor Jim Harding, you're from Manhattan?"

"Yes, I'm Matt Barns, FDNY. Brandi and I met at Ground Zero on Tuesday. She wanted to be sure I'd go to heaven." He grinned at the older man and took his hand for a warm handshake. "I am, Sir, because we read together about God's love for me. We read from that tract that had your church's name on it."

Jim Harding swallowed and in a voice not quite his own, he said, "That's great!"

Brandi's face looked positively angelic. Her hand was still in Matt's, but she was nearly dancing beside him. "He's gonna come here to church when he has time off! Isn't that super duper, Pastor Harding?"

"Yes, it is, Brandi. I think it's about time for the bell to ring. Just this once, you can go down the steps here inside to get back to your classroom. I think Mr. Barns and I have a few things we'd like to talk about, okay?"

"Yes, Pastor, but you don't have to tell him how to get to heaven, 'cause I already did that and he is!" Brandi's face was positively radiant.

Brandi pulled her hand from Matt's, waved to him and ran from the office while the three adults stood and watched. Matt hadn't held such a tiny hand in a very long time, but his hand felt just a little empty after Brandi's warmth left. The pastor turned and watched the child run from the room and sighed, shaking his head. "That child is something else! We all wondered how she'd take her daddy's death, but all she says about it is that he's gone to heaven to be with Jesus." Jim shook his head. "Her mom is responsible for that."

"Oh?" Matt asked, "When was this?"

The pastor looked to Marian, but then, before she could answer, he said, "It's been three years now, I think."

Not even knowing Brandi's mother's name, he knew that should not be the first question across his lips, but now that he knew there were several years that the lovely lady was single, he wanted more than anything to make her acquaintance, but he didn't voice his thoughts. The pastor motioned to him, so he smiled at the secretary and followed. Surely, the name of the lovely lady would come out while he and the pastor talked.

When they were seated behind the closed door of the pastor's office, he said, "So Brandi really led you to the Lord?"

Matt grinned at the man sitting behind the desk. "Well, she didn't use fancy words like that, Sir, but she had me read from this tract." Matt had found himself each day sliding the tract into his shirt pocket before he left his sleeping room, so he pulled it out now. "Later, when I went to my station, I read the whole thing and discovered the address of the church, so I decided to find out where it was."

The older man shook his head again. "That child is so amazing! You say she found you at Ground Zero to give you that tract?"

Nodding, Matt said, "Yes, Sir. She came under the yellow tape quite a ways and handed it to me, but she wouldn't go away until I read the verse, John 3: 16 and put my name into it. Then she had me pray with her." Matt was a little choked up, as he said, "It was an awesome experience, in all that fire, smoke, screams and cursing to bow my head and pray. I won't ever forget it. Some time later, I went to the table where ladies were giving out water and I saw her mother, but Brandi wasn't there. I imagine she was somewhere else handing out those tracts."

Pastor Jim took a hanky from his pocket and wiped his eyes, then leaned back in his chair and said, "It's no wonder Brandi is like she is, Faith's a wonderful lady and a mother of the highest quality. It's too bad Max died, her calling is to be with children. She's been the best mother to Brandi, as you can tell."

"She did seem lovely," Matt muttered.

The pastor pulled in a deep sigh. "So you'll join us perhaps this Sunday?"

"Yes, I'm off in the morning."

"Well, let me invite you to our singles class. It meets at nine o'clock and the teacher is one dynamic man! Church is at ten fifteen." The man cleared his throat. "I do most of the preaching, but hopefully, you'll stay awake while I do."

Matt laughed. "I'm sure that won't be a problem, Sir."

"Say, is that tract all you have to read?"

"Well, I have a book or two in my room." He wasn't quite sure what the man meant from what he said.

Jim chuckled self-consciously and waved his hand before he said, "I'm sorry; do you have a Bible so you can read more than John 3: 16?"

"No, I don't have a Bible, I guess, but yesterday afternoon, there was a man standing almost at the same place where your ladies were handing out water on Tuesday and he was handing out what he called Testaments. He said it was God's Word and it gave hope in all the tragedy. I took one; I was pretty sure John 3: 16 was in there."

"Yes, it's there." The pastor reached behind him and pulled a Book that matched several others from the shelf. "This is the entire Bible. That Testament is good to carry in your pocket to read when you have a minute. This Bible is good for when you have more time. It has a few helps so you can start doing some Bible study. I'd also recommend that you come when we have Bible study here. It'll help you know where you're going now that you've taken the first step in the Christian life. It's wise you start in the New Testament. A new believer can get bogged down if they start in the Old Testament. Can you come back for Bible study some times?"

"My work schedule is on duty for twenty-four hours, off forty-eight. I'm on starting this afternoon at three, so I'll be on starting Sunday at three."

Standing, with one hand holding out the Bible and his other hand to shake, Pastor Harding smiled at the handsome fireman and said, "Matt, thanks for coming today. Soul winning is what being a Christian is all about. Brandi has learned that early at her mother's knee and I'm happy she found you in all that awfulness. Be sure you come on Sunday, I'll look for you and I know Brandi will be, too."

"Thanks, Sir. I'll plan to make it." As he shook the pastor's hand and then turned to go, he didn't say it out loud, but to himself, he said, *I'll be here not just to see Brandi and to hear you, but to meet Brandi's mother.*

Pastor Jim held Matt's hand a moment. "Thanks for coming by, it's been a pleasure."

Matt gave the pastor his smile. "Sir, it has for me too. Thanks. Oh, and thanks so much for this Bible, I'll be reading it as often as I can."

Outside the church door, Matt looked at his watch. He realized he must move fast. Instead of long strides, he broke into a rather fast jog, he must catch the very next train and the station was several blocks away. As fast as he could he must get to his room to change to his uniform. His shift started in two hours. If everything went right, he'd make it, but a short delay, and he'd be late. Not something he wanted to do, especially when Colin was so good to them all in this crisis. The man had kept his head. That's why he was a good commander.

He read in the paper he bought on the newsstand before he boarded the train that some fires were still burning and cleanup would take days. Something else he read and that saddened him profoundly, they hadn't found the Fire Chief, he was one of those who was considered lost, as one of the first responders. However, he remembered Colin saying they'd stay at the station and do a regular shift. Maybe there weren't any fires in their precinct right now, but given the size of NYC, some unrelated ones could call them to action.

Only a few minutes after Matt left, a car pulled onto the parking lot and drove to where the teachers parked. Faith put her windows down a little, it was a hot day and there was no shade on the church parking lot. After getting out, she opened the back door to retrieve her sewing machine, and left her car. She and other mothers were making costumes and scenery for a play the third graders would perform later in October. She was always glad to help the teachers out.

Faith met the other mothers who put her sewing machine to work after only a few minutes of talking over their ideas. They didn't have much time to work, their October deadline was fast approaching and the kids needed the costumes. Some of the dads had volunteered to work on the sets and Faith was glad, she wasn't too good at swinging a hammer or building things; she left that for Max. As she thought about it she wondered if any of the dads had died in the catastrophe. From the newscasts she watched and listened to there were too many deaths to comprehend and even more reported missing. It saddened her to think about it.

She looked at her watch some time later the last bell was about to sound. "Well, Ladies, school's about out, we better get to our cars before the stampede hits. I'll call you all or talk with you about another time to meet. Thanks for coming, I think we got a lot accomplished."

"Yeah, we did," another mother sighed. She also looked at the clock. "Yeah, the hordes are about to strike, see you all again." Each lady grabbed her purse and headed for the exit.

Faith's assessment of the end of school was definitely right. Any adult wanted to be out of the hallways when the last bell of the day sounded. Today especially, the sun was out and heat didn't bother the children nearly as much as it did adults, they just wanted to be outside. Faith sighed, there was a time when she felt that way and so full of energy. Becoming an adult did things for you that weren't always what they were cracked up to be.

Faith had to box up her sewing machine, but she did it in record time, so she was lugging it out the door as the bell sounded. She knew she had a few minutes, the kindergarteners were the only ones to leave at the bell, the other children had to stay in their seats until the bell rang, then they could go to their cubbies for their book bags and lunch boxes. That way, the older children wouldn't trample the little ones as they left school. Even so, Faith hurried as fast as she could while lugging her barely portable machine. Being in the middle of a swarm of kids wasn't what she wanted to do today.

Brandi was one of the first out of her class. She loved school, but when it was over, she wanted to be outside in the sunshine and today was perfect. When the bell sounded, she jumped from her seat, grabbed her book bag and lunch box from her cubby and ran down the hall to the door onto the parking lot. She knew her mommy was here today, she was glad; she wouldn't have to wait to get home to tell her about Matt. She couldn't wait to tell Mommy the answer to her prayer! She only prayed last night! Wow! God was fast about answering that prayer!

Faith always tried to park in the same place when she came to school, so Brandi knew where to meet her. She was still walking to the car when the hordes of children came through the doors and of course, the noise level hit the ozone layer. With her book bag still in one hand and her lunch box in the other, both arms flying out beside her, her curls bouncing and flying in the breeze, Brandi had a huge grin on her face as she ran toward her mommy who stood beside the car still unlocking her door.

"Mommy!" she called; still several cars away and running full out, "Guess who came here to the church today! Mommy, it was so way cool! It was lunch time! Oh, you'll never, never guess!" Brandi skidded to a stop beside the car. "Mommy, it is so awesome!"

Faith straightened up from unlocking the car and thought, but came up with a blank. "I have no idea, Brandi. Who?" Except for the mothers who come to help her, hardly anyone came to the church who wasn't involved with the school when it was in session. It was too quixotic.

By now, Brandi was beside her mom, and her smile couldn't get any bigger. Her arms were still stretched out at her sides and she did a little dance. She exclaimed, "Matt! He came so he could find out how to get here so he can come back on Sunday for church. I showed him where your class is, 'cause it's right there inside the door. I think he'll come to Sunday school! Mommy, how cool is that?"

Despite herself, Faith's heart did a jig, but she quickly controlled it. No one, especially Brandi, could know how, just hearing the man's name affected her. After all, she only saw him for five minutes and she only knew his name because her daughter had told her. Sensible, Christian ladies didn't have heart flutters about strange men! She knew that for a fact. It didn't matter that she lost all rational thought when their eyes met over the water jugs on 9-11.

She cleared her throat to get that frog cleared away, and opened the driver's door so she wouldn't have to look at Brandi. "How do you know that, Brandi?" she asked, after unlocking the rest of the doors with the inside remote opener.

Brandi ran around the car to get in the passenger side, as Faith hoisted her heavy sewing machine onto the back seat. Brandi slammed the door, reached for her seatbelt and said, "Oh, Mommy, 'cause he let me take him inside the front door. I showed him your class and he told me that's the class he'd go in, too. See, I told you he didn't have anybody and we could have him. I knew Jesus was right! Real soon after that, we saw Pastor Harding. He talked to him some more after I went back to class."

And this will bring him back to Sunday school? she asked herself. *I'm a widow with a little girl, for goodness sake! I have too many liabilities; no single man in his right mind'll ever be interested, especially some good looking man like Fireman Matt.* Faith sighed, for goodness sake; she wasn't all that pretty, either. Red hair, curls that wouldn't be tamed, good grief! What would fireman Matt see in her? *Faith, get your head down out of the clouds!* She had to get Brandi away from thinking that Matt was destined to be her new daddy, immediately. Goodness, the man didn't know what he was in for!

"But Brandi, he's a fireman, downtown Manhattan," she said, patiently. "It's quite a ways to come all the way out here. Probably Pastor Harding told him about a good church closer to where he lives. Goodness, Sweetheart, it takes about an hour to get from the Long Island train station there in Manhattan to Thomaston."

"Mommy," Brandi said, sternly, putting her hands on her hips. Mostly, the act was lost on Faith, since she was fastening her seatbelt and putting the key in the ignition. Several seconds later, when Faith finally looked at her, Brandi continued, "Matt is gonna come here! Remember, you told me to pray that he finds a *good* church and we both said ours is the best. He can't be our new daddy if he doesn't come here, you know."

Pulling in a long breath and turning the key to give herself a little time, she said, "Brandi, we have no idea if Matt's even interested in having a relationship with me...."

"Mommy," Brandi interrupted. As if talking to a slow learner, she said, "Mommy, he is! Jesus told me he'll be my new daddy. You gotta trust that Jesus knows best."

"Yes, we both know that Jesus knows best." She wondered many times why the Lord thought the best was to take her wonderful husband at such a young age. However, he was injured in the Middle East and those injuries only worsened until he died. The autopsy finally showed the doctors what really caused Max's health problems, they were insidious, no wonder the doctors hadn't found what was truly wrong with him. With Pastor Harding's counseling, she finally accepted that.

What she didn't say was, *We don't really know if it's Jesus or you just making this up, who can tell. Brandi'll be so disappointed if nothing comes of my meeting Matt. After all, I still don't know his full name.*

Faith swallowed a sigh, three years without a mate was a long time. Sometimes at night it seemed like a very, very long time and her bed seemed so very cold and empty. Sometimes, she hugged the cold pillow where Max used to sleep. Of course, it didn't change anything. The pillow was still lifeless and cold when she woke up. Sometimes in the quietness of her own room she shed some tears.

Almost as soon as Brandi learned how to talk, Faith and Max realized there was no stopping Brandi. Once she could string words together into sentences, she did. Faith found that the best way to get off a subject was not to argue, but drop the subject. Faith learned that Brandi would get the last word, even if it killed her. She knew that today would be no exception so she nodded her head.

With the engine running, Faith looked behind her and to the sides and seeing a space Faith quickly pulled the stick into reverse and maneuvered out of the parking space. That was no small task; there were several minibuses and other cars between them and the exit, not to mention scores of children, all eager to find their way home. Faith eased ahead and turned behind the minibus that usually brought Brandi home. Some of the children were looking out the back windows and several waved.

"Mommy," Brandi waved absently at the back of the bus and said, looking at the hot street, "can't we go for ice cream? We haven't had any softswirl in so-o-o-o long."

Faith thought for a minute. "You know, that does sound like a good idea. Lets. We could even sit under the tree there at our favorite place."

Brandi clapped her hands, but because her seatbelt was fastened, she couldn't reach to hug her mommy, but her grin told Faith everything she needed to know. She'd skimp pennies some other place so they could have a treat. After all, she hadn't bought that refill and that cost way more than two softswirls at the ice cream stand. At the next intersection, Faith turned and headed to their favorite ice cream store. It wasn't often she indulged her daughter, but she felt like having some ice cream, too. If she was at home instead of at school when it let out, Brandi would have ridden the bus and they wouldn't be getting ice cream.

Soon they were in line behind several other cars, some they both recognized from the parking lot at school. Faith laughed. "Look at that! I think there's about three in front of us from your school, Brandi." The little girl giggled right along with her.

Rather than pull into the line, she found a parking spot. Brandi had her seatbelt loose and said, "I'll find us a table, Mommy!"

"Okay, Brandi, I'll get you a cone, I know that's what you want."

"Oh, yes!"

"Be sure you get one in the shade, it's awful hot!"

Getting out of the air conditioned car, Faith felt the sweat immediately start to trickle down her back. Brandi was already headed away from the car and Faith had to call after her. Brandi nodded. "I will, Mommy. I see one right over there."

In line, Faith greeted one of the other mothers, but after their orders were filled, the other lady said, "We're on our way to the beach. See you, Faith!"

"Sure! Have fun!"

Only moments later Faith joined Brandi at the table in the shade. As they licked their cones, Faith asked, "Do you have homework?"

Brandi sighed, "Yes, a little, but I can swing until you get supper ready, can't I?"

"You know that depends on how much you have, Love."

"Oh, not really much. Miss Lambert spent lots of time talking about that awful time. She said it'll be in place of our current events for this week. Why do you think those awful men came and did that to those buildings?" Brandi asked as she licked her ice cream cone.

Faith looked over Brandi's head at nothing in particular; it took several counseling sessions for her to get through her anger. It was Arabs in a different country who started the Gulf War that eventually snuffed out the life of her husband. She knew all about terrorists and what they did all over the world. In her heart, she was sure those who still lived, who had sent their flunkies to do the deeds, were gloating in their success. Yes, God was in control, but Satan sure liked to let people know about himself, too. The Bible said Satan had power just that God could overrule when He saw fit.

Faith weighed her words, but she was sure Brandi was old enough to understand. "Honey, there are some people in the world who believe differently than we do. They think that the fastest way to get to heaven and gain favor with their god is to do something like what happened on Tuesday. For them, they think that is to hurt people, even kill people of other religions and faiths. I believe we Christians are the biggest threat they have. That's why they sent those planes into our buildings. They hate us because we don't believe as they do."

Brandi gasped, "But Jesus said God loves everybody! People aren't to kill other people at all! God doesn't like people who do!"

"Yes, Sweetheart, that's true, but these people have learned the wrong thing. They do not believe in our God."

Brandi scowled fiercely. "They need to know John three sixteen!"

Softly, drawing into her own thoughts, Faith said, "Yes, they truly do. Still, most of them live thousands of miles away and we'll never know who they are."

"That's too bad!" Brandi exclaimed.

Once Matt reached the train station, he was glad it wasn't rush hour and the train into the city was on time. It steamed into the station moments after he arrived, but he was ready with his ticket. He slouched into his seat and the train sped down the track. He reached his sleeping room with minutes to spare. He stripped quickly and literally jumped into his uniform, transferred his New Testament and his tract to the pocket of his shirt and left for the fire station. If they were staying at their own station for this shift, the men would fix their supper. It seemed forever since they were there for a normal shift and he couldn't remember if it was his turn to help fix the meal. It didn't matter, he had to get there, but the heat was oppressive, especially in the canyons of the high rises. Before he reached the station the sweat ran down his back.

Matt's fire station was far enough uptown from Ground Zero that none of the devastation affected them. There was still smoke drifting in the air, they could smell it. However, since it was so hot, the men were glad to come inside and keep the weather out. Unlike downtown, the smoke smell hadn't permeated the walls. Matt met Mario at the time clock, so they punched in, and hurried to the conference room to learn their assignments for this shift. Several men would be assigned immediately to check out the equipment that always had to be in tiptop condition at a moment's notice and others would start their evening meal. Even if they weren't fighting fires, there was always something to keep them busy except during times of sleep.

Matt's fellow firefighters for this shift had barely gathered around the large table when the horn sounded summoning them to the fire trucks for a run. Chairs scraped back and the men were on the move, as Colin said, "Okay, men, we'll meet here when this is over."

"Yes, Sir!" several men yelled.

They returned to the fire station in time to fix a late supper. Any ideas of a huge meal went out with the fire trucks at three o'clock. Their meal was simple, nourishing and fast. The men sat around the table in the big room and talked about the last few days since the happenings of September eleventh.

Many of them hadn't seen the others, since there were no real shifts until this afternoon. When they were finished with their meal, the big board that showed the streets and alleys of their precinct was still quiet. Most of the men got up to refill their coffee cups, then came back to their seats for more talk. Matt hadn't told anyone about meeting Brandi down amidst the rubble. Mario knew about it because he was so close.

Someone looked at Matt and asked, "Say, Barns, what's this I hear about some little girl gettin' behind the lines?" Maybe somebody else liked to gossip, there were other rescuers on the scene, maybe somebody saw him and reported.

He shifted and pushed back from the table, stretching out his long legs. "Yes, I couldn't believe it, but there she was!"

"What, for heaven's sake, was she doin' down at Ground Zero? What was wrong with her mother, didn't she keep her corralled?"

Matt shrugged, as if it was the most natural thing for a little girl to be beside him in such a disaster. "She was handing out tracts and wanted me to take her last one."

The other man smirked. "And of course you did."

"Yeah, I did. She wouldn't leave until I did and we read it together."

"Man!" the man exclaimed, "What are you, crazy? You both could've been killed, you not payin' attention like that."

Matt shrugged, not repentant at all. "Yeah, I know, but what we did was very important and nothing did happen."

"Could have been, though."

Someone else started talking about some other happening at Ground Zero. It was an easy thing to do; almost every man had some different experience he needed to talk about. Before long, everyone was talking about the rescues they made. It was something most of the men needed to say the words and let out the tension. Everyone knew how tense the whole situation that surrounded the terrorists attack was.

The rescue on Wednesday that Matt and Mario made of the young woman was almost the last of a live person. Of course, there were many bodies, but all the firefighters knew there were many who became part of the rubble, burned up in either the exploding planes or in the terrible heat they created as they sent the towers to their doom or crushed beneath the tons of rubble. So far, no one had heard about their fire chief, the city considered him lost.

Mario didn't say much most of the time, but he had a good heart, so he finally said, "I called the hospital earlier this morning to find out about that woman we found. They knew right away who I was talkin' about, 'cause she was so close to the end of the live ones. The nurse I talked to said she's recovering okay. When the medic told them what we told him, everyone was surprised. Bein' buried under so much, she had lots and lots of bruises, but only had a fractured collar bone. They said she should be discharged in a few days. She was pretty weak and dehydrated, that's why they kept her."

"Man! That's somethin' else!"

Mario nodded. "That's what we thought, too. You know, I think everybody's got a time to live and a time to die and that lady's time to die wasn't up yet."

"Yeah, I believe you're right, Man!" Matt agreed.

"I'm still having nightmares," another man exclaimed.

"I hear ya, man! It's hard to go to sleep!" Matt had experienced that the night of the attack, but since then, he was able to sleep quite well.

The breakfast dishes were rinsed and in the dishwasher when the horn sounded, calling the firefighters to their trucks. The light on the board showed that the fire was at the very edge of their precinct in one of the warehouses close to the harbor. None of the men liked to go there, often the fire started in the storage part of the huge building and whatever was there acted like a torch. More than a few times there was foul play involved. For some reason, mobsters loved to use abandoned warehouses to further their activities. Sometimes the fire was set intentionally to lure firemen so someone could do them in. The firemen had to be really careful at a warehouse fire; they could be shot by some gangster just for being there. However, they knew it was their job to suit up in seconds, hit the trucks on the run and get down the road with sirens screeching.

This particular warehouse had been standing a long time. The office seemed well maintained and was still intact when the trucks arrived. However, flames were coming through the roof behind the office. The warehouse part was totally engaged when they arrived. Just as the men surmised, something in the storage area ignited and now there was quite a blaze. It took the men several hours and lots of water to extinguish the blaze. However, they were able to keep the flames from reaching the office, which was a feat in itself.

However, that was always a good thing, sometimes the owners kept valuable records there.

When the fire was finally out, Matt and Mario, along with others, were doing clean-up, going through the burned out shell, making sure that the last of the flames were out. They were very careful, since some of the roof had caved in. Other crew members shut off the hydrant at the street and put the hoses in place on the truck, getting the truck ready to go back to the station.

Much to Matt and Mario's surprise, as they headed for the office area, in the quietness that followed all the activity, they heard whimpers and sniffling in a corner behind the office. They hurried toward the sound, a totally foreign sound for an abandoned warehouse. They had walked through the whole expanse of the structure except for this area that had a common wall with the office. Stepping over some of the rubble from the caved-in roof, Matt a few steps ahead of Mario, they came face to face with two tiny children.

They were the same size, but one was a boy and the other a little girl who coward behind the boy. Both of them were filthy, their faces covered with soot. Matt looked a little more closely at the children, but neither of them looked like they were burned. At one time, he was sure; the whole storage part of the warehouse was in flames. He glanced around, wondering where they could have hidden. He didn't see any place at all; these children must have had their guardian angel wings completely covering them for them to come out without a singe.

Matt's heart turned over as he looked into the children's eyes. He immediately abandoned his pickaxe and crouched in front of the little boy, knowing how much bigger he was than they, he was sure they felt intimidated by his size. As he reached for the boy's hand, he asked, as kindly and quietly as he could, "Didn't you get out with everyone else?"

The little boy shook his head. "No, Sir," he murmured.

Matt looked around, then up at the blackened wall. "Goodness, I can't believe you made it! You're both all right."

"Yes, Sir," the boy whispered.

As Matt thought about it, this area was close to the office area, in fact, that was the common wall. Across the huge room was the loading dock, there were gaping holes even before the fire. He knew that, because there were no doors, just the hardware for them, outlining the holes. Probably the air coming in those openings had fueled the fire. Perhaps this area was safer, since nothing in the office area was damaged. It made him wonder if these children were living here on their own. But they were so tiny!

Deciding there was no harm in asking, he said, looking first at the little girl, then the boy, "Have you been living here?"

The boy didn't answer, but looked down at his feet, the little girl didn't answer, but stuck her thumb in her mouth as she looked at the back of her brother's head. "Don't you have family? A mom and dad?"

The boy still looked at his feet, but the little girl, sucking her thumb vigorously, peeked around him and Matt could see her barely shaking her head. Hoping to gain their trust, Matt put one knee on the floor and held out his hands to the children. The little boy didn't move, so the girl didn't either, although she looked like she wanted to. His heart twisted, these children were undoubtedly abandoned or perhaps runaways. Obviously, something or someone made them really skittish. He could feel his eyes scratching; he loved children and hated seeing them suffer.

"Why don't you guys come with me? There's nothing here for you now, I'll see that you get a place to live and food to eat. We need to get you out of this smoky place."

The little boy moved his hand out from his body, not to take Matt's hand, but in front of the girl as she tried to move. Shaking his head, the boy said emphatically, "We don't go no place by ourselves! She's my sister and I won't let you split us up!"

As kindly as he could, Matt said, "I didn't say I would split you up. Sonny, you two can't stay here, not now that it's all burned up." He pointed over his head. "Look at the huge hole in the roof! All kinds of stuff can come down on you."

Belligerently, the boy said, "We can so! We done it before!"

FOUR

TIME STOOD STILL.
Matt couldn't speak for several minutes.

Seeing the tears in the little girl's eyes, Matt tried to stay as calm as he could. This was always the hardest part of their job, finding abandoned children. Almost whispering, trying to counteract the boy's loud voice, Matt said, "Why don't you come with us back to the station? None of us got lunch and you can eat with us. How about that?"

It was no mistaking the sound that came from both of their tummies just then. The mention of food told how hungry the children were. It couldn't be hidden; no cars were going by outside and the fire truck that was waiting for the two men was out beyond the building. "Okay," the boy said, grudgingly. "I guess we are kinda hungry."

Mario was several feet behind Matt, they were both big men, one that size was enough to frighten children this size. However, as Matt stood up, Mario moved and picked up Matt's pickaxe. The look on his face told anyone how compassionate he was. As soon as Matt had the children going, he followed the trio as they made their way across the rubble, down beside the wall into the office. Several times, Matt picked the little girl up to get her over the piles of rubble. She went willingly into Matt's arms, but the little boy would have none of that.

One time when Matt held the little girl, feeling how tiny she was, like skin drawn over bones, he asked her, "What's your name?"

"She don't talk," the little boy answered before the little girl could swallow.

"So what are your names?"

"Karin and Karl."

There was a very definite family resemblance and they were just about the same size. "Are you twins? How old are you?"

"Yeah, I'm five minutes older'n her. We're five."

"Wow!" was all Matt could say. Five years old and on their own!

Mario pulled in a noisy breath, he had a five year old girl at home, but he couldn't imagine her living on the street. This little boy grew up fast, needing to find food day after day for them and also a place of shelter, not only for nighttime, but also from the elements. Matt was blinking fast, intent on keeping the tears from coming to his eyes. He knew he couldn't cry in front of these two little urchins, but his eyes still hurt.

The shoes the children wore were several sizes too big, but they were full of holes. The first time Matt picked Karin up she lost one and they had to stop for it. What clothes they had on hardly covered them and were filthy. Neither one of them carried anything away from the spot, there was nothing where the two firemen found them. Matt wasn't sure but that the children had found the clothes in the same place they found most of their food - the local dumpster. It made his stomach turn over. Thinking about the one close to his sleeping room, it had huge rodents in it! He stifled a shudder; he couldn't imagine a tiny little boy climbing into one of those.

As they neared the front of the office, but before Mario opened the door, Matt thought of something, so he said, "You know, we're both firemen and we ride on a big fire engine. You won't be scared, will you, Karin?"

She was walking beside Matt, holding tightly to his hand, but as soon as he asked his question, she skipped in front of him and held up her arms. He smiled at her and as he scooped her up, he said, "Ah, you'd feel better if big, strong Matt carried you out there, is that it?" She nodded and gave him a shy grin.

He smiled back at the little girl, then perched her on his arm and gave her back a little pat. At that moment he wanted to kiss the tiny child, but he didn't. Instead, he took Karl's hand again and smiled at him, before he said, "How about you, Karl, will you be scared?" He was sure he knew what the little boy would say.

Without hesitation, Karl said, "Nah, I'll just hold your hand, mister fireman." Which he did, *very* tightly.

Karin laid her head on Matt's shoulder, but when Mario pushed the outside office door open and the loud engine noise burst upon them, the little girl tried to burrow closer to Matt's chest. He couldn't see her face, but her left thumb went in her mouth. He wondered when he first saw the children, why her left thumb was so clean, now he knew. A shudder went through him as he realized how much dirt that little thumb had on it. He wondered how long these children had been on their own. If the amount of dirt was a barometer, it was a very long time. He had to revise that, they were in the fire just now; some of the dirt could be ashes.

Matt and Mario were the last of their crew to reach the truck. Immediately, when the firemen on the truck saw Matt and his charges, they began to move. Matt and Mario ordinarily rode on the back and others of higher rank rode inside. However, the two men sitting beside the driver got out and went to the back, leaving the door open so Matt could have the seat. He looked at Colin's assistant and grinned, as he moved back, but said nothing. With one hand, he helped Karl in first; then sat on the seat, still holding his tiny burden. Karin wouldn't have let him go anyway. Mario set Matt's pickaxe beside him inside the truck, then closed the door behind him. He gave Matt a subtle salute and went on to the back of the truck to claim the last seat for their return to the station.

Colin, sitting behind the wheel, said, "Who have we here?" as he looked down at the two little people, with a kindly smile.

Since neither of the children seemed to come up with any words at all once they saw the huge truck, Matt said, "This is Karl and Karin. They're five year old twins Mario and I found on the other side of the office wall."

"Wow! and they lived to tell about it?"

"Yeah. I was shocked myself. They weren't that far from where the blaze was and the roof collapsed, yet they aren't burned, not even their clothes."

Over their heads, Colin murmured, "What'll we do with them?"

Matt shrugged. "Split up is out of the question." Karl's little tummy growled just then and he stared up at Matt. "I promised them lunch."

Colin chuckled softly, as he put the big truck in gear and started down the street. "I'd say we got two hungry little people! We better make time back to the station and get some lunch. I know I can eat, breakfast was a pretty long time ago."

"I'm with you on that!" Matt exclaimed. His stomach added an appreciative rumble to the suggestion of food.

Colin brought the fire truck up in front of the station. Several of the men jumped off and two of them stood to direct him as he backed into the spot where the engine was normally parked. By the time Matt had his door open, Colin had the big truck shut off so that the noise of the big diesel wasn't vibrating inside the closed area. Even so, Karin hid her face in Matt's neck and he felt Karl's little hand holding tightly to his pant leg. Matt loved children and these two easily captured his heart.

"Wow!" the little boy murmured.

"It's a big place, isn't it?" Matt asked. It was a big place, even from Matt's perspective, what was it from down at a five year old level?

Looking around, Karl nodded. "Yeah," he whispered.

"Let's go find us some food!"

By now, the next shift was on duty. Immediately, they started their inspection of the big truck, making sure it was cleaned out and ready for another run, which could happen at any moment. Matt knew, as soon as he ate, he was off duty. The big clock on the wall confirmed that three o'clock had come and gone, by an hour.

He decided to go to his locker first, leave his gear; and then head upstairs with his charges to feed them and also himself, plus give them showers and perhaps some clean clothes that hopefully fit better. By now, their stomachs were growling almost constantly. That sound made him wonder when the last time these tiny waifs had anything to put in their stomachs.

As he walked, he said to the little girl, still plastered to his side, "Karin, I must take off my coat and boots. I'm going to have to put you down so I can get them off." When she tried to move even closer to him, he continued, "It's not near as noisy back by the lockers and there won't be as many people."

In fact, when he arrived in the locker room, all the other men from his shift had left, he and the children were all alone and it was very still. Once the door shut and both children saw that they were alone with Matt, they relaxed a little. Karl let go of Matt's pant leg and Karin pulled her thumb from her mouth. That last action made Matt extremely happy. Because he was a fireman he got into dirty places often, but he didn't put it in his mouth! In fact most of the time he had his mouth covered with a mask.

Getting ready to take off his turnout and his boots, Matt crouched down and let Karin's feet touch the floor. Immediately, she moved to her brother's side and put her thumb back in her mouth. Matt tried not to show his dislike of that action by standing up and shrugging out of the coat. Mario had already left his axe beside the locker door, so Matt put his gear away as quickly as he could and pulled out his shoes.

He smiled as he looked down at the children; then held his hands down for them to take. "So, are we ready to go find some of that lunch Colin was talking about?"

Both Karl and Karin nodded solemnly. "Uh huh," Karl whispered. Both children took his hands, and Matt headed for the stairs at the back of the station.

"Great, I'm hungry, too."

Matt fixed them each a peanut butter and jelly sandwich. That was, he knew, universal fare for little kids. What he hadn't expected was that both children stood right beside him watching every move he made. He had barely made his own sandwich when both the children's hands were empty and they starred hungrily at the three mouthfuls he had left. He still stood at the counter as he ate, so he fixed another sandwich for each of the children, and poured them each a glass of milk. Those disappeared nearly as fast as the first sandwiches. Matt hurriedly slapped another sandwich together for himself and pulled out a box of cookies he discovered when he was looking for the peanut butter. After snagging one, he set the box where the children could reach them and they disappeared almost as fast as the sandwiches. It made Matt wonder when the children had eaten last.

The phone rang at the Bible Church in Thomaston and Marian Fisher answered as she usually did. A deep voice said, "Hello, Mrs. Fisher, you may not remember me, but I'm Matt Barns, FDNY. I came in yesterday and you gave me some information about your church."

Oh, yes, Marian could remember! A very happy smile spread across Marian's face immediately. "Yes, Mr. Barns, what can we do for you?" She chuckled. "By the way, it isn't Sunday yet, that was when we thought we'd hear from you."

Matt didn't hear Marian's obvious interest; he was too intent on his mission. "Would you mind if I talked to the pastor, Mrs. Fisher? I certainly hope he's still in and not gone home!"

The secretary wanted to listen to that voice for much longer, but she said, "Sure, Pastor Harding is in his office, let me put you through to him."

"Thank you kindly, Mrs. Fisher."

Only seconds later, Jim Harding answered, "Hi, Matt what can I do for you today?"

"Pastor, last night I had some free time and read the literature Mrs. Fisher gave me about your church and ministries. I noticed you have a foundling ministry through your church." Jim swallowed, but kept silent as Matt continued, "About two hours ago my buddy and I found a set of five year old twins, who were in a warehouse where we were summoned to put out a fire. Amazingly, they were unharmed! According to the little boy, they have no family. I've contacted the children's services offices in every borough, but with the nine eleven tragedy, they're swamped. Would you have any room in your foundling operation for these children?"

The pastor listened as Matt spoke, all the time turning over in his mind what he could do. He was convinced he must do something. It was some time since the church voted to start that ministry, usually the children's services had places for abandoned children in their own area, but Jim could understand, after the catastrophe, that they would be overloaded. Just before Matt finished, the name of the perfect person came to Jim's mind.

"Matt," Jim said, "where can we meet? I think I have just the place for these little tikes. You say you've gone through all the possible channels?"

Matt was slouched in the only comfortable chair in the room, but two little people crowded around his knees, as he said, "Yes, I'm still here at the station and I've spent an hour or so calling all the boroughs, but with the results of nine eleven, no one can take them."

Jim leaned back in his office chair and ran his fingers through his hair. "You say you're still at your station? That's downtown Manhattan?"

"Yes, well, not at Ground Zero, but we can hop the train and be there in an hour or so. I'm free until Sunday afternoon."

"All right. Why don't you do that? While you're on your way, I'll call around and see if I can't locate someone, even if it's for a temporary period of time. That ministry hasn't been operational in a while but that doesn't mean we can't activate it when it's needed so badly like this. We'll wing it from there after you arrive. You say these children are five?"

"Yes, that's right, a boy who's going on twenty and a little girl who doesn't talk."

Jim sighed, "Poor children. I'll see you in a short while."

"Yes, Pastor, thank you."

Matt hung up and looked into the little faces that were both trained intently on him. He took them to the shower room there at the station and supervised a joint shower. Karin wouldn't go in by herself, so he stuck Karl in with her. Now the thumb was the same color as the rest of her. There at the station they had a very small closet where they kept a minimal supply of clothes, mostly things that the men brought in from home that their children outgrew. Thankfully, Matt was able to find one set of clothes that each child could wear, along with some shoes. Both children were sparkling, compared to when he found them. The clothes and shoes fit and didn't have holes.

"Okay, guys," he said, smiling at them. "Let's be out of this place. I talked to a nice man I met yesterday and he's going to see if he can find you a good home. Maybe you can even sleep in a bed tonight. Neat idea, huh?"

"Yeah," Karl muttered.

Even after he had them in the nearly empty room beside the conference room, neither child told him much. Of course, Karin hadn't let out a sound, even though she followed directions or answered with a shake or a nod of her head. Karl either couldn't or wouldn't tell him where they lived before the warehouse and he wouldn't let it slip who his parents were. Grudgingly, he told Matt their last name was something like Kaufmann, but he mumbled and Matt couldn't be sure.

Matt checked his wallet to see if he had enough money with him for the train fare for all of them and him back. He never carried much cash to work, but he had plenty, then reached for their hands and left the building. He found he must adjust his long stride to match that of two five year olds, but he found he enjoyed the company of these little people. Even after six in the evening it was pleasant and still being September it wasn't dark and wouldn't be when they arrived in Thomaston. He wondered who Pastor Jim would find to take the children on such short notice. He didn't know much about pastors, but he was sure the pastor of as large a church as Pastor Jim had along with being principal of an elementary school, he was too snowed under to take them himself.

When they reached the train station, the noises of the trains had Karin clamoring to get into Matt's arms. Karl moved much closer to Matt, gripping his hand in what for an adult would be bone-crushing. Matt moved to the ticket window and paid the fare, then took the children to the departing train level. Minutes later a train roared in next to the platform where they stood and Karin buried her head in Matt's neck and put a strangle hold around his neck, while Karl whirled behind him. They wouldn't become unglued until they were safely on the train and the doors shut. Thankfully, the noise was shut out by the closed doors. Matt sat in a seat in about the middle of the car and let the children look out the window when the train left the tunnel.

"WOW!" Karl exclaimed.

"We sure are moving fast, aren't we?"

"Yeah, super fast!" Karl said, but wouldn't take his eyes away from the window. The train moved about as fast as a subway train, obviously Karl and Karen hadn't ridden either one.

As soon as Jim Harding hung up from talking with the fireman, he dialed a number. It was indeed Friday about suppertime, but the person he had in mind to start with didn't usually go out on Friday, in fact, she and her daughter usually spent Friday evenings at home for a quiet family night. Jim was always impressed with the little Lankaster family; Max had provided a stable, loving home. He was one of a kind; and it tore Jim up to have to preach the funeral for such a good man. God had His reason for taking Max home, but he left a devastated, grieving widow behind and a tiny child for her to raise on her own.

After the third ring a breathless Faith picked up the phone. "Hello?"

"Hi, Faith, did I get you from something?"

"Oh, Brandi and I were coming in from the yard when we heard the phone ring. I had to run the last few feet. What can I do for you, Pastor?"

He wondered how to broach the subject for a single mom, but he made the call, now he must get her to agree. She was the best person, actually, the only one he would consider. He drew in a long breath and said, "Faith, you know about our foundling ministry, don't you?"

"Y-yes, Pastor," she answered, hesitantly. How could this relate to her? That ministry hadn't been mentioned in a business meeting in a few years.

"I just hung up from talking to Matt Barns. I guess he's the fireman whom Brandi led to the Lord when you ladies were there handing out cups of water on nine eleven."

At hearing his name, his full name finally, Faith's heart skipped a beat, but she quickly put a clamp on it. She still couldn't understand where this had anything to do with her. "Yes?" she asked, tentatively.

Jim took another deep breath, scooted his chair back and rested his heels on the desk. He knew he had to do this in one; there was no one else he wanted to place these children with. Perhaps there was another home who could better afford the children, but no home could do what Faith could do. Perhaps if he were relaxed he could pull this off better.

He took a deep breath and plunged in. "Matt worked another fire today, not at the Towers disaster, but somewhere else and found a set of twins in the burned out building. He said that fortunately they were unharmed. He spent some time calling the children's agency in each of the boroughs, but they're swamped and have no one to place any children with. He read our literature and called me about our foundling ministry, hoping we could help them. He was concerned that they were living in this abandoned warehouse. I immediately thought of you. Would you be able to help out, maybe even for a day or two?"

Thinking of her nice home, that had four bedrooms and lots of yard space, where at one time she hoped to raise several happy children, she along with her husband, she sighed. Being a practical woman, she said, "Pastor, I'm a single mom. As you know, we have a limited budget which Brandi and I manage to live on, if I'm careful. I've never had to, nor do I want to take charity, but a set of twins could be a handful. I might not be able to do a good enough job."

While Faith talked, Jim did some fast thinking. "Man! I forgot to tell you, they're a boy and girl about five years old. Believe me, we wouldn't expect you to stretch your budget that much, Faith. This foundling ministry has funds available to help." *He would make it happen!*

The ministry was set up several years ago, because the church found out that a missionary's family, whom the church supported, had returned home without the father, but other arrangements were made, so it was never used. So no funds were set aside for it, the deacons couldn't see any reason for that. There was an emergency fund that the church dipped into occasionally to help out people who came asking for assistance. However, even if he and Marcia had to do without something, he'd make sure Faith had some money to work with.

After a moment's silence, where Faith was contemplating the pastor's words, she asked, "When would this start?"

Jim chuckled softly. "Well, Faith, as we speak Matt's bringing the children out here to the church. I think it'd start as soon as you could get here."

Faith also chuckled, looking up at her kitchen clock. "My, you don't give a body long to mull this over, do you?"

A smile in his voice, Jim answered, "Actually, I don't, Faith. Matt said he's still at the fire station and he'd leave with them immediately. He said it'd take about an hour to get here."

"Five years old, a boy and a girl," Faith mused out loud. "Fireman Matt found them in a warehouse where he helped put out a fire? They weren't hurt, burned?"

"That's what he said. He said they weren't harmed and that really surprised him."

She let out a long sigh. "I guess, Pastor, since I'm sure you called me because you felt I was the best you could find, I'll help you out. You say it's for a day or two? Can they go home after that? Is that what you're saying?"

Jim pulled his hand over his face, cleared his throat and said, "Well, it could be longer than that, I guess."

Faith laughed again. "I heard that, Pastor. I'll get Brandi cleaned up and we'll be there in, say, twenty minutes."

The man would not let the sigh of relief sound over the phone! "Great! Thanks so much, Faith. Your crown in heaven is sparkling!"

"Pastor," she warned, "none of that! As I'm sure you know, I love children, maybe some don't but I consider them a gift from the Lord."

"I know, Faith, I know. Even so, I do believe that you have a special crown in heaven that the Lord's polishing up just for you."

Brandi stood at her elbow when Faith hung up. "What was that about, Mommy? Was that Pastor Harding?"

Faith replaced the phone on the wall, sat in a kitchen chair and drew her daughter to her. Nodding, she said, "Yes, Honey, that was Pastor. Fireman Matt called him. He found two little kids in a burned out building and he's bringing them to church. They have nowhere to live...."

Brandi's face turned into brilliant sunshine. "Mommy! They can come here! We'd love them to pieces!" She looked intently at Faith. "Matt can be our new daddy, like Jesus told me!"

Faith mentally shook her head. There was that....

"Come on, Brandi, wash your hands, you've been playing outside. I've been digging up some carrots from the garden, we both need to wash up; and then we'll go to church."

Knowing any argument she might have was already lost, Faith said nothing more. She and Brandi washed up, and with a smile, she reached for her purse and keys. She wouldn't say it out loud, Brandi was not to know that recently Faith hoped and prayed for a man to come into her life. She remembered clearly her reaction to the handsome fireman at the water table on Tuesday. Even with all the grime, the horrible circumstances hadn't changed her reaction. She sighed, as she and Brandi headed out the back door to the garage, with Brandi skipping happily ahead. She was already in the car when Faith raised the door, then came to her side and got in.

"Mommy! This is so exciting! A sister and a brother," she finished happily. Clapping her hands, she exclaimed, "This is super-duper!"

"Brandi, you must remember this is probably temporary, if their mommy and daddy can be found, they'll have to go to them."

Brandi let out a big sigh, "Mommy, you just don't seem to understand. Fireman Matt's bringing them and we're all gonna be a happy family one day." *Real soon*, but she didn't say that out loud. Mommy probably wouldn't listen to that part.

Faith pushed the key into the ignition, but didn't turn it. She knew there was no time like the present to get some things said. Taking Brandi's hand, and looking sternly at her, she said, "Brandi, look at me!" This had gone quite far enough, at least for now. The car was silent, Faith hadn't started it. As soon as she knew Brandi gave her full attention, Faith said, "Fireman Matt will not be your daddy today! That much I can guarantee you. Tonight, when we come home and you go to bed, there will be two other children in the house and in beds in another room, but Matt will not be there. Do you understand?"

A very subdued little voice said, "Yes, Mommy."

She waited until Brandi answered, this was very, very important. "Another thing, you are not, absolutely *not* to say anything to anyone, not Pastor Harding, not Fireman Matt, not Mrs. Fisher or Miss Lambert or these children what you've been telling me about Fireman Matt being your daddy. Do you understand? Am I making myself clear, Brandi?"

Brandi looked down and twisted her hands in her lap. "You mean it's our secret?"

"Yes, that's exactly what I mean, Brandi. Absolutely nothing is to cross your lips about it. In fact, if you were to say something like that you could very well scare Matt off, instead of bringing him to us. Do you understand?"

Brandi raised her head and gave her mommy a brilliant smile. "Yes, Mommy, I won't say anything about him being our daddy, not ever." Brandi gave a long sigh and sank back into the seat. "But it's gonna happen!" she whispered, ever so quietly.

"Fine!" Faith turned the key.

After only a minute of silence, Brandi had obviously thought that through and found the thought not quite to her liking. She looked at Faith and asked, "Mommy, when Matt does become our daddy, can I tell him then?"

Faith sighed, "Brandi, you will be the death of me! Goodness, we haven't even been introduced! A relationship develops over time. Brandi, remember, Matt lives alone, he doesn't have a daughter, I know he rescued these twins, but that doesn't mean he's ready to be a daddy."

Nodding, Brandi said, "But he will one day soon. Jesus told me and I believe Him. Besides, He can make Matt love us."

Faith backed out and drove to the church without another word. A couple of miles later, she turned the corner to drive onto the parking lot of the church. Already turning from the sidewalk, from the other direction came a tall blond man, carrying a tiny child with another holding his other hand. Brandi saw them and began bouncing in her seat, a smile covering her face. She could hardly sit still, she was so excited!

"Mommy! Mommy! That's fireman Matt! Hurry!"

"Brandi! Calm down!" Faith said and turned into the parking lot.

Matt had worked two fires in the last twenty-four hours. That was not unusual, but the time he spent at Ground Zero was still taking its toll. He was starting to feel the results of a long day. However, he hurried the children off the train at the Thomaston stop and into the station before the train left the platform. Of course, the platform was outside and the sound would dissipate wide open space much more than in the tunnel-like terminal when they boarded, however, he knew it could be quite loud and these trains weren't known for their slow, quiet departure from the stations. They had a posted schedule to meet and the experienced trainmen knew how long each stop should take to get them to their destination on time. He knew each engineer ran a tight schedule. They waited in the station building until the train left.

As they walked along, Matt wondered who the pastor would talk into taking the children. It was a big undertaking to take two five year olds without any warning. Most families would have to scramble to find places and seeing how quickly these two put away the food he fixed for them, that might be an issue, as well. He wondered when they had their last decent meal. Matt sighed, as Karin put up her hands to be carried, goodness knows he did his best to get them placed inside the city.

He picked up the tiny girl and kept on walking, at least today that was not an option. As he thought about it, he was convinced that these twins were getting a much better deal just because they wouldn't be in foster care in the city. He was in homes where there were foster kids. There was a mom and dad, but often the dad was drunk or some of the household was into drugs. What kind of home life was that for any kids, especially traumatized kids like these?

He glanced down at Karin and saw that she wasn't sucking her thumb, nor was she burrowed into his chest, but looking around, wide-eyed at the surroundings. Karl, too, had slowed down considerably, he was also looking around. Of course, down by the warehouse where he found them, there were no trees and certainly no green grass or flowers as there were along the sidewalk where they walked.

"Pretty," Karl murmured.

"Yeah, if you listen real carefully, you can even hear some birds," Matt said.

Karl cocked his head listened a minute, and said, "Wow! I hear 'em. Mister! Them's big houses, too."

"Yeah, they are nice."

Up ahead, he saw the steeple for the church, but Karl was not about to be hurried. He made sure his hand was firmly in Matt's, but he wanted to see everything. He never saw sky so blue and green grass was something that was foreign. He never saw anything so pretty as the flowers beside the sidewalk. Matt turned off the sidewalk onto the parking lot and headed for the front door of the church. Karl's head seemed to be on a swivel and his eyes were bigger than Matt had ever seen eyes on a child, even when he was pulling that child from a burning building. The child in his arms was also wide-eyed. He knew there were many tenements around Manhattan where trees, grass and flowers were non-existent.

Around the corner from the other direction came a car, a very serviceable four door sedan. Probably the kind of car a widow would drive out of necessity. His heart lurched at the thought. He kept watching as the car approached, its turn signal came on and that's when Matt recognized the child bouncing in the passenger seat. Faith Lankaster was the person whom the pastor had contacted; Brandi was too excited not to be aware of why they were here. It was then that Matt remembered what Jim said about Faith. He said that she was a good mother.

Matt's breath caught. His feet wanted to sprout wings and carry him quickly inside. Ever since Tuesday, he wanted to meet this lady, his chance had come, but now there was not one child in the picture, but three. He stifled a groan as he set Karin down and reached for the door handle to open the front door of the church. Brandi was out, her car door bouncing and running toward them. More slowly, Faith closed her door and made her way around the car.

Brandi was one big, happy smile as she came up, but Faith's smile was much more shy. "Hello," he said, "I guess we get to speak at last." Matt couldn't help but smile at the lovely lady he would finally be introduced to.

Brandi reached up and clasped Matt's hand. With eyes that fairly danced and feet that absolutely would not stand still, she said, "Fireman Matt, my mommy says you never told her your name." They both stood silently looking at each other. "Mommy, this is Fireman Matt Barns. Mister Matt, this is my mommy, Faith Lankaster."

Nodding to Brandi, Faith said, "Very good, Brandi, that was just the way Miss Lambert has taught you to make introductions." She turned immediately to Matt and said, "I'm pleased to meet you. It's much better out here, isn't it?"

By now, all five were inside the front door of the church. Matt looked down at the lovely lady and couldn't help the smile as he said, "Yes, much better, I'm pleased to meet you, too." *You don't know how much.*

Jim Harding's office door was open. By now, Mrs. Fisher's time was over and she was gone. Jim would have left too, except he knew these folks were coming. He heard voices in the foyer, so he stood and came around his desk. He decided, since they came in together, they could say a few words to each other first. Matt hadn't told him that he also met Faith briefly on Tuesday at the water table. Knowing Brandi as he did, he was sure the child would make the introductions quite well. That child was smart, the most out-going child he knew in their school.

All three children were eyeing each other. Of course, Brandi was taller than the twins, but that didn't matter, not to Brandi. Brandi never met a stranger, whether it was a child or an adult. She loved everybody and usually, the first words out of her mouth were to tell them how much Jesus loved them. Brandi smiled at the twins, but the minute Karl glanced at her his eyes dropped to the floor and almost at the same time, Karin's thumb went into her mouth.

It only took Brandi a minute to assess the situation. She knew her mommy, Pastor Harding and Matt needed to talk about everything, so she reached out for the twins' hands. She gave them a big smile, but since they didn't take her hands, she said instead, "You know what, guys? We got the best play place in all the world! It's right around the corner from here." As if it was the clincher, she added, "It's even better than McDonalds! Come on; let's go play while these big people talk! Want to?"

Matt had to chuckle at that, but he realized the twins were looking at him. He looked down and smiled, letting go of their hands. "Hey, go ahead with Brandi. She knows this place really well, she goes to school here. I'm sure if she says you'll have a good time, you will."

That was all the encouragement the twins needed. Much to his surprise, both Karl and Karin grabbed Brandi's hands and the three skipped off together and out of sight through another doorway. Matt was even more shocked to see that Karin's thumb wasn't in her mouth, but her free hand was swinging beside her.

Jim Harding mentally shook his head, as the children disappeared. That child was the best PR person at nine years old! He never thought the children could use the play place they had set up for temporary use when people came with different needs. Without being asked, Brandi made a sensible meeting possible for the adults. That child was worth her weight in gold! Of course, wasn't that why he contacted Faith, because she was the best mother?

Watching until all three disappeared and the door closed, Jim said, "I'm sure glad we made that room into a play place, McDonalds? well, I don't know about that, but it does serve the purpose right now." As he closed the office door, he said, "Okay, I guess Brandi got you both introduced? Is that right?"

"Yes," Faith whispered, that's all the sound she could make come out of her dry mouth. It seemed her mind and heart stuttered in this man's presence.

"Yes," Matt said, hardly taking his eyes off the lovely lady, "we met almost as close to Ground Zero as I met Brandi. Faith handed me a cupful of water, actually filled my cup several times. I couldn't help seeing the resemblance between her and her daughter." He grinned at the lovely lady and continued, "I bet she's watching herself grow up."

"I can believe that, Faith's mom always says she's watching Faith grow up all over again. Have a seat and let's talk over the particulars Faith needs to know about these twins."

Matt waited for Faith to sit and said, "Yes, we couldn't say much over the phone."

Faith's heart seemed to flutter around in her chest, and beat very ineffectively, but Matt's voice did serious things to Faith's inner working parts. As Jim moved around his desk and Matt sat beside her, Faith pulled in a deep breath, she was sure she would hyperventilate in only minutes if she didn't, with Matt sitting so close. There at Ground Zero, Matt was in full fireman uniform, even to his helmet and she hadn't seen his blond hair. Also, with all the dust and debris, she couldn't tell that his eyes were blue – a deep sky blue.

He was one extremely handsome man and very well built. At Ground Zero she thought he was older, but she realized as she looked at him, he certainly wasn't. He still had on his white shirt with his name on the pocket and the FDNY emblem on the sleeve, as well as the blue pants that he always wore under his turnout coat and boots. Putting everything together, Faith decided he hadn't had the time to go to his room to change.

Pulling them both from their daydreams, Jim said, "Matt, I've asked Faith if she will take the twins on a temporary basis. I assume that the children's services will continue to look for a place or places for these children?"

Matt shook his head slowly, stretched out his long legs and solemnly said, "That was one of the problems, Pastor. Karl refused to have them come with me even from the warehouse, until I assured him that they would not be split up. I never even mentioned to anyone that I talked to in each of the boroughs that that was an option. One case worker said there might be a far out chance she could place one, but none of them could place two together. Because of nine eleven, no one would give me any time element for an opening."

Quickly, Faith spoke up. "That's okay! Brandi and I have a large house with a nice yard and a swing. Brandi's daddy built her a sandbox several years ago, but it's been covered, she doesn't play in it much, but I'm sure the twins would love it."

Jim nodded at Faith, but he said to Matt, "I noticed you didn't bring any other clothes for the children with you."

Matt shook his head. "The things they had on when we found them looked like Karl had found them in the local dumpster, they were holey and filthy. Of course, add to that we found them in a burned-out building. What they had on their feet could hardly be called shoes, they were so awful and they flopped on both children they were so big. They were just something to keep their feet off the floor. The children themselves were in pitiful shape."

Faith didn't comment, but she gasped, as Matt continued, "At the station, I cleaned them up in the shower, but I threw away everything they had on, which wasn't much. We have a tiny closet at the station where the men with children bring in things their kids have outgrown from time to time. I was only able to find one outfit each and one pair of shoes for each of them."

Jim looked at Faith. "We used to have a closet here, didn't we? Yes, come to think of it, I think someone left some clothes in the office not long ago."

Faith thought a minute, then nodded and said, "Yes, Pastor, I think you're right. I'm pretty sure it's in a little room off the teens classroom."

"Let's go see what we can find, surely we can find them something to sleep in tonight. Faith, would you be free tomorrow to get them some other clothes?"

With a great lump in her throat, her voice wasn't what she normally sounded like as she said, "Certainly, Pastor. Five year old children can't be expected to keep one outfit clean all day. I can vouch for that, because even a nine year old can't do it very often."

Faith couldn't believe such a big man could speak so quietly, as Matt said, "I have all day tomorrow off, I'd be happy to come back and go with you. You shouldn't have to do that alone, besides, I feel some responsibility for finding them and bringing them here."

"You would?" she asked, "That would make it lots easier." *Three children, one adult to go shopping for a boy and a girl? Nearly impossible.*

Matt nodded. "Count on it!"

The three stood up and Jim led the way out of the office area, but Matt stood back like a true gentleman, and ushered Faith out the door. As they rounded the corner to the stairs and passed the door where the children were, Faith put her head in the room and said, "Brandi, Pastor Harding, Matt and I are going downstairs for a few minutes. You keep playing we'll be back."

"Okay, Mommy! We're having lots of fun!"

Without being obvious, Faith looked at the twins, hoping to get an idea what size she should look for in the 'Helping Hands' closet. She would be grateful for anything, especially for a little boy. She was sure she still had some of Brandi's clothes from that size stored in the attic, but of course, she never had anything for a boy.

She wondered if Matt would expect her to foot the bill for any clothes purchased or if he would offer to pay for some. Perhaps Pastor would come up with some money for clothes. When they talked briefly on the phone, she assumed the church would give her money for food, she hadn't thought about clothes. It was good the weather was still warm, these children had absolutely nothing and winter clothes cost more than summer clothes!

Until today she had head knowledge that there were people, children included, who had nothing, but when she saw Matt with those children, it struck her, these children had nothing. Nothing at all! From what Matt said, they didn't own the clothes on their backs. Firemen had supplied them. It made her very thankful for the small dividend check she received each month from Max's investments and the other checks from his employer and military stipend for widows and dependent children. She also got a small check for one dependent child.

By the time Faith caught up with the two men, they had the closet door open. Matt was the one who dressed the children at the fire station, so he knew what sizes best fit them. He squatted inside the tiny room, going through things on several shelves. On one side were girls' clothes and on the other were boys. Faith looked in the room and knew she would be claustrophobic if she tried to get in there with him, he filled the tiny area. It seemed like his broad shoulders hardly fit between the shelves on each side.

She quickly took up a station on one side of the door, as Jim stepped to the other. Matt pulled things from the boys' side first, filling Jim's arms with several things, then turned to the other side and pulled out quite a few girls' things and handed them to Faith. After several minutes of looking through other things on other shelves to see if there were any other things, Matt stood up and took a step out of the closet.

He looked at the small piles each of the others held and said, "That looks like all the things in there in their size. At least those are the sizes that they have on now."

Faith looked at her stack and said, "I think I have several boxes in the attic that I saved of Brandi's. Maybe I can pull them down tonight and go through them before we go shopping tomorrow. There's no sense of spending more than we need. Of course, I have nothing for a boy, but this and what I have will help a lot."

Faith had lost track of time. Actually, she hadn't looked at the clock at home when she raced into the house to answer the phone, so she happened to glance at the big clock on the wall in Marian's office when they returned upstairs. She gasped; it was nearly eight o'clock! She couldn't have told anyone the right time if they asked. She looked at the big man walking beside her, remembering how long it took to ride the train into the city. "You walked from the train station here, didn't you?" she asked.

The big man smiled at her and she noticed a dimple in his right cheek. She had to drag her eyes from it and her heart… well….. it gave an erratic jerk. His eyes twinkled as he said, "Yes, Ma'am, I've lived in the city for several years. When my car was vandalized the third time a few years back, I got rid of it and I haven't gotten another. When I'm not riding on a very big truck, I use the subways or trains to take me where I need to go. Where can I meet you tomorrow and what time? Any time's fine with me, you name it. Remember, I'll be happy to come help corral the kids and also help put some clothes on their backs."

Nodding at the clock, she said, "I'm thinking of right now. You'll be very hungry by the time you get back to Manhattan, won't you?"

Realizing that he was hungry and that he only had two sandwiches he threw together while he fed the twins and also hoping his stomach wouldn't betray him, he said, "The kids and I ate a late lunch, but yes, it'll be a good hour before I get back."

FIVE

J IM LAID THE STACK OF CLOTHES HE HELD ON MARIAN'S DESK, WENT TO A FILING
cabinet and unlocked one of the drawers. "I have a better idea! I planned
to give Faith money for groceries and those clothes she'll buy tomorrow with
your help. Since it's after six... well more like going on eight, why don't I give
you a bit more and you can take all three of those kids out for pizza. That
would get you all fed without too much hassle and in a relatively short time."

Faith's heart turned around in her chest. To eat a meal in a restaurant
with a man, a very handsome man, a man close to her own age and three
children would feel like a family. She took a deep breath; she must put a cap
on her feelings and thoughts! Just because the man was coming back to help
her shop for the twins meant nothing... well, maybe it did... He probably felt
responsible, since he found them and now was dumping them on the church.
To go out for pizza was the simplest way to get them all fed and also the fastest
way. She stifled a sigh; she would accept whatever help she could get.

Any other way, she must take three hungry children home and keep
them occupied and out from underfoot while she thought of something fast
she could put on the table. Come to think of it, she used up her last two cans
of chunky soup, was it only last night? She wasn't sure what she had in the
house that would qualify as 'fast food'. What she put on the table probably
didn't matter the children looked like they'd blow away in a strong wind. Not
to even think about Matt with an hour's ride before he could get his supper.

Matt smiled at the pastor and said, "It works for me, Pastor! The way the
kids stomachs growled before I fed them two sandwiches, they'll wolf down
several pieces." He gave Faith a crooked smile and said, "Not to mention that
I can eat." She smiled at him, but didn't comment.

Jim chuckled at Matt's last statement. "Fine! Then it's settled." Pastor Jim pulled out a cash box from the open drawer and with another key, opened it and pulled out several bills. "Ahhh, this is great! Nobody's been in to ask for any emergency funds since the beginning of the month." As he counted out all the bills into Faith's hand, he said, "I wouldn't normally worry to count it out, but you know what a stickler Randy is, Faith. I can't replenish this emergency fund until he gets a receipt from me, so I'll need you to sign for this."

"That's fine, Pastor. This seems like an awful lot!" Faith looked at the stack in her hand, then back up at the pastor.

"Faith," he waited until she looked up at him, "this is more than giving a cup of cold water to one of these little ones." He turned the receipt book toward her, then picked up one of Marian's pens and handed it to her.

Knowing the scripture he referred to, Faith said, "Thanks, Pastor. I understand what you're saying."

Faith laid the stack of bills down on the table while she signed the voucher the pastor gave her. Jim picked up one of the bills from the pile and handed it to Matt. As he winked, he said, "Men always feel better paying for a meal at a restaurant, don't they? I know Marsha always thinks it's my job to shell out the bucks."

Matt chuckled, taking the money the pastor held out. "Yes, I think we do." He didn't care how much money the pastor gave him, he'd make sure all five of them were well fed.

Matt was watching Faith and as soon as she picked up the money on the desk, he turned to Jim and extended his hand. "Thanks, Pastor, didn't expect to see you so soon again, but I'm glad your church has this ministry. I know the twins will be well cared for, probably much better than any home the state would put them into."

Looking at the lady whose face had turned pink from the compliment, Jim said, "Yes, I'll agree with you there, Matt. One hundred percent! I think I may have told you, Ms. Faith is wonderful with children. We have living proof in that older child playing in the other room. We'll see you Sunday."

"Yes, you sure will, Pastor and thanks for the money. I'll see that these folks get all the pizza they can hold." He let out a sigh. "It'll probably be the best meal those twins have had in quite a few days."

Jim's throat suddenly clogged, so he whispered, "Yes, I'm sure that's true. They really look like a stiff wind would blow them away."

Jim didn't say the words that came to his mind so easily, but here was the perfect couple, Matt was a perfect substitute for the man Faith had lost. It was more than three years, she came to his office many times after Max's death for counseling, but she was long over his death now, he knew she was ready to move on and here was the perfect man. It didn't take a rocket scientist to see that both Matt and Faith were uncomfortable together; he could almost see the sparks! It wasn't hard to see the looks that passed between them. Being a man and…well… a minister as well…, it wasn't his place to be matchmaker, but then again….

He chuckled, as he saw them out the office door. "That's great!" He called after them. "Get 'em all to sleep early, Faith. We'll see you."

Faith and Matt both went to the room around the corner to collect the children. Before they could leave, however, they had to help put away the toys and cover the sandbox. "Mommy," Brandi said, "Karin and Karl are just the right size to play in this sandbox. We can uncover mine tomorrow for them to play, can't we?"

"Yes, I think we can, Brandi, but in the morning, Matt's coming back so we can go shopping together to get them some clothes."

Brandi's mouth opened immediately and a grin spread across her face, but Faith looked sternly at her and shook her head slightly, but enough to make Matt wonder what that silent communication meant. Brandi closed her mouth without saying anything, but she clapped her hands. Faith could just about see the words that were ready to pop from her mouth. She was afraid Matt could also see them, but for the moment, she had diverted them. She swallowed the sigh that had every intention of coming out. She could only hope that Brandi wouldn't spread her words about what she thought Jesus had told her.

As soon as the children saw the adults, the twins ran to Matt. He smiled, but continued to help Faith and Brandi straighten up the playroom and lifted the heavy sandbox cover into place. He stood up, but not about to ask about the silent mother/daughter exchange, Matt said, "Okay, kids, how about we go see if we can round up some pizza?"

"Pizza?" Karl said, in awe. Karin turned huge eyes on him.

"Yup! We're gonna all have pizza!"

"Wow!" Karl couldn't help but say. Karen didn't speak, but she clapped her hands once and her eyes were dancing.

Faith knew she was a decent driver, but she always felt strange getting into the driver's seat when there was a man with her, Max always drove when they were together. However, she knew she was the one who knew where the pizza restaurant was. As they walked to the parking lot, Matt went with her to the driver's side and opened the door for her. Acting perfectly at ease, helping her into the driver's side, he smiled at her, as she looked up at him. It turned her heart all the way over and she almost didn't raise her foot high enough to put it inside the car. When she was comfortably in, Matt looked down into her eyes and murmured, so only her ears could hear, "I'm usually a passenger in a rather large truck." Faith chuckled. Hearing that sound nearly turned Matt's knees to jelly. He closed Faith's door and hurried around to the passenger side.

While Matt helped Faith, Brandi was ushering the twins into the back seat. Like a mother hen, she shooed Karl in first and said, "Be sure you buckle your seatbelt, Karl. Come on, Karin, you're next. Oh, wait a minute, maybe I'd better sit in the middle, that seatbelt is harder to fasten than the two on the outsides." She climbed in and closed the back door, then stepped over Karin and sat down.

Matt came around the front of the car and opened the front passenger door, then looked down at the seat Brandi usually sat in. He let out a good-natured growl and said, "Do I need to scrunch into that little place?"

Both Brandi and Faith laughed, but Faith said, "Brandi usually sits there and she likes to be close so she can look out the windshield. Go ahead scoot the seat back, your long legs would never fit in that little space."

"Thanks, that helps a lot."

While Matt moved the seat, Brandi asked, "Mommy, what was in those two bags you put in the trunk?"

"Those were some clothes from the 'Helping Hands' closet that'll probably fit Karl and Karin. They'll probably even wear some of them for bed tonight. Really, that was all there was in their size. We'll get some of those boxes down from the attic and see if there's anything Karin can wear in them. Tomorrow, when Matt comes back, we'll know for sure what we'll need to buy for both Karl and Karin."

Brandi clapped her hands. "So we all get to go shopping?"

Matt was feeling more and more a part of this family. His heart expanded as he looked in the back seat. He grinned as he listened to Brandi and grumbled, "Just like a female, excited about going shopping."

Brandi laughed. "Oh, yes, Mister Matt! Shopping's fun! And we'll get to go in the huge children's department, too!"

"Yes, Sweetheart," Faith said, as she pulled the stick into drive, then turned to Matt and asked, "What time would you be coming back tomorrow? You have so much farther to come; it should be you who makes the decision."

Hearing her call her daughter sweetheart did strange things to Matt's insides and turned his brain to mush. He realized that he'd be most happy if she used that word on him, rather than her daughter. But, no, they only met – to know names – today! He looked away quickly and swallowed, his throat had turned to sandpaper only seconds ago, but he didn't want her to see how much he was affected.

He realized she directed her question to him, so he had to swallow again and clear his throat before any sound came out "Umm, I'm free all day. I went off duty today when I left the fire station and I'm not on again until three Sunday afternoon. I only have a sleeping room; I'll eat in the diner on the way to the train station. I could be here any time you'll get the kids ready, Faith. I think you should be the one to say."

"How's ten o'clock?"

"That'll be great! I'll be here. Umm, where should I meet you?"

"We'll pick you up at the train station. We'll drop you off there tonight after we eat, too. The best and most reasonable pizza place is several blocks from the train station." She grinned at him. "You'd have all the calories used up from your meal by the time you got there, if you had to walk that far and the same to get to our house."

"Thanks." He chuckled. Her smile did things to his insides.

There was a man on his shift at the fire station whose wife was a Christian, or at least that's what he said. Matt had never met her, but to hear the fireman talk, he had little respect for her religion and made a point that he did not share her belief or go to her church. By his many actions and speech, Matt was sure the fireman never professed any belief.

Matt wondered what was different. He was sure if this lady was interested in him that he'd make a point to go with her every time she went to church whenever he could. It would not be a hardship. In fact, she was the most gracious lady he ever met. A thought rushed into his brain. *You're a Christian now!* Was his brain trying to tell him something?

He looked out the window at the city going by. This was a very different ending to this day! Who knew when he left the cot this morning that he'd be in the company of a lovely lady, her nine year old daughter and a set of five year old twins? If he cultivated this relationship he knew he would take on a ready-made family. Faith had Brandi and there was a good possibility that the twins would be with her for some time, maybe a long time.

He lived on his own all these years as a fireman, he was an only child, but there were other kids on the ranch in Montana. He had a roommate in college, but that was way different from a wife and kids! Was he up to it? Looking over his shoulder, with the pretext of checking to see if the twins were okay, he looked at all three.

A ready made family of one nine year old and two five year olds looked back at him. His heart overflowed. If Brandi, Karl and Karin were the ready-made family; he knew he could handle every minute. It would definitely *not* be a hardship! He cleared his throat; perhaps he was getting the cart before the horse? The lady, the mother figure in this situation, also was a very significant player. Perhaps she still had very deep seated feelings for her dead husband.

At the restaurant, Brandi said, as three seatbelts snapped open, "Mommy, Karin and Karl and I gotta go wash our hands and umm, maybe go potty, too, but should we go get a table while you and Matt order?"

"No, Brandi, go wash up. I see that round booth open in the back. Matt can handle the pizza while I get the table." She looked at the twins and said, as she smiled, "Wash your hands really well, that sand gets stuck under your fingernails very easily."

"Okay," Karl said, seriously and Karin nodded. The three children skipped off toward the restrooms without another word.

Before Faith moved down the aisle to the large booth, she looked up into Matt's eyes and said, "I didn't mean to take away your authority role in the twins' lives. That's okay, isn't it?"

With a tender look in his eyes as he looked down at her, he said, "Of course, Faith." At that moment Faith wasn't sure her heart would stay in her chest.

Matt was only a few minutes behind Faith, since there was no one ahead of him. He placed the order and they would bring it to the table. When he sat down, he scooted up right beside her. He really wanted to put his arm across the back of the seat, but he kept his arm by his side. At first, Faith felt boxed in, she thought Matt would leave room between them for one of the children and one on each side, but obviously, he had other plans.

She turned and into the relative quiet in the restaurant she asked, "So Karin doesn't talk?"

"Karl said she doesn't and he answers for her before she can even take a breath. I know she can hear, she's followed directions quite well."

Faith shook her head. "They've both been traumatized, I'm sure. They're pretty children. Karin's really sweet."

Grinning at the pretty lady, he said, "She, along with your Brandi, will be a heart stopper one of these days."

"Oh, please," Faith whispered, knowing a blush crept up her neck. "Don't say that! I dread the day when Brandi wants to go on her first date."

His eyes twinkling, Matt chuckled and said, "Be prepared, it'll come upon you really fast." He knew the affect he had on her; she affected him nearly the same way.

Faith let out a sigh. "Believe me, I know that! With a child, time never stands still. It seems like every morning something new comes up."

Matt chuckled. "I believe that!"

He watched as the children left the restrooms, but he said, "You and Brandi look very much alike. Do you feel sometimes like you're watching yourself grow up?"

"Absolutely! Except I can't remember being such a live wire. Mom tells me she's watching me grow up again, so maybe I had such energy once upon a time." She shook her head. "But now not so much."

The children, the pizza, the pitcher of soft drink and the table settings all arrived at the table at just about the same time. The waiter was pushing two large, steaming pizzas onto the table, just as Brandi brought the twins up to the seat. Matt wondered how this would work, Karin was so insistent that she would not go in the shower without Karl, but it was obvious Brandi was intent on splitting them up, just like she had in the car.

"Karl, you go sit by Mister Matt and Karin, you get in first next to Mommy and I'll sit next to you. It's better to have the men sit together and us ladies over here. You know."

Without any fussing, surprising Matt completely, Karin climbed up on the vinyl seat and slid her bottom along until she was right next to Faith. Surprising both adults, Karin gave Faith a huge smile. Brandi was right beside her in only seconds. Faith looked down at the child and smiled. Matt had to check himself; he could easily become jealous of the look Faith gave that little girl. It should be made a law that women could only look at men like that!

To cover his thoughts, he looked down at Karl and said, "So, I guess that means we gotta stick together, doesn't it?"

"Yeah. Me'n Karin never been in a place like this before," he whispered, in awe. "We never got no real pizza."

"Really? Wow!" Matt exclaimed.

"Yeah, the old man sometimes ordered, but we didn't get but a little piece." Hearing what the child said, Faith's heart turned over but she didn't comment.

Pulling one large pie close in front of them, Matt lifted a piece onto a plate and pushed it in front of Faith, then lifted the next onto a plate and slid it over to Karin. Immediately she picked it up; then looked at first Faith, then at Brandi. Before Faith could say anything, Brandi said, "Wait till Matt gets a piece for everybody, Karin, then we gotta say grace before we eat."

Karin's forehead wrinkled, Matt was sure she had no idea what Brandi was talking about. The next piece reached Brandi and the next went to Karl. Lastly, Matt served himself. He looked at Faith; the first prayer he ever prayed was at Ground Zero, with Brandi. He wasn't sure how you 'said grace' over pizza.

"Okay, kids," Faith folded her hands in front of her on the table so the children could see them and said, "Let's bow our heads. God in heaven gives us food to eat and we need to thank Him." She waited a minute while the twins dubiously did as she said. "Brandi, you say grace."

"Dear Jesus; thanks for the food and thanks for sending us Mister Matt and Karin and Karl. Mommy and me love 'em lots. Amen."

Time stood still.

Matt couldn't remember ever feeling like he did right then, the cotton filled his throat. *A family,* he thought, *a real family - I could be part of a real family! Brandi has just included me in her prayer!*

The moment passed, Brandi raised her head and said, "Come on, guys, let's eat!"

Both Karin and Karl picked up their piece of pizza and took a huge bite; Brandi's bite wasn't too much smaller, only Faith was dainty, as she picked up her slice and took a bite. Just as they ate at lunch, the twins had their pieces gone even before Matt could get his much larger mouth around his piece. Faith ate half of hers, then laid it on her plate and filled glasses with the soft drink for each one.

"Here you go, guys, here's your drinks," she said.

After dinner and almost as soon as the twins were buckled into their seats in the car, they fell asleep. Their tummies were full, they knew they were safe. Brandi was also quiet, because she didn't want to wake them. She couldn't move much because she was sitting between them again. However, she watched the adults in the front seat and wished they were all going home to their house. Matt could start right now being their daddy, it just seemed so right. She wanted to tell him what Jesus had told her, but she said nothing as Faith drove to the train station and in the empty parking lot drove right up beside the well lighted station.

At the train station, Brandi whispered, before any doors opened, "Mommy, I'll stay here with Karin and Karl, you can go with Matt to get his ticket."

Matt would have liked for Faith to come with him, not only to the ticket window, but all the way to his room. However, he knew there was no reason for her to get out of the car. This was the first time they were formally introduced, a kiss, even a light touching of the lips, was probably more than he should give. They hadn't even touched, except there at the restaurant their knees brushed once or twice. He wouldn't say anything, he'd let Faith come or not and certainly she was the one to answer her child.

Faith would like nothing better than to walk Matt into the station. This time of the evening, trains weren't quite as frequent and they missed the last train to Manhattan by ten minutes. The next wouldn't come for twenty more and Faith knew there was a place down at the far end of the platform that wasn't as well lit as the rest; a good place for a kiss... However, she took herself to task. After all, now she not only had *one* liability, she had *three*. What single man would be interested in a widow, a not too pretty widow, she had to add, who was now responsible for three children? She sighed. However, she swallowed immediately; she didn't want Matt to hear that sigh. After all, she was a responsible, independent adult!

Matt looked at her and as her eyes came slowly up to look into his face, he smiled. Without being obvious, he slid his hand across the space between them and took her hand. It pleased him immensely that she didn't pull it away. He squeezed it, keeping her attention on him, and moved his head, giving just a nod toward the outside. Faith's heart stood still. Was he really asking her to come, or was her brain playing tricks on her? That thought made her wonder if she'd been out of a man's company for so long that she didn't remember the signs. Matt was coming back tomorrow, she better get her head on straight.

Still holding her hand, Matt opened his door. Of course, he had to drop it, she wouldn't get out on his side, but he looked over his shoulder and said, "Okay, Brandi, we'll take you up on that. I'll see you in the morning."

A smile, with radiance to rival the sun burst across her face. "Okay, Matt! I'll be right here; and we'll be okay, Mommy!"

"Thanks, Brandi."

Wondering where she ever got the nerve, Faith released her seatbelt, pulled the keys from the ignition and opened her door. By the time she had her left foot on the ground, Matt stood beside the door holding it. With that lopsided grin on his face, he looked down at her. Her heart took a turn around the parking lot as she looked up at him. The streetlights were still buzzing because they only came on a few minutes before. The sun was very low behind the buildings, but there was still a bright glow in the sky. Between the two, his hair positively glistened.

Before Faith moved she hit the door lock, then she stood up and stepped away from the door. Remembering that two of the three still in the car were asleep, Matt pushed the door to the first catch very quietly, and reached down for Faith's hand. They walked toward the station together, but were comfortable not speaking. Actually, Faith realized, she couldn't have said a word if her life depended on it. Matt realized as he walked beside this lady that he felt he finally found his nitch in life. Would there be a way to convince her that he'd like nothing better than to make her his better half? He nearly sent up a prayer that she wasn't still grieving for her husband. Pastor said her husband died three years ago, was that long enough?

Perhaps that wasn't the issue. She was a Christian for quite some time that was obvious from her life and that of her daughter. The praise the pastor gave her couldn't be earned in a heart beat. He'd been a Christian, or he asked God to forgive his sins only four days ago. On another level, he was a fireman. Realizing she knew there were many firefighters lost because of their line of work on nine eleven, would she even consider him as a possibility because of his chosen field? She was a widow, she already lost one husband, he didn't know how, but that had to be something she'd think about.

He had no way of knowing her financial status, but she couldn't be outrageously rich or the pastor wouldn't have emptied his cash box for her to keep the twins. What had Jim implied when he volunteered to come back that he'd help pay for the clothes? She and Brandi dressed as any woman and daughter would. He made a decent wage and he was up for promotion soon. He was single, had no monetary obligations other than a sleeping room, a few clothes and food. Would that be something he could bring to interest her in wanting to join forces with him?

He swallowed a sigh, as he stood behind her to open the door into the lighted station. She stood with him as he purchased his ticket, and walked with him out through the door onto the platform. There was no one else on the platform, so they sat down on one of the benches.

He slid his ticket into his shirt pocket, and laid his arm across the back of the seat behind her head. It was quiet; they could hear a few peepers in the trees at the end of the platform. He realized he could get used to sounds like this. He always lived in a city as an adult. This quietness was more like he was used to as a child, he lived on a huge, working ranch, but a place like this and a woman like this were very appealing. In fact, he could see the stars in the sky, not something he ever saw from the streets of Manhattan. There were mountains and canyons where he came from, but the canyons he was accustomed to now were man made, tall skyscrapers.

Finally, she found her tongue. "So you can stay with us all day tomorrow and then come back for church on Sunday?"

"Yes, I can, Faith. I'd be most happy to do just that. Oh, I forgot to ask before, but when does church get over?"

"It's over about eleven thirty, at least that's usually when we get home. Pastor Harding's pretty good about getting out on time. If I had dinner in the crock pot so we could eat right away would you be able to eat with us before going back for work?"

Absently, Matt's fingers picked up one of Faith's curls and let it slip through his fingers, this was another feeling he'd like to cultivate. She felt him, but didn't pull away. However, she had to swallow before she said, "Oh, we'll bring you back here after dinner; we live beyond the church from here.

There again, you'd burn up all the calories you ate long before you arrived here at the station."

Loving the feel of her hair, he was sure if he could feel a morning sunbeam that it would feel just like what he held in his hand. He finally made his lips move and said, "Sure, my room is really close to the fire station. That place holds no fascination for me. I must eat all my meals out, so I'd be delighted to join you for dinner. I'll be happy to join you for all day tomorrow, too, Faith. I'll check the schedule at the train station when I get there and I'll be sure to be on the train that gets me here as close to ten as possible."

She gave him one of her brilliant smiles. "Great! We'll be here." He couldn't have made his vocal chords say anything right then. Instead, what he really wanted to do was seal his lips onto those absolutely lovely lips that were turned up and looked almost as lovely as those last rays of sunlight slipping over the western trees.

The sound was unmistakable. The train was coming into the station; blowing its horn as it crossed the streets. One last time, Matt lifted the curl he toyed with and let it glide through his fingers. He wished he could do so much more, but they were only introduced this evening! He felt like he'd known this lady for years. He felt the connection at the water table on nine eleven, it hadn't lessened this evening.

She lifted her head at the sound and the light from the engine shown on her beautiful face. He almost clamped down on her curl, in fact his fingers tightened just a little, but a great urge came over him as he watched the fleeting expressions on her face and he wanted so much to kiss her. He looked at the lady by his side and winked at her. If he had any affect on her as she had on him, him playing with her hair was doing a number on her.

He cleared his throat and said, "Don't do too much tonight, Faith. We don't have to go straight from here to the stores, I'm more than happy to get those boxes from your attic tomorrow if you like." He stood up as the train pulled in. "Thanks for this evening, Faith. Pizza, everything…" *You don't know how much!*

With the hiss of the train, he almost missed her whispered one word answer. "Yes."

"See you in the morning!" She watched him swing up onto the second step of the train car, he was very athletic. That was probably how he boarded a fire engine, too.

She wished he could have kissed her goodbye, but of course, he wouldn't, they only met formally this afternoon, for goodness sake! As he waved and disappeared into the car, she waved and had to keep a tight reign on her hand so she didn't take it to her lips and send him a kiss. She saw him slouch into a window seat and wished she boarded the train with him; forget about the three children in the car sitting close by!

When he was seated and the train started to move she raised her hand and waved again. He grinned at her and gave her a saucy salute. She watched until the train was out of sight around the corner, sure her heart had left with it. Matt slouched into a seat; he left his heart on the platform with the lovely auburn-haired lady. He saw her wave, so he grinned and put his fingers to his forehead as the train left the station and watched until he couldn't see her anymore.

Faith knew that Matt had cleaned the children at the fire station, he said he did. Still she wondered if she should put them in the tub when they reached home. Brandi needed her bath, maybe they'd want to play in the water for a while. When she slid behind the wheel from seeing Matt off, all three children were asleep, maybe she didn't have to even think about it tonight.

When she turned the wheel onto their gravel driveway, however, Brandi woke up and gently shook the twins on either side of her. "Come on, guys, we're almost home!" she said softly, but loudly enough that both twins could hear her.

Karl raised his head first and stared into the near darkness outside the car. "Wow!" he said in awe. "Wow!" The big tree beside the driveway made a huge shadow, making it even darker before they reached the house. Faith and Brandi left the house in daylight and in such a hurry they forgot to leave a light on, so the house was just a hulk of darkness looming ahead of them. Faith turned beside the house and headed for the dark, yawning opening that was the garage. However, as she turned toward the garage the motion sensor light came on over the back door. Her car lights illuminated the empty space ahead.

Only a minute later Karin looked up and tears slid silently down her cheeks and her thumb worked its way into her mouth. Big sister, Brandi, quickly slid her arm around the little girl and said, "It's okay, Karin, this is home! Mommy's parking the car and we're going in so you guys can go to bed now. Don't cry you'll get to put on some new jammies! Mommy got some today at church, isn't that cool?" Karin sniffed and nodded trustingly. "And remember that pizza? It was really good!"

Faith was so glad for the motion lights on the garage that came on. At least it wouldn't be pitch dark in the garage when Faith turned off the car lights. If anyone was looking, they saw the twins' eyes were huge. Faith shut off the engine, released her seatbelt and reached for her purse. Brandi's belt snapped as it hit the end. She reached for both fasteners of the twins' belts and released them as the light came on when Faith opened her door. Both Karl's and Karin's eyes were wide, staring around them into the darkness outside the car. Faith stepped out of the car and two pair of eyes moved to watch her. Faith looked in the back seat, and reached for the door handle, because Karl was on the move.

As soon as the door was open Karl jumped to the ground with Brandi right behind him, but Karin's eyes were full of tears, there were shiny tracks on her cheeks and her thumb was squarely in her mouth. Faith didn't have to look hard to see the fear in her eyes. She moved into the doorway, looked at the tiny girl and smiled, holding out her arms to the wee person. After only a second hesitation, Karen reached both arms toward Faith.

As she bent into the back seat, she murmured, "Come here, pumpkin, everything's just fine. There's nothing to be scared of. Brother's going with Brandi inside and we'll be right behind them." To emphasize her words, Faith leaned in and kissed the little cheek.

Faith must have said the magic word, because Karin went immediately to her knees and held out her arms to Faith. Only a second later, the trusting little soul was firmly wrapped around Faith's chest as she straightened up. Faith was shocked at how little the tiny girl weighed. She could only assume that the children hadn't been eating nearly enough to keep body and soul together for a long time. Quickly, she pushed the door closed and turned to follow the other two children into the kitchen. It was several years since she carried a child from the car to the house, but it felt so right. It would feel 'righter' if one big, strong fireman were also going in that house. She didn't question where that thought came from.

Inside the kitchen door, Faith came in on Brandi's words, "...and I gotta take a bath now." She turned to Faith and asked, "Mommy, should Karin and Karl take baths?"

Karin had a death grip around Faith's neck, so she couldn't see the child's face, even so, she looked down at Karl and saw the fear on his face and made a split-second decision. "Matt gave the kids a shower at the fire station, I think if they changed clothes and we found them a comfy bed that would work. They only played in the sandbox at church, so I don't think they got dirty. Probably after we roam the mall for several hours and they swing and play tomorrow they'll be dirty enough for a bath. Besides, it'll be church on Sunday and they'll need to be super clean for their Sunday clothes." Where they would come from, she wasn't sure.

"Mommy, you didn't get the clothes from the car...."

Sitting down in her chair at the table and carefully taking both of Karin's hands from around her neck, she let a sigh escape, then she answered, "I know. Why don't you go turn on some lights and take Karl and Karin upstairs. Maybe they can decide while I'm getting the clothes which rooms they like. How's that?"

Brandi grinned at the twins and grabbed their hands. "Okay, Mommy, we'll go right up now, but you must hurry!"

"I will, Brandi."

Karin's tears were dried and she left, holding Brandi's hand, just as Karl was holding her other hand. Faith swallowed and watched them leave the kitchen; then she grabbed her keys and headed out the back door. She was glad for the motion light that one of the church men had installed for her last fall, it made the few steps outside between the house and the garage much easier to navigate at night. By the time she came back in the house with the two bags of clothes, lights were on upstairs, glowing in each room. Big sister was doing her job.

Faith locked the back door behind her and turned off lights as she headed for the stairs. Once she put the twins to bed and got them quiet, then said goodnight to Brandi, she knew she needed a long, relaxing bath herself. She'd read in bed for a while and that would finish out her day. Her day would end much differently than she could ever have imagined!

Remembering what Matt said about Karin refusing to shower by herself, she wondered where the twins would sleep, but of course, Brandi hadn't figured into the shower at the fire station. And once Brandi was introduced to the twins, she was calling the shots. Only Brandi's room was a little girl's room, the master bedroom was hers and the other two were furnished as guest rooms that she and Max hoped to fill with other children someday. That was not to be, but now there were two children who needed a loving, stable home. She wondered again if she could provide it. She sighed; Pastor Jim seemed to think she was the one to do it. Could she? Would her budget stretch that far? She absolutely hated to take charity, but that's what the bills in her purse were, weren't they?

The light was on in the large bathroom and Karin sat on the toilet with the door wide open. Brandi stood guard, probably making sure she didn't fall in. Karl, the little man that he was, stood just outside the door facing the hallway, not looking at the girls, but wide-eyed through the doorways into each room that he could see.

Faith reached the top step, still holding a bag in each arm. She didn't comment on the girls in the bathroom, why should she, but instead she said, "Karl, did you decide which room will be yours?"

In awe, he whispered, "You mean I could have a room all by myself? Wow!"

"Yes, that's right." Faith smiled at the little boy.

She crouched down in front of him and placed the bags on the floor beside her. She reached for one of his hands and said, "Maybe, little by little, we could make your room look more like a little boy's room. Would you like that?"

"Oh, yeah, Miss...." He acted a little confused and Faith sensed it was because she never told the children what to call her.

Still crouched in front of him and holding one hand, she looked into his eyes. Speaking softly, but definitely wanting to know the answer, she said, just to him, "Karl, do you have a mommy? Should we be looking for her?"

His eyes dropped to his shoes. He pulled his lower lip between his teeth and forlornly shook his head. Faith was glad she was so close to him, as he finally whispered, "No." He gave a huge sigh as if letting a huge weight fall from his shoulders. "The old man was really mean to Mommy and Sister for a long time." Faith didn't say another word, she was sure if she stayed quiet the little boy would say more, what was weighing on his heart. Instead, with all the love she could convey only with her eyes, she put her hand on his shoulder and waited.

After another long sigh he continued, "He didn't like me much either, but it wasn't so bad. One night, long time after Mommy put us to bed; he came home bad drunk and started beatin' Mommy. He thought I was asleep, but I wasn't, I heard Mommy screamin', but then he shot her. I heard the shot go off and then Mommy didn't scream no more. I waited a long time. I heard him fall on the couch and start snorin' real loud. When I heard him I made Sister come with me, we ran down the stairs to the street. We ranned far away."

"Is that when you went to the warehouse?"

He shook his head again. "Uh uh. We slep' in a doorway that night, but people made us move in the mornin', but we didn't go back to the apartment. I didn't want nothin' to do with the old man when he woke up. We didn't go to the garage till that day those big buildings fell down. We went in there away from the smoke and stayed until Matt found us. Umm, could you be our mommy like you're Brandi's mommy?" he asked hopefully, his eyes coming up to look at her.

Faith's heart was nearly breaking. Tears glistened in her eyes, but she wouldn't let them fall. She took her hand from his shoulder and put her arm around him and hugged him. "Karl, I think that would be okay," she choked out. "Come on, let's find your room, shall we? Will Karin sleep by herself?"

Crestfallen, as if he forgot about his sister for a few minutes, he said, "Oh, no, probly not. She'll sleep with me."

Just at that moment, Brandi led Karin from the bathroom. "Mommy," she asked, "Could Karin sleep in my room? There's that other bed nobody sleeps next to mine. Would it be okay?"

She and Karl stopped talking. She stayed on their level, but kept Karl's hand in hers. The girls were coming, but Faith held out her free hand to Karin and asked, "Karin, do you want to sleep in Brandi's room or do you need to sleep with Karl? It's okay either way, pumpkin."

Karin took Faith's other hand and looked at her for several minutes, then her smile burst across her face and she turned to Brandi. No words came from her mouth, but she made her desire known very easily. That smile was just like the one Karin gave her at the pizza place and Faith's heart turned over. It would be very, very hard not to play favorites, that tiny girl was wrapping Faith around her finger, smile by smile.

Kissing the little hand she still held, Faith said, "Okay, it's fine with me if you two sleep in the same room, but right now, Brandi needs to take her bath. How about while she's doing that you come with Karl and me while he decides which room he wants. I'll read you both a story and he can go to bed. When Brandi's finished, you two girls can get in bed in Brandi's room." She looked from Karl to Karin and asked, "Will that work?"

Karl was grinning, as he said, "Yeah!" Karin was still smiling and nodded.

Brandi ran into her room and pulled her pajamas from under her pillow while Faith, with Karin tagging along, took the bag of girl's clothes in and put them on the second bed in the room. Karl, of course, didn't go in; he was a boy and didn't want to go in a girl's room. Karin was Faith's shadow and followed her, even after Brandi ran back out and into the bathroom.

Brandi's room was in one corner up stairs and Faith's was across the hall. The other two bedrooms were in the other two corners, one much smaller than the other, because two bathrooms were between it and Faith's room. Karl walked into the room next to the bathroom and looked around silently, then without any comment, he walked across the hall to the much bigger room and looked around. He shook his head and walked back to the smaller room across the hall, walked in and hopped up on the bed.

Grinning broadly, he looked at Faith and said, "I want this for my room! It's great!"

Faith and Karin followed him in and Faith said, "That's fine, Karl, we'll start tomorrow at the mall and get curtains for these windows just like you want." She thought a minute and then said, "Actually, there's a store in the mall where we could get some material. I could get enough to make curtains and a cover for the bed. Okay?"

The boy looked around the room and saw that there were two windows. His eyes turned to saucers and he exclaimed, "Oh, wow! Yeah, that's great!" Faith gathered Karen in her arm, with a story book in the other hand and sat down beside Karl. She took her time and looked from one child to the other before she opened the book.

Not really surprising, Brandi's bath only lasted about five minutes. Faith didn't say anything, but she wondered if the child had even used soap. Of course, it wasn't like the day when they spent all day in the dust and debris of nine eleven. It was about half an hour later that the story was finished and Faith had all three children settled in their beds. Much to her surprise, even though the twins had slept in the car, as soon as the lights went out, they fell asleep. She left one night light on in their bathroom.

As she drew water in her tub and dumped bubble bath in, Faith wondered if the children would sleep through the night. After hearing Karl's story, she wondered if perhaps the children or Karin in particular would have nightmares, it could easily happen. In the same situation, she was sure she'd have nightmares. She sent up a prayer right then for these dear children who had lived such hard lives in so short a time. She ended the prayer by saying, "And Lord, give me the strength and wisdom to love and care for these dear children as You would have me do."

Matt reluctantly boarded the train, not really wanting to leave the lovely lady on the platform. He handed his ticket to the conductor before he turned into the car to find a seat. He wondered if they had tokens or commuter passes that were cheaper than each individual ticket. He had a feeling that he'd be riding this train often in the next weeks or months. He decided to get to the terminal early in the morning and look into that.

He assessed his day, well, two days. They had sped by like a speeding freight train. Thursday he came out to find the church, only with the intention of knowing where to come on Sunday for church. He talked with the pastor and promised to come back for Sunday school as well. He had to hurry to catch the train, then moved so fast when he reached his room he hardly had time to change his clothes, certainly not read any mail. This noon, well, late morning, he found homeless twins and spent the rest of the day in the company of a wonderful lady, her daughter and those twins. He quickly admitted that the time since he left the fire station was the most enjoyable he spent in a very long time. He readily admitted he would love to be the daddy those three children needed – as long as the mommy was the delightful lady he'd been introduced to at the church.

SIX

A S HE SAT IN THE SEAT AND LOOKED OUT THE WINDOW, WATCHING THE SUNSET turn to night, he also realized that he was still in his uniform. He hadn't had the chance to change since he scrambled into it almost thirty hours before. Of course, he had a good dousing from the waist up when he put the twins in the shower and cleaned them up. Still, he felt as if he was sewed into this uniform. He could use a shower and shampoo in the worst way. He didn't dare raise his arm; other passengers might catch an unwanted whiff! He felt his chin; a shave might help, too. He'd save the shave till morning. Morning… he couldn't wait! *I'll spend it in Thomaston with the loveliest lady in the world!*

Much to Faith's surprise, the next time her eyes opened, sun was shining in her window. However, she knew it wasn't the sun that woke her. She opened her eyes slowly and there were three sets of eyes silently looking at her from beside the bed. Two sets were big, solemn brown and the other set was sparkling blue just like her own.

"Mommy," the tallest one said, "come on! It's time to get up! It's long past the time you usually get up and we have to meet Matt at the train station and we're all hungry. It's time for breakfast, you know."

"Are you sure," she muttered.

"Oh, yes, Mommy!"

Faith groaned to herself. It was bad enough when Brandi came in to wake her up, now there were three. She glanced at the alarm clock beside the bed, it was barely seven o'clock. There was plenty of time to get to the train station by ten o'clock, even if she broke down and made French toast, which she sometimes did on Saturday.

Turning and pushing with her elbow, Faith sat up; glad she had on a cover-up nightie. She knew her hair was a mess, but whose hair wasn't when they just woke up? She smiled at all three of the children and said, "Okay, kids, I see you're still in your jammies. I didn't put away anything from those bags. You go to your rooms and search out some clothes to wear. By the way, did you wash your faces?"

Brandi sighed, "Of course we did, Mommy! I even found those toothbrushes Dr. Kyder gave us, so now Karin and Karl each have one. We'll go get dressed, but it won't take us long, we'll be to the kitchen before you. What's for breakfast? You know it's Saturday and you sometimes fix French toast."

Faith nodded. "Yes, I remember. Why don't you get out the electric skillet, the bread and the eggs? You know how to break the eggs in a bowl, you can do that, it'll be a big help. I'll plug in the skillet, don't you do that, but you can pour our orange juice and milk, if you're so sure you'll be in the kitchen before I am." She smiled. "I can move really fast, you know."

"Mommy," Brandi sighed, "you aren't really that fast at all!" *No, it's been a long time since I've moved at warp speed!* She grabbed the twins' hands and said, "Come on, guys!"

"Yeah, let's go!" Karl said.

The three children skipped out of Faith's room and she watched them with a smile until the door closed behind them. Quickly she scooted into her bathroom, thankful that she could have a few more minutes before she had to deal with three children. She washed her face, brushed her teeth and ran a comb through her curls, knowing that as soon as she opened the kitchen door the wind would send her hair flying. She went back in her room and found a pretty sundress to wear. She found a hair clip to match and pushed it into her hair. The sun was out and it would be another warm day. She knew she would go in the attic…that could be a very warm place. Hmm, that would be with a very handsome man….

Maybe Karl did talk and Karin didn't, but he didn't say too much and given his body language when he told her about his parents, he was embarrassed. She decided she'd begin encouraging Karin to speak, she was sure it wasn't that she didn't know how, it was undoubtedly the home she came from that shut her down. Just from the little that Karl told her, she couldn't imagine such a home life for them. Her home had been a loving, Christian home and each of her two siblings were fine Christian men.

She did her best over the years to make the Lankaster home as loving as possible before, as well as after Max died. She wondered if Karin would need counseling, if she did, someone else would have to pay for it, she couldn't stretch her budget that much. The money Pastor gave her would buy groceries and a few clothes for Karl, but not too much else. She wondered at her statement of buying material to make the room Karl slept in into a boy's room. She was definitely biting off more than she could chew with that statement!

French toast went over like every other bit of food that was put in front of the twins. However, this time, Faith noticed that the twins took smaller bites and didn't inhale their meal as they had last night with the pizza. Maybe seeing a stack of French toast when they sat down at the table helped them know there was plenty to eat.

It was still a pleasure to watch them eat, they made no complaints about the food, but they dug in and put it away. Their glasses of milk and orange juice emptied quickly, too. Their table manners were sorely lacking, but that would come eventually. That was not something she needed to correct right away. At this point loving these two little people was the highest priority.

Faith stacked the plates, then stood up to take them to the sink and said, "Okay, kids, off to the bathroom to brush your teeth. As soon as you finish, come back here so we can go to meet Matt. I'll get these dishes into the dishwasher while you do and we'll be all ready for a big day."

Brandi pulled out Karin's chair and helped her down, as she said, "Okay, Mommy, I know Karin and Karl are excited to use their new toothbrushes. We'll be back real soon." Just like a mother hen, she added, "We'd better go to the bathroom, too."

"Yeah," Karl added, "I never had no toothbrush before." Quickly, Faith looked at Karin and she was shaking her head, too.

"Okay, brush your teeth well!" She tried for an upbeat sound, not her real feelings at such a statement from a five year old boy who should have been brushing his teeth as soon as he had one and seen a dentist at least once a year for probably three of those five!

To think these little human beings hadn't even had their own toothbrush! They were five years old! That was something she took for granted for years! She took Brandi to the dentist faithfully and he gave her a toothbrush each time she went. They had so many Brandi gave two of them to the twins. She knew there were still several more where they came from. The children left and the room was quiet, but the noise in the hall and on the stairs sounded like a herd of elephants. She smiled; it was a good sound the house had been quiet for a long time.

As she loaded the dishwasher, she was glad for it. It would fill up twice as fast now. Her heart skipped a beat, tomorrow, there would be five putting their feet under her table, even if it was for only one meal. Matt had already consented to come for Sunday dinner. As she thought about it, he volunteered to come help her get the boxes of clothes from the attic. There was a good chance they'd still be here at lunch time and very probably here for supper this evening. She must remember to keep her heart under wraps, if she let it out on its own, it might get the idea that this man would be here all the time..... *Not that it would make me mad*, she admitted. Soon, the children were back and Faith found herself smiling.

Faith's purse was where she left it last night. She dug out her wallet and checked to see how much money she had, of course, she could always use her credit card, but she hated to use that much. She picked up her keys and ushered the children out in front of her. Just as she assumed from looking out the window in her room, it was a beautiful day. There was a warm, gentle breeze. In fact, later on, it could be quite warm. That was just fine, summer clothes were a lot easier to dress in than having to bundle up in winter clothes.

She looked at the children. She was sure Brandi helped Karin dress, both she and Brandi had on pretty tops and shorts that matched one of the colors. Karl obviously picked out his own outfit. He also had on shorts and a top, but like many boys, he hadn't been too fussy about color coordination. However, neither of the twins looked like little waifs as they had when Matt brought them to church. Again, Brandi ushered the twins into the back seat and sat between them, making sure their seatbelts were buckled.

"Mommy, I'm sitting back here with Karin and Karl, because you'll be picking Matt up, so he'll ride up there with you."

"Yes, thank you, Brandi. I'm sure the twins like it that you sit with them."

Out of the blue, only a few blocks before the train station, Karl asked, "Can Matt be our new daddy? Would it be okay?"

Quickly, Faith looked in the rearview mirror straight at Brandi. She scowled, thinking that possibly Brandi put that thought in Karl's head. Brandi was grinning back, but her lips were closed. Obviously, Karl thought that one up all by himself. She had to think a minute as to how to answer, knowing what Brandi kept saying ever since Tuesday. She really didn't want the little boy to be embarrassed, either. She would be totally embarrassed if Matt ever got wind of what Brandi said and now what Karl asked.

Her fingers grew white as she gripped the steering wheel; she knew she had to say the right words. "Karl, Brandi and I only met Matt the day the Towers came down. Actually, he and I only talked for the first time yesterday when he brought you to our church. I think it's a bit early to say yes or no to that question."

"Oh, okay, but he's gonna be here all day, isn't he?" *Like that would be long enough.*

"Yes, he is. He's helping us get you guys some clothes."

"Wow!" Brandi exclaimed. "Won't it be fun today?"

Very importantly, Karl said, "And we're gonna get some stuff to make my room into a boy's room, too. Mommy told me last night!"

Faith silently groaned he hadn't forgotten that. "Yes, that's right, Karl. We'll have to look in that department to see what they have."

"Okay, that's great!" He bounced a little on the seat. Faith breathed a silent sigh Karl's question was forgotten for the time being. *Maybe!*

A train whistled into the station just as Faith pulled into a parking spot. Before she had the car shut off, she heard three seatbelts click and snap in the back seat. The children saw the sun sparkle on the train's silver skin and heard the brakes hiss. Quickly, she pulled her key from the ignition and released her belt. She glanced down at her watch as she opened the door. At the same time the back door slammed. Obviously, this wasn't Matt's train; it was bound for the city.

Quickly, she pushed her door open and called, "Kids, wait, don't run ahead too much, this isn't the train Matt's coming on. He won't be here for another twenty minutes." She might as well have saved her breath. The twins grabbed Brandi's hands as their little legs scrambled to keep up with her longer ones.

Since Brandi knew no speed but run, she was half way across the parking lot before Faith had the doors locked. She followed them more slowly, but kept them in sight as they ran. Since it wasn't Matt's train, she didn't need to get all out of breath, but she did need to keep them in sight. That was a challenge all on its own. Who knew how many people were in the station or how many would come in. Faith's heart kicked her, surely here on the island the kids were safe! She nearly ran to catch up.

Brandi flung open the station door and Faith ran to keep them in sight. The station could be full of people, and that was an excellent place to lose children. As she reached the door, she saw a glimpse of the trio darting between adults standing at the ticket counter and milling around, waiting for the people to get off the train. Inside the station, it was nearly impossible to keep the children in sight, but she did her best. The passengers who were planning to board this train were heading out the door and Brandi scooted the twins into the middle of the pack, while Faith was left to join in at the back.

"Well," she murmured, "They'll learn soon enough it's not Matt's train. Thank goodness we aren't boarding a train! I'm really glad we're meeting someone who's getting off, he'd already be inside if this was his train."

It was still fifteen minutes until ten o'clock when they were all on the platform. Saturday morning, there were almost as many people going into the city as other mornings, only later in the day, so the trains ran every twenty minutes. However, those coming from the city didn't come as frequently. What the children hadn't realized was that this train was one going into the city, not coming from it. Obviously, Brandi didn't know her directions too well. The one Matt was on would get in in another twenty minutes or so and come from the other direction. Maybe a short lesson on directions was in order one day soon.

She quickly scanned those still leaving the cars, he might have come earlier than she expected. Matt would be easy to see, he was nearly a head taller than most of the people. His blond hair in the sun would be a beacon, at least to her. She looked at the benches scattered around the platform and into groups of people standing around, but didn't see anyone that sent her heart into a flutter. Since she was alone she let out a sigh, there was no use telling her heart to behave, she was pretty sure she was sunk already.

Since the children were still milling around, she decided that if she sat on a bench they would come to her. When the passengers began to board after the others were off, Brandi brought the twins back to where she was. All three of them crowded in beside her and all three of their faces were long without a smile. Karl plunked down next to her, and the two girls crowded onto the seat on the other side. Right away, Brandi said, "Mommy, where is he? Isn't he coming? I didn't see him at all!"

Faith pulled in a deep breath, glad she didn't have to hurry to board a train often. "Of course he's coming, Brandi, but trains come into this station going both ways. Once this one leaves this station, there's a double track before it reaches the next station, it'll go over to that other track so that it can pass a train coming the other way. That train right there is going into the city and the one Matt will ride is coming from the city. Besides, the next train coming from the city won't get here for another fifteen minutes."

"Oh, goody, I'm glad we didn't miss him!" She looked at the twins, Karl sitting beside Faith and Karin next to Brandi. "We can look around at all the people now!"

"But Matt's gonna come?" Karl asked.

"Yes, he is, Karl," Faith assured him. "He'll be here real soon, you just watch!"

"Yeah, okay."

Just the way he asked made her understand that the man in the twins' lives hadn't kept his word or been at home when he should have or when he told the family he would be there. She guessed the children were disappointed often by their dad. She didn't say anything, but she made sure she would not disappoint either child. Why didn't parents realize how very important keeping their word was to children? That was one thing about God's Word, it said what it meant and it meant what it said. Always!

Matt was up soon after the sun peeked over the horizon. He took longer than normal to dress. On a Saturday that he was off in this kind of weather he wore shorts, not even thinking about it because he normally went to a buddy's place in Connecticut to fish with his friend. At first he reached for his shorts, but remembered that Faith didn't have shorts on when she came to the church for the twins. Did church people not wear shorts? He had no clue, so instead reached for a cool pair of slacks and a polo shirt.

He hadn't really wasted time dressing but he hurried to the diner for breakfast. He would be on the right train at the right time to reach Thomaston at ten o'clock! He and the cook were the only people in the diner when he walked in, so the man served him his cup of coffee. Matt relaxed in the booth and looked at the clock as the cook started fixing his eggs the way he like them. The older man wasn't much of a talker, so the diner was quiet.

Matt reached the train station in plenty of time to check into how to get passes or tokens for multiple trips. He would ride the train four times just today and tomorrow. The teller at the window where he went assured him and quickly sold him nearly a pocket full of passes for his riding enjoyment. His wallet bulged as he put them away. The terminal was crowded; he didn't realize how many people used the commuter line on a Saturday. But then, who wanted to drive in the over-populated borough of Manhattan?

Only minutes later, the train roared in and he made sure he was on it. He rushed through the door and found a double seat by the window. In the terminal the trains were underground, but soon they emerged into the sunlight. He couldn't ignore the pounding of his heart, as he anticipated the trip he was about to make and the lady who would be at the end. He readily admitted he was excited to see her… well, them.

There weren't many people on the train leaving the city, so he had his pick of seats. His seat by a window wasn't far from the door. As the train left the terminal he wondered what he was doing. He, a solitary fireman, was going out on the Island to spend his free day with a lady he hardly knew and three children. He wondered if he needed to make an appointment to have his head examined. It had obviously taken leave of its senses.

Normally, on a free Saturday, he joined a buddy from his shift who owned a fishing cabin on the shore in Connecticut where they could spend the day. It would be quiet and restful. He knew, even before he got there, that this day would be anything but quiet and restful. But then, life was like that. At that moment, he knew he was ready for a change. His athletic heart picked up its cadence, his life was about to take a one-eighty!

He wondered how the night had gone. Did Faith have any problems getting the twins to go to bed? He was pretty sure they hadn't slept in a bed in quite a while. They fell asleep almost as soon as they were belted in after pizza, but would they insist on sleeping together, would they even sleep? Did either of them routinely have nightmares? Again this morning, he realized how much he hated dumping the twins on Faith with only Brandi to help her. But then, Pastor Jim's statement came back to him, "Faith loves children. She's an awesome mom!"

He looked at his watch as the train slowed for the street crossings of

Thomaston to come into the station. He realized that his normally slow-beating, athletic heart was beating much faster. He chuckled, he was about to see his lovely lady. Well, maybe she wasn't his just yet, but... maybe one day soon. He wondered if he had any allies in the twins or Brandi. He had to be one hopeless critter, wanting to take on twin five year olds and a nine year old - a ready-made family. Him, the closest thing to a sibling he ever had was his cousin who was four years older and another who was five years younger and whose family lived three hours away. He shook his head, what was he thinking?

The horn was blaring intermittently and the train was slowing. The brakes hissed and he was on his feet. The conductor yelled, "Thomaston!"

Just before leaving the two seat bench, he glanced out the window and saw a welcome sight. On a bench, out of the sun, sat a lovely lady with three children crowded around her. That heart of his betrayed him yet again and picked up more speed and a grin spread over his face. He whirled around and headed for the door. He grabbed the handrail down the steps and swung down the last step to the platform. He grinned at the conductor and gave him a two finger salute.

Before his feet even touched the cement, he heard running feet. He only had time to step away from the train when three little people launched themselves at him. He crouched down and opened his arms. All three plowed into him, nearly sending him onto his rear. However, even though his arms were around the children, his eyes went over their heads drinking in the sight of the lovely lady who followed more slowly. As far as he was concerned, her smile rivaled the sun in brightness. The realization hit him right between the eyes that he could stand seeing smiles like that for a very, very long time.

"Hi, Matt!" Brandi and Karl said together. Karin put her arms around his neck and planted a wet kiss on his cheek.

"Hi, guys!" he exclaimed, the words strangled in his throat. With Karin wrapped around him, he stood up so he could greet the lady who just walked up. He knew the smile on his face was about to stretch the skin of his face. He was so happy to see the lady. "Hi, how'd you make out? I see you're all cleaned and pressed."

Without realizing it, he reached out his free hand toward her, but she never hesitated, she reached for it and took it. After kissing Matt again on the cheek, Karin wanted down. When Matt looked, Brandi was holding out her hand for her. He put her on the ground and the three children took off running toward the parking lot. Excitement was hardly explanation enough for the way they acted.

Watching them, he said, "Guess Brandi's got them corralled just fine." He grinned. "I should have guessed."

"Oh, she's been little mother hen since we got home last night. We made out just fine last night and this morning. The only thing, what woke me up this morning was not the sun streaming in the window, although it was shining, or the alarm, but three sets of eyes solemnly watching me catch my last few Z's."

Matt chuckled. "Mmm, that would be disconcerting. So they slept okay?"

Nodding, Faith laughed. "Must have, I never heard a thing."

"Well, I'm glad of that. On the way out here I wondered if they had nightmares. So we go to your place to fish some boxes from the attic?"

"Yes, I'm hoping to find quite a few things that Karin can wear. There is no sense buying new when Brandi's things from Karin's age are still in very good shape. Of course, I have nothing for Karl, at least not at his age." She sighed, "He picked out the room he wants and I made the promise to get him some curtains for a boy's room or some material to make curtains and a bedcover." She sighed, "What was I thinking?"

"Would you have time to do that?"

"It's not the time, Matt."

"It's the extra money, isn't it?"

"Yeah, it is," she agreed, reluctantly.

"We'll see about that."

He wondered how she'd feel if he paid for some things Karl needed. The pastor gave her money, but he knew how much it was, not even a hundred dollars, since he picked a twenty off the top for their pizza last night. She probably had enough money from month to month to keep herself and Brandi comfortably, but not extravagantly. A widow wouldn't make an extravagant amount, he was sure. He knew groceries for two, even children, weren't cheep. That one little bag of clothes for Karl wouldn't go far; there was nothing in that closet he could wear to church. He could wear those things to play in or to school, but there was nothing fancy.

Licking his lips, Matt said, "How 'bout I help you with some of that? I've told you I live in one room, it's in an old converted Victorian that doesn't cost much. I eat lots of my meals at the station that's part of the FDNY budget. I make a decent wage, let me help you some. Will you do me that honor, Faith?"

She squeezed his hand. "Matt, I won't refuse you, believe me."

He looked down at her and grinned. "Thanks."

She shook her head. "No, thank you, Matt."

Matt watched closely when Faith turned onto her gravel drive, he was anxious to see where she lived. That was not something that came into the discussion at all last evening when the three of them were talking in Pastor Jim's office. This had to be on the outskirts of town and looked very inviting. There was a slight rise, enough so that only the roof was visible from the road. She drove under the branches of a large shade tree. The large tree was on the bank, and on a sturdy limb opposite the drive a swing hung down. It swung slightly in the breeze. They crested the rise and Matt looked at the house, a house he could imagine filling with children he and Faith would love and raise together.

They were passing the tree, when Brandi exclaimed, "Mommy! Stop! Karin and Karl and I want to swing! We can do that while you and Matt bring down the boxes, can't we? It's such a perfect day to swing!"

Faith applied the brake and stopped. Three seatbelts snapped and both back doors opened and bounced, making the car lurch back and forth. Only moments later both doors banged shut. Matt turn to watch the two who climbed out on his side, running behind the car with arms pumping to catch up with Karl who got out on the side closest to the swing. Faith hardly had her foot on the gas before Karl was in the swing, pumping his legs for all they were worth. Brandi came up and gave him a push. Karin stood next to the tree, a grin on her face.

The car started moving slowly toward the house, but Matt couldn't help himself, his left hand snaked across the back of the seat and rested on Faith's shoulder. Still playing with her hair, but looking at the three children, Matt asked, incredulously, "Did you hear anybody say anything about swinging?"

Faith chuckled. "No, that's mother hen again."

Matt looked ahead and exclaimed, "What a perfect place! You must love it."

As she eased down on the gas, Faith glanced over at Matt. "Yes, I've loved it since the very first time I saw it. My late husband worked at the WTC, but he wanted his family to live outside the city. We looked for months even before I became pregnant and finally found this place. It's this house and more than an acre of land."

She was quiet for just a minute and then she said much more quietly, "Perhaps Max had a premonition, I've wondered about that a few times, but his insurance had a clause that stated this house and property would be fully paid for upon his death." There was a wobble in her voice, but her eyes were clear.

"Wow! That was terrific! I'm sure it made his passing much easier on you."

"Yes. I hope to never have to sell." She parked beside the house and smiled at him. As both their seatbelts clicked, she asked, "So, Fireman Matt, are you ready to climb those pull-down stairs into that stuffy attic to find some little girl clothes?"

He chuckled and let the auburn curl slide through his fingers one last time. "Lady, I'm forever climbing stairs. You just lead me to them." He grinned at her. "You know that is one reason I came out today. I'm here to help clothe those twins."

She led him into her kitchen. "Okay, we're about to do just that!"

The kitchen was a smaller version of an airy room where a farmer's wife would cook for a large family. There was a large table set into a large bay with three windows. The white curtains at those windows were bordered with the same fabric as the table cloth. The same blue was echoed in the checkered cushions on the chairs. The kitchen sported every modern convenience from the built-in dishwasher to the microwave. He noticed there was also a pantry on the opposite wall. What a wonderful place to feed a family! The sun found a spot and made the table sparkle. The centerpiece of silk flowers was magnificent in the sunlight.

She didn't comment on the kitchen, but led him through to the hallway. Of course, at one end was the front door. At the back were a set of stairs that she went to immediately. He followed more slowly, glancing into each room that he came to. He took longer to look into her living room. It was large and sunny and each piece of furniture looked inviting and comfortable. This was not an extravagant home, but one that had been furnished with good taste. He was absolutely sure who that person was with good taste. It reminded him of the home his mom made for her little family. He was sure it was still just as cozy after all these years.

At the head of the stairs, Faith waited. She pointed to the room on the left and said, "Karl picked this as his room. I said we'd make curtains and a cover so it'd be more a boy's room."

"The twins didn't sleep together?" he asked, astonished.

"No, Brandi convinced Karin that the two girls should be together in her room. She has twin beds and the room is very girlish, so I'm glad that worked out."

Nodding, he asked, "So where are these stairs?"

Without taking him to the girls' bedroom, she headed for a room close by and said, "They're here in Karl's closet. They're near the center of the roof, but I hope you don't have to bend double to get up there. You are a big man."

"I'll admit to that, but I'm sure it'll work out. Lead the way." His smile made his eyes twinkle and that set her heart fluttering. She almost smacked her hands together in an effort to put a lid on that treacherous heart. Matt saw the look on her face and had to reign in his hands, they almost reached out to take her in his arms!

As they entered the room Karl claimed, Matt looked around again. The bed was full sized; the child must have rattled around in it last night. He could picture in his mind how his room was when he was growing up. Every inch of wall space was covered with banners and posters. He could envision this one in a few years. A boy had to have his own domain he knew this would be Karl's. Matt was excited for him.

Soon, the stairs creaked down and ended several feet into the room. Matt didn't really expect Faith to go up, but she never hesitated and climbed the stairs in front of him. He waited until she was several steps up then watched as she gracefully moved from step to step in front of him. He licked his lips, then looked on up to the slanted roof above them, knowing what turn his mind was taking. The lady was well made with nicely shaped legs, his fingers itched to mold to them and run up and down on them. Of course, his eyes could look, his mind could fantasize, but not a word must leave his mouth and his hands quickly found the railings. He was impressed, the stairs felt quite sturdy.

Faith reached the attic and pulled the string that hung down. A bare light bulb came on and showed all the filmy cobwebs hanging from the rafters. Faith moved immediately aside so that Matt could also come up. He had to bend over; his head would get into the cobwebs if he didn't. She looked up, then at the top of his head and smiled at him sheepishly. "This isn't one of my weekly cleaning spots, I'm sure you can tell."

He chuckled. "I never knew of an attic that was. Are these the boxes?"

"I've put the sizes on the tops, so let me find the ones I want. We won't have to look through everything up here; we can take them down and put them in their room. It'll be much easier that way." Fanning herself with her hand, she added, "Besides, the iced tea is two stories away up here."

"Yeah, I hear that! Those trees don't keep much of the heat out of up here."

"That's true and attics don't usually have air conditioning ducts."

Soon, they had four boxes on Karl's floor and the stairs were back in place. Matt carried them to the girls' room and Faith shook out the clothes, putting them either in the drawers of a dresser or hanging them on one side of the closet. Matt broke down the boxes getting them ready for recycling when they heard the back door slam behind three excited children.

"Well," Faith sighed, "it sounds like the quiet time is over. We are about to be invaded by little people, I'm afraid."

"I kind of figured that, too."

From the doorway, Brandi said, breathlessly, "Mommy, what did you find for Karin?"

Faith smiled at the two girls, as they burst into the room. "Just look, girls! What do you think of this?"

Brandi held Karin's hand and nearly dragged her to the closet. "Karin, look what Mommy found for you! These'll all be yours!" The little girl's eyes nearly popped.

Karl came reluctantly to the door, but when he saw that Matt was already there, he walked in and stood beside him. Matt squatted down and put his arm around the boy as they watched the girls. He smiled at him, as he said, "We'll get yours this afternoon. I saw your room it'll be the best room for a boy like you. What're you thinking of getting for curtains?"

"I don't know." He looked at Matt with his big brown eyes. "Will you help me pick out stuff? I never had a room of my own."

"Of course! Isn't that why I came along?"

Karl's smile burst across his face. "Yeah! 'Course you did!"

In only a few minutes Faith had a simple lunch on the table. Brandi helped the children wash their hands in the half-bath under the stairs, while Matt helped Faith by pouring drinks and setting out the plates she handed him. He realized he didn't want to be far from her, she was fast becoming a very important person in his life. He couldn't help but wonder what she thought of him. Could he convince her that she meant more to him than just a lady to mother some orphaned children that he happened to find while in his line of work? He watched the children eat, their table manners weren't the best, but there was no vacuum sucking up the food. He hadn't heard any tummies growling before they found their seats. Obviously their extreme hunger of yesterday had been satisfied.

Right after lunch they left for the mall. However, Faith parked very close to the big department store that not only had children's clothes, but also had a good sized fabric department. She hoped they might have some sales, but there was every possibility that everything was regular price, any Labor Day sale was long over. She had to buy school clothes for a growing Brandi not long ago; she knew how expensive children's clothes could be. Matt, of course was quiet; he had no experience in this department.

Of course, Brandi knew where they were. There was a much smaller store, with only an inside entrance into the mall that she loved. It was close to this big store and before they all released their seatbelts, she said, "Mommy, can I take Karin and Karl to my favorite store so we can see my friend?"

"Well, let's think about this first, Brandi. How can Karl pick out what he wants for his room if you take them there right now?" Faith asked.

After a moment's thought, Brandi said, "We could go to the fabric place first and then we could go after he picks his favorite. You don't need him to pick out clothes, do you?"

Faith smiled at her child. "You like to be there when we pick out yours, don't you? You did when we came to get your school clothes."

Brandi sighed, "Mommy, he's a boy, why should he care?"

Matt had to laugh. "So only girls have to know what they wear?" he asked.

Brandi looked at Matt. "Boys just wear clothes, not pretty outfits."

"Ah, I see. I think I understand this reasoning."

"How about we compromise," Faith said. "Since it's Karl who needs all these things, you and Karin can go to your store while Karl stays with us. How's that, Karl?"

Feeling very important, since he was the one to get all the things, he grinned. "Yeah, that's great! I can stay with Matt and you."

"Okay," Brandi said, cheerfully. "Karin and I'll have fun."

Matt looked at Faith and asked, "Should I go with them?"

Listening as the three seatbelts clicked in the back seat, Faith said, "No, it's a very secure place and Brandi goes there a lot. One of the ladies who works there goes to our church. They'll be fine; we'll only have to go get them."

"Okay, sounds good to me." *Actually, it sounds great!* Of course, anywhere Faith was was the best place to be.

As they reached the roadway, a car passed, so Faith said, "Be careful, kids! You need to watch the traffic."

"Yes, Mommy, we'll watch," Brandi said.

All five of them went to the mall entrance of the big store and watched as Brandi took Karin across the way to the much smaller store. Faith saw her friend and waved as the two girls walked in. Now that he didn't have Brandi's hand to hold, Karl immediately reached for Matt's hand. Matt felt the little hand creep into his. He looked down at the little boy and smiled and gave the hand a gentle squeeze. He loved kids and hoped one day to have some of his own, but he discovered a long time ago that there had to be two people to have kids. Until yesterday he hadn't found the lady he wanted to be the mother of his kids.

"So, now that it's the three of us, we need to do some serious shopping for this guy," he said, smiling down at the little boy and squeezed his hand again. Karl looked up and grinned.

Faith also looked down at the little boy and smiled. "Yes, both departments are here on this floor, so let's find the boys department right away."

Probably because he could never remember being the focus of attention, Karl whispered, "Wow! For me?"

When they walked into the boys' department, Karl looked around in awe. It was obvious he'd never been to a big store for his clothes; his serious brown eyes looked like saucers as he looked around. He never said a word, just clung to Matt's hand more tightly, but his head was going back and forth as he looked at all the clothes.

Matt looked at some of the prices on the casual clothes and beckoned Faith over close. "How much do you feel you can spend?"

She shook her head. "Not near as much as I'd like."

"Let's get everything we need and don't look at the prices too closely. When we get to the counter, you pay what you feel you can and I'll cover the rest. Remember, we're going to get stuff for the bedroom, too."

"You'll do that?" she gasped.

Giving her his lopsided grin, he said, "I feel like a spending spree coming up."

He was rewarded with a very obvious lady's giggle. Looking around at all the aisles in the department, she said, "It's a good possibility that's what you'll get."

Matt shrugged. "It's just fine with me!"

It seemed as though Matt's hand had a mind of its own. He stepped close to her when they looked at the price tag on a pair of jeans and it seemed natural to put his arm around her. He was very pleased when she didn't stiffen or try to pull away from his hand or side. Faith felt his warm hand touch her waist. Just as when he put his hand on her shoulder or when he took her hand, it sent ripples of awareness throughout her body. In recent years, since Max had been gone, only Pastor Jim put his arm around her and that was only as a Christian brother.

According to the way her heart acted, she knew this was no brotherly touch; at least it wasn't for her. She didn't want to move, even though her brain told her that a good looking fireman wouldn't want a widow with three liabilities, but she really wanted to stay inside the circle of his arms for a very long time, if he put them around her. She could feel her heart thumping in her chest and wondered if Matt could hear it. Surely he could, it wasn't that noisy in the store. Without asking, Matt tossed the jeans in the cart.

While Matt's arm was still around Faith, Karl saw a shirt with several bright colors hanging on a rack. He let go of Matt's hand and ran over to it. "Wow!" he exclaimed. "Look at this! Is that in my size?"

Matt moved over to the rack, bringing Faith along with him. With his free hand, he picked up the tag and said, "I do believe it is, Karl. Do you like this one?"

"Yeah, it's neat!"

Soon, they had a shopping cart over half full with shirts and jeans, tops and shorts, underclothes and another pair of shoes. Matt reminded Karl that they needed to find a nice outfit for him to wear to church, so after they had everything he needed, they continued to look and found just the outfit. Faith could imagine what the boy would look like in about twenty years, just like his daddy....

Faith watched as the checkout lady began ringing up the items. It was obvious she couldn't pay for nearly half of the things. However, Matt had put several of the clothes into the basket without consulting her, including the outfit he and Karl picked out for Sunday. The little boy's face was wreathed in smiles. He obviously never had so much positive attention in his life. She ached for him. Brandi didn't have a daddy and that troubled her, but boys needed a daddy. A good daddy who was a good role model and who kept his word and his promises. She didn't dare let her mind wander to the obvious next step, even though there was a big, strong, warm hand settled on her hip.

When the total came on the screen, Faith set her purse on the counter, but while she reached into her wallet to pull out her money, Matt slapped his credit card down on the counter and motioned for the clerk to use it for the purchase. Faith had her hand around her money and looked up just in time to see the lady lay the slip down for him to sign his name. He did, while the lady started loading bags with the clothes.

When they left the counter and Faith said, "You didn't let me pay anything!"

Matt chuckled. "Is that so?"

With the bags in the cart, Matt had to push it. Until they reached the counter, Matt could push the cart and keep his arm around Faith, because they only moved a few feet at a time. However, with their mission in the clothes department completed, they must move on to a different department, but they found that Karl was hanging back, still looking at the clothes and ultimately getting lost in them.

Matt looked around for him and said, "Hey, Karl, why don't we get you this front row seat up here. You're getting lost in all these aisles and we can't see you."

Karl came immediately and Matt swung him up into the child's seat. "There, now you can see it all, man!"

"Yeah!" Karl said enthusiastically. "Yeah, this is great!"

Faith had to chuckle. She gave up long ago putting Brandi in the child's seat of the cart, she had too much energy and was forever trying to climb out, but Karl was happy to look out over the entire department. Faith walked beside Matt and they left the clothing department, heading down a wide aisle toward another department in the store.

They came to the kitchen and bathroom department first and Matt said, "Do you have everything you need from this department?"

As they continued to walk, Faith thought for just a minute, and said,

"Yes, I can't think of anything I need. I'm not one to buy special things for the bathroom; I have plenty of towels, sheets and blankets. I think just material to make curtains and a bedspread for that bed in his room will be plenty."

"That sure is a huge bed in his room, but I guess he'll grow into it someday."

Looking sideways at the big man beside her, Faith chuckled. "Yes, the male of the species has a way of doing that."

Matt chuckled and certainly didn't deny her statement. The lady beside him was delightful as well as practical. He kept pushing the cart down the aisle going from one end of the store to the other. It was also wide enough that shoppers could go either direction and not get in each other's way. Matt was glad for that, he loved having this exceptional lady right beside him.

Karl loved his seat in front of Matt, his head constantly moved from side to side, looking at everything in the huge store. Often he made comments about things, but never whined or wanted anything he could see from his perch. Soon, Faith took them down another aisle until they reached the department with hundreds of bolts of cloth standing on their ends. She led them directly to one end of an aisle.

SEVEN

WHERE FAITH STOPPED WAS THE SHORT END OF A LONG STRETCH OF MANY BOLTS of fabric. She caught Karl's attention and said, "So, Karl, here are some designs you can look through and choose from for those curtains and your bedcover," she said.

"Wow! I can choose any one of these?" He flung his arms out, as if to take in every one of the choices in front of him.

Smiling, Faith rubbed his arm and said, "Yes, that's right. Be sure and look at each one and get just the one you want."

"Wow!" he whispered in awe.

Never asking to get out of the seat on the cart, he leaned over, putting his elbows on the side of the cart. Faith and Matt were both quiet, but as Karl's eyes went back and forth, looking at each design, Matt's arm snaked out again and pulled Faith back to his side. He was glad she didn't pull away, but as he looked down at her, she looked up at him and smiled. The look in her eyes warmed him straight to his heart. Looks like that could turn his brain to mush in a heartbeat, he was sure of it.

Karl's eyes were going from one end of the rack to the other. Never a word came from his mouth, only his eyes moved. Finally, his right arm went out and he said, triumphantly, "That's what I want!" Figures on the fabric he pointed to were of characters from a popular children's movie that had toys for sale in the toy department.

Matt leaned over and just before he lifted the bolt to place it in the cart, he said, "You're sure about this?"

Nodding, Karl exclaimed, "Oh, yes!"

"Okay, we're good, then."

While she stood inside of Matt's arm, Faith silently calculated how much yardage she'd need. Along the way to the cashier, she picked up thread and hardware for two sets of curtains and a bedspread. At the counter, she pulled the bolt from the cart and laid her accessories down with it, and pulled her purse around to find her wallet and some bills. However, Matt slapped down his credit card which he put in his pocket instead of his wallet.

With this last purchase, Matt said, "Do we have everything?" His grin was wide enough the dimple showed in his cheek. He anticipated what Faith would say.

"Matt, you've bought everything today!" Faith murmured. Trying hard to give him a disgusted look, she said, "I was supposed to pay *some* of it, you know."

He winked at her. "So? My phone bill, my life insurance premium last month and the rent for my one room were the last time I spent any large amount of money. Except train fare and meals at the diner which I pay each time I eat, and, like I say, lots of those are compliments of FDNY. Was last month the last time you spent any large amount of money, Faith?"

She chuckled. "Don't I wish!"

He squeezed her close and put his finger over her lips, wishing that he could put his own lips there instead. "Well, then, that's it. Don't say any more about it. Do we have everything? By the way, shall we all go for the girls or should I get these in the car while you get them?"

"I thought Karl might like to play over there for a little, but since we have the store cart and there's too much to carry around, maybe we better do it your way."

Matt looked at the little boy and asked, "Karl, do you want to go with Faith or me?"

They could almost see the wheels turning in his head. He was torn, they could tell. Finally, he looked at Matt, then scowled before he said, "I wanna go with you, Matt. Us men need to stick together."

Matt chuckled and brushed his hand over Karl's head. "Well, that's fine with me, Karl. I think I could use a big strong guy like you out at the car." He seemed to give it some thought for just a minute, but then he said, "How about we let Faith go back for the girls and we'll empty the cart, then we'll come back in the store. We'll walk through real fast and if they're still playing we'll meet them there."

"Yeah, that's okay!"

Faith grinned. She knew she and the girls wouldn't meet Karl and Matt inside this big store. "Okay, guys, I'll see you in a few minutes." Matt knew that Faith understood, so he winked and as only a fireman would, he jogged through the store, pushing the cart toward the door to the parking lot, but giving Karl a ride he wouldn't forget right away. Faith watched for a few minutes, a soft smile on her face, then turned the other way, intent on finding an empty bench in the concourse outside the store and across from the smaller store where the girls were.

Brandi loved the Christian store. They had lots of pictures and usually there was some music playing that she knew. She could sing along most of the time. In the back at one side, they had a small play area, because lots of children wanted to come here while their parents shopped in the mall. In fact, the store employed an extra person just to keep an eye on the play area. Brandi took her time moving through the store, showing Karin all her favorite pictures and the many knickknacks she loved. Most of the time Karin held Brandi's hand tightly.

Brandi showed Karin something and said, "Isn't this store neat, Karin?"

The little girl nodded and grinned up at Brandi. Her thumb never found her mouth all morning and even now was dry, as she looked around. The little girl trusted Brandi completely, just as any younger child would trust an older sibling. When the two reached the play area, Brandi grinned at the lady, but walked on by with Karin in tow. Soon, however, Karin found something she wanted to see and she let go of Brandi's hand. Brandi let her and went on to the kids books section. At nine, she was into books lots more than a five year old was, especially since the twins had never been to school. However, Karin found something that totally fascinated her. It moved and Karin stood and watched; her eyes as big as saucers.

Knowing that Karl would have some time to play, Faith didn't go in the little store, but sat on a bench outside the big store, but where she could see the little store to wait for Matt and Karl. She was sure they hurried. Very soon she looked down the long aisle to the mall entrance and saw the tall blond man with a tiny brown-haired boy holding tightly to his hand coming toward her. The minute she saw him that muscle in her chest did some strange gyrations.

Her treacherous heart was doing it again; it would absolutely not listen to her head, especially when Matt was around.

Matt was grinning at her and she stood up. She fell in beside them and walked with them into the little store. Matt had never been in a store like this, so he slowed and began to look at everything. As soon as they reached the back of the store, at the end of the first isle, Karl saw Brandi and Karin in the play area and quickly let go of Matt's hand. Matt, with Faith at his side, continued to look at everything in the store.

Finally, he said, "This is a neat place."

"For several of us it's our favorite. At Christmas they go all out. The front window is totally taken up with a large manger scene and the music is nothing but Christian Christmas music. It's a great oasis from all the stuff the other stores play."

"Oh, I can believe that!"

After they looked through the whole store and the children were still playing happily, Faith said only for Matt's ears, "I have something I want to tell you. Could we go back out to that bench and talk for a few minutes?"

"Sure! Lead the way."

They sat and immediately Matt's hand went across the top of the bench behind Faith's neck. She scooted over, but turned to look at him. She told him what Karl had told her about his home and Matt shook his head. "It's no wonder Karin doesn't talk! If they both witnessed his abuse of their mom and he abused Karin, I'm not surprised she sucks her thumb, too. He didn't say he knew his mom was dead, only that she didn't scream any more after he heard the shot?"

"Yes, that's right. Do you know their last name?"

"He mumbled when I asked him, but I think he might have said Kaufmann. It doesn't matter, they won't be returned to a home like that anyway."

Looking down at her hands clasped in her lap, she said, "Matt, my heart goes out to them. I hope I can make a good home for them."

He clamped his hand on her shoulder and pulled her back, snug against his side. Wishing he could kiss her, he did turn her head to look directly into her eyes and exclaimed, "Faith Lankaster! Don't you say such a thing like that again! For heaven's sake! In this time, it's not even been twenty-four hours they've lost most of their fear. You, and Brandi too, have done wonders for them!" He debated a second and added, "Pastor Jim gave you a great compliment on Thursday. He said you were meant to be a mother, that Brandi was a terrific child."

Her face turned red instantly at the compliment. She shook her head and said, "No, surely he didn't say that!"

"Oh, but he did. There was no interference on the phone line."

He looked at his watch, then up at her and grinned. When he grinned like that his blue eyes twinkled and Faith nearly lost it. "On Thursday when I told Brandi nine o'clock was early to come to Sunday school, she said all I had to do was go to bed earlier so I could get up in time to get here. If that's what I must do, I better get back to the train station and I know you'll need help unloading your car of all those clothes."

Faith laughed and the sound bathed Matt's heart. Along with her smiles, Matt knew he could get used to listening to Faith laugh. In his line of work, people didn't experience very many laughs. "That's so like her," she said. "I tell her all the time she needs to go to bed early for this or that. Usually, though, it's so I can slow her down from a constant run."

Having seen Matt's watch, she said, "If we go home now I can get supper on the table and you could eat with us before we take you back to the station."

Knowing there were four of them and only one of him, he scowled and looked at her, before he said, "That would be okay?"

"Of course, Matt," she whispered, through the cotton that had clogged her throat. "Surely you know I enjoy your company."

"Believe me; I enjoy yours, too, Faith."

She looked up at him, something he wouldn't identify shone at him, as she said, "I'm glad to know that." She cleared her throat and said, "We better round up the kids and be off."

They stood and went back into the Christian book store and found the kids still playing. However, when Karin saw Faith, a smile burst across her face and she ran to her and wrapped her little arms around her legs. Matt's throat went dry. Brandi looked up and knew it was time to leave, so she took Karl's hand and they both left together. As they made their way out of the store, Faith smiled and waved at her friend who was waiting on a customer right then.

As they walked together behind the children, across the mall into the department store, Matt whispered, "Is your friend the gossiping type?"

Faith giggled. "Well, she doesn't work in a store like that for nothing."

"Mmm, I wondered. She watched us all the way by."

"I'm not surprised."

It was about four o'clock when they arrived at Faith's house and Brandi said, "Mommy, can Matt open the sandbox so we can play before supper? It hasn't rained in days, you know."

"Maybe if you asked him he might."

Brandi leaned forward and tapped his arm that was lying across the back of the seat. "Mister Matt, could you open the sandbox for us, please?"

He looked over his shoulder and grinned at the little girl. "You show me where it is and what's to be done and I'll see if I'm up to it."

Brandi giggled. "It won't be hard for you, I know."

"Well, I'll never know until I see this box."

Faith parked beside the house, knowing they would go back to the train station after supper. The three children jumped out and grabbed Matt's hands, while Faith went to the trunk for the bags of things they had purchased. She took two bags in, but left the trunk lid up so that Matt could get the rest after he opened the sandbox in the backyard. Faith took the bags up to Karl's room, she knew just what she wanted to fix for supper and it wouldn't take long.

Matt felt extremely lonely going back to the city. He enjoyed every minute with Faith and the children. As he told Faith, he hadn't spent much money in over a month. He spent a good amount on the clothes for Karl, but it made him feel great doing it. He couldn't wait to see Karl in that suit they picked out together. That reminded him, he better dress so he looked nearly the same, but he hadn't worn a suit in a very long time and it was summer. He grinned; he didn't want a five year old boy to show him up! He chuckled. He had so much fun today. As he climbed the steps from the train station was the first he remembered his friend's invitation to go to Connecticut. It had never crossed his mind all day!

It was dark when he arrived at the old Victorian. The neighborhood was quiet, but quietness in New York City could be deceiving. Who knew what or who lurked behind the big house? The Victorian was nestled with several other older places that had been converted into rooming houses. Several times there were disturbances behind the houses. Inside the door were the mailboxes for the six renters and he used his key to open his.

Of course, there was the usual junk mail, which he stuffed under his arm, intent on throwing away as soon as he reached his wastebasket, but there was a letter from a law firm in Tucson, Arizona. He scowled at the letter; fifteen years ago was when he moved his Aunt Mable there. She was his mom's sister who never married instead became a career woman and had retired. How in the world could a law firm from Tucson get his address to write to him? He knew he moved here to New York City since he moved her.

He climbed the stairs and opened his door. As usual, the stale odor wafted out. Inside he flipped the switch for the overhead light. After locking the door, he lifted his arm over his wastebasket and let the junk mail fall into it. He walked over to his desk and slumped into the chair, then used his letter opener and pulled out the one sheet of paper from inside. Carefully, he smoothed out the paper with the impressive letterhead at the top. It was dated September eleven.

> "Dear Mr. Barns;
> It has come to my attention that you have not been informed of the death of Mable Germain. You were probably not aware that you are her major beneficiary.
> Please reply by return mail if you can come to our office to sign the forms needed to release to you what her will states is your inheritance. If you cannot come to our office, we will be happy to send the forms by overnight express for your signature.
> Thank you for your attention to this matter. We hope to hear from you in the near future.
> Yours truly, Arnold B. Cochran"

Matt leaned back in his chair, holding the letter up. He felt light-headed he hadn't seen his great-aunt Mable in fifteen years. The only significant thing he could remember doing for her was to drive her car, with a U-haul trailer on the back, from her home in Buffalo out to Tucson when she decided that the winters were just too much for her in Buffalo. He had emptied the U-haul into the apartment, returned the trailer and flew home. He pulled in a deep breath, he was her major beneficiary? What could she be leaving him? Surely not that furniture that was now fifteen years older!

He pulled a sheet of stationery in front of him and dashed off a reply:

"Dear Mr. Cochran,

Please send me the forms I need to sign. I work for FDNY and we have been exceedingly busy in recent days, as I'm sure you can understand. We also have no available substitutes so that I could take some time off.

I will be waiting for your reply.

Thank you, Matt Barns."

He would mail the letter on his way to the train station in the morning. He had no idea what the letter meant that he was her major beneficiary. She worked in the corporate world for as long as he could remember until her retirement sixteen years ago. He wasn't that close to her, and had no idea if she had investments or anything. Perhaps it was only the contents of the apartment he emptied the U-haul into. Whatever it was, he was not going to Tucson in the near future. The farthest he wanted to go away from this room was the house he spent some time in today in Thomaston. Since the man said they could over-night the things that he must sign, going there didn't seem to be necessary, either. He sealed his letter, put it where he'd remember to pick it up in the morning, then hit the shower and soon fell into bed.

He was up early, excited to return to Thomaston. He dressed in good clothes. He must leave Faith's house soon after their Sunday dinner to get back to change into his uniform and get to the fire station on time. Taking a change of clothes was foolish. There would be another Sunday when he was off all day and could spend it with them.

He chuckled as he walked out the door of the Victorian, the house was quiet, it was only seven o'clock, but his first stop was the diner for a quick breakfast and then on to board the train no later than seven forty-five. Yes, he went to bed early, just as Brandi said he should and now he was on the move early so he could go to Sunday school. Sunday school - he'd never been to Sunday school, it was not something his parents, or their parents, for that matter, felt was important in the life of a young boy who rode a bus for a long time to school. He had no idea what went on, especially for adults, but it gave him another chance to sit beside Faith and that made him very happy.

Obviously, there was one person from her church who saw them together, but this would be the first time most of her friends saw her with a man since her husband's death. She had been a widow for three years, for most people that was certainly long enough. Faith didn't seem to be still grieving. However, he knew a few people never let a widow forget about her loss. It was unfortunate, but he enjoyed her company too much to worry about that occasional bitter person who would talk.

The train came, he handed the conductor one of his passes just before he swung up onto the second step of the car. The man gave him a silent grin, which made him wonder, but he thought perhaps he had a silly grin on his face. So what! He was off to see the best lady in the world and the three children who lived with her. Life was good! In an hour, it would be better!

He saw her car in the closest space when the train pulled into the station. It was early; she had to get three children ready for church. He realized his athletic heart was betraying him again and beating double time in his chest as he caught a glimpse of her in the morning sun. Again today, he swung off the train onto the platform and took off at a jog toward the car. He would not waste one minute getting to her. He easily admitted, at least to himself, that he would gladly spend the rest of his days making this lady his better half and loving her, along with any children that would fill that house. Life had taken a very great turn on nine eleven.

Faith saw the man on the train steps and her heart took off, thumping madly. On Friday, his uniform fit him very well. Yesterday his casual clothes set off his muscled chest and arms, but today, in his dress clothes, he looked magnificent. She heard none of the commotion in the back seat the only thing that registered was the man coming toward her. He opened the passenger door and slid into the seat. Even running that distance he wasn't breathing heavily.

"Hi, everybody! How's the gang?" he asked.

"We're great, Matt!" Brandi exclaimed, immediately. "I guess you went to bed early so you could get up in time for Sunday school."

"Yup, I sure did, Brandi!"

He looked at the lady behind the wheel and she was looking back. She was taking in the whole man and could hardly look away. She swallowed before she could get the words out, "I'm great, too, Matt." She didn't add the words out loud, but she thought them, *now that you're here.*

"Great! I'm on top of the world!" and he meant it! Life since Friday had turned into the most fantastic time in his life.

His eyes caressed her. He knew he shouldn't let his eyes linger on any one part, but her pretty dress fit her perfectly, lovingly molding to her curves. Of course, it would be better when she stood up, but she was one pretty lady. Those legs he admired yesterday as she climbed the attic stairs peeked out from under the end of her dress as she moved them to drive the car. He had to lick his lips and clear his throat.

"You look sensational," he whispered, as he slid his hand across the top of the seat. He didn't miss the instant pink color that flooded her neck and cheeks. Not to dwell on that, he asked, "Was last night as good as the night before?"

The only reply she could think of and almost came off her tongue was, *No, my bed was lonely, I missed you.* She swallowed those words and said, "Yes, everybody slept through the night again. I managed to wake myself up, though. No eyes bored into my skull this morning." Her eyes twinkled as she looked up at him. "Did you get to bed early? I know Brandi told you that was how to get up early."

He chuckled. "Yeah." Not wanting her to see the hunger in his eyes, he turned his head and looked out the windshield. "Yeah, I went to that grand Victorian, got my mail, got rid of the junk, took a shower and hit the sack. I had to open the window a smidge, the room gets really stuffy sometimes."

A few minutes later, he looked in the back seat and said to the twins, "You two are lucky, your first time in Sunday school is when you're five years old. I had to wait all these years before I could go for the first time."

"Wow!" Brandi said. "That's a really long time!"

Faith chuckled, but didn't comment, but Matt laughed. "Thanks, Brandi, I needed that. Here I thought I was a young guy..."

"Well," she said, ever the diplomat, "you aren't really old, but your mommy should have taken you a long time ago. Sunday school is fun and you learn a lot about Jesus. Mommy says I can take Karin and Karl to their class and introduce them to their teacher."

"That's great, Brandi! I'm sure they'll have a good time."

"Yeah, I know they'll like it."

Only a few minutes later, Faith parked in the church parking lot with all the other cars that were arriving. Matt was out his door in an instant, even before Faith pulled the key from the ignition. Brandi, of course, was helping the twins with their seatbelts, but Matt opened Faith's door and reached in for her hand. As she took his hand was the first time she realized that her friends and acquaintances would see her with a man, a very handsome man, she quickly admitted as she looked up at him. His blue eyes seemed to caress her and his blond hair sparkled in the sunshine. She felt a bit dowdy, even in her Sunday dress.

As he helped her to her feet, he let his eyes skim over all of her. She had her hair tamed with some very pretty combs. Other days, she hadn't worn any makeup, but today she added a touch, making her even more lovely. Her dress was sleeveless, letting him see quite a bit of her flawless skin, the dress hugged her upper body to her waist, then flared a little over her hips and hung to within an inch or two of her knees, a demure, but lovely sundress. The strappy shoes she wore added some height, but the top of her head was still lower than his neck. He didn't comment, but he surely approved of what he saw.

Knowing that many of these people had never seen him before and therefore her with him, he asked, "Will you feel more comfortable if we just walk together? Will the kids be walking with us?"

When she was beside him, even before she answered, she slipped her hand behind his elbow. She looked up and said, "Let 'em all look! They all may as well know we're together. They can eat their hearts out while I walk with this handsome man." Watching Brandi herd the twins away from the car and towards the education building, Faith nodded toward where they had gone and said, "Oh, by the way, I don't think we'll be walking with the kids."

He chuckled; looking where she was, then back at her. "No, I'll agree on that. Looks like Brandi has them well in hand."

By now, Brandi was nearly to the doors leading into the education wing. With his free hand he touched his shirt pocket and said, "I should stop in the men's room and put on my tie."

She looked from his lips to his shirt that was opened one button. "Not for me you don't. The way you look right now is just fine!"

The look in her eyes made time stand still. He cleared his throat. "Thanks, Faith."

"Oh, no thanks needed."

By now, Brandi and the twins were long gone. Instead of going in the front door of the church, Brandi took them across the parking lot to the door to the educational wing. That door was closing as Faith put her arm around his. They disappeared even before Matt and Faith moved away from the car, of course, that wasn't surprising, knowing what gear Brandi moved in. Whether she meant to or not, what happened to Karl and Karin couldn't have bothered Faith one whit at that moment.

Matt wondered how she would introduce him, but he didn't have long to wait, a white haired lady came and as she looked Matt up and down, she said, "Faith, who have we here?"

Faith never took her hand from around his arm, when she said, "Hi, Mom, I'd like you to meet Matt Barns. He's the fireman whom Brandi introduced to Jesus down at Ground Zero on Tuesday. Matt, my mom, Laurel Mills."

Knowing he needed to start off on the right foot with this lady, he turned on what charm he had and smiled. Holding out his hand, he said, "I'm pleased to meet you Mrs. Mills. You have a charming daughter and grand-daughter."

"Yes," she said, taking his hand and shaking it once, "I think they're very special. I'm very glad you came today and I hope you enjoy your time in our church. From what I've heard, we have a great singles group that I'm sure you'll enjoy."

"I'm sure I will." He felt the pressure on his arm, so he turned with Faith and went with her toward the classroom inside the front door.

The older lady turned toward the educational wing, so when Matt and Faith were out of earshot of the lady, Faith whispered, "I didn't dare tell her when she called the other day that Brandi met you so far beyond the yellow tape. She wouldn't have been content to tongue-lash me over the phone, she'd have been at my house within twenty minutes, so I told her Brandi gave you a tract and told you about Jesus and how to go to heaven."

Matt chuckled. "Fearless Faith, now the truth comes out. At your age lying to your mother. Tisk, tisk."

She grinned, as they sat in seats in the next to the back row in the class. "It wasn't *quite* a lie; I just didn't tell her *exactly* the way it happened."

He grinned at her. "Never fear, your secret's safe with me."

They were barely comfortable when the teacher left the small podium at the front and came to them. He held out his hand and said, "Welcome to the singles class. I'm Ron Walsh, I'm always glad for new blood coming into the class." He gave the young man a sheepish grin. "Especially men, they're a rare breed around here."

Matt stood and shook the man's hand warmly. "I'm Matt Barns. It's good to be here this morning." His eyes twinkling, Matt added, "I'm glad to oblige on the men's part. You know, a little person told me a secret about that, if you go to bed early, you can get up early for Sunday school. You know, it works!"

The teacher chuckled. "Yes, my wife's always telling my kids that's the way to do it; but as they get older it doesn't always work."

It was obvious to both Matt and Faith that the man was dying to learn how he came to be in the church and even more so, how he happened to be with Faith. However, he didn't ask, so neither Matt nor Faith volunteered that information. Matt sat down and his arm slid across Faith's chair even before the teacher moved back to the front.

Faith was sure that word would be out soon. Brandi had no inhibitions, she loved people and she would tell her class all the events that happened in hers and her mommy's life since September eleventh. Her only hope was she wouldn't say her line about Jesus telling her that Matt would be her new daddy. Somehow, words like those spread like wildfire. This church was made up of nice people, but some of them didn't always show it….well, not all the time.

Matt was impressed with the Sunday school teacher. The lesson was good and class participation was lively and the hour sped by very quickly. He felt like it was time he spent well. Not only that, he sat beside Faith. He also enjoyed the church service and Pastor Jim's sermon. It was a big church, Matt discovered, but he was made to feel as if he came home. People came up to him and spoke to him, even though Faith was never far from his side. However, the thing he liked the best, the two of them sat together, without any children for the full two hours. Not only were the children in Sunday school, they also went to junior church, a concept that was brand new to Matt.

Brandi took the twins to the class for five year olds. Karl waded right in, because he saw a fire truck standing in the corner with some other toys, but Karin looked around and quickly back to Brandi with fear in her eyes and immediately stuck her thumb in her mouth. Brandi still stood beside her and decided to stay for a few minutes. It was more important that Karin be happy than that she have perfect attendance in her class. Besides, she could tell her teacher she was there in the building, she knew that would count.

As soon as Brandi saw Karin's thumb go in her mouth, she took her hand

and said, "Look, Karin, I see some dollies that need their clothes put back on. Want to help me?" Karin turned happily with her and picked up a naked doll. As soon as she saw the clothes she wanted to dress the doll, her thumb came out of her mouth and her hand reached for the clothes nearby.

A few minutes later, the teacher came bustling in the room and stopped short as she saw the three children. "Hi! Who have we here?"

Brandi turned around and said, "Hi, Mrs. Milan. Mommy and me got twins at our house. This is Karin and that's Karl. A friend of mine and Mommy's found them in an old warehouse, so they came to live with us." Brandi grinned at her friend. "You know, we love them to pieces, but it's their first time in Sunday school."

The lady looked at the children as she put her things down on the short table and said, "Hi, Karl and Karin, I'm glad you came."

Karin hid behind Brandi, sucking on her thumb and Karl looked at the woman, then turned back to play with the truck, without saying a word. The lady turned to Karin and asked, "What do you like to do best, Karin?"

Karin took her thumb from her mouth when she picked up the doll, but she dropped it and stuck her thumb back in her mouth when the lady spoke to her. Brandi put the doll back that she was dressing and smiling, she said, "Mrs. Milan, Karin hasn't said anything since she came to us, but I kinda know what she wants. I'll stay with her until she's not scared any more. Okay?"

Mrs. Milan sat down in one of the low chairs and said, "I see. I guess that's okay, but what we do here in class is much too young for you, Brandi."

Picking up the doll again, she grinned at the lady and said, "I know, but Karin and Karl have never been to Sunday school ever in their whole lives before, it's kinda new and Karin gets afraid easily. It's okay; I won't mind staying with her." She grinned at the lady. "Besides, I remember being in your class, I like your teaching."

Wow! How to win friends and influence people! The lady thought. "Okay, Brandi, I'll be happy for you to stick around then."

"Great!"

Before the class started, ten more children came in the room. Another little girl came over to play with the dolls. She was quite a talker and soon, she and Karin were playing very well together. As soon as Brandi noticed, she left the two of them alone and backed off. Finally, Karin acted like she didn't need Brandi beside her, so the nine year old slipped quietly from the room and headed for her own class room. Mrs. Milan was impressed.

After Sunday school, Brandi came and took Karl and Karin with her to junior church. This was also a new experience for the twins, but Brandi stayed in the same room with them this time. It would be next school year when Brandi graduated from this room to the next for junior church. They learned a new song, but Brandi noticed that neither Karl nor Karin sang or even opened their mouths. However, by the time they sang the song through three times, Karin was smiling and nodding her head in time to the rhythm.

Karin's little friend from Sunday school sat beside her in junior church and the little girl's eyes sparkled, it was obvious she was having fun. The teacher told a great story, one that caught everyone's attention, even Brandi's. Both Karl and Karin were spellbound and hardly moved. Brandi was glad this was the teacher this week, she was the best. This teacher made the story just as interesting as anything could be. By the end of the church time both of the twins were smiling and their eyes were dancing.

It was the custom that parents came to the room where the junior church was held when the service ended in the auditorium. It was the best way not to have children lost while trying to find their parents. Faith and Matt walked down the hallway and Faith looked through the glass in the door to see the children singing a last song.

She looked up at Matt, her eyes sparkling, as she said, "What do you think, are they having fun?"

Karl wasn't moving his hands, he just stood next to Brandi his hands in his pockets, but Karin was watching her little friend and copied every movement that she did. Of course, Brandi was singing loudly and doing all the motions, she knew the song well. Matt watched and a smile twinkled in his eyes as well as covered his lips.

Softly, in her ear, he said, "You can't imagine how glad I am that there wasn't any room for them in the foster care system in NYC."

"Yes, so am I." However, Faith had a double meaning for her statement. If these children hadn't come to her, probably Matt wouldn't have either. Yes, they had a stellar moment at Ground Zero, but that would have been that if he hadn't brought the twins. She had never doubted God's hand in her life, but He worked some impossible happenings since September eleven to bring her and Matt together. She would absolutely not complain!

Not long after dinner was finished, Matt reluctantly let Faith bundle the kids in her car and drive him back to the train station. He absolutely hated leaving what he considered his little family. Karin had tears in her eyes and Karl had a very long face as they watched the train come in and then Matt swing up onto the second step. Of course, his last look was to the lovely lady. From that distance he couldn't be sure, but he thought perhaps her eyes were sparkling with unshed tears. There definitely was no huge smile on her face as she waved to him. As he sat down on the bench seat and looked out the window, he could swear he left his heart.

That evening, at church, the twins sat with Faith and Brandi. Karl took up the seat on one side of Faith, while Karin sat between Faith and Brandi. Of course, Brandi knew not to make noise in church, and Faith had no worry that Karin would, but Karl didn't know how to act in a church service. She needn't have worried; Karl was a quiet child and looked around the huge room in awe as it filled up for the service. No sound came from his mouth and his little bottom stayed right beside Faith.

The evening service wasn't geared for children, but there was lots of singing and they had to stand several times. Finally, during the sermon, Karin fell asleep with her head on Faith's lap. Karl also leaned heavily against Faith, but didn't fall into her lap. Brandi smiled at her mommy; she had a really neat day being big sister to the twins.

After the service, Faith waited until most of the people were in the aisles before she moved. She didn't know if she should carry Karin, but Brandi took care of that, she gently shook her and soon had a twin on either side, leading out through the doors to the parking lot.

Faith was collecting her Bible and purse when a woman not much older than she came between the seats and stopped in front of her. Faith braced herself, she knew she needed to guard her tongue and say as little as possible, this woman talked, her phone was almost always busy, to church women and non-church alike. To say that the woman was the church's self-proclaimed gossip was to put it mildly. Faith swallowed a sigh she wished she could have hurried out when Brandi left with the twins.

"Who were those children with you tonight, Faith?" she asked, watching

Brandi take the twins out. The words were said very sweetly, but the look in the woman's eyes was anything but sweet, as sharp as a hungry hawk's. Probably by morning her tongue would be just as sharp.

Fondly, Faith's eyes followed the trio. In less than forty-eight hours she couldn't imagine not having the twins in her home. "They're children in our foundling ministry, Maryann." *Not that I'd tell you, but I'd like to make them my own,* she knew in her heart. It was better to tell her they were with her because of the church, rather than say there was no room in the city's foster care system. She knew that for a fact.

The woman scowled, she never heard of such a thing. Had Pastor Jim pulled something over on her? "And what is that?"

Intending to say exactly what she meant, but not too much, Faith said, "That ministry was set up several years ago, Maryann. It's for children who have no home. As I remember, when it was discussed in one of the church business meetings, I believe some missionaries were captured overseas, in some hostile country, but their children came home and until some family members could take them, our foundling ministry took care of them. It's been a while, but I remember when we voted on it. The vote was unanimous, if I recall. Anyway, that's how come I have them, Pastor Jim recommended me."

Not too kindly, the woman asked, "And *you* have them? Those kids aren't missionaries kids, are they?"

Faith scowled, not really sure why the emphasis. "Ye-es, Pastor Jim asked me if I would take them. No, they aren't missionaries kids, but just as needy."

"For goodness sake!" the woman huffed loudly. "Why did he ask a single mother? Surely there are couples who could do the job. I mean, after all…." Not that she would take them; she was too busy for childcare.

Faith shrugged. "Perhaps he felt we had the room." Since she had her purse and Bible, Faith turned to head out of her row.

Not about to end the conversation, of course, she hadn't gotten all the scoop, Maryann said, "Yeah, I guess that could be a reason. After all, Max left you that big house. You and Brandi must rattle around in it."

Knowing that the woman had never been to her place and it couldn't be seen from the road, Faith wondered how she knew what size her house really was. Faith also knew that Maryann loved to spread tales; she was not one of Faith's close friends for that reason. That was also exactly why Faith only answered in short sentences. Faith smiled and turned, making sure she had her things then flung her purse strap up on her shoulder, ready to leave her pew, because Brandi had been gone for several minutes. However, the woman didn't seem ready to leave her alone. Even so, Faith started to move toward the end of the row. Like a magnet, Maryann paced her in the next pew. Faith swallowed a sigh, nothing like showing the woman how exasperated she was and how much she didn't like gossip.

Finally, Faith looked toward the door where Brandi had gone several minutes before and said, "Was there something else, Maryann? I have to get going, there's school tomorrow, of course, you know and Brandi's already outside."

"Yeah, didn't I see you with a man this morning?" She looked around as if to see where the man might be hiding this evening.

Again, intending to only say the absolute minimum, Faith said, "Yes, Matt's a fireman and had to go on duty this evening. Maryann, I really must go, Brandi took the twins and they're probably out on the parking lot by now."

"Yes, yes, of course! You have a good week, Faith," she said, airily and waved, as Faith hurried away from her.

However, Faith didn't make it directly to the parking lot. Pastor Jim and Marcia stood at the door to greet people and Marcia stopped her. "Faith, Jim told me all about those twins when he came home on Friday. You've done wonders with them! Jim said they looked so forlorn and lost - why I just saw them with Brandi, they look so happy and all.... Even Jim commented on how happy they look." Marcia pulled Faith into her arms and whispered, "Faith, you are one phenomenal woman! Just terrific!"

Faith looked out the door to the parking lot, but couldn't see the trio. "Yes, they seem to be adjusting really well at home." She smiled. "They are really such loveable kids, they gobble up every bit of attention Brandi and I give them."

The other lady kept her arms around Faith and hugged her. "You're great, Faith! Maybe Brandi is great, but you are the best of the best." She turned her head and whispered into her ear, "I also saw that handsome man who couldn't take his eyes off you this morning in church. I think that's great, too, girl!"

Faith blushed and licked her lips. "Thanks," she whispered back. "He's the one who found the twins, but he's much more than that now."

Marcia winked. "I had that figured out already."

Wanting to change the subject a bit, Faith pushed her purse strap up on her shoulder and said, "Actually, Brandi found Fireman Matt at Ground Zero on nine eleven and gave him one of our tracts. She actually led him to the Lord!"

"Ah, but he has eyes only for you now, dear friend." Again she winked at Faith. "It is quite obvious, believe me."

"Maybe so," Faith conceded.

On the parking lot, Brandi stood with the twins beside the car. "Mommy, hurry, it's hot here and we're hungry for our snack."

"Okay, kids, it's home for a snack. Hmm, I think I've got…"

"Mommy!" Brandi scolded. "You do that all the time! What is it?"

"Well, if I told you…"

Brandi let out a long sigh. "I know, it wouldn't be a surprise."

Faith chuckled. "Yup, you got that right!"

EIGHT

As Faith put the children to bed, after their snack, she wondered what would be the outcome of today. Maryann wasn't subtle at all and she had a tongue that wagged a lot. She knew Marcia, as the pastor's wife, wouldn't say or do anything that shouldn't be done, but Maryann could be a trouble-maker if she chose and very often she chose to cause trouble out of spite, it seemed. She had several women who listened to everything she said, if she shaded things just a little, well, those women took it as gospel. Faith let out a sigh, those were women from church, she had no idea who Maryann knew outside of church, but she was sure her tongue wagged there just as much as with church friends. Faith shook her head. She never learned to gossip and she was never impressed with women who did. As far as Faith was concerned, Maryann sported a red beacon on her head.

She turned off the lights in the children's rooms, then went to her own bed and pulled back the light covers. It had been a warm day and even now, the breeze coming in the windows was warm. After curling up against the pillows stacked at the headboard, she picked up her Bible and daily devotional and started reading. She knew she did her best today, with Matt's help they spent an exceptionally good day. She couldn't help but feel good about it.

It was after nine and she had put her Bible down when the phone beside her bed rang. She let it ring again, but didn't let the answering machine downstairs pick up. "Hello?" she asked. "This is Faith Lankaster."

"Hi, Faith. Had a minute and decided to call. We had a run earlier, but we're free right now. How did church tonight go?"

That familiar flutter started in her heart the moment Matt spoke, so Faith swallowed and said, "Just fine, Matt. Karin especially, loves the music.

She watches Brandi's book and her eyes sparkle. Karl stands there like he'll do this if it kills him."

He chuckled. "I can see him. Like this morning with his hands in his pockets. Your friend from the store didn't find you?"

Still remembering the disturbing scene, Faith said, "No, but another of her sort did. I didn't let her talk long Brandi was on the parking lot by the time she closed in on me. Pastor's wife was encouraging, though. She made me feel really good." Faith chuckled. "She even saw the handsome man with me this morning."

Matt chuckled. "Did you tell her he skipped town?"

"Nope. I told her no such thing! So you're not busy right now?" She couldn't hear any sound in the back ground.

Matt looked around the lounge at the guys, as he said, "Not right now. They're playing cards, but I decided I'd sit out so I could hear your voice. Mind if I come out on Tuesday?"

With those words her heart went into overdrive. "Matt, that'd be great! Sure! Let's see," she chuckled, "I'll make a list...."

"You do that, sweet lady. I haven't been behind a mower in years."

They talked for a few more minutes, then the unmistakable horn started blaring and Matt said, "Oops! Gotta go!"

"Be safe!" she said immediately.

The line went dead and Faith replaced the receiver more slowly on her night stand. She smiled, as she reached for the light switch. It wouldn't be quite so hard to sleep tonight since she talked to him. She wondered if he missed her as much as she missed him since she waved to him on the train this afternoon. Of course, now his mind had to be totally on the fire run, but she'd go to sleep thinking about him and about all the things they did since he brought the twins out on Friday. Things she hadn't done or even thought of doing in... at least three years.

She laid her head on the pillow and sighed. Her bed was still only half full, the pillow on the other half was cold and empty, but Faith's heart was still pattering fast. Matt had called her! He wanted to talk to her, even when he was on duty! She sighed and snuggled down under her light blanket. Maybe one day in the not-too-distant future, she'd have a bed-mate! Was that too much to ask the Lord for? She hoped not.

As she closed her eyes, she murmured, "God in heaven, keep Matt safe."

The morning paper was delivered to the station early and Matt usually was the first to pick it up and take it to their multi-purpose room on second floor. He usually read most of the paper, just to keep abreast of what went on in the big city. He read the major article on the front page then turned to the back page of the first section to finish it. After the few lines of the article, his eyes glanced down at a much smaller article that started there on the back page. Curiosity made him read it.

> Police were called last night to the third floor apartment in the seven hundred block of Forty-fifth Street. Neighbors had noticed an odor coming from the apparently abandoned apartment and called the landlord. He called police, then met them and unlocked the door for them.
>
> When the police entered the apartment, they found two dead, a woman, about twenty-four, had been shot and a man, about twenty-seven. The male body is still undergoing tests to determine the cause of death, but drugs have not been ruled out. There were also numerous beer cans and bottles strewn around the apartment. The coroner has not ruled out a deadly mix of alcohol and drugs as the cause of death.
>
> Evidence in the apartment lead police to assume that there were small children, possibly a boy and a girl, but they were not found. When asked, neighbors said the people had moved in only recently and kept mostly to themselves. They couldn't verify if there were children or not.
>
> After checking the four room apartment, police determined the odor was the decomposing bodies, which had been in the closed apartment for over a week.

Matt's stomach knotted up. "That's Karl and Karin's parents, I'll lay odds to it," he muttered, as he laid the paper aside.

Matt wondered if he should say anything to anyone about what he knew. He and Mario were the ones who found the children, but he was the only one to interact with them. The children were being very well cared for, in a safe place and goodness knew they didn't need to be moved any time soon. Besides, there was no room in the city's foster care system. This couple was dead. After listening to what Faith told him Karl told her, the time frame fit perfectly. Being so young, probably the children would never be able to tell how long it had been or where they had lived.

He realized as he found a pair of scissors, that there were no names given in the article, probably identification would have to be made of the man and woman. If they looked through the apartment enough to find out there was evidence of children, why hadn't they found any identification? That was puzzling. Surely, the man, at least would have his ID with him.

He shrugged; this could fester all day. If nothing came of it he would call Pastor Jim and talk to him when he got off duty this afternoon. Tomorrow, when he went to Faith's would be soon enough to tell her. He decided not to cut out the article until just before he went off duty this afternoon. He'd see if anyone said anything about the article or made a connection. He really doubted anyone would. His shift mates saw the children, but no one heard their names. No one was around when Karl told him their last name. As he recalled, not even Mario was there. It was well after his shift ended that he called the welfare and foster care agencies.

One thing was for sure, the warehouse where they found Karl and Karin wasn't anywhere close to Forty-fifth Street. Karl really took them far from where they lived! Except that Karl told Faith about his dad shooting his mom, no one at the fire station would put two and two together about the children he found last Friday. He knew he wouldn't have, except that Faith had told him. Matt wondered if Karl had some idea that his dad was into drugs and that was why he only mumbled his last name.

He shook his head; if things could stay as they were those children had every chance in the world to turn out great. They would not become a statistic for New York City. If there was not money in the church budget for them, he'd gladly pitch in whatever it took. Again he thanked the good Lord that there was no room for them in the city's foster care system and that Faith had gotten them.

He smelled fresh coffee and knew that the cooks were feverishly working to get breakfast on the table. They knew that when men are hungry, nothing else matters. Soon, other smells; bacon, sausage, pancakes, eggs, all worked on the senses and soon Matt's stomach growled appreciatively. Mario was one of the cooks this morning he always did a fine job. He folded up the paper and left it on the table, then picked up his mug that still had half a cup of stale coffee in it and made his way to the kitchen to pick up a plate and help himself.

Others followed the same appetizing smells; he wasn't the only one in the kitchen. He was right, there was a huge bowl of scrambled eggs, a plate piled high with bacon and sausage and another full of toast. Of course the coffee maker was full. He dumped out what was in his cup and got a fresh cup. He could always use a good cup of coffee.

Soon, several men sat with Matt at the long table in the multi-purpose room. Breakfast was always good, most men didn't botch up breakfast food and usually, there was lots of it. Matt thought about the article he read and what to do about it, so the conversation went on around him. He was glad to block out the conversation in fact, his thoughts went directly to Faith.

He laid down his fork and leaned back to drain his mug when another man down the table said, "Hey, Barns, Justin told me you didn't go with him to his fishin' cabin. Where'd you go?"

"I had those twins, remember?"

"Yeah, didn't you get them in with Children's Agency?"

Matt shook his head and said, "No, Man, believe me, I tried, but they didn't have any room, even in all the boroughs. Nine eleven, you know."

"They ain't at your place!" he said, aghast.

"No, they're in a home in Thomaston."

Justin scowled and asked, "How'd you get 'em there? Thomaston, that's on the Island, isn't it? They got room in their foster care there?"

Matt reached for the tract in his pocket. Holding it up so the men could see the back of it, he said, "I called the pastor of this church and he found a place for them."

Scowling, because he was confused, the man said, "So you took 'em there Friday night? You had Saturday off, how come you didn't come up?"

Matt shrugged, as if it was the thing to do and said, "I went back to help put clothes on their backs and stayed the day."

"You know where they are? When the Children's Agency gets 'em, they disappear, don't they? At least that's what I hear."

"No, these kids didn't disappear. They didn't go into foster care. Like I said, this big church took them as their responsibility. They're in a good home, but it's not over loaded with money, so I went to help out."

"Yeah, you got a soft spot for kids, I remember. At a fire you always ask about any kids." Justin scowled. "But you came in here like a house-a-fire yesterday barely in time for shift. Busy all weekend?"

"Yeah, I was."

The man looked at him closely. "Was it a woman?"

Matt couldn't hide the smirk. "You could say that."

"Ah, so out with it, man!" Justin exclaimed. "If it's a woman, that's something brand new for a jock like you!"

Matt shrugged. "A single lady goes to that church, she's pretty and I like her."

"At a church? How'd you meet her?"

"Simple, I went to church at her church. With the twins there, why not?"

Justin looked closely at Matt and said, "So, do I get this straight?" He held up his hand and clicked off one finger, as he said, "You took the twins to this church in Thomaston on Friday." With his second finger, he said, "You spent the day there on Saturday puttin' clothes on their backs." Holding up a third finger, he finished, "you went to church on Sunday, gettin' back just in time to come to work. You had a place to stay?"

"Yep, it's up the street about three blocks."

"Excuse me?"

Matt shrugged again. "It's quiet in here, I think you heard me."

Justin leaned his chair back on its back legs, eyed his fellow firefighter and frowned. "You didn't bed her?"

Matt scooted his chair back, intending to get up soon. "Nope. Wouldn't think of it. Not only does she now have three kids in the house with her, but she's a fine Christian lady. It's not something I'd even mention to her."

Justin shook his head and looked at his friend incredulously. "You got a chance to bed a woman and you didn't?"

Matt scooped up his plate and empty mug. As he stood up, he said, "Yup, that's the size of it." Not that he ever did! He had never bedded a woman! He wouldn't be anyone's one night stand! His wasn't a Christian home, but his parents raised him to hold a woman in high respect. He always had, he always would.

The horn started blaring; Matt set his things back on the table, as chairs scraped back. Men were on the move, there was another run. It was ten o'clock; would this be another long haul? The men never liked runs at ten o'clock. Many times they didn't get back to the station in time to get off at three o'clock. Soon, the men were suited and on the trucks. The garage doors went up and two engines roared from the station with their sirens blaring. Matt was glad, he didn't have to tell Justin all that much about Faith. He was proud of her, in fact, his feelings said she was more than a friend, but he didn't want to drag her through the mud as men in general and firemen more specifically, could do. After a fire run no one would think to bring up the subject. That was one thing about being a fireman; you had to have your head all in the game to survive.

After everyone was gathered at the breakfast table on Monday, Faith said to Karl, "Have you been going to school, Karl?"

Shaking his head, the little boy said, "No. The old man moved us a lot. He said we was smart and didn't need to go to school this year."

"Oh!" Brandi said, nearly jumping out of her seat. "At my school we got the best kindergarten teacher! You know that room where you went to Sunday school yesterday? That's her class room. You'd have lots of fun with her."

Karl's face lit up. "Yeah?" He turned his brown eyes to Faith and asked, "Can we go? I really liked that fire truck in that room!"

Always mindful that Karin wasn't participating verbally, she looked at the little girl. No one ever had to question if Karin knew what was being said, but they had to know how to read her body language. Faith didn't have to wonder what she thought on the subject of kindergarten, Karin was not smiling and her thumb was securely in her mouth. She would not look at Faith.

Faith decided on another strategy. Smiling, she looked first at Karin, then Karl and said, "How about this idea? I haven't got a full day planned for today; I'll take you to school. Brandi can go to her class and I'll enroll you guys in kindergarten and then go with you to class. I'll stick around until you're all settled in and then we'll see what happens. Think that'll work?"

Karl nodded, enthusiastically. "Yeah, that's cool! I liked that fire truck they had there in that room. Would I get to play with it?"

Faith didn't want to discourage the little boy, but she knew they did many things besides play with toys. "Maybe some of the time, Karl, but remember, there're lots of other things to do in kindergarten. The teacher reads stories and you learn to count. Sometimes she helps you learn about letters, too. Then you could learn to spell your own names. There are all kinds of things and the teacher is really a nice lady," Faith said, enthusiastically.

"Oh, it's super, guys!" Brandi exclaimed.

"Oh, okay, cool!"

Faith turned to Karin and said, "Karin, how about it? Will it be okay if I come to the room and stay with you?"

The little girl still kept her head down and sucked on her thumb as if it was the world's sweetest candy, but after a few more sucks, she looked at Faith and saw that she was still looking at her, so she moved her head up and down a miniscule amount. If Faith hadn't been looking right at her, she would probably have missed it. Karin was not very enthusiastic about going to school she was quite clear on that subject.

However, with Karin's nod, Faith stood up immediately, gathered up the breakfast dishes and took them to the sink. Glancing quickly at the way the children were dressed, she was glad they could wear what they had on for school. "Okay, guys, it's on the move! Brandi, go to the road, it's almost time for your bus to come, so you'll need to wave her on. When she's gone, come back and help me with lunches. After I get everybody settled, I'll have to go see if I can find some book bags and lunch boxes for Karl and Karin. I hope they aren't all sold out."

As Brandi pulled on her jacket, she came along side of her mommy and as they walked toward the front door, she said, "Mommy, I have the one from last year in my closet, Karin could use it, it's still good, you know. There was a boy in my class last year who didn't come back this year. I heard Pastor Harding say when school started that he left his book bag and he didn't know where to find him. He said he thinks they moved away."

Faith nodded and opened the door for her. Giving her shoulders a quick squeeze, Faith said, "Thanks for letting me know about that, I'll ask Pastor when we go this morning, Brandi. You know you're being a big help, thank you." Brandi grinned at the praise.

After Brandi was out the door and skipping down the drive, Faith hurried up to her room, straight to her closet. She didn't know exactly where the book bag was, but if it was possible to be found, she was the woman to find it! This bag also had an insulated section for a small lunch, ideal for Karin. Faith knew the bag was still in fine shape, but Brandi's best friend got a new one this year and convinced Brandi she needed one just like it. She sighed; she didn't realize peer pressure started in third grade. Then again, peer pressure probably started when two people were together – just think of Adam and Eve.

She almost gave up, since she knew she still had lunches to make for the twins, when her toe connected with a strap and when she pulled her foot back, the strap looked like what she remembered the old book bag looked like, so she reached down to the floor and pulled until the missing bag came out from under a pile of school papers and dirty clothes. Faith sighed; it was time for Brandi to clean out her closet. Faith sighed and headed for the door; perhaps there should be some pressure - peer or not - mother to child.

Only a few minutes later, Faith herded the children out the door and into the car. The drive to the church wasn't far, Brandi wouldn't be late and the twins wouldn't miss much of what happened in the kindergarten class. Surely even getting enrolled wouldn't take too long.

Just before Brandi took off for her class, Faith said, "Brandi, I'll be back this afternoon, since I'm not sure how this'll go this morning, so you don't need to ride the bus today, but it'll probably work out for you three to ride tomorrow."

"Okay, Mommy! I'll see you guys later!" She waved and skipped across the parking lot toward the educational wing of the complex.

"Yeah!" Karl said. Of course Karin didn't speak, but she still sat in the back seat, hadn't unbuckled her seatbelt and her thumb was securely in her mouth. It took Faith a bit of persuading to move Karin from the car. Faith smiled to herself – maybe Karin didn't talk, but she was her own little person and anyone getting to know her found that out quickly.

Karl was becoming a little independent, so he walked into the office with Faith, but didn't hold her hand. However, Karin was holding Faith's hand in a death grip, with her thumb firmly implanted in her mouth. Faith wondered if this would work, Karin was obviously not excited about being away from her, not only that, she didn't speak and she wondered if Angela Teagarden could handle that.

Marian Fisher looked up from her computer when Faith walked in. "Hi, who's this?"

"Hi, Marian, we have two potential kindergarteners, Karl and Karin." Matt had told Faith what Karl had mumbled was his last name, but Karl hadn't told her, so she didn't tell Marian. She wondered if she should put the last name on the form.

Marian grinned at Faith. "That's great, Faith!"

Marian saw the children yesterday, so she pulled out some forms and handed them to her, then came around to the twins as Faith began filling out the papers. She squatted down and looked at the children. Only Karl glanced at her. "Hi, guys, so you're coming here to school?"

"Yeah," Karl said, "Brandi told me I'm gonna be in the same room as that big fire truck I played with yesterday."

Marian smiled at the little boy. "Ahh! I bet I know which room you're talking about! You like fire engines?"

"Yeah, we rode in a huge, big one with Matt the other day! It was cool! It had the hugest window ever and all them firemans climbed on. When we went down the road real fast cars went everwhere!"

"In a big fire truck?"

As if the child hadn't been scared speechless, he said, enthusiastically, "Yeah! But we didn't get to hear no siren, 'cause we rode in it after the fire was out. I sat next to the driver, but her sat on Matt's knee." Karl conveniently forgot that he was really scared too when he added, "Her was scared and hid her face."

Marian shook her head. "I could do without the siren! It's so loud you can hear it for a long ways down the blocks."

Karl shrugged. "Well, yeah." Enthusiastically, Karl added, "Me and Sis, we rode with fireman Matt to where they keep them fire trucks!"

Marian looked at Karin, who had scooted as far back into the seat as possible and had her thumb firmly in place. "How about you, did you get to ride the fire truck?"

The child ducked her head, but she nodded, her chin hitting her chest. Marian patted the little girl's leg. As she stood up, she put her index finger into her cheek, acting like she was thinking. After a few seconds, she said, "I bet I know what'd work here. I have some suckers one would fit just right in that mouth of yours."

She came back and handed one to Karl, but squatted in front of Karin again. Holding it in front of the child, she said, "Want to tear off the paper? I think you'll like strawberry."

Karin raised her eyes to see the sucker. As she saw the size, her eyes turned to saucers. Keeping her thumb in her mouth, she reached for the sucker then pulled her thumb from her mouth. Marian didn't say anything, just watched as Karin pulled at the paper wrapped around the sucker. The paper vanished and the sucker was in her mouth. The thumb, of course, didn't go back in the mouth, but it was free, real close and stood at attention just in case it was needed, the other hand held the sucker.

The pastor heard Faith speak to Marian, so he came from his office, but stood and waited until Faith was finished with the forms. He came over and took them from her and asked, "Did you find out what the children's last name was?"

Shaking her head, Faith looked at Karl, perhaps hoping he would tell them, but said to the pastor, "Karl never did tell me."

Jim looked down at the forms Faith handed him and saw what Faith had written, then looked up at Karl. "Can you remember your last name, Karl?"

Just as it had with Matt, his chin hit his chest; he looked at his shoes and mumbled around the sucker, "Kaufmann." Only Faith who was sitting beside him could hear by straining. Obviously, it wasn't something he wanted people to know.

"I didn't hear what you said, Karl. Was it Kaufmann?" The little boy still looked at his shoes, but he nodded. That was the name Faith put on the forms, so he didn't add or change anything she listed.

Pastor Jim looked at Faith and asked, "Should I call Angela to come meet you here? You could explain about things without all the other ears."

"That might be a good idea. I planned to go to the classroom and stay a while, but that will probably work really well."

Jim nodded. "I'll call her." He went to the intercom that sat on Marian's desk and pressed the kindergarten room number. "Miss Teagarden, will you come to the office for a few minutes, please?"

Not too much was said while the adults and children waited for the teacher to come. When the pretty young woman came in the door, with a ponytail a little lopsided and hands that she obviously wiped quickly, she looked at both children and smiled. "You mean I get to have these perfectly charming children in my class?"

Boldly, Karl slid off the seat, went up to the lady and said, "Yeah, my new mommy said I'm to go to kindergarten today!"

"Is that so? What's your name?"

The little boy's chest expanded. "I'm Karl. That's my sister, Karin, but she don't talk."

"I see."

Marian Fisher looked at Faith, then down at Karl and said, "How would it be if I took Karl down to the classroom? Would you come with me, Karl?"

Anxious to get where the big fire truck was, Karl said, "Yeah, okay." He looked up at the lady and also at the teacher and asked, "Can I play with the fire truck now?"

Before Angela could answer, Marian said, "I don't know what's going on in the class. Maybe there's something just as interesting going on, Karl."

Not quite as enthusiastically, Karl said, "Yeah, okay."

The minute the new lady entered the room, Karin scooted as far back in the seat as possible, tucking her head into her chest and pulling her legs up onto the seat. While Angela and Marian talked with Karl, Karin fought herself, one second she had the sucker in her mouth; then she pulled it out with her right hand and stuck her thumb in its place. Her thumb was a little pink from the juice from the strawberry sucker and quite sticky. She was holding her thumb up, but at the moment the sucker was in her mouth.

As soon as Marian and Karl left, Angela squatted in front of Karin. "Hi, Karin. I'm your teacher, Miss Teagarden, but the kids call me, Miss T. Did you come to Sunday school yesterday?" Karin nodded, still keeping her eyes averted. "Then you've been in our classroom already!" she said, enthusiastically. "You know what we're gonna make right after lunch? We're gonna make stamps out of playdough. Karin won't be hard to make into the stamp. Karin is such a pretty name and you'll get to learn how to spell your name! Will you come with me?"

Karin let go of the sucker with her right hand, took it with her sticky left hand and reached for Faith's hand. Her left thumb stuck out from the sucker stick as if it was at the ready. She still wouldn't look at Angela. There was no smile as she looked up at Faith, but she could see the trust in the child's eyes. Slowly, Karin inched her bottom forward toward the front of the chair, letting her feet dangle off. Little by little she inched toward the edge. Faith smiled at the little girl. "Shall I come, too?" Karin smiled as she reached the edge of the chair then tentatively took a step toward the door, but holding Faith's hand tightly.

As Angela stood up, Faith said, "Okay, I guess we'll follow you, Miss T." Jim stood back in the doorway of his office with a gentle smile on his face. He had been so right to put the twins in Faith's capable hands.

Marian was returning as the trio went down the stairs. She smiled and said, "Karl's sitting in the circle listening to the story. He found a little friend he knew from Sunday school."

"Thanks, Marian," Angela said.

Karin moved slower and slower as they came closer to the room, but Miss T. opened the door and led them in. Faith sat on a low chair near the door, but Karin's little friend from Sunday school saw her and came rushing over. She exclaimed enthusiastically, "Karin! You came! Cool! Come on, we're workin' in the paints! We get to make pictures with our hands!"

Reluctantly, Karin took two steps away from Faith, but then she ran behind her friend. The helper found an extra large shirt that totally covered her clothes. Giggling with the other girls, she put her hands into the paint and smeared them over the papers hanging on the easels. Faith stayed ten minutes, watching both Karl and Karin, but neither of the children looked at her. Silently, she signaled to Angela that she was leaving and the teacher nodded. On her way back upstairs to the office, Faith decided she had done the right thing by bringing them today.

After Faith left the church, she went home and started working on the material Karl picked out at the department store on Saturday. She took the measurements for the two windows and started working on the set of curtains for the bigger one. Her intention was to get both of them finished before she went back for the children. She was excited, almost as excited as Karl was on Saturday when he saw the bolt of cloth.

Her sewing machine was in the den and before she began sewing, she opened both windows. It was a lovely day and the breeze that came in the windows had a fresh smell to it. It was days like today that made her love late summer and early fall. It wasn't hard to sew several straight lines and no boy wanted ruffles on curtains for his room. As Faith's foot pressed the control, she knew it didn't take much concentration to make the curtain, so her mind soon wandered to the handsome man who paid for this material she was working with.

She smiled. Yesterday he left them at one o'clock, but he called her at nine thirty. He said he wanted to hear her voice. She wondered if he'd call her again tonight. Tonight he was off and in his room. Of course, she hadn't seen it, but she wondered how much time he spent in it. It sounded like he ate all his meals out, so that meant he only slept in his room. She came to the end of the hem and snipped the threads. Shaking her head, that was not much of a life. He hadn't told her much about himself, what family did he have, anyway?

She ate a quick lunch and rushed back to work on the second set, but she finished hanging the second curtain in Karl's room when she looked at her watch. Only seconds later, the clock her parents gave them as a wedding present began to play. "Oh, my goodness! That's quarter to three! I must move!"

Faith pulled into the church parking lot with only minutes to wait before the last bell. She left the car and hurried into the educational wing and along the hall to the kindergarten room. Only for a moment the hall was quiet, the bell hadn't sounded. She decided not to look in the room, but wait in the hall for the twins. They needed to get used to doing their day at school themselves. She didn't intend to bring them to school; they must ride the bus beginning tomorrow. She was a firm believer in helping a child to independence as soon as possible.

However, the instant the bell sounded, the kindergarten door burst open. One child escaped, but right behind her was Karin holding tightly to Karl's hand, but the minute she saw Faith her smile burst across her face. She dropped Karl's hand, flung her arms out wide and ran to Faith, her book bag strap held tightly in her little hand. She paid no attention to Faith's arms, but ran and wrapped her arms around Faith's legs. Karl came up a few steps behind her and his grin was wide and infectious.

Smiling, Faith crouched down and gathered the twins to her, kissing each one on the forehead and asked, "So how was your day?"

"It was great!" Karl enthused and Karin nodded immediately. "We did all kinds of neat stuff. We come back tomorrow?"

"Absolutely and tomorrow, you'll ride the bus with Brandi."

Karl's eyes turned to saucers. "Wow! We can do that?"

"Yes, I know you'll like that. Today I found a book bag for you, too."

"Really? My very own?"

"Yes, your very own, Karl." Looking at the quiet little girl, Faith said, "I'm glad to see you remembered yours, Karin."

The little girl looked at the brightly colored bag Miss T. had draped across her arm that slipped immediately to her hand, then looked up and grinned. Faith stood up and reached for the twins' hands, but she knew it was only minutes until Brandi's class let out, so she stayed close to the wall. When the older children left their classrooms there was usually a major stampede!

Only minutes later, Brandi came down the hall, holding her book bag and lunch box in her left hand. Miss Lambert told her class not to run in the hallway and Brandi was trying hard, but when she saw her mommy and the twins, she skipped quickly to them, her smile spreading. Beside them, she reached for Karl's hand. He grabbed it and they hurried out together into the sunshine and headed for Faith's car. They weren't the only children on the parking lot. Several minibuses were there with children crowded around them.

As Faith eased the car out of the parking lot, Brandi asked, "When's Matt coming back, Mommy? Will he be there when we get home?"

"He called me last night before I went to sleep. He asked if he could come out tomorrow, but it'll be after you guys leave for school."

Brandi sighed, "Mommy, come on, you need to get with the program. Ask him to marry you so he doesn't have to ask, he can just come home."

"Yeah!" Karl added. "I like that. He'd be our daddy then!"

"Guys," Faith looked in the rearview mirror and said, just a bit panicked, "do you know how long Matt and I've known each other?"

"Well, it was a week ago tomorrow I showed him how to go to heaven and you gave him a cup of water." *As if that was quite long enough for them to wait for Matt to be their daddy!*

Faith sighed, as she inched ahead. Sometimes she wished there was another entrance. "True." Faith remembered the instant reaction, in all that chaos, terrible noise and flying debris that she and Matt had toward each other, she chuckled. "Brandi, my dear, it doesn't mean we knew each other that long. We only met to talk on Friday. I know we've spent lots of time with him Saturday and Sunday, and we all got to know him, but I think he and I need to get to know each other a little better than that. Goodness, I don't even know if he likes spinach or not!"

Instantly, Brandi started laughing. When she finally took a breath, she exclaimed, "Mommy, spinach? Who cares if he likes spinach!"

"Well, you know what I mean." Faith had to grin, amused at her own choice of words. She didn't even care for cooked spinach too much.

"But Mommy...." Faith, knowing just by the inflection of her voice where this speech was headed, shook her finger at Brandi. "I know, it's still our secret. I'm tryin' hard to remember, Mommy, really."

"Thank you."

"Can we play in the sandbox when we get home?" Karl asked, he wasn't too much into conversations he didn't understand. "That was lots of fun and they don't got one in our class." Faith didn't miss the fact that Karl called her house home. It was only three days; it sent a streak of warmth down her spine to think that so soon, this little child felt at home. A silent prayer went heavenward thanking her Father for His goodness. She also knew, at least she was sure in her heart of hearts that the twins were God's way of bringing a good man into her life.

"Is the cover still off?" Faith asked and glanced in the mirror. "You know it's too heavy for any of you to get off and it's also too heavy for me to get back in place."

"We sorta pulled it over top of the sand, but Matt didn't put it back, not like it was."

Pushing down on the accelerator, Faith said, "Then I guess you can, but we'll need to pull the cover over right when you're finished playing, it may rain before you get back to it. Brandi do you have homework?"

Really exasperated with such a mundane question, Brandi looked at Faith in the rearview mirror and said, "Mommy, I got some I can do after supper. It's pretty now, it's time to play, we been in school all day, you know."

"All right, but you come in and wash up when I call you for supper. Maybe we can go to the park after supper for a little bit. We haven't been there for quite a while."

"Oh, yayee!" Brandi exclaimed. "There's a teeter and a slide we can go on. We'll see some other kids there, too. That's the most fun. Right, Karl?"

Not really sure what he was agreeing to, Karl said, "Yeah!" Karin, of course didn't add anything verbal to the exchange. In fact, she was busy inspecting her book-bag. Perhaps she wasn't enthused about the park.

Some time after school was out and the complex was quiet, the phone rang and Marian Fisher answered. Without identifying himself, Matt asked to speak with the pastor, so Marian put him through, also without asking who was calling. When Jim picked up the phone and answered, Matt said, "Hello, Pastor, this is Matt Barns, did you see the paper today?"

"No, I didn't. It's sort of hectic around home in the morning and then I get to school... well need I say more? Why?"

"I've cut out an article from today's paper that I think may pertain to the twins. I need some advice as to what I should do, if anything." He read Jim the article and then said, "Karl told me his last name was Kaufmann, rather reluctantly. He told Faith about his dad shooting his mom and then falling on the couch and him taking his sister and running away. Of course, he didn't have any time reference. The warehouse where we found them was blocks and blocks from Forty-fifth Street. I didn't say anything here at the station and I'm sure some of the men read this, because the commander reads every word of the paper, but nothing has been said. What do you think I should do in this case?"

Jim pushed his chair back from his desk and raised his feet to rest on it, before he said, "Matt, Faith brought the twins to school today. Karl didn't want to, but he finally did tell us his last name. I didn't hear you read any name in that article."

"No, that's why I'm wondering what to do, especially since there wasn't any room in the foster care system anyway."

Holding the receiver to his ear, but with a very thoughtful look on his face, after a short silence, when he absently rubbed his chin, Jim said, "Matt, I think I'd leave it alone. If someone asks is time enough to see what happens. Right now, the children are happy and doing fine. I know that for a fact, I saw them."

Matt couldn't hide his apprehension, as he said, "How did Karin make out in school?"

Jim grinned and slapped his hand on the desktop, as he said, "Perfectly! We were all surprised, but she did just great! Faith didn't even have to stay but a few minutes in the classroom with her. She found her friend from Sunday school. Kids seem to be so resilient and these two especially."

"Yes, that's so. Say, Pastor, has anything been said about me being with Faith?"

The pastor chuckled. "Not that I know about, Matt. Personally, I think it's great! She's well over Max's death, it's time for her. You keep coming around."

Matt chuckled. "Believe me, I plan to, Pastor. Thanks for your advice."

Matt hung up and looked at the clock on the stand beside the bed. He got off on time and now it was four o'clock. He asked Faith if he could come out in the morning, but now he was looking at a very long, boring evening with only the diversion of going to the nearby diner for supper. He'd give just about anything to be on the train going home to Thomaston to Mrs. Faith *Barns* and three children whom he was daddy to. He wondered if that was a possibility or if it was a pipe dream.

His shift was relatively calm, with three runs in twenty-four hours and he got about six hours sleep at the station, so he wasn't tired. That was his usual time to sleep. He thought about the route between the train station and Faith's house, trying to remember if there was a motel or boarding house along the way. For a while, he needed a place to stay, but it didn't need to be in this Victorian on Manhattan, it could be in the city of Thomaston, he was sure.

Not that Faith wasn't capable, but he'd sure like to be part of putting the children to bed, Karl especially, when he could. He also wouldn't mind helping them get ready for school. He wasn't even sure if she had to take them to school. If so, that would be a major undertaking each day. She had three to get ready in the early morning! Two of them were thrown at her with no advance warning. That wouldn't be easy, even if you were a morning person.

He scraped his hand down his face, continuing his thoughts. Never mind doing things for the kids, he very much wanted to be part of Faith's life and maybe, in the not too distant future, he'd like to put her to bed, right beside him. His single bed was getting pretty stark and lonesome. After all, they weren't getting any younger. They hadn't exchanged ages, but he'd wager that she was about thirty-two, maybe thirty-three, since Brandi was nine and from the way Faith talked, she was married to Max at least a year before she was born.

She hadn't told him she went to college, the topic never came up, but she seemed too cultured, refined not to have. Anyway, he was pretty sure she was very close to his age, give or take a couple of years. He must admit, he was never in love before, but he didn't have a name if what he felt for Faith wasn't love.

He looked at the clock again. "Wow! Five minutes went by since I looked last," he grumbled and shook his head.

Finally, after sitting at his desk and deciding that the air in the room was stifling him, he decided it was time to go to the diner, maybe if he walked around the block first he could interest his stomach in getting hungry. However, when supper was over, it wouldn't be dark and much too early to sack out. Maybe he'd take a real walk and go down to Ground Zero to see what was done about clearing away all the rubble and debris. The fires were controlled, but there were massive amounts of useless cement and steel to move. It made him shudder to think of all the burned up bodies that were beyond recognition still in all that rubble.

Now that he had that thought, he decided to walk there first. If he ate when it was dark that was no problem, but he'd like to see some of what was being done and you couldn't take that in too well after dark. He wondered if that cross still stood like such a beacon for him last week. As he began his walk, he realized it would be a week tomorrow that time stood still.

The horn had sounded, they were the second alarm and as they rode the fire truck toward the scene, only the first tower had been struck. Much to their horror, they saw the second plane coming in much too fast and much too low, then realizing that whoever was the pilot meant to plow into the second tower. They watched as it burst into flames on impact. It was then that they realized it was no accident that a plane had hit the first tower. One of the other firemen on the truck had shouted, "That plane just plowed into that tower!"

Later, they learned that almost at the same time another plane hit the Pentagon in Washington and another went down in Pennsylvania, but because of some fast thinking of some passengers it hadn't done any damage except that the plane and its passengers were lost. All the planes had been hijacked by terrorists who wished to see America tremble. Tremble she did, but it had galvanized her into immediate action.

NINE

A S HE BEGAN HIS WALK, THE SUN WAS IN THE WEST, BEHIND THE SKYSCRAPERS AND casting its waning light onto the high windows of those buildings, but at this hour, they were mostly abandoned as he neared Ground Zero. There were still yellow tapes stretched across the streets and gaping holes that silently told people not to go closer. He stopped at the intersection where Faith and the others gave out water. He looked beyond the tape to where he knew he and others were working and where Brandi met him, but that spot was too far away. Since that time too much had changed for him to recognize the spot.

He saw the bulldozers abandoned for the night and wondered if the workers were finding bodies in the debris or if all that was left was cement and steel. A cold wind touched him and he shivered. He knew he would never, ever be the same again. Nine eleven had changed him forever. As he stood there gazing over the silent carnage he knew it wasn't nine eleven that had changed him, but God Himself and He used a little child to make that drastic change.

He stood at the spot where he first saw Faith at the table where she gave him a drink. She was as refreshing as that water she gave out. He found out since then what a lovely person she was. Now he was about to admit that he loved her. He definitely had feelings for her he never experienced before in his life, could he call that love? Maybe.

From where he stood, at the spot where her table was all he could see was carnage. There was only rubble and destruction, but he would carry that little tract that Brandi gave him. Things had changed so much, but he looked beyond the yellow tape, imagining the slab of concrete where he prayed his very first prayer. Since that fragile start, he read the Bible Jim gave him whenever possible. He was anxious to go to a Bible study, but he knew it wouldn't be again this week. He would be back on duty again at that time.

Where he stood it was silent, an unnatural silence, there were no buses or taxis or even people and subways were diverted onto other lines. After some time, he turned around and started back toward his room. It would be dark by the time he reached the diner and now his stomach was telling him it was time to eat. However, even after he ate, he still had a long hour or two before he could fall asleep. He sighed and stuck his hands in his pockets. Being a bachelor wasn't too interesting any longer. For him, bachelorhood never was that exciting time with lots of free women and lots of parties. Sowing wild oats was not his thing. His parents hadn't been church going people, but they raised him to have high standards in his life.

After supper, as Faith loaded the dishwasher, Karin stuck her thumb in her mouth and wandered into the living room. She climbed up on the couch and curled up in the corner on a pillow. About ten minutes later, when Brandi and Karl went looking for her so they could go to the park, she was sound asleep, holding one of Faith's throw pillows in one arm while the other thumb was in her mouth. Tears crowded Faith's eyes but didn't fall. That tiny child was precious; she was also precious in God's sight. Faith never thought about the extra work she was now doing, she was so glad the twins were safe.

"Mommy," Brandi whispered, as Faith followed, "I guess we'd better not go to the park. Karin's too tired to play. She needs a bath so she can go to bed."

"Yes, I think you're right. I remember you were pretty tired your first day of school."

Looking at her mommy incredulously, she shook her head and said, "I was? I can't remember that. Are you sure?"

Silently Faith said, *No, I'm sure you don't remember. It's never happened again.* Still looking at Karin, Faith nodded and said, "I'm sure you don't remember, after all that was four years ago when you started school and you've met so many new kids since then."

Again, as she did on several other occasions, Brandi gently shook Karin awake. The little girl opened her sleepy eyes and looked from one face to the other. Brandi smiled at her and held out her hand. As Karin trustingly took it, Brandi said, "Come on, Karin, it's time for your bath. I know you had a really big day today, but there's school again tomorrow! I gotta take a bath, too. We wanna be all clean for school!"

Karin yawned and nodded as she slid off the couch. Faith wouldn't play favorites, but this silent child was absolutely precious. Karin took Brandi's hand and headed for the stairs. Karl looked up at Faith, who smiled at him. She had to admit, Karl was not far behind his sister in her heart. These two children were a wonderful addition to her family. Now just to add a wonderful man for their daddy....

After her bath, Karin went straight to bed and Karl jumped in to play. He didn't take long and Faith wasn't surprised when he asked Faith for a story and headed for bed, too. After Brandi finished her homework, she took her bath, and went in her room to read her Bible while her mommy took her bath. She read her Bible for a little while, but then put it away and went back her favorite chair to pray before Faith came. There was something she wanted only Jesus to hear. She knelt in front of the big chair, folded her hands and scrunched her eyelids together.

"Dear Jesus," she whispered so she wouldn't wake Karin, "You know we need Matt as our daddy real bad. Mommy gets real tired since we got the twins. Like I told You before, us three kids need a daddy and I kinda think Mommy likes Matt a lot. He likes her, too, I can tell. Can You work it out real soon? And Jesus, Karin needs to start talkin' pretty soon. Mommy and I and Karl can understand, but she's gonna meet lots of people who can't. Could You work on that, too? I love You, Jesus. Thanks, I gotta stop now, Mommy's coming. Amen."

Faith came in Brandi's room and Brandi climbed into bed, she whispered to Faith, "How do we know when it's the twins' birthday?"

Faith wrinkled her forehead. "Hmm, I guess we could ask Karl, but if he doesn't know, I don't know how we could find out for sure."

"Mommy, it'd be horrid if we couldn't find out! How do they get birthday presents? They couldn't take cupcakes to school to celebrate!"

Faith nodded. "Yeah, that is something to think about. Let's ask Karl in the morning, okay? Maybe he can remember."

Looking over at the sleeping child in the other bed, Brandi said, "Yeah, I'll try real hard to remember, Mommy. Every kid needs to celebrate his birthday, so he's gotta know when it is! Tomorrow's good." Brandi lay down and smiled at her mommy. "I love you, Mommy; you're the best mommy in all the world!"

Faith's heart swelled and tears glistened in her eyes, as she said, "Oh, Brandi, you're the best girl any mommy could have! You've been great with Karin and Karl."

Brandi gave her mommy an angelic smile. "I love 'em, too!"

"Honey, I know you do! And I'm so glad, they are precious children."

In the morning, Brandi poured cereal in three bowls and set them at three places. She poured milk in glasses and orange juice into some smaller glasses. Faith came in the kitchen and started a pot of coffee brewing. She pulled out a bagel and cream cheese for herself and sat down while the kids were wolfing down their breakfast. She was sure both Karl and Karin had put on a few pounds, which they desperately needed. However, they still hadn't lost their zest for eating everything on their plates.

Just before they finished, Brandi said, "Karl, when's your birthday?"

He scowled, obviously trying to think hard. At that moment a thought flashed across Faith's mind that perhaps there never was a celebration for the twins' birthday! It was entirely possible they came from a destitute or abusive home.

A minute later he asked, "You mean when we had a cake with candles on it?"

"Yeah!" Brandi exclaimed with a grin. Maybe this wouldn't be so hard after all.

"Umm, it was by a holiday...."

"This year? Since Christmas?" Brandi asked, helpfully.

"Nah, it was a long time. We got a coat for Christmas, but it was before that our afore mommy gave us a cake."

"Ween..." Karin said out loud.

Instantly, three pairs of eyes turned to Karin and Faith's mouth flew open. It was the first sound that came from her mouth since Matt placed the twins' hands in Faith's on Friday. Immediately, Karin dropped her eyes and her chin hit her chest. Her spoon clattered into her bowl and her thumb went straight to her mouth. Faith couldn't be sure, but she'd put money on it that Karin had tears in her eyes.

In awe, Faith said, "Did you say something, Karin?"

Before she could answer, Karl exclaimed, "Halloween! We had cake with candles and the next day was Halloween!"

"Thank you, Karl." However, she stood up immediately and crouched down beside his chair. She took his hand, and said, "Karl, I think from now on, we need to give Karin a chance to say something if she wants. Okay?"

"I'll try and remember. She don't talk for so long, not since Daddy started hittin' her." Tears glistened in his eyes, as he murmured, "We couldn't eat our cake Daddy come home, even afore we blew out our candles and…and shoved us in our room real fast and locked the door. We heard stuff goin' on outside our door and our cake was all gone when he let us back out. Karin cried then and Daddy whipped us with his belt. She ain't talked since that night."

Faith's eyes watered up and she hugged the little boy, "Oh, Karl," she murmured and kissed his cheek. Then she turned and hugged the little girl, "Oh, Karin, you sweet thing." The little girl threw her arms around Faith's neck and held on. Faith kissed her, too

Matt hadn't slept too much over night. He usually only slept about six hours, that's all they could manage when they were on duty, usually a fire run interrupted any long stretch of sleep. On his long walk and then as he ate supper, he continued to think about how he could live in Thomaston to be close to those he now considered his family…. and loved dearly.

As he showered and put on clean clothes, he smiled, yes, it was no slip of his mental tongue; he considered Faith, Brandi and the twins his family. With water sluicing off his body he gladly admitted that he loved the lady with auburn curls. Since he left them on Sunday he missed them terribly. He wanted to call Faith last night, just to hear her voice, but he didn't know how she'd take it, would she feel he over-stepped his rights? He didn't know, so he didn't.

He knew it would stretch his work time to about twenty-seven hours, since he needed an hour and a half of travel time each way not to be late, but he wouldn't mind, if he could be with Faith and the kids. On nights like this, he could stay later in the evening. He and Faith could spend some quiet time together after the kids were in bed. At least he hoped that could happen.

He looked at his watch as he left for breakfast at the diner. Faith would be busy getting the kids off to school. He didn't know if she had to take them, since they went to Christian school, or if there was a bus, but he planned to be on the train by eight to see if he could find a place to live. He didn't remember a place between the train station and her house, but there must be something where he could hang his hat and clean uniforms in a city the size of Thomaston. He would ask the station master at the Thomaston station, surely he'd know.

Matt hurried through breakfast at the diner, then on the street corner outside he found a newspaper dispenser, so he bought one for something to do while he rode the train for the hour. He took long strides down the street and rushed into the Long Island train station. The timetable board overhead said a train leaving for the Island was due in any minute, so he dashed down one level to the platform. A train going out on the Island roared into the station as he reached the platform. If he had a hat on, it would be gone with the wind the train made and the noise…. The doors opened and since he was leaving the city in the early morning, he had the car to himself. Only a moment later the trainman came into the car and took his coupon. Obviously, there weren't many passengers, the trainman gave Matt a silent grin and sat down with his own paper.

He had the article about the dead couple in his wallet, but he scanned most of the first section. There again on the last page, he found an article about the unnamed couple.

> The dead couple, found in the third floor apartment in the seven hundred block of Forty-fifth Street have been identified as Sylvester Kaufmann and his common-law wife, Amanda. In some circles, Kaufmann is well known for his dealings in stolen goods. After a more thorough search of the apartment where he was found, many stolen items were found and confiscated. It is believed at this time that Amanda was shot by a gun Kaufmann had concealed in his trench coat, which investigators have found close to the body. His death is being attributed to drugs and alcohol. However, investigations are still going on.

The article ended and Matt breathed a sigh. "No mention of any children." However, he was sure now that these were Karl and Karin's parents. He shook his head. That little boy had been wise beyond his years to take his sister and run. If he hadn't, they would be lost in the foster care system by now Matt was sure and he shuddered. The timeline seemed like this all happened only days before nine-eleven. He was never in foster care, of course, but since coming to New York City he had dealings with foster families. Not what he'd recommend for any child who could have another chance.

It would soon be his stop, so he folded up the paper and leaned his head back. As he looked out the window at the land bathed in sunlight, he tried to think if he ever heard of Sylvester Kaufmann. However, the name didn't ring a bell, he didn't make a habit of getting into the police territory, fighting fires was enough for him. The man was obviously part of a theft ring, if there was contraband in the apartment. There hadn't been a hint of what kind of stolen goods they found and if his death was caused by a combination of drugs and alcohol, a dealer could have drugs in the apartment. He shook his head, what a home life for two small children and the woman wasn't even his wife by marriage!

As he stood up, while the train slowed, he thanked the Lord again that Karl took his sister and ran. He wondered how much the children saw in their young lives. Some very evil people could come to their home. He jumped to the platform, not expecting Faith to be waiting. He hadn't told her when he'd arrive, even on Sunday, he thought of finding a place to live in Thomaston. Immediately, he began walking, leaving the train station behind. However, he stopped even before he finished crossing the parking lot, and turned back to the station.

Inside, he walked up to the station master, who was now away from the window, sweeping the large waiting room. Giving the man a broad grin, Matt asked, "Hi, do you know Thomaston very well?"

The man nodded. "Pretty well, I've lived here most of my life."

"I'm wondering if there's a boarding house, bed and breakfast or a motel close by or at least on this side of downtown," Matt said, still smiling.

"We're too close to the city for a boarding house, but I do believe a lady just recently turned her parents' old home place into a nice bed and breakfast."

"Ahh, so where is this place?"

Leaning on his broom, he said, "Once you cross the parking lot at the street, turn to your left and go about four blocks. It's a big gray house on the corner; she's done a real good job gettin' it fixed up. I believe it has a white picket fence around the two sides that border the streets. You can't miss it."

"Great! Thanks!"

The station master grinned back and said, "Not a problem!"

Matt gave the man a two finger salute before he left the station. He was grinning; the day was perfect and would continue to be he could feel it. He wanted to whistle, so he did. Today was Tuesday, past the middle of the month. He paid the room rent for the month, but only paid by the month, so he could clear out a little at a time or bring it all at once. Whatever!

He didn't have much, he could have the room empty in two or three trips, by bringing out a piece of luggage each time he went off duty from the fire station. A bachelor fireman didn't have too many things to weigh him down. Besides, the room didn't lend itself to hanging pictures and other such personal stuff.

He found the place easily from the man's instructions. It did look nice and the picket fence set it off from the buildings around it. He went up on the porch, lifted the knocker, that was sparkling in the early morning sun and let it fall. It broke the silence of the morning as it hit the solid door. As he waited, he turned to look around him and liked what he saw.

Soon a middle-aged woman came to the door and smiled at the handsome man. "Yes? What can I do for you?"

"Hi. The man at the train station said you are operating a bed and breakfast here. I'm wondering if you have a room available by the week or month?"

"Yes. Come on in." She held the door then turned to lead him down the spacious hallway and into a large dining room. The table and chairs dominated the room obviously several decades ago this house was filled with a family. "Since there's only about half a month left, why don't we go with a half month rent, then in October, you can rent for the month. Would that work for you?"

"I believe it would. I'm Matt Barns and you?"

"I'm Silvia Piper. I have my form here. Could you fill it out for me, please?"

"Certainly, I'd be happy to!"

Silvia tried to look busy while Matt filled out her form, but she was definitely not immune to the handsome man seated at her dining table. When Matt had filled out the lady's form and paid his money, she led him back to the hall and up the wide stairs. "I have a large room right here on the front of the house. It has its own bath and there's a large closet."

The room she led him to was huge, much larger than the room in the

Victorian. The room was bathed in sunshine through the two windows. There were matching drapes, all the furniture matched and lovely pictures added spectacular color to the room. Of course, the sunlight in the room was because there was actually a yard around this house not like the Victorian that was wedged between two others just like it. If any sunlight filtered in the window, it had to be a crooked beam that did it! He looked through the open doorway beyond and saw the very nice private bath. This was luxury; he hadn't had his own bath, other than to call the one at his parents' home his own, because he was an only child.

He looked around and exclaimed, "Wow! This is great! I can move in today?"

"Certainly. You paid starting today."

He grinned at her, accepting the key. "I'll just do that! This room is spectacular and the bath… well, I'm happy!" Actually, he was ecstatic and his grin showed it. He never thought of such a perfect place to hang his hat or his uniforms this close to Manhattan. He swallowed a chuckle, actually, close to his family was more to his choosing. Except that Silvia was still in the room, Matt wanted to leap into the air and click his heels. He wished he thought to bring a piece of luggage with him this morning!

Silvia was single and as Matt smiled at her, her heart did an extra pitter-patter. She guessed he was too young for her, but she could fantasize just fine. She smiled back, then turned and preceded him down the stairs. She turned toward the kitchen then when Matt reached the bottom step, she said, "Oh, in keeping with the name, I serve breakfast each morning from seven to ten. My residents find it easier if I have a buffet."

Matt nodded. "That sounds perfect. I'll take you up on that tomorrow." He was almost positive he could find another table to place his feet under for the other two meals. He grinned as he went out the door, in fact, the grin felt as if it was permanent.

Two excited twins walked with Brandi and Faith down the driveway to the road. Today would be the very first time they had ever ridden a school bus. Of course, this wasn't a big yellow school bus, it was a twelve passenger van with the name of the church school printed on the side, but they were riding with other kids to school. Importantly, they had their book bags on their backs. Karin's lunch was in the special part of her book bag, but Karl's lunch was in his new lunch box. He was so proud when he came home last night and found that Faith found a lunch box that had the same movie characters on it as his curtains.

Big sister, Brandi walked with them, but made them stop under the tree so that they could see the bus coming, but be back from the road in case any traffic came before the bus arrived. All four were watching when the van turned the corner and came to the drive. The driver stopped and opened the door. She smiled as the three came running to the steps.

"Hi," Faith stood at the edge of the road and said, "I checked with Pastor Jim yesterday. He said you'd have room for two more."

The lady was a young grandmother who loved children. She smiled at the twins as they came up the steps, but Brandi took them down the aisle. The lady, who also went to the church, turned to Faith and said, "Of course! He also told me yesterday while I loaded to expect a couple more here at your place. They're precious darlings. They go to kindergarten?"

"Yes, I took them and enrolled them yesterday; they're excited to ride your bus today. Brandi's doing a great job of being big sister."

The lady winked at Faith. "Yes, I can see that. I'll bring 'em back later on." Karin reluctantly followed Brandi to a seat, but she had her thumb in her mouth before she reached it. As soon as she saw that the children were seated, the lady closed the door.

Faith waved to the back of the bus as it pulled away then she turned to walk back to her house. That was the first time she thought about the fact that Matt had never said when she should meet him at the train station. She knew he could walk it, but it was quite a few blocks, as she said before he could use all his breakfast calories walking from there to here. She sighed, he must walk today, they hadn't agreed on a time. Until he came, she planned to work on Karl's bedspread. She couldn't believe what a hit the curtains were when he first saw them. The twins were so appreciative of everything she and Brandi did for them.

The dishwasher was still going, so she went upstairs to make the beds. After putting in a load of wash, she sat down at the sewing machine to cut pieces of the material to pin around the big center piece for the bedspread. She heard a knock at her front door; however from the den she couldn't see her driveway. Her heart took wings and fluttered into her throat as she dropped everything and ran from the room. She wiped her suddenly sweaty hands down her slacks as she headed for the door. It never occurred to her that it might not be Matt.

She flung the door open, expecting to see Matt, but instead a large delivery truck sat idling in the driveway and a man, just as large as Matt stood on her porch holding a package. She wasn't sure, but it felt like her heart crashed when she saw it wasn't Matt. "Good morning, Ma'am, package for Mrs. Max Lankaster."

It wasn't often she received packages and most everyone she knew addressed her as Faith Lankaster, but she said, "Yes, I'll sign for that, if you wish."

Faith took the electronic device to sign, signed her name then reached for the package the man had in one hand, as she handed the device back. The man seemed reluctant to hand her the package, so she looked up into his face. What she saw sent a cold shiver down her spine. The man had no intention of handing her the package, then leaving, it was obvious. She felt very vulnerable standing there holding out her hands.

Suddenly, before she could think to draw her hands back, the man dropped the package on the porch and grabbed her wrists. She held his electronic device, but the thought to clobber him with it never came to her mind. "I have time for my morning break," he said, menacingly, "and it'll be right now. No one can see from the road, and I know you're by yourself."

Faith continued to look at the man, her mouth felt like cotton, as she stood powerless before the man, he was much too strong for her to resist and she had her hands out in front of her. However, she knew she had one weapon. In her heart she cried out to her heavenly Father who had been her Protector for many years. He was the Protector of widows and children. Only seconds later, even before the man could push her from her doorway into the hall, she heard whistling coming closer down the drive, but the man obviously didn't hear.

Matt saw the large delivery truck sitting in the drive only feet from Faith's front door. He walked a little faster, now that he could see her house, he was anxious to get to her. It was more than twenty-four hours and he missed her. He rounded the truck and saw the man holding Faith's wrists. It took only seconds for Matt's mind to register that the driver had no intentions of leaving his parcel and moving on.

"Hey!" he yelled and took a bounding leap for the porch. "What are you doing with my lady? You think you have some right to her?"

The man was so startled, he let go of Faith's wrists as if they were scorching him. Faith, of course stepped back immediately into her doorway. He grabbed the electronic device that was still in her hand and whirled around, but the package stayed on the porch floor. By this time, Matt was on the porch within inches of the delivery man. With his device in his hand the man tried to take a step, but instead nearly collided with Matt. Matt's hands came up and grabbed the man roughly by the shirt on each shoulder.

Looking intently into the man's face, he said, "Planning on a pleasant coffee break here, with the lady, were you?"

The man licked his lips and tried to take a step away from Matt. "Ahh, delivering a package, sir. I was retrieving my, umm, device."

"Ahh, yes, it took both hands on her wrists?"

"Not exactly."

"I think an apology is in order, mister."

Matt was still holding the man's shirt with both hands, but he turned his head and said, over his shoulder. "I'm, ah, sorry, Mrs. Lankaster."

"That's fine, be on your way, get out of here." Faith was unconsciously rubbing her wrists, as she looked at the man.

"Y-y-e-e-s-s, I-I'll just do that."

Matt thrust the man from him, who stumbled backwards for a step. Holding his hand out, he gained his balance before he fell from the porch and bounded down the three steps and in three long strides was in his truck. Quickly, he backed around in front of her garage and gunned his truck out the driveway, spraying a few stones of gravel from the driveway onto the side of the house. Matt moved to Faith, put his arms around her, but turned so they could both watch the truck disappear over the crest of the hill.

"Whew! I'm glad I was so close!"

"I am, too!" She smiled, as she stepped closer inside the circle of his arms. "I was pretty sure you'd come right then, I prayed that you would and you did."

"Oh, Faith..." he breathed into her hair.

She was so close. There was no one around that could see them. He felt her putting her arms around him, so he took one hand from her back and put his finger under her chin. As her head went up at his insistence, she looked into his eyes. She didn't know what he could see in hers, but even in the broad sunlight, his pupils nearly blotted out the blue, his look sent another shiver up her back, but it wasn't from cold.

Looking at her lips, he whispered, "Would you be upset if I kissed you, Faith?" His lips turned up, as he said, "You look kissable, you know."

A smile whispered across her lips and her eyes sparkled. "No, I wouldn't mind at all, Matt. I'd like it a lot, actually."

His lips moved toward hers, but she was so anxious, she rose to her tiptoes to meet them. He took his finger from her chin and buried his hand in her hair. He knew her lips must be soft and pliable, but the real thing was far better than the imagined. Finally, his lips settled on hers and he felt her sigh. At first, the kiss was only a light pressure, but at her response, he drew her closer and deepened it, luxuriating in the feel of her lips and her body yielding to him. At that moment he knew she was why he never felt anything for another woman!

Several minutes later, he lifted his head, but continued to hold her. After he swallowed, knowing his voice would crack if he tried to speak, he said, "Are your plans firm for today?"

Faith licked her swollen lips, but even so, only a murmur came out. "Only to be here at three thirty when the kids get home."

He gave her another quick peck and said, "Want to make a trip into the city with me?"

"Why?" she asked, perplexed. A scowl marred her pretty face.

"I've moved," he said, succinctly.

Even more perplexed, she asked, "Where?" She couldn't imagine where he could have moved, she had no idea.

His smile spreading farther with each of her questions. "About four blocks the other side of the church to a bed and breakfast."

A grin spread across her face and her arms tightened around him. "Here? Here in Thomaston?" When he nodded, she squeezed him tightly. "Wow! Sure, let me get my keys and purse. We can leave right away!"

Matt's twinkling eyes looked down at her and he said, "Lady, I like how you think!"

When they were in her car driving to the train station, she said, "So when you leave work, like yesterday, from now on you'll come here?"

"Yes. Last night I thought I'd go bananas after I got off work. Our shift ended on time, so I was at my room by three fifteen. I took care of my mail and still couldn't think of a thing to do, it was too early to eat. I finally decided to walk down to Ground Zero and got back after dark to the diner. I still had so much time before I could fall asleep that I read fifteen chapters in the Bible Pastor gave me."

Faith chuckled and leaned close again for a kiss. Matt was quick to oblige. "You wouldn't have been bored if you were here, believe me."

"No, I didn't think so. So even Karin rode the bus to school?"

Faith's smile rivaled the sun as she said, "Yes, that precious child! Her little friend from church is in kindergarten and bless her, she grabbed Karin the instant she walked in with me yesterday. I sat down to watch, but within minutes, neither of the kids even looked at me. They never missed me when I left."

"That's great!"

"Yes, I was so glad! Believe me; it was not like that at home! And there in the office at church… well, lets just say, each step was quite an ordeal."

Faith parked and they walked onto the platform. With rush hour over, the trains weren't coming as often. However, they only had ten minutes to wait, so they waited in the warm sunshine. Matt pulled two coupons from his wallet to have ready when the train pulled in for their ride. Only a few minutes later, they heard the train whistle blowing as it came into the city.

When they were settled in their seat for the hour ride, Matt pulled yesterday's article from his wallet and handed it to her. "What do you think?" he asked.

She took the small piece of paper and read it, before she said, "Wow! That has to be the twin's parents! It has to be, after what Karl told me."

"Yes, that's what I decided. I didn't cut the article out of the paper until just before I left yesterday afternoon, but I didn't hear any comments. I assume no one put two and two together except us. I called Pastor yesterday to see what he said and he said to leave it alone. However, read what's in the paper today."

She took the paper he held out to her, opened to the article. Of course, it didn't take long to read, so when she had, he asked, "Who knows besides us and Pastor what their last name is? Well, maybe there at school. Did that woman ask you on Sunday night? That gossip?"

"No, Maryann didn't even ask what the twins' first names were. Yes, I'm sure that's it. I filled out registration forms for them yesterday. Only Marian was there when Pastor Jim asked Karl what their last name was. I imagine Angela, their teacher knows now, but I haven't told anyone else." She sat thinking, then said, "Wouldn't it be awful for five year olds? What a terrible home life that must have been!"

"Terrible! Karl is a smart little boy for getting them out of there."

"He is." She handed the paper back and Matt rolled it up, as Faith said, "Guess what happened today?"

Matt slid his arm across the back of the seat and turned to look at her. She had a marvelous smile on her face he wanted to kiss her all over again. "What? I can't imagine, but you look like you're about to jump out of your skin!" he said. As he spoke, he let his hand slide onto her shoulder.

"Karin said her first sound!"

"Really? What was it?" That excited him, too.

"Last night, Brandi asked me how we could find out when the kids birthday was. I said we could ask Karl, but if he didn't know I didn't know how to find out. Of course, she remembered and asked him at breakfast. We had to give him several hints; even then he didn't come up with it." She turned to Matt and with the brightest smile, she exclaimed, "Karin said, 'Ween.' We were all so shocked that we all looked at her and of course, it embarrassed her, so she dropped her eyes. That was enough for Karl; he said it was the day before Halloween."

"Oh, Faith!" Matt exclaimed, "That's terrific! I'm so glad she's talked already." He shook his head. "I was afraid it was something that might last a long time. It just shows me how comfortable they are in your home."

Her cheeks turned pink at his compliment, but she said, "Karl said it was their birthday when she stopped talking."

"Oh," he groaned, "what happened?"

"Their mother gave them a small cake, he showed me how big. But when their father came home with some thugs, he locked them in their room. When they were allowed out, the cake was gone and Karin cried. The man beat her and she hasn't talked since."

Shaking his head, Matt whispered, "I can't imagine!" Fiercely, he drew Faith close and as he lowered his head for another kiss, he said again, "I can't imagine treating anyone like that, especially tiny kids." Meaning it with all his heart, Matt said, "I'm so glad you got those kids."

It was a good ways from the train station to Matt's room in the old Victorian, so they left the station and boarded the subway. At his stop, he took her up the stairs to the sidewalk. It was a nice day, the temperature wasn't too hot, but it seemed more oppressive, since it was in the city. Holding her hand, he set a pace she could easily keep. She looked up at the older building as they approached and saw the peeling paint and the railing that needed help to stand up.

Not even taking hold of the rickety railing, she said, "No love lost on this place, was there? This thing looks like it could fall down in a brisk breeze."

"No, you can say that again!"

As they walked up, a mail truck came and the mailman called, "You're Matthew Barns?"

"Yes. You have something for me?"

"I need a signature." Matt signed the man's paper, who then handed Matt a large 'express mail' envelope.

As they exchanged articles, Matt said, "Say, do you have a change of address form? I've moved and I'll need my mail forwarded, starting immediately."

The older man grinned, looked at the shabby house, then at the lovely lady at Matt's side. "You are moving away from this perfectly lovely house? Why, I can't imagine where else you would want to hang your hat! I mean, a Victorian on Manhattan, why what are you thinking?"

Matt took the man's form and started in filling it out. "Mmm, I know what you mean, but yes, I'm moving today. So have a good life, sir." Matt finished filling out the form and handed it back. "Believe me, I'll be on the next train."

"Can't say as I blame you."

He and Faith left the mailman and went up the stairs to go in the old house. Matt didn't bother to check the mailbox, he had last evening and he just now got what the man had for him. So he led Faith up the stairs to his room off the stairway. Faith wrinkled her nose. The place didn't smell bad, just old and well used. The carpet on the stairs was worn very thin. She wasn't exactly sure what color it had been when it was installed.

Inside the room was one window with dingy white curtains and a shade to pull to block out what light came in. There was a desk and chair, a dresser and a single bed with a drab cover on it. The closet was tiny and the floor had two small rugs also a drab beige, one beside the bed, the other, a little larger, had the desk sitting on it. Old and well used were the words that came to Faith as she looked around. No wonder he wanted to be out of here most of the time! Since it was a rooming house, no meals were served, no wonder he ate all his meals out!

Quickly, Matt pulled out two suitcases from the closet. Faith began taking clothes from the hangers and bringing them to the bed, while Matt went to his dresser and pulled out the things that were in the drawers. Last of all, he laid his three uniforms on top and closed the lids, then set the two cases beside the door. There was a backpack lying under the desk. He pulled that out and set it on the chair, then emptied the desk drawers into it, last of all, sliding the unopened express mail envelope inside.

He looked around the room and sighed. "Oh, I have a few things in the bathroom. I'll only be a minute."

Chuckling, Faith said, "I won't be going anywhere."

As he left the room, Faith went to the dingy window and pulled back the gray curtain to see what was outside. Dust flew out of the curtain as she pushed it back. She had to cover her nose quickly to keep the sneeze from forming. The window was a useless addition to the room. She realized the only thing it was good for was to bring in city air, probably hot in the summer and cold in the winter. There was a register, but she didn't feel any cool air coming from it. Across a narrow alley sat another building with a window staring back at her. She shuddered; glad she never had to live in something like this. Matt came back, opened one of the suitcases and stuffed the things in it, then snapped it shut without comment.

He turned to Faith with a big smile. "Ready to get out of here?"

"Absolutely! Let's go!"

It was nearly time for the kids to board the bus and Matt and Faith were still at his room at the bed and breakfast. Matt took Faith for lunch at the diner where he ate so many meals, but before they left he said goodbye to the owner and some of the staff who worked there for so many years. Time got away from them a little and now they had to hurry to get home before the kids. It didn't take long to put away Matt's few things in the big closet and dresser. However, Faith couldn't remember having so much fun in years.

The few moments of terror when the delivery man tried to molest her were all but forgotten.

Matt was emptying his backpack into the lovely rolltop desk in his room when Faith saw the express mail envelope he took out and laid on top. "What is this?" she asked, picking it up. "You had to sign for it and it came express mail."

"I think it's from some lawyer," he said, making light of it.

She grinned, looking more closely at it. "Yeah, from Tucson, Arizona. Well, by all means, get it out so you can see what's up!" She held the large envelope out to him.

He chuckled. "You mean you can't have unopened mail around?"

"No! When the mail comes, I'm out there to get it and it's opened before I get back to the house, usually. Unless it's bills and I know the envelopes they come in."

"Just like a kid at Christmas," he teased.

"Yes, that's me!"

His eyes twinkling, Matt took the envelope and laid it back on the desk. "It can wait until I get back. Even if I must send something back it can't go out until morning."

Faith sighed, "What a party pooper!"

"Yup, that's me! Besides, we gotta get home for the kids."

"Yes, I guess."

Matt chuckled and put his arm around her. He was so happy that he moved! He pushed the door lock in the knob and pulled it as they went out together. With the door closed, the hallway was dark and Matt turned Faith into his chest. He kept his arm around her, moved his other hand and combed his fingers through the hair at her temple, loving the silky texture.

With a tender smile, he bent his head and kissed her, savoring her sweetness. "You are so lovely, my sweet Faith," he murmured. The deep sounds of a grandfather clock rose to their ears as it struck three o'clock and Matt added, "I would say we must be out of here or we won't be home before the kids."

"Oh, Matt, I've had the best day with you! Having you move out here is the best thing ever!" She rose on her tiptoes and kissed him again.

"I'm glad it meets with your approval. I was bored to tears last night."

As they went to her car in the driveway, Faith handed the keys to Matt.

"I'd just as soon you drove us home. And tonight, you can drive it back here. I won't need it before the kids go to school." She chuckled. "Believe me, there was nothing boring about our house last night!"

Reluctantly, he took the keys from her and said, "Are you sure?"

"Of course! I have no long-standing sentiments about this car! It's a good serviceable car that's gotten us around for several years."

Matt pulled in the driveway only minutes before the school bus made the turn around the corner down the block. He pulled up beside the back door where Faith usually parked and they got out. It was sunny when they left in the morning, but now the clouds had moved in and it felt like rain. In fact, it was a little chilly this late in the afternoon. Matt, of course, didn't notice, but Faith felt the goose bumps on her arms before she opened the back door into the house. She pushed the door open and they enjoyed a few seconds of quietness.

Very soon they heard voices and soon the back door burst open. "Mommy!" Brandi said, excitedly, "What's that box on the front porch?"

This was the first time all day she remembered about what the delivery man had done, but she said, "I forgot about that. A delivery man brought it this morning."

"Mommy!" she scolded. "You mean you left it there *all day* and didn't open it? What is wrong with you? You never leave a package like that!"

Matt chuckled as he listened to Brandi and remembered what Faith said at his room. He guessed it was no secret that Faith opened the mail on the way in from the mailbox. "Brandi," he said, "I sort of spirited your mom away this morning. She didn't have time even to bring it in."

By now, the twins were also in the kitchen and the minute Karl saw Matt, he rushed over and hugged his legs. Knowing that Karl considered it sissy to be picked up, Matt bent over and ran his hand through the boy's hair a few times. "So how was school, big guy?" he asked. "You got that fire engine licked yet?"

"It's good! I got to play with the fire truck today!"

"That means one of us did. I never even saw one today."

TEN

Not to be outdone, Karin came shyly over and looked up at Matt. He bent a little more, reached out and scooped her up. He smiled and asked, "How was your day, Li'l Bit?"

Except for the one syllable she had said at breakfast and some soft giggles, Karin didn't make noise, but when Matt called her Li'l Bit, Karin threw her head back and laughed. She threw her arms around his neck and gave him a big slobbery kiss on his cheek, then rubbed it in with her hand. Matt also laughed, even though tears wanted to clog his throat and went to the kitchen table, pulled out a chair and sat down, putting Karin on his leg. Karl came right along and stood beside him.

"Guess I said something funny?" he asked, solemnly.

"I guess so," Karl said, softly. "She never, ever laughed like that before. The old man didn't like us makin' noise much."

Karin's hands were still around Matt's neck, but she brought her lips to his ear. He couldn't imagine what she was going to do, but he never pulled away from her. In the softest whisper, she said, "My daddy."

Immediately, Matt was completely choked up. His vocal chords were knotted in his throat. He swallowed and tears nearly worked their way from behind his eyes. He put his other hand around Karin and finally whispered, "We'll work on that, Li'l Bit."

After Brandi asked about the package she rushed out of the kitchen into the hall and opened the front door to retrieve the package. She called from there, "Mommy! I can't lift this thing! You'll have to get it."

Faith was in the laundry room running a load of clothes; Matt could hear the washer running, so he knew she didn't hear. However, Karin scrambled from Matt's leg and Karl also hurried to the hallway, so Matt followed a little more slowly. Brandi still stood by the box, but she looked up and saw him, so she said, "Matt, can you pull this box inside? I think it's even too heavy for Mommy."

"Sure, I'll get it."

"Oh, thank you!"

Remembering that the delivery man held it along with his electronic device, he was sure it wasn't heavy, but he bent over and for the sake of the children, he grunted and staggered as he lifted it. He even tipped it, letting it nearly fall off his hands, just for good measure. The children thought that was the funniest thing, seeing such a big man straining to lift a package not nearly as big as any of them, they held their sides and laughed and tears streaked their cheeks.

Faith finally heard all the noise, so she came from the laundry room to see what all the commotion was about. "What's going on?" she asked, looking at the laughing children and at Matt, now standing straight holding the package in his hands. She even scowled a little. "What's so funny about Matt holding that package?"

"Mommy!" Brandi exclaimed, still laughing, "Matt's havin' such a hard time getting that package in the house! It must be really, really heavy! You know, he barely got straightened up and brought it in before you got here."

Grinning, as she watched the big man with the package, she said, "You know what I think? I think he's putting on a show for you guys."

Faith stepped back letting go of the door, the twins came inside and Matt followed them grinning. He gave Faith a wink, meant only between adults. That, of course made her heart do flip-flops. Just before she closed the door, Brandi turned and looked out toward her swing hanging on the big tree. Large drops of rain were coming down, so she sighed, "Oh, we can't play outside, it's raining! We barely got home and it rains! Bummer."

"You know where you can play," Faith said. "Take Karl and Karin downstairs until supper's ready. Why don't you?"

"Oh, yes! Come on, guys! We'll have lots of fun and we won't get wet."

Knowing that nothing had ever been said about what was downstairs, as the cellar door closed behind Brandi, Matt asked, "What's downstairs?"

Grinning, Faith said, "A big dollhouse Max made for Brandi when she was tiny, it has everything, including painted furniture and people and a realistic looking dog and because he loved them so much, a train set he set up for the big boys to play with." Faith laughed, as she saw the look on Matt's face. Immediately, she added, "I'll be okay with supper, Matt, if you want to go down and help Karl play with the trains."

Putting his hands on her arms and kissing her, he said, "You won't mind?"

Giggling, she said, "Pre-breaded chicken fingers, French fries, cold slaw, chocolate cupcakes and coolaid can't be too hard. I can manage a pot of coffee for the grownups. Go on! It's the kind of stuff I fix all the time for Brandi and me, I'll just triple the amount I usually use."

Matt chuckled, as he turned toward the door beside the pantry. "Thanks, Love, I haven't played with trains since I was a kid."

Faith stood with her mouth hanging open as she watched the door close behind him. Once he spoke, he never looked back, but stepped down and closed the door. She heard the name he called her. Her mouth finally went shut and she swallowed. It had been three years since she was called anything besides 'Faith' or 'Mommy' and the word Matt said sounded like the most natural thing in the world for him to say. A tear slid down her cheek, as she whispered, "He called me, 'Love'. I know he did!"

She stood staring at the door for several minutes. Finally, in slow motion, she turned back to her refrigerator and opened it, but didn't take anything out. *Is that how he feels? Does he love me? I'm not beautiful, I have liabilities. He's a single, very handsome man he could have any beautiful woman he wanted.* Insecurities kept dancing through her head. She was a widow, past thirty, with a child, now she had two extra children she was mothering. How could Matt, or any man, for that matter, want to call her 'Love'? However, the overpowering thought that conquered all the others burst upon her whole body. *I love him!*

With a smile on her face, she set the table for five. It was a large table, it could easily accommodate more. She set Matt at the head and Karl at the foot. Brandi and Karin sat beside each other with their backs to the windows and she set her own place with her back to the kitchen so she could easily get to the refrigerator or the stove in case she had forgotten anything. She smiled again, she'd love to use candles and rush out to her tiny flower bed for a few flowers to make the table special, but she'd only inspire questions from the little people that she didn't think should be asked yet. A celebration could wait.

It was much later that Matt turned the key in the lock for his room at the bed and breakfast. It was a rewarding day. He had his wish; he played with the kids for a while and helped put them to bed. While Faith read a story to the girls, he sat on Karl's bed and let him climb on his lap while he read a story. Faith had several wonderful picture storybooks, all telling Bible stories. He decided he'd learn right along with Karl. That thought excited him.

He also had another of his wishes. After the lights were out in the children's rooms, he and Faith tiptoed downstairs into the living room. She sat on the couch, but left nothing to his imagination, she patted the seat beside her and he sat in it, sliding his arm across the back as he sat. Only moments later, he gathered her in his arms for a long, wonderful kiss. It seemed he couldn't stop kissing her now that he started. *Not that I want to*, he thought. He smiled, because she was the most kissable woman and WOW! did she respond! Yes, sir, she was his cup of tea!

As he stripped and went in the bath for a shower, he smiled. As he let the wonderfully warm water sluice over his body, he sighed. Tomorrow at this time he'd also be preparing for sleep, but wouldn't know if he could sleep uninterrupted until morning or be roused by the horn to make a midnight dash to save a building or some lives. It was his job, what he got paid to do. He wanted to be a fireman for a long time, it was a challenging profession, but he couldn't say he loved it. Not any more.

The question still not far from anyone's mind who lived in or around New York City was: 'Would terrorists strike again and if so, where, when and how?' He knew lots of people still lived in terror. Others were going about their business as if nothing had happened. Many others were grieving a death in the family. He thought perhaps he was somewhere in the middle, of course, he wasn't grieving a loved one. As a fireman, you took each day as it comes, you put out fires if you can or contain what you can't put out and you by all means save the people you can. His heart hurt again as he remembered the thousands of people who were lost during that catastrophe on nine eleven, including the many firemen who were the first responders. The mayor was still debating who would be the new fire chief.

As he brushed his teeth and shaved, he grinned at his reflection in the mirror. Maybe he wouldn't be using the second part of what this house was advertised for. He was invited enthusiastically by three little people and one big person to come back for breakfast. He willingly agreed, because he must leave while the children were still in school. He wanted to be there even earlier, he wondered how much work she had to do to get the kids ready for school. At least now he knew they rode a bus to school.

Tomorrow at breakfast would be the only time for twenty-four hours he'd see them. He wouldn't see the kids again until suppertime on Thursday. Tears tried to work their way around his eyes, but he blinked them away. Karin called him 'my daddy'. Only he had heard her and what he said in response hadn't given any hint to Karl, but it was a very special moment for him. He never in his life was called 'Daddy', and to think a non-verbal child said it.

He rushed over to the bed, picked up the phone on the night stand and dialed a number. On the second ring a soft voice answered, "Hello?"

"Hi, Love. Are you just about asleep?"

"Well, I'm in bed. I had my devotions."

"Hmm, I still need to do that, but I really wanted to call and talk for a minute."

"It's great for you to call, Honey."

He swallowed; she called him 'honey'! The thoughts those words conjured up in his mind were not thoughts he should dwell on today. However, the thoughts did things to his body he knew couldn't be fulfilled for an unspecified period of time. He never was in her room, but as nice as Karl's room was, he knew hers must be lovely, like her. His imagination showed him a large bed with creamy white sheets, several fluffy pillows and in the center, with curls fanning out on those pillows, holding a phone receiver to her ear was a lovely, smiling lady....

He cleared his throat, before he could say, "I just showered in this magnificent bath. That's a luxury I never had back there on Manhattan." He chuckled, "I didn't have to wait my turn to get in tonight, either."

"I know. If the size of your room was any indication of the size of the bathroom, it was miniscule. How many of you had to share it, anyway?"

"Depending on the number of renters, but as many as six. As you can imagine, we took short showers, the hot water didn't always go all the way around."

"Wow! I'm so glad you have that room and that it's so close to us." Her voice took on a wistful sound, as she said, "Matt, thanks for calling."

"I wouldn't miss it! I'll see you in the morning."

"Yes, I'll be expecting you, good night."

"Goodnight." As he replaced the phone on the cradle, he added, "Sweetheart." Of course, the receiver was far enough from his face he was sure she didn't hear him.

After savoring the few minutes with Faith on the phone, he went to the desk and pulled out the chair. He picked up the express mail envelope, opened it and pulled out the cards and a single sheet inside. There was also another express mail envelope folded inside, so Matt knew he must sign whatever the lawyer sent and return it. He was surprised, the return envelope already had postage, so all Matt had to do was find a mailbox and put it in. That was easy, things could be taken care of fast. He still couldn't believe he was his aunt's beneficiary!

Matt opened the lawyer's letter and read:

> Dear Mr. Barns,
> Enclosed please find the documents you need to sign. There are several CDs that need a signature. I assume that since you cannot come to Tucson, that you will not be able to cash out these documents at the local bank. If you will sign and return these forms, I will take them to the banks involved and have them wire the money to whatever bank you designate. Miss Germain specified that all her hard assets be liquidated, which we have done. This money was used to take care of her final expenses and my fees.
> What you see enclosed is free of any indebtedness and is for you to dispose of as you wish.
> I will be looking forward to hearing from you at your earliest convenience.
> Thank you, Arnold B. Cochran.

Matt laid the letter aside and pulled out several small cards and as he looked at each one his eyes grew larger. By the last one, he knew when this money was transferred to his bank he would be a very wealthy man. Actually, if he didn't want to let it sit and grow marginally in the bank, he should either invest it or he could use it to start a business, something he thought about on several occasions. He wrote the name of his bank and his account number on each card then wrote his name below that. He wouldn't have writer's cramp, but it would be close! After he put everything back in the express mail envelope, he sealed it and went to bed, still not sure what to do when the money actually arrived at his bank As his eyes closed, he knew he had a few days to think about it.

Matt and Faith stood on the porch and watched the children run down the drive toward the road to catch the bus for school. Each of them had a brightly colored book bag on his back and Brandi and Karl carried their lunch boxes. Karin held Brandi's free hand, but Karl ran ahead, set his lunch box on the ground and jumped onto the swing. They couldn't hear what Brandi said, but Karl only took two turns of back and forth before he jumped off, picked up his lunch box and ran after the girls. Of course, they were lost to sight before they reached the road, but they heard the engine noise of the minibus.

Faith sighed, "That's it for another school day!"

Matt looked at his watch, as they went back inside. "What'll we do till one thirty? I sure don't have anything else to move."

"I'm so glad you moved out of that place! It was depressing."

Faith went to the coffee maker and brought back the carafe. She cleared all the dishes to the sink except their two mugs, since they hadn't had a second cup yet. She filled them and splashed some milk into hers, then quickly loaded the dishwasher and came back to sit down in her seat. "I know you know the way from the train station to the church and here really well, but how about a drive down to the shore?"

"Sure! We wouldn't pass the bed and breakfast on the way to the train station if we came right from the shore, would we?"

"No, but I could pack a lunch then we can stop there on the way so you can pick up your uniform. If you want, you can change at the train station and I bring your clothes home to wash. Those and any others, actually."

Swallowing the last of his coffee and placing the mug on the table none to softly, he said, "You're on, Lady! That sounds like a fantastic day."

"Great!"

Soon, they were in her car, with Faith behind the wheel, Matt insisted, since she knew the way she wanted to go to the shore. They stopped briefly at the bed and breakfast and he came out with his backpack and his uniform on a hanger, which he hung in front of the back window. He slid in beside her, moving his arm across the back of the seat as he did. She turned her smiling face toward him, as she watched the driveway behind her and backed onto the street.

The rain overnight cooled the air, but the sun was shining brightly. Faith wore a sweater, but Matt was sure before they came back that it would disappear. After all, she wouldn't need it if he had his arm around her and he intended to do that for most of the day. As far as he was concerned, if he didn't have to let this lady out of his sight, he'd be a happy man!

Thomaston wasn't far from the Long Island Sound and soon Faith drove down to the parking lot close to the public beach. It was Wednesday, just passed the middle of September. There weren't very many cars parked in the lot and only a handful of people on the beach. Most everyone worked at nine to five jobs, either in Thomaston or in the city and children were in school. There were a few women out pushing baby carriages and some older people doing some power walking on the sand. When Faith opened the trunk to pull out the cooler she packed, Matt grabbed it, while Faith pulled out the blanket beside it.

They made their way toward the water and Matt noted that the sand farther away from the water was damp, so the tide was going out. They spread the blanket on the dry sand then held it down with the cooler, but before she did anything else, Faith sat down and pulled off her sandals, so Matt took off his shoes.

She looked up and said, "I hate getting sand in my shoes. It doesn't matter that sandals are so open sand still sticks to my feet. Besides, I love the feel of sand on my bare feet."

Smiling, Matt said, "I know what you mean. Of course, in Montana, where I grew up, we didn't have any salt water, just creeks and lakes. Also, we didn't have waves or tides to contend with like there's plenty of here. Still, I've become addicted to the ocean. On my days off I used to go to Connecticut with some buddies and spend time at a fishing cabin."

"Oh, I bet that was fun!"

"Well, it was until I met a certain auburn-haired lady who also has an auburn-haired daughter. Have any idea who those two could be?"

Pink crept up Faith's cheeks. "Umm, could their last name be Lankaster?"

Matt pulled her to his side and kissed her forehead, before he said, "You know, I do believe that was the name I heard."

They joined those that were walking on the sand, but they didn't do any power walking. Matt immediately put his arm around Faith and they set a leisurely pace. Faith loved the beach and what better way than to spend the warmest part of the day with the man she loved? Even though there was city very close to them, right here, right now, they felt as if they were in a world all their own, with hardly a care to effect them. Faith's head had finally caught up with her heart and acknowledged that she was in love. If this man could love her, with all her liabilities, she would happily spend the rest of her life showing him her love.

There was a gentle breeze off the water and at first, Faith was glad for her sweater, but as the sun rose higher and before they returned to the blanket for lunch, she shed it and tied it around her waist. Matt was right, his arm snuggling her close to his side and the sun shining warmly down on them, warmed her quite well. Besides, she'd much rather feel his arm around her without the sweater in the way.

Soon after lunch, it was time to pack up and head to the Thomaston train station. When they arrived, Matt took his uniform and backpack into the station to the restroom. When he came out moments later, Faith's heart skipped a beat. Her handsome, cocky fireman was back. He smiled at her, there was a twinkle in his eye, as she came to him and they walked back to her car for him to put his backpack inside. They were only on the platform a few minutes when they heard the train whistle. He knew it was inevitable, but he didn't have to like it, no, not one bit!

No others were on the platform, so Matt took Faith tenderly in his arms and hugged her close. She put her arms around him and lifted her face. He, of course, immediately lowered his head and as the train whistled into the station, they were still sharing a long kiss. The hissing, steaming brakes brought them back to reality.

Putting his finger under her chin, he said, "I'll do my best to call you about nine thirty, Love. Tell the kids goodnight for me."

"I will, you be safe and come right out. We'll be here about four thirty waiting for you tomorrow." However, she didn't say the words she wanted to: *I love you.*

She smiled and waved as he strode the last few feet to the train. She stayed right where she was and saw him sit down in a seat and scoot over by the window. As the train slowly began to move, she waved and he waved back, he had to admit he was missing her very much already, his arm felt extremely empty. Before he lost her from view, he kissed his hand and sent it to her. His eyes were glued on her until the train moved around the corner.

She sighed and sent him her own back. "I love that man," she murmured. "I love him with all my heart."

Faith went home, intent on working on Karl's bedspread she dropped on Tuesday and hadn't had a minute to return to since. In a matter of days her life was full and wonderful. She parked beside the house, there were kids clubs and ladies Bible study tonight. She knew Matt wanted to go to a Bible study when he could, but it wouldn't be this week. She opened the trunk for the cooler. They shook out the blanket very well, so she decided to leave it, there might be another nice day when she and Matt could go back to the beach. As she headed for the back door with the cooler, she sighed, she hadn't had such a happy two days in a very long time. Tomorrow, before he came home she needed to clean, but tomorrow was soon enough.

Inside the kitchen, she set the cooler on the floor, in case there was still some sand on the bottom. Quickly, she emptied it, wiped it out and put it in the back of the pantry, then headed into the hall to the bathroom. It wasn't until she returned to the kitchen that she noticed the red light flashing on her answering machine.

She pushed the button, wondering who would call while they were gone and listened, with a sinking heart, as the voice said, "Mrs. Lankaster, this is Maranda Fulton of Child Protection Agency here in Thomaston. I was informed that you are housing twins, a brother and sister. I need to get with you at your earliest convenience. My office hours are eight to five, Monday through Friday. Please call immediately to set up a time so we can discuss this." She left two phone numbers, and then she added, "You have a good day."

"Mmm," Faith groused, "I'm sure I'll have a good day after that. Have a good day? What in the world does the child protection…"

She poured the rest of the tea from the thermos they took on their picnic into a glass and sat down at the kitchen table. Matt would be back tomorrow about four thirty. She didn't want to meet anyone about the children until he could go with her. She guessed that Pastor Jim would be a good one to go along, too. She looked at her watch, there was over an hour until the children came home, so she reached for the phone.

"Marian, would you put me through to Pastor Jim, please?"

"Sure, Faith. Those twins are the cutest little buttons I ever saw! You're doing great with them, girl! Pastor went in his office; hold on a minute, he'll pick up."

"Hi, Faith, what can I do for you?" his voice came immediately on the line.

She heard the click as Marian disconnected, so she said, "Pastor, Matt and I've been gone today until now when I put him on the train for his shift on Manhattan. I walked in and my answering machine was blinking. The message was from some woman with Thomaston's Child Protection Agency. She wants to meet with me."

Acting a little irate, Jim exclaimed, "What for? Child Protection…?"

Faith tried to curb her groan, those words and what on earth they could mean sent her heart into a frantic rhythm. However, she said, "Jim, Maryann Swain cornered me Sunday night and asked about the twins. I didn't tell her much only that they were with me because of the church's foundling ministry. However…."

Jim let out a long sigh, before he said, "You don't need to say anything more, Faith. It's anyone's guess how it grew from there. You and I both know how she likes to gossip." He sighed again, "Have you called this woman? Now that she's found out somehow, I'm afraid we'll have to meet with her."

"No, I called you first. She says her office hours are eight to five, but I don't want to meet with her without you and Matt there, too."

"Good. When will he be back?"

"His shift is over at three tomorrow, but of course he can't get here until about four thirty. He'll be free all day on Friday."

Faith could hear him shuffling papers, but he said, "You call that woman back and set it up for Friday sometime. It won't matter to me, I'll clear whatever I have and go with you. Those kids need to stay where they are."

"Thanks, Jim that makes me feel really good."

"Of course!" Jim said fiercely. There wasn't anyone better to care for the twins than the lady who had them now! It didn't matter one whit that she was a single mom. He grinned, he didn't think that would last much longer. They finished their conversation and Jim hung up.

Faith hung up, then waited a few minutes. However, she decided to get the nasty task over with as soon as possible, especially before the kids came home, so she called the number the woman left. A woman answered on the second ring, identifying the agency. Faith asked to speak with Ms Fulton and soon the woman came on the line. Just by the way she answered the phone Faith was not impressed with her.

Faith said, "Ms Fulton, this is Faith Lankaster. I'm returning your call."

A heavy smoker's voice answered her, "Yes, Mrs. Lankaster. Would you be able to come in tomorrow?"

Not liking the woman's voice, Faith answered, "No, my day's already tied up, but Friday would be all right. Why the urgency, anyway?" she asked.

The woman cleared her throat. "I should think you'd know the answer to that!" she exclaimed, but wouldn't tell her anything else.

"No, I really don't," Faith said, honestly. "From your message and what you're saying now, I'm not sure I want to know, either. Perhaps I'll wait for my answer until Friday. What time should we have this meeting?"

"How about nine? Will that work for you?"

"Yes."

"You'll bring the twins?"

Knowing that would be the worst thing to do, she answered, "Oh, no! No, they're in school. I'll see you at nine on Friday." She hung up before the woman could say anything else.

She walked in her den and sat down at the sewing machine. Around her feet was the material that Karl picked out. The thought circled through her mind that there might not be a reason to finish the bedspread the children might be taken away from her after the meeting on Friday. She immediately squelched that thought. She'd have two men with her, both of whom told her there was no better place for the twins than where they were right now. No, she would absolutely not have that thought!

She watched the clock and as the little clock on the desk flashed three o'clock, she reached for the phone and dialed information to get the number for Matt's fire station. She couldn't wait until he called at nine thirty. It was only minutes after three when her call went through to the commander's office. After the man identified the station, Faith asked, "Is Matt Barns available so that I could speak with him a minute?"

"Ah, yes, I see him out in the bay, just a minute I'll call him in."

Soon, a voice she loved to hear answered, "Barns, here."

"Hi, Matt, I won't keep you long, I know you're busy, but I had to tell you."

"What is it, Love?" She could tell he had his other hand around the receiver.

Unconsciously, she put hers around her receiver also. She cleared her throat, it unnerved her to think someone had turned her in to an agency about protecting children. "When I got home there was a message on the answering machine from the Thomaston Child Protection. The woman wants to meet me at my earliest convenience."

Anger welled up in his chest and with difficulty he kept it under wraps, as he said, "What did you do about that?"

"I called Pastor Jim right away. He said I should make the appointment for Friday when both you and he could go with me."

"Absolutely!" he exclaimed. "Think it was that blabber-mouth Sunday night who got hold of someone in that department?"

"Yes, I think it was, even though I didn't tell her hardly anything. I called the woman back and it's set for nine on Friday."

"You know I'll be there! Thanks for calling, Love. I miss you."

"Oh, yes! I miss you, too."

She didn't have time to say goodbye when she heard the horn start blaring. It sent her heart into overdrive. Of course Matt didn't say goodbye, only seconds later, the line went dead and Faith knew her man was racing to the locker room to suit up and jump on the fire truck. She prayed for him right then that he'd be safe. This was the second time they were talking when the horn went off and he had to run. She wasn't sure she'd call the fire station too often, that horn sent chills up her back.

By now, she had the hem sewed on two of the long pieces, so she put the third piece under the needle. As soon as this one was hemmed, she could put everything together. She made the bedspreads in the girls' room several years ago. The piece on top was flat, but the three parts that hung to the floor were gathered and frilly. However, she knew this one would be different. When she cut the pieces she decided to pleat the sides as she attached them to the top piece. It would add fullness over blankets, but it wouldn't look like a girl's bedspread. She hoped Karl would like it, but she decided it'd have to do if he didn't.

She was still in the den when Brandi called from the back door, "Mommy, we're home! We're thirsty, can we have some coolaid and then can we swing?"

"Yes," she called, "that's fine."

Curious as ever, Brandi, with the twins following came looking for her.

No one had to say anything, because Karl scooted into the room. His eyes turned to saucers as he saw what she was doing. "Oh, WOW! That's my bedcover!"

"Yes, it is, Karl, I have it almost done. We can put it on your bed really soon."

"Cool!" His eyes sparkled, as he looked up at Faith.

He took a step then hesitated, but Faith saw his action. Her heart turned over, so she bent over and held out her arms over the fabric on the floor. A smile covering the frog in her throat, she whispered, "Could I have a kiss, do you think?"

The little boy threw his arms out wide, then took that step and hugged her fiercely. "Yeah, a real big one!" He bestowed a wet kiss on her cheek. Faith, of course, pulled him closer and returned a kiss to his cheek. This was one of the most satisfying parts of being a mother. Kids loved to be loved and when they felt secure, they returned that love in spades.

Not to have Karl do it all, Karin waded right in beside him and before Faith could straighten up after Karl let go, Karin threw her arms out and wrapped them around Faith's neck. She deposited her own wet kiss on Faith's cheek. The little girl's eyes were sparkling as she kept her arms around her neck, but leaned back to look at her. Faith was sure the child didn't need to say a word her eyes told her how much she knew she was loved. Faith wrapped both arms around the children and gave them each another kiss.

Faith smiled at the little girl and said, "Thank you, Karin! Both your kisses are great. Why don't you both go with Brandi and get your drink. I'm sure you're thirsty after riding the bus home. You'll have a good long time out on the swing while I finished this bedspread and get supper for us."

"'Kay!" Karl crowed, as the two children skipped from the room, following Brandi.

From the kitchen, Faith heard, "Oh, look, guys, it's grape!" Yes, it was grape, Brandi's favorite but Faith's least favorite. Fortunately now there were three who could drink it and she wouldn't have to help out before the stuff went sour.

Faith decided as soon as she listened to the woman's message to erase it and not tell the children. There was no reason to traumatize them, and very possibly, nothing would come of it by the time she and Matt and Pastor got done with the woman. She only wondered how she could be civil with Maryann this evening in her Bible study. She sent up a quick prayer about it.

Only a few minutes later, she had the last piece sewed to finish the bedspread. It was a huge wad of fabric; it had to be for a double bed. She looked at the clock on the desk and knew she had to hurry, so she shut off the machine and grabbed up the wad that was partly in her lap. She turned off the light as she left the room and headed immediately for the stairs. She only pulled the bed clothes together this morning there hadn't been time after the kids left for school.

That meant she had to make Karl's bed first before putting the bedspread on. She dropped the spread in the chair close to the bed and quickly arranged the sheet and cover, then threw the spread over it all. Immediately, she hurried downstairs to start supper. Again tonight supper was for speed and comfort and to fill three hungry tummies, not really of great nutritional value – save that for another time.

Faith was glad that everything the twins did at church was in the same room. Their Sunday school class met in the kindergarten room and Wednesday night club also met there. The only thing that changed from one time to the other was the teacher. She took them, Brandi stopped off at her own room on the way, so she could introduce the twins to their club teacher.

Faith stopped in the doorway, but Karl and Karin walked right in. They both looked at the new teacher, but they were very familiar with this room now, so they went on to do other things. Faith turned to the teacher and said, "Elli, Karl and Karin have come to live with Brandi and me. They've been coming to kindergarten this week, so they're pretty familiar with this room. Just so you know, Karin doesn't talk, but she knows what you say and understands perfectly. Karl doesn't say much, but he does talk and he'll often answer for Karin. I figured you needed to know this ahead of time."

The pretty lady smiled. "Thanks, Faith, good to know. We'll have a good time, we always do. On such a nice evening, we'll probably be outside when you finish Bible study."

"Great! I'll see you later."

Praying as she left them and walked to the church lounge that she be at least civil to Maryann, she walked in the room. Maryann was already there and of course she sat beside one of her favorite friends, but as Faith walked through the doorway, she stopped talking and gave her a saccharine sweet smile. Faith tried hard to cover the shudder that went up her spine.

Before she even found a seat - one as far from Maryann as possible - the woman said, "Hi, Faith, how are the twins? You do still have them, don't you?"

"Just fine, Maryann, thanks." She sat down and quickly pulled her study guide from the back of her Bible and began reading. She was not about to tell the woman anything, especially not about the phone call. If that piece of information never surfaced it was fine!

Maryann, because she liked to hear herself talk, usually dominated the Bible study hour. The leader was not a forceful woman, she only interrupted her occasionally, but because Faith had read her lesson thoroughly and also didn't want to hear Maryann talk too much, she determined not to let Maryann have all the say tonight. She prayed before the discussion leader came that God would help her to be tactful; something Maryann often was not.

By the end of the hour Faith had accomplished her goal. Maryann was frustrated several times and when the buzzer sounded that the clubs were over, the leader didn't ask her to pray. Several other women agreed with Faith and didn't care for Maryann, so they helped Faith carry the load of conversation. Faith was pleased with the way the study turned out.

Knowing that Maryann would try to corner her again, as she had Sunday evening and Faith had no intention of talking to her, she skipped out quickly and hurried down the hall toward the door leading outside. The door leading to that playground was at the end of the educational building, but the door to the parking lot where Maryann parked wasn't near as far. Faith turned the corner at the end of the hall as the other ladies reached the door to the parking lot.

Faith turned and disappeared from sight for all the other ladies, but she heard, "Faith, wait, I need to talk to you." Faith didn't even grace the sentence with an answer she kept on and hurried out onto the playground. When she reached the playing area, she was giggling she saw the look on Maryann's face in the classroom. She knew the woman was totally frustrated, Faith could only laugh. "Thanks, Lord!" she exclaimed outside the door. "You more than helped me accomplish my goal! I think the other ladies and I had a great Bible study!"

Elli looked up to see who came through the door and saw Faith's lips move. Grinning, she said, "What, talking to yourself?"

Faith laughed. "Having five year old twins and an always-on-the-move nine year old will do that to you!"

Elli nodded. "I can just imagine! We had a great time this evening! Hey, kids, it's time to get on the move. Your parents'll be here any minute."

"Yeah, we know!" some loud-mouth little boy yelled.

It was eight o'clock, Friday morning. Matt filled bowls with cereal, while Brandi pulled out the milk, and orange juice and Faith took down the glasses for the drinks. The coffeemaker wheezed and Faith pulled out two mugs for her and Matt. After the first meal that Matt ate with them at the house, the children claimed their seats and now they were eager to fill their tummies. Sometimes, Faith ate when the children did, but usually, she had coffee before they left, since she also had to fix lunches. However, while she made three lunches, Matt pulled out a bag of bagels and the cream cheese for Faith's breakfast and fixed himself some fruit as well as cereal.

They stood on the porch and waved to the children as they ran down the drive to catch the bus, but as they disappeared over the rise, Faith turned into Matt's chest and hugged him. He felt her arms tighten around his waist, so he tightened his hold on her and asked, "What is it, Love? You seem distressed."

"Oh," she whispered, "I can't bear the thought that we might loose them!"

Fiercely, he put his finger under her chin and raised her head so she had to look at him. "Don't even consider it, Love! What in heaven's name could be a reason for that to happen?"

"I don't know, Honey, I don't know, but it's so scary thinking about it." *Time stood still.*

He looked at her, his lips only inches from hers. "You called me 'Honey'!" he murmured. "Did you know that?"

Uncertainly, she looked into his eyes. "Was that okay?"

His arms tightened around her and his lips captured hers. Moments later, when he raised his head, he said, "Oh, yes! It was the best name I've ever in my whole life been called!"

The mantel clock in the living room started the first half of the Westminster chime and Matt said, "Sounds like we better move. I think we need a few minutes to meet Pastor first."

"Yes, we sure do! I'll get my purse and keys."

He chuckled, as she handed him the keys then allowed him to help her into the passenger seat. As she raised her legs to put them inside, he said, "You know, I'll need to get myself a car or some rag-tag thing if I'm living here. I'll park at the station so you won't have to come wait for hours like you did yesterday and at the B and B when I'm there, it'll get me here sooner."

"We don't mind at all. Believe me, the kids watch every train that comes through and ask if that's your train. Even if it's going the wrong way!" She shook her head. "That first time you came out I nearly lost them! Brandi was dragging them behind her. They were really disgruntled when they learned it wasn't your train."

As he started up, he said, fiercely, "I mind that you had to wait two hours for me yesterday! You had already left when I was able to call, so you sat there at the station waiting all that time. It was such a waste! The kids could have played at home and not cooped up in that car and you could get supper. Perhaps after this meeting we can go to auto sales row and see about getting something for me to drive." Another thought came to him, as he drove downtown. *Actually, what we really need is an SUV big enough for a family. Faith could have that and I could use her puddle jumper on my trips to the B and B and the station. In a day or three I can easily afford that.* He didn't say anything out loud, but the thought made perfect sense.

"Well, if you insist."

Nodding, he grinned and said, "Yes, I insist."

With a little help from Faith, since Matt was not totally familiar with downtown, they pulled into the parking lot outside the building where the Child Protection Agency was housed. Pastor Jim was already there and stepped from his car immediately when he saw Faith's car drive in. Matt pulled right beside the pastor's car and motioned for the man to get in with them.

As soon as he was seated, Matt said, "Pastor, Faith's a little scared, could you pray for this meeting this morning?"

Immediately, he reached over the seat and took both their hands, so quickly, Matt and Faith completed the circle. "Of course! I feel we need divine guidance to say the right words to stop this wicked thing! Heavenly Father, please be in this meeting this morning. You know what is at stake here, we have no idea. You lead our words and keep us focused on what needs to be said and perhaps what needs not to be said. Guard our lips, Lord. Thank You for Your guidance and direction. In Your Son's Name, amen."

Faith breathed a sigh and said, "Thanks, Pastor, I guess we better go, we surely don't want to be late."

The three exited the car and Jim said, "No, we better not be, even though we don't really know what's going on."

They walked in the building and looked at the directory to find where the office was, then took the elevator up to the third floor. It seemed the whole floor housed the Child Protection Agency. It must be a big department and there must be a much bigger need in Thomaston than any of the three realized. The pastor opened the door with the opaque glass window and then Matt followed Faith, with the pastor coming last. There were several seats, but most of the chairs were already full.

A young woman smiled as Faith stopped at her desk and said, "Yes, may I help you? Could you give me your name?"

"I'm Faith Lankaster; I have an appointment with Ms. Fulton this morning at nine o'clock. I guess we're a few minutes early."

"That's fine, I'll call her. Who are these gentlemen?"

"This is Mr. Matt Barns and this is Pastor Jim Harding. They've come with me for this meeting with Ms. Fulton."

"Have a seat, I'll call Ms. Fulton." At least this woman was friendly.

ELEVEN

MATT'S WATCH BEEPED THE HOUR AND A DOOR OPENED. A WOMAN ABOUT MATT'S age came toward them, looking only at Faith, holding out her hand, a briefcase at her side. Both men rose along with Faith, the woman's smiling face immediately turned to a deep scowl. "Good morning, I'm Maranda Fulton. I presume you're Mrs. Lankaster and these men are...?"

"Yes," Faith stepped back next to Matt; it felt like the woman was crowding her, trying to intimidate her. "This is Matt Barns, he's with FDNY and this is our pastor, Jim Harding."

Her scowl only deepening, the woman looked between the two men and asked, "And why have you come? What is the reason for that?"

Jim looked around at the large reception area that, at the moment, had several other people sitting in it and the receptionist who sat at her desk looking at the four with open interest and said, "Surely you have an office or a conference room where we could meet with you to discuss whatever needs to be said?"

The woman cleared her throat, looking for the first time at Jim and realizing immediately that her intimidation tactics weren't working and said, "Yes. Yes, I do. Come this way."

It was obvious to Faith and the two men that the woman planned on a speedy meeting, perhaps even there in the reception area, in front of everyone there, overwhelming Faith and doing as she pleased with the twins. However, all four of them knew nothing would happen to the twins, since they weren't there.

The woman walked first, very purposefully, her briefcase snug at her side. Matt had his hand on the small of Faith's back, she was extremely happy for his support and the pastor came last. Faith's heart pounded, she had a bad feeling about this meeting ever since she listened to her answering machine on Wednesday. The woman's message and the way she spoke to Faith on Wednesday were menacing and the few words spoken so far this morning weren't the least bit cordial. The woman was unfriendly, almost antagonistic, especially when she heard that one of the men was a minister. Faith was convinced the woman had man issues and most probably issues with anything that related to church or religion, too. It didn't matter to Faith, she was extremely glad that she had the total support of these two men.

Maranda led them into a smaller room with a table in the center and seven chairs around it. It was an unpleasant room, with four plain white walls and two long fluorescent lights against the ceiling that began buzzing when the woman flipped the switch, there were no windows or pictures. Obviously she hadn't planned to use the room for this meeting; there wasn't a pitcher of water or glasses. Maranda went to the head of the table, expecting the others to find a chair.

Matt took Faith around the table and held the chair for her, while Jim took a seat in a chair on the side near the door. Faith wasn't even seated, before Maranda said, arrogantly, "Now then, Mrs. Lankaster, since this meeting was to be *you* and *me* discussing the twins you are housing, tell me why are these *men* here?"

Praying in her heart for wisdom and strength, she replied, "First of all, I think you owe me an explanation as to *why* we needed this meeting at all. The other day, when I called to make this appointment at your request you told me it should be obvious why this meeting was necessary. I had no idea then and even a day and a half later, I have no idea why you called me, other than it has something to do with the twins I am housing."

Stalling for time, Ms Fulton took her eyes from Faith and focused for several minutes on her briefcase which she still held. She set it on the table, clicking it open. She raised the lid, effectively hiding behind it for a few seconds. She shuffled through several folders, finally pulled one out, then deliberately closed up the case and set it on the floor. She laid the folder on the table in front of her and opened it. Inside was a single sheet of paper. Faith was close enough to see it was blank.

Finally, looking up, she said, "Ma'am, that's precisely why I wanted a meeting. You're housing twins, you are a single woman therefore, I have no idea why these *men* are here." The woman cleared her throat. "Usually when there's a case for the protection agency, if there's a *man* involved…" Her voice faded away, but the others in the room understood her meaning. However, she had not answered Faith's question.

Becoming irate because of Maranda's insinuation, Faith exclaimed, "Fine, you like to stall and not give an answer! I've had a few dealings with bureaucrats, no one wants to answer questions that are asked in a straight-forward manner. Yes, I'm a single mother. Mr. Barns found the twins when he was putting out a fire that's why he's here. Pastor Harding is the pastor of our church. It is through a program of our church that the twins are with me. I will say no more until you tell us plainly why you called for this meeting."

The woman obviously thought she'd have the upper hand when she met with Faith. She looked from Faith to Matt and then to Jim, who were looking back at her, without saying anything. Maranda cleared her throat. When no one else said anything, she turned back to her briefcase, lifted it again to the table, raised the lid and shuffled through it for several minutes before she finally pulled out a pen. Faith decided it must be her favorite, why else would she waste so much time finding it? Of course, the most obvious reason was that she was stalling.

Clearing her throat, latched the briefcase and put it on the floor again before she put a few scratches on the paper, then cleared her throat again and said, "I had a message on my voicemail on Wednesday morning when I arrived at work that there was some irregularity about the placement of some children in your home. It wasn't said in so many words that there was abuse involved, but it was strongly implied. That was why I called you originally and wanted you to bring the *children with you* to this meeting. Of course, we should have met before this!"

Scowling, Jim Harding asked, "Did this person identify themselves?"

Drumming the pen against the paper, she dropped her eyes and said, "Um, well, yes, but I don't think that's relevant here."

Jim leaned forward, his elbows on the table and looked directly at Maranda. "If the accusation is false, you don't think there should be some identification?"

Maranda cleared her throat again and said, "I told you, the person did identify herself. However, I don't think it's relevant to this meeting now."

"I see. It was a *woman*, however, that's what you're saying."

Clearing her throat, realizing she was now at a disadvantage and knowing she shouldn't have even made reference to the sex of the caller, she said, "Um, yes, that's true."

Speaking quickly, so Jim couldn't pursue his thought, Maranda said, "What have you done with these children, Mrs. Lankaster? You should have brought them in, just like I asked."

"What have I been doing with them?"

Maranda was obviously unnerved by being asked her own question. She swallowed noticeably before she said, "Yes. That's what I asked you."

Acting as if the question was totally foolish, Faith said, "They arrived here in Thomaston at our church on Friday in time for supper with only the clothes on their backs. They were clean, but very hungry. The church supplied them with a few pieces of clothing apiece and we fed them supper. I took them home and put them to bed. Saturday, Mr. Barns and I took them shopping for some more clothes, not an exorbitant amount, but enough to have several changes. Sunday he and I took them to church and Sunday school, *since that is our way of life*. They were in an age appropriate class. Monday I took them to the same school my daughter goes to and enrolled them in kindergarten where they have been going and are there now. Their teacher is quite pleased with their progress, I might add."

Her lip curling, the woman said, "You *made* them go to church?" Maranda obviously wanted her words to feel like a slap in Faith's face. Faith had no trouble determining that was her wish as she looked back.

Faith looked straight into those hard eyes and said, "Ms. Fulton, as I said, it has been my way of life for as long as I can remember that I was in church whenever it is open, both my late husband and I were raised that way. We took our daughter to church with us from the Sunday after she was born. Believe me, my daughter, who is nine, wouldn't miss her Sunday school class for anything. She took the twins and we followed along to the classroom where their age met. Yes, we *took* them *with us* to church, we didn't *make* them go. They came away very excited about their class."

"I see." The coldness and the hardness didn't change. Fiddling with the pen again, then closing the folder on the single sheet of paper, then opening it again, she said, "From the message on my voicemail, I understood that you had them out at an evening meeting where they were disruptive before they fell asleep."

Before Faith could answer, Jim said in his commanding church voice, "Ms. Fulton, I have no idea who gave you this information, but our evening service starts at six o'clock and is over at seven, hardly late for children. I have seen these twins on several occasions and they are definitely not disruptive! They were certainly not disruptive in any way in that evening service. Once I saw them with Mrs. Lankaster, I never noticed them again. Perhaps the children did fall asleep, could that be disruptive to you if you were in a meeting geared mostly to adults?"

Deciding to switch subjects rather than answer Jim's question, Ms Fulton asked, "Why is it you have these children, Mrs. Lankaster? You say Mr. Barns found the twins and he works for FDNY. This is hardly New York City."

Looking at the woman with cold eyes, Matt said, "Perhaps I should answer that question for you instead of Mrs. Lankaster."

Glancing at him, the woman said, "As you wish." As Matt took a breath, Maranda rushed on, "It seems to me that Mrs. Lankaster set up this meeting with me, having you *men* here is irrelevant. It should be just she and I."

Matt shook his head emphatically. "I must disagree, Ms. Fulton. Mrs. Lankaster called me and told me that you called telling her that she must make an appointment with you. Therefore, she was accommodating you. Also, she has every right to have someone with her for such a meeting as this and since Pastor Harding and I know the situation from the first minute, it was very appropriate for her to ask us to be here. Do you have a problem with having *men* in your meetings, Ms. Fulton?"

Looking extremely uncomfortable, because indeed she did have a big problem dealing with men, Maranda cleared her throat. She fiddled with the folder again and picked up the pen, but didn't write anything on her paper. She licked her lips and said, "You were about to answer my question about why you should be involved in this meeting, as I understand it."

Smiling, not knowing how nervous he made her, he said, "I work for a mid-Manhattan fire station. We were called to a warehouse fire only days after nine eleven. After putting out the blaze, my buddy and I find the twins unharmed inside the burned out shell. We took them to our fire station. I cleaned them up, fed them and called the Children's Agency in each of the boroughs. Because of the recent tragedy, each agency was overloaded and could not take the twins. I remembered that Pastor Harding's church has a foundling ministry, so I called, took them to the church and he brought Mrs. Lankaster in as the lady who could best care for them."

Without acknowledging Matt, Maranda turned to Jim and asked, "Why did you place these children in a home without a father?" Her tone of voice changed and she said, cynically, "I should think, a *church* agency would by all means work with a home with a man and woman."

Jim had decided if the woman ever asked him something again, he would ask his own question first – the real issue for the meeting. "Why were you so anxious for Mrs. Lankaster to call you for an immediate interview? Why is *your* department involved at all?"

The woman glanced at her paper, where she had obviously written down the names of the three people in the room with her. "Mr. Harding, I believe I'm asking the questions today."

"No, Ms. Fulton, you were asked this question not only at the beginning of this session, but also on Wednesday. Both of those times the subject was brought up by Mrs. Lankaster. She deserves an answer. Before I answer anything else and I feel I am speaking for both Mrs. Lankaster and Mr. Barns, you *will* answer my questions."

"I received word on my voicemail that there was a problem," she conceded.

"So you're telling me that since you are with the Child *Protection* Agency and you were called, that this person insinuated there was problem warranting protecting children."

The woman cleared her throat. "Well, yes."

Again looking the woman squarely in the eyes, Jim asked, "What kind of *protection* did these children need, according to this call?"

The woman began to nervously tap her pen on the paper lying on top of the folder. It was obvious that her hands were sweaty, the pen slipped from her fingers. She cleared her throat and picked up the pen. Not answering Jim's question, but said instead, "We have a children's agency here in Thomaston, these children should have been placed through them. That way we could be sure they were placed in a safe home as well as a home with two parents, as is required."

When Maranda finished speaking, Jim waited several minutes, deciding to wait her out. Becoming more agitated the woman finally looked at him. He asked, "Why is that, when they came from Manhattan, Ms Fulton?" Leaning almost into Maranda's space he said, "You realize, of course, that you have completely sidestepped my question, not only this time it was asked but before. What kind of *protection* did these children need, according to this voicemail message?"

Looking down at her paper again, the woman said, "We're getting way off base, here. I think we need to get back to my question. Mr. Harding, why did you place these children in a home without a father?"

"What kind of *protection* did these children need, according to this voicemail message, Ms. Fulton?" Jim asked again.

Maranda's voice was quite loud, she was obviously very agitated. "Mr. Harding!" she nearly yelled. "I cannot divulge that information to you, we must keep our contacts protected, it is the law!"

Very calmly, as if he dealt with situations like this each day, Jim asked, "But without contacting this person again to talk with her personally to find out what *kind* of protection was needed, you took the call at face value, didn't confirm it at all, and called Mrs. Lankaster to come in for what reason?"

Miranda's face was beet red. She again looked down at her folder and said, "I have to verify each call, each potential problem!"

"Without calling the person back who left you the message?" Jim leaned forward on his elbows and looked hard at the woman.

Maranda couldn't hide her agitation. Beads of sweat were obvious on her forehead and her hands trembled. Loudly she said, "Yes! I'm not required to return the call from the person on my voicemail. The situation can be quite urgent and children in serious danger. We are trained to act with all speed on the behalf of the children involved. That is why I asked Mrs. Lankaster to come in yesterday and bring the children! I was very concerned for the welfare of these twins. I hoped she would call earlier on Wednesday so I could ascertain the situation even then, but Mrs. Lankaster didn't call until quite late, and then she said she was tied up yesterday."

"But you did nothing in almost two days to insure their safety?"

Maranda cleared her throat, her face beet red, realizing the bait she had swallowed. "No, I didn't," she murmured, the sweat ran down her face by now.

"Is that the way you usually handle these calls? By the way, I'm still waiting to hear you say what kind of protection was needed for these twins."

"No, I... I usually call a police officer and we go to the home immediately, but when I called initially, there was no answer."

Still looking at the case worker very intently, Jim calmly said, "I find it interesting that you didn't do that at all, Ms. Fulton."

Just then, another woman opened the door and all four turned to look at her. Another woman trying to be as formidable as Ms Fulton, said, "Excuse me, Ms. Fulton, is there a problem here? I heard some loud words. Would you mind if I sat in on the rest of your meeting?"

"Ah, no, that's fine." Maranda was unsuccessfully rifling through her pockets and her briefcase for something, but obviously not finding it.

Maranda tried not to show the sigh of relief she felt escape from her chest. Surely now that her supervisor was in the room she could handle the situation, if only these men hadn't come! She raised her arm and wiped her face on her sleeve, smiled what she hoped was a genuine smile and said, "Thank you, Ms. Wheatly. This is Mrs. Lankaster, who is housing a set of twins in her home. Mr. Barns is from FDNY and Mr. Harding is a preacher at a local church." Nodding to the new woman, Maranda said, "This is my supervisor, Ms Georgiana Wheatly."

"How do you all do? This is a protection problem, Ms. Fulton?"

The woman licked her lips and swallowed, before she said, "Ah... well... yes, that was what the message on my voicemail led me to believe."

"I see. Mrs. Lankaster, what is your home like?"

Before she could answer Jim interrupted again. "Ms Wheatly, we are still waiting for Ms Fulton to answer a question that we have asked several times – beginning on Wednesday when Mrs. Lankaster returned Ms. Fulton's call. What kind of protection did these twins need your agency's intervention for."

The woman cleared her throat and looked at Maranda. "Is that so?"

"Yes."

Without waiting for Maranda to answer, Ms Wheatly turned to Faith and said, "I'm waiting for your answer to my question."

Quite forcefully, Jim said, "Ms. Wheatly, we are waiting for the answer to our initial question. Robert's Rules of order states that there is only one question on the table at a time."

Instantly uncomfortable, Georgiana looked silently at Maranda. "Ms. Fulton?"

Maranda opened her mouth – like a fish out of water – then closed it. Sweat still poured down her face and she tapped her pen nervously on the paper. She swallowed and opened her mouth again, but no words came out.

Wanting to help her employee out and also hoping to steer away from Jim's question, since it was this question that was making Maranda very uncomfortable. Georgiana asked Faith again, "What is your home like?"

Faith looked at Jim, but when he said nothing she answered, "My nine year old daughter and I live in a house on an acre of land left to us by my late husband. I have four bedrooms."

"There is no man living in your home?"

"No, I just told you, I am a widow."

Looking significantly at the man sitting beside Faith, not touching her, but with his elbow on the back of her chair, the woman said, "That doesn't mean too much in this day and age."

By this time, Ms. Wheatly had taken a seat at the other end of the table. Faith leaned forward on the table and looked directly at her. In fact, Faith's look was so focused that the supervisor cleared her throat, instinctively pulled her head back and clasped her hands together on the table, somewhat like a barrier in front of her. Speaking very distinctly, Faith said, "It means a great deal to me, Ms. Wheatly. No man would be welcome to live in my house unless I was married to him. Perhaps it means nothing to you, but to me it does."

The woman cleared her throat, leaving that hot potato alone immediately. "I see. Mr. Harding, you placed these twins in a one parent home? Why is that?"

"Because I felt it was the best home possible," he answered without hesitation, looking the woman in the eyes. "Ms. Wheatly, as I understand, this is a child *protection* case. Ms Fulton called Mrs. Lankaster and told her this much, but to this point has refused to say what the reason for the concern was. Would you care to explain why she has refused to answer this simple question or why a protection agency was contacted? Mrs. Lankaster asked this question several times, I believe she deserves an answer."

Ignoring Jim's question completely, the woman answered, "But our foster care system, our adoptive agencies all require homes where children are placed be inspected and approved and have two parents. Only when these criteria are met can children be placed."

"Ms. Wheatly," Jim said, looking at her squarely in the eye and waiting for her to look at him, "You never deal with churches and church members do you? Our foundling ministry takes care of that Who is it who makes the inspection for these agencies that you've mentioned?"

"Well, members of their staff, of course."

"Precisely, Ms. Wheatly. Of course, it is members of our staff who take care of these matters for our foundling ministry."

Matt had great respect for Jim Harding right from the first time they met, but his respect was growing exponentially with each word that came from his mouth. At this point, he had bamboozled one woman and was about to do the same to another getting her totally off base. He was doing that with an utterly calm demeanor, while throwing both women into confusion. From the way he saw it, the twins had nothing to worry about, Faith was their new mother they would be staying with her. He wanted to jump to his feet and wave a flag, this was great!

"They approved someone who is a single mother?" Ms. Fulton asked.

"Obviously. Another obvious observation is that you are not telling us why it was your agency that was contacted or why there was a need for child *protection*."

"Who is paying for housing these children?"

"Ms. Fulton," Jim spoke again, "you are not with the foster care system or any of the adoptive agencies. It is quite obvious that there is not a problem or a need for protection for these twins. Therefore I think it is irrelevant for you to know who is paying for keeping these children. This meeting that you asked Mrs. Lankaster to come for has been totally a waste of time for all three of us. I think we will see ourselves out." Giving both women a tight smile, he said, "However, this meeting has been very enlightening, to say the least."

Without giving anyone a chance to speak Jim rose from his chair, moving his head back and forth so he could keep his eyes on Maranda and her supervisor. Matt immediately stood and put his hand on Faith's chair to help her up. Of course, they must circle the table and go behind either Maranda or Georgiana, but Matt followed Faith's cue and they went behind Georgiana.

Realizing she handled this meeting badly, so much so, that her supervisor appeared because she heard Maranda raise her voice. She put her hands down on either side of the sheet of paper in front of her and stood up, glaring at Jim. However, he looked at her in such a way that even though her mouth was open, no words came out and only seconds later, she closed it.

Glancing quickly at Georgiana and seeing surprise on her face, she looked back at Jim and exclaimed, "I shall dismiss this meeting!"

Still moving toward the door, Jim said, "No, you're only wasting our time. We shall see ourselves out, Ms. Fulton. Perhaps next time you should check into these matters more thoroughly, perhaps contacting your source first." Nodding to the other woman, he said, "You have a good day, Ms. Wheatly. I don't believe it was any of the three of us who raised our voices, but I do wish you both a good day."

Jim took one more step to the door, opened it and held it until Matt ushered Faith out. Scrambling ineffectively with her folder, Maranda still stood at the table with her mouth open as if to speak, but nothing came out. Just before he closed the door behind him, he said, looking first at Maranda, then at Georgiana, "Oh, you might try to find out how our *foundling* ministry works, ladies, and how *church* people operate before you try to make judgments in the future – especially about a *protection* case."

Jim quite deliberately closed the door. Both Maranda and Georgiana were still in the room. Georgiana had jumped to her feet and was only three steps from the doorway and quickly yanked on the door. Jim moved up to flank Faith on her other side, neither man touched Faith and the three walked down the hall together, without looking back, even though they heard the door open. None of them said anything to each other, they wanted to get out of the building as quickly as possible. Even though he wanted to, Matt kept his hands at his sides he wasn't sure how his actions in the conference room would affect what was said.

Behind them, the open conference door make a loud noise as it slammed closed, echoing through the hall. However, none of the three turned to look. Only seconds later, the door opened again and Maranda, standing in the doorway called after them, "I'll be reporting this!"

Jim turned slightly, but kept walking along with Faith and Matt. "What will you report and to whom, Ms. Fulton?"

"My report will state that Mrs. Lankaster was very uncooperative! My questions were not answered to my satisfaction."

"I see," Jim said. "Since I'm in charge of the *foundling ministry*, perhaps you could have whomever you give this report to call me in the future. After all, this *foundling ministry* was started and is maintained by our *church*." Giving the woman a tight smile, Jim said, "You have a good day, Ms. Fulton."

Trying to curb her frustration and act as professional as possible in light of how she acted in the meeting, she said, "Well….well…." Matt, Faith and Jim didn't wait for the rest of her words they disappeared into the big reception room. The door between the hallway and the reception room closed before Maranda said anything more. Maranda watched the door close. Nothing about the meeting went how she wanted or expected. She was totally unraveled.

Jim, Matt and Faith reached the reception area and headed for the door, but the conference room door slammed again, because Georgiana called Maranda back inside. She was sure there were others in the reception area waiting to meet other counselors, so there was no reply to Jim's statement. Georgiana motioned Maranda back to her seat, she took several steps and collapsed into the chair and heaved a long sigh. She wiped her sleeve across her face. She was still sweating profusely.

"What happened?"

Knowing how terribly she fouled the interview and realizing that having her supervisor come in was not a good thing, she didn't look at Georgiana instead she fumbled with her paper and the folder still on the desk and took a deep breath. She cleared her throat and said, "A friend of mine called late Tuesday night and left a message on my voicemail about a set of twins who were brought over from New York City. She was led me to believe that it was an unsuitable place for children, that there might be drugs or alcohol and I should look into it."

Scowling, Georgiana looked at her calendar. "Maranda, it's Friday. You got the message first thing on Wednesday…."

Nodding emphatically, she said, "Yes, I… I know. I called this Faith Lankaster, but got only her answering machine, so of course, I left a message telling her how urgent a meeting was. She called around three and said she had commitments and couldn't come in until this morning."

Looking directly at the agitated woman, Georgiana asked, "When she did call, did you tell her you would be coming to make an inspection immediately? By the way, are you sure that younger man isn't a live in? They seemed sort of chummy."

Shaking her head, still looking at the folder in front of her, she said, "No, I agreed with this time." Shaking her head more emphatically, Maranda said,

"You heard her, Georgiana, she was most emphatic that no man would live with her, she would be married for that to happen."

"Umm, well…. So why was that man involved?"

"He's the fireman who found the children."

"In New York City?"

"Yes," Maranda whispered.

"Did you find out if there were drugs or alcohol?"

Shaking her head, dismally, Maranda said, "No, I asked what Ms Lankaster was doing with the children, but the preacher dominated the conversation. After only a few questions that the other two answered, he took over and did all the talking. Just the way he talked and… and looked at me… He made me so nervous I couldn't find out anything." She pulled in a deep breath. "I mean, you heard him! He was like a broken record! And the way he looked at me… I… I'm sure glad I don't go to *his* church!"

"What's this foundling ministry he's talking about?"

"I have no idea. It's something run by his church."

Shaking her head, Georgiana said, "You should have found that out immediately! I can't believe how you've handled this! You're one of my better investigators! Maranda, everything about this situation was handled wrong, right from the first call! Who is this friend of yours?"

"A woman I've been friends with since we were in high school, Mel Sample."

"Does she go to that church?"

"No, but a friend of hers does. It was this friend that told her."

Shaking her head, Georgiana said, "That was second or third hand information! I think you botched this one royally. Perhaps we should let it sift through the cracks and get lost. Those church fanatics stick together you can't hardly crack something like that."

Maranda sighed, "I figured that out after only a few minutes. But Georgiana, it was someone from that church who told my friend!"

"Maranda, what you got was second or third hand information. Who knows how it was first reported! I still have a big problem with this whole thing. I think you better let it drop."

"Yes, I guess that's the best thing to do," Maranda breathed out a big sigh.

Meanwhile, when the trio reached the parking lot, Faith hugged Jim.

"Jim, you did great!" She stepped back beside Matt. "I was so glad for both of you! I'd have broken down long before the interview was over and probably the kids would be gone by this afternoon."

"Faith," Jim said, looking very seriously from Faith to Matt, "don't consider this the end of this inquiry. I'll keep an eye on the twins and I'll warn Katie not to let anyone on her bus she doesn't know. For the next few days, we must be more than careful. Don't let anyone in your house that you don't know. These agencies are inter-related and have a fast grapevine. Believe me they are not above passing on false information. That's a fact! We found that out just now. Someone from the children's agency or the foster care system may be after you within hours."

Matt finally gave in to his desire and circled Faith's waist. He nodded, but also squeezed her close. "Yes, I'd say that's true."

"How can people do things like this to innocent children?" Faith asked, her eyes glistening with unshed tears.

"It's called greed and kickbacks," Matt said. "Believe me, it happens all the time and not just in these agencies. It happens even in the foster homes as well."

"Oh, my!" Faith whispered.

Nodding, Jim said, "That was why I suggested that any further contact come through me. However, now that they have your number, they'll probably contact you instead. Your phone may be ringing when you get back home."

Seeing the look on her face, Matt said, "I'll be with you the rest of today and it's the weekend tomorrow, they won't call or come by then, I'm sure."

"I can only hope so," Faith murmured.

Jim patted her on the back. "It'll all turn out fine, Faith, don't give up the ship. As I've said before, those children are in exactly the home they belong!"

"Thank you, Pastor," Faith murmured.

Maranda and Georgiana left the conference room. Georgiana's office was next door, so she went in and smiled as Maranda went on. Maranda's smile in return was only a raising of one side of her mouth. She hurried on to her office, but as she went in, she closed the door quickly behind her. She was angry, not only because her supervisor heard her loud words and come, but especially because the interview turned into a royal fiasco and she felt she accomplished nothing. It was no wonder she hated dealing with men! That problem for her started at an early age.

On Wednesday when she listened to the voicemail message, she wondered why her friend contacted her, but she assumed it was because she was a friend. Maranda realized too late, that she should have passed the message on immediately to the children's agency there in Thomaston. After all, a friend of hers was in that department and probably could have handled the meeting much better. She sighed they were housed in the same building, after all.

Maranda dropped her briefcase beside her desk chair, fell into the chair and wiped her sweaty hands down her thighs. Immediately, she found her huge mug, rushed to her private coffeemaker and poured herself a cup. As she set the carafe back down she wished for something stronger to slip into the brown liquid, but of course, that couldn't happen at work! Taking it back to her desk, she took a big gulp, wishing the caffeine would wipe out the adrenalin that was rushing through her veins. However, as keyed up as she was she wasn't sure anything would calm her.

Still with her cup in one hand, she hunted through her rolodex until she found the private number of the woman she usually contacted in the Children's Agency. "Come on, Railene, answer the phone!" she muttered.

On the fourth ring Railene answered and Maranda said, "Railene, this is Maranda Fulton. I have something I need to run by you."

Another smoker's voice answered, "I'm all ears, Maranda, be about it, I have an appointment in five minutes."

"On Wednesday morning, I had a message on my voicemail from a friend of mine that a set of twins was being housed with a single mom here in Thomaston."

"Hmm, sounds interesting. Why don't I know about this?"

"I wasn't able to get all the particulars I hoped to obtain but, it seems a fireman from FDNY found them and took them to a church here locally. The preacher called in this woman and put them in her home."

Railene's pen started tapping on her desk. "No proper channels, it seems. By the way, why was your agency contacted?"

"A friend called and left me a voicemail, but the impression she gave there was some type of abuse. Drugs, alcohol, it was quite vague. So I didn't contact you immediately."

"A church and there was abuse?" Railene nodded, but said out loud, "In some circles I'd say there's mental abuse through churches. Go on, I think I need to hear the rest of the story."

Maranda cleared her throat and said, "That was my impression. The woman who has the children, the fireman, who, by the way, seemed quite chummy with the woman, and the preacher of this church were all here a few minutes ago. I didn't get much out of them, other than uncooperativeness and to be informed that there was no abuse. By the way, I only asked for the woman and the twins to come in, but she brought those two *men* with her and not the twins."

"I see. You made a home visit?"

"Ahh, no. They came here."

"It was Wednesday when you received this call and today's Friday. This is the first time you saw this woman and these children?"

"I never saw the children, they were in some kindergarten at the time, but yes I saw Mrs. Lankaster this morning."

"How long have these children been in this home?"

"I understand it was Friday last week."

"It's a week later. Who inspected this home? Why were these children placed in a single parent home?"

"Ahh, this preacher said his church took care of the inspection. He felt Mrs. Lankaster was the best person to take the children."

"Who's paying for their keep?"

"I wasn't able to find that out."

"Where can I see these children and inspect this home?"

Clearing her throat, Maranda said, "The preacher said to deal with him first. He said to call the church before contacting anyone."

Curbing her frustration, but just, Railene said, "Is that so? Give me the church name and the woman's name and phone number."

After Maranda gave Railene the information, she said, "So you'll handle this?"

Maranda heard the woman pound her desk, as she said, "Absolutely! This is very irregular, but I'll have it straightened out today!"

"Thanks, Railene, I should have contacted you immediately. I'm sorry," Maranda said.

"No problem, Maranda. I will take care of it today!"

Railene summoned her secretary and told her to reschedule her afternoon appointments. She debated calling the church, but decided to cut to the chase and deal directly with the woman. The twins were in her home, improperly placed, since she was a single parent. There was a nebulous suggestion of abuse. Railene would love see a man of the cloth squirm. Men of that ilk needed to be brought down and she was the woman - the force of one woman - to do just that!

Just after lunch Faith's phone rang. She and Matt had talked and decided not to answer the phone, but let the answering machine pick up. Matt knew the woman from Child Protection heard Jim's request, but he was skeptical that the request would be heeded. After all, the woman never answered the straight forward question that Faith and Jim had asked her. Why should anyone expect that she would either drop the incident or contact the church as requested?

They sat in the kitchen and listened as the outgoing message finished. "Good morning," It was now afternoon - a smoker's voice said. "This is Railene Rolans from Thomaston Department of Children's Services. I need to set up an appointment to make an inspection of the home where I understand a set of twins have been placed illegally. I must do this today. As soon as you receive this message, please call me. I'll give you my cell phone number, I can be reached at that number at any time and I can come within fifteen minutes...."

As the woman spoke, Faith picked up her cordless phone and took it in the den where Matt picked up another phone. She and Matt opened the line, but Faith said, "Yes, Ms. Rolans. What is it you need? By the way, did you call our church office, as Pastor Harding requested?"

Railene had to swallow; she didn't expect a live voice. The woman's voice made her feel uncomfortable, it was much more cultured than she expected. Still, she plowed ahead, totally ignoring Faith's last question. She cleared her throat and said, "I need to make an inspection of this home where twins were placed! Why are they in Thomaston if they come from Manhattan?"

Faith and Matt had talked about what kind of questions someone would ask, so Faith said, "Why do you need to make an inspection? By the way, did you contact Pastor Harding and clear this with him?"

The bitter anger came through in her voice, as she said, "Of course not! You're housing twins. You're a single parent, which is not tolerated."

"Ms. Rolans, you'll have to contact Pastor Harding before I'll submit to anything you want. I'm sure you can reach him at the church office." With great satisfaction and a smile that covered her face, Faith pushed the disconnect button and Matt hung up.

Railene had her mouth open, but heard the dial tone, so, totally frustrated; she slammed the phone into the cradle. This was why she hated dealing with church people, men....

Matt chuckled as he stood up and went to the loveseat where Faith sat. He sat beside her and slid his arm around Faith's shoulders. He grinned and said, "Well done, Mrs. Lankaster! I have every confidence that Jim will handle this perfectly and that you won't have to deal with this lovely Ms. Rolans. She sounded like a real gem, just like those other two were earlier."

Faith smiled at Matt, and said, "Yes, I agree. Why is it that women like that are the ones who end up with jobs like that? I wasn't impressed with either of those women at the Child Protection Agency, that they had anyone's best interest at heart, especially not Karl and Karin's."

"That's for sure! This woman gave me the same impression. Love, let's see if we can make your garage back into a two car garage, shall we? You better take that phone along, Pastor may have some advice for us, or heaven forbid that woman may call back."

"Yes, let's go!" Faith held the phone as she stood. Matt pulled her close and they walked outside. She sighed, as the sun's warmth hit her. "I'm so glad you're here. I'm glad the woman didn't insist on making an inspection before."

"Mmm, so am I, Love." His reason might not be exactly the same as Faith's, but he was extremely glad to be with Faith and also glad he could be in her corner about the twins.

An angry Railene slammed down the receiver, but picked it up immediately and called the number of the church and Marian answered. After Marian had identified the church, Railene, who barely let Marian finish speaking, said, "I need to speak with Mr. Harding."

"I'm sorry, Pastor Harding's on the playground right now. It's lunch recess, could I have him call you back when he comes in?"

Railene looked again at the name and phone number she was given. "What is this place? I thought it was a church!"

Quite congenially, Marian answered, "It is, but we have an elementary school here and he's the principal."

Having her preconceived notion about churches totally demolished with that one sentence, Railene said, "I see." Trying to regroup, Railene cleared her throat and said, "Yes, I'll give you the number, have him call immediately. My business is very important." She gave both her name, the name of the agency and her phone number to Marian.

Congenially, Marian said, "Thank you, Ms. Rolans, I'm sure he'll call you back as soon as he's available." Marian wondered at the vibes she got from the woman.

Railene fumed, as she hung up. She hadn't eaten lunch and her stomach growled loudly. She noticed her hands were shaking, but she didn't know if that was adrenalin or her diabetes, so she took her coffee mug to the kitchen, filled it, and pulled her brown bag lunch from the refrigerator. Her frustration level was high, so she slammed the refrigerator door, and rushed back to her desk. When she pulled her tuna sandwich from the wrapper it was juicy and some salad dressing dripped on her hand, and onto the paper she was using on her desk. She slammed the sandwich on the wrapper, grabbed the whole thing up and threw it forcefully into the trashcan. Even more frustrated, she pulled out the apple and took a huge bite. She set the apple down and grabbed her napkins to wipe off her paper before she couldn't read her writing.

The phone rang.

TWELVE

RAILENE THREW HER HANDS IN THE AIR AND CHEWED FEVERISHLY. AS SHE HAD IT programmed, her voicemail kicked in after two rings and since she didn't have it on speaker, she couldn't hear who the speaker was or what they said. She heard it click off before her mouth was empty enough she could be understood. Immediately, she pushed the button to retrieve the message, only to find that the caller was Jim Harding. He left his message, telling Railene he would be out of the office for the remainder of the afternoon; she would have to contact him on Monday. Totally frustrated, the woman threw the rest of the apple against the wall, where it left a huge splatter. She stamped a foot and let out a scream that ended in a curse. Of course, her face was beet red. Fortunately, her office door was closed tightly, no one heard her…. she hoped.

As they cleaned the garage, Matt said, "I've been thinking; what do you say I buy an SUV and unofficially, we trade vehicles. Something like that would give you more room with three kids and I'll borrow this car to go to the train station and the B and B. What do you say?"

"It sounds okay," she scowled, but said tentatively, "but you'll buy a new car like that and then not drive it?"

He came from beside the car and put his hands on her upper arms. He smiled at her, bent his head and kissed her, before he said, "It's like with Karl's clothes, Sweetheart, was your rent on the first the last thing you spent money on?" He shook his head and answered his own question, "I hardly think so."

"No, of course not! But that's so much money!"

He put his finger under her chin, kissed her lips and whispered, "Don't worry about it, okay? Besides, I'm sure I'll get to drive it."

"You're sure?"

"Absolutely!"

"When'll we do this?"

"Want to go now or wait for the kids?"

Thinking of her very active nine year old and adding two more four years younger, she sighed, "We better go now. I can't imagine trying to do something like that with three kids running all over. One of the car dealers goes to our church, I'm sure he'll do you a good job."

"Okay, let's be on our way!"

He helped her into her car, then went around and sat in the driver's seat. She directed him across town to a huge new car lot. After he parked, Faith waited for Matt to come open her door then she led him inside the big showroom. There were cars in several lots around the showroom area, but she didn't stop to look at them.

A salesman walked up and asked, "Can I help you folks?"

"Is Marvin Service in today? If he is, I'd like to speak with him."

"Yes, Ma'am, I'll get him."

Soon, a distinguished older man walked from an office and as soon as he saw Faith a smile broke across his face. "Faith Lankaster, what can I do for you?"

"Hi, Marvin, this is Matt Barns. I told him you'd give us a fair shake here."

Matt held out his hand. "I'm in the market for a nice SUV."

Marvin grasped Matt's hand and shook it, but he said, "Ah, one of our most popular items. We received a shipment last evening, just got them showroom ready. I'd say your timing's perfect." He led them out to a lot and waved his hand in the direction of about fifteen vehicles. "Take a look. If you see something you like, I'll get the keys and you can test drive it. If you want a color in a model that isn't there, it can be ordered and here within a week."

Matt smiled. "That's great, thanks!"

Matt turned Faith to look over the display. They stood on the showroom level, but the outside lot was several feet below them so that they could look out over them. With his arm around her waist, Matt bent his head close to hers. He couldn't seem to get enough of this lovely woman. After only a few minutes of looking, Faith turned her head and smiled at Matt. Her smile usually turned Matt's knees to mush.

"Honey," she whispered, so that Marvin couldn't hear her, "why don't you do the picking? After all, Brandi and I picked out my car."

Matt shook his head and bent even closer to her. "Nope! I want this to be our choice. Which one'll it be?"

Giggling like a school girl, Faith hadn't been anywhere to spend a lot of money since Max died, she pointed. "I really like the color of that maroon one. It is pretty and I think it's big enough for three active children."

Smiling at her, he agreed, "Yes, that one caught my eye, too. Since we both agree we like that one, let's test it out."

Matt straightened and looked behind him. What he saw was a man looking at his hand on Faith's waist with a deep scowl on his face. "Ahh, Marvin, do you have the keys to that maroon one out there? Faith and I'd like to take a drive. You did say we could test drive it, didn't you?"

His eyes immediately moving back to Matt's face, but his neck turned a bright red, as he cleared his throat and said, "Oh, um, yes, I'll get them."

When the man left, Matt lowered his head to Faith's ear. "He didn't seem to like it that I had my arm around you, Love. He doesn't have any designs on you does he, by any chance?"

Faith gave him an incredulous look. "Honey, you can't be serious! He's married, and I like his wife a lot. He better not have any designs on me!"

"Okay, I wondered."

Soon the man was back, not quite meeting Matt's eyes, handed him the keys. "Take it for a spin, Sir. You should have some open spaces to test it out. Drive it to Faith's if you want. The day's young, it's no problem."

"That sounds fine with me, we'll be back shortly."

"Yes, okay."

Matt drove to Faith's house, listening carefully as he drove, then got out and raised the hood. He went over everything, intent on having a car in as good shape as possible. He had Faith drive back and listened while she drove. It was hard to hear any sounds; the vehicle ran like a top. He felt it handled well, both for him and Faith. She drove on the lot and hopped out, coming to Matt's side as he stepped out. They walked in the showroom together, but Marvin must have been watching, he came from another part of the building almost at the same time.

"So, how did it drive for you?"

"I think we'll take that one," Matt said. "It handles really well."

Marvin smiled broadly. "Come on back to my office and let's get these papers signed so you can be on your way."

"That sounds fair to me," Matt said.

However, Matt wouldn't accept the sticker price. Maybe he would be a wealthy man in a few days, but that didn't mean he should squander his money. Matt knew when his dad bought cars, he never took the first price quoted as the price he would pay and he had raised his son to be just as discerning. He knew that the sticker price included a hefty commission for the salesman who persuaded the customer to buy and this was the owner. Matt was totally level-headed and never lost his cool, even though Marvin tried to weasel more money from him. Faith was impressed yet again with this man who had come into her life.

"Now," Marvin said, after the negotiations, gathering his papers around him, "am I correct, there's no trade in?"

"That's true. I'll give you a hefty down payment today, but we'll need to set up payments with you for the rest."

"That's fine. We can do our own financing here," he said, starting to fill out the first page in front of him.

Matt nodded. "Good, that's even better."

Matt hadn't told Faith about the CDs and savings accounts he signed withdrawal cards for his first night at the B and B. He wasn't sure if he wanted to. He hadn't decided if he would invest everything and let it accumulate for retirement or start his own business. Whatever he did, he knew he could easily afford this vehicle and he would have it paid off in only a few months.

It was still an hour before the kids were to get home when Matt took the keys and the receipt from Marvin. He turned from the man, put his arm around Faith and led her from the showroom, not caring what Marvin or anyone else thought about it. This lady was the love of his life; he wanted to be as close to her as he could be.

Outside, he took his hand from her back, lifted her right hand and placed the keys in her palm, then closed her fingers around them. "Here, Love, you drive this and I'll follow you in your car back to the house."

She looked at the keys in her hand, then to his face, her head going back and forth slightly. "Me drive it? You can't be serious!"

He looked at her with so much love in his eyes, she had to see. "Yes, I insist, you'll be driving it most anyway. You might as well get used to it."

"Whatever you say," she murmured.

With a grin and a wink, he said, "Yes, Love, I say."

He led her to the driver's door, opened it and helped her in, then turned and went the short distance to her car. She sat in the very comfortable bucket seat and looked out over the much shorter nose of the wonderfully new smelling car and decided that her life had just about turned all the way around. She and Brandi had a good life the past three years, but she knew she had never been so happy in that time as she was now. Was she placing too much hope on one man or had God truly seen her loneliness and given her a wonderful man to be her soul mate? Finally, she turned the key and the machine purred into life. Only moments later, she left the dealership and drove home, pulling up beside the house.

Matt's thoughts as he drove behind her were centered on the lovely lady in front of him. He couldn't see her, of course only momentarily catch a glimpse in the outside mirror, but his mind was full of her. He knew he loved her, even though he was never in love before. He dated several women in his life, and been considered one of the eligible jocks in high school and college, but he never felt for any of those girls or women as he felt for Faith. If that wasn't love then what could it be? He wondered if it was too soon to ask her to marry him. How long did a man wait after meeting a lady to ask that question? Besides, did it make a difference if she was a widow? He had no clue.

He turned behind her on her driveway and decided to put his thoughts on ice for a while. Maybe it was a bit too soon to proclaim his love, he wondered if he needed an ally and if he had it in the children, but that could wait for a few more days. She stopped in front of the garage, but he pulled up beside the house, quickly shut off the car and got out. Matt hurried around the car and in only minutes was beside her.

He asked, "What do you think, will the kids want to go for a ride when they get home?"

Faith laughed. "As if you need to ask! Is the sky blue? Is the grass green? Do fish swim in the water? Umm, what else?"

Matt chuckled. "You think it's that certain, huh. Shall we go pick them up?"

"That's a good idea." Thinking about what Jim said earlier, she continued,

"That way, we could be sure no one would pick them up who shouldn't." She looked at her watch. "We better go pretty soon, then."

They had walked around the new car, headed for the back door, instead, Matt opened the passenger door, then helped her in. He grinned and said, "Let's be on our way, then! Time's a wasting, as they say."

She grinned. "That's fine with me!"

Before he closed her door, he squeezed her arm a little and winked at her. He walked around the back of the SUV, but when he was at the corner where he was sure she couldn't see him, he pushed his fist into the air. He felt like jumping up and clicking his heels. He was in love for the first time, if Faith would have him, he was hers for life and he couldn't be happier. He opened the driver's door, grinned at the pretty lady already seated, slid in and started up.

Railene was so angry after listening to Jim Harding's message she yanked her drawer open and pulled out her phone book. She had the woman's name who had the twins and the phone number, so she took her ruler and went down each listing of Lankaster until she matched the name and number. She hoped telephone companies never stopped printing books with addresses. Jotting down the address, she slammed the book closed and threw it in her drawer. She couldn't remember being so angry. Purposefully, she grabbed out her purse, briefcase and keys and headed out to the parking lot. She wasn't out of the building when her stomach growled, reminding her she hadn't eaten her lunch and she needed to for her diabetes.

As she sat in her car, she slammed the door so hard that the car rocked back and forth then she hit the steering wheel with her full force. She gritted her teeth, since she noticed her hands were shaking. "I'm not going to wait for any weekend! I'll have those kids out of there today! This whole thing has gotten totally out of hand and it's about to stop!" she yelled, then looked around at the parked cars close by to see if anyone saw or heard her. After all, she was a professional and in that capacity, no one saw her lose control. No one had in the past and no one would now or in the future! However, her stomach growled again. She slammed her fist on the steering wheel and growled, "I forgot my water!"

Not knowing what they drove, or Faith and Matt, and they not knowing who she was, they passed each other only two blocks from Faith's home. Matt drove on to the church and parked in a spot very close to the door to the educational wing exit so they would be sure not to miss the children when they left after school.

Railene pulled in the driveway to Faith's house and smiled, there was a car parked beside the house. This problem would be solved very shortly and those twins would be shipped back to Manhattan, to the children's agency there where they belonged, if she had her way. So it was Friday afternoon, they could deal with these kids however they wanted to. No kids from the city had any business being in her jurisdiction and that was final!

Railene pulled up right behind Faith's car. This woman would not be rushing out the back door for a quick get-away! Not on her watch! Quickly, she grabbed up her briefcase and confidently walked to the front door. She rang the bell, expecting a woman to come answer her summons. The children were probably still in school, but they would be on their way as soon as they stepped off the bus. However, she heard nothing.

She rang the bell again, still there was no answer. *If this woman is a single mother and there is a car parked beside the house, where could she be? She couldn't have gone out the back door and gotten away, I'm parked too close to her car,* she thought. The woman rang the bell again and at the same time thumped the door with her briefcase; her frustration level had reached its limit. However, there was still no answer. She left the door and went to a window and peered inside, everything was dark and quiet. That is, everything in the house was dark and quiet, however, in the silence, her stomach growled very loudly.

Now she was angry, in hitting the door with her briefcase she hit her leg on the rebound and it hurt. She stomped off the porch, thumping down each step. "I'll wait! Something is going on here and I'm getting to the bottom of it!" she yelled, then looked around, but realized no one could hear her; no other house was in sight. She was glad, if things got ugly, no one would see. She went to her car, yanked open the door and fell onto the seat, throwing her briefcase onto the passenger seat. With the same hand, she reached into her purse for her cigarettes, pulled one out and lit up, then took a long drag. After inhaling, she opened her mouth and let a huge puff out through her mouth and nose. However, her stomach growled again.

Brandi made it a habit to stop at the kindergarten room for the twins, so they came out together. Karl didn't hold anyone's hand anymore, so he walked beside Brandi, but Karin very willingly held Brandi's hand, she was much more timid and very feminine, not like the tomboy that Brandi was.

Since it was Friday, they and all the other children were excited to leave school. Matt and Faith heard the bell and seconds later, the door burst open. It was the weekend and the children could play all day Saturday and this time of year, that was the most important thing about a weekend for elementary aged children. Besides, for Brandi and the twins, there was an added happiness; Matt would be with them until after lunch tomorrow. He was also looking forward to spending time with them. Not just the kids, but especially with Faith. Except that he was a grown man, he felt like dancing and skipping like the kids coming from the building.

Matt sat behind the wheel watching the door to the education wing along with Faith, but Faith saw Karl push open the door and Brandi's auburn curls right behind him. Not wanting the children to miss them, she opened her door and stepped onto the parking lot. She closed the door, which drew Brandi's attention. As soon as she caught sight of Faith, Brandi's mouth dropped open when she saw what her mommy stood beside. She started running, pulling Karin along. Karl ran beside her. He ran because Brandi was, he didn't see Faith right away.

"Mommy! Why are you in that?" Brandi asked, breathlessly coming up to her.

"Matt bought this." Quickly, she opened the back door and all three scrambled in. "Be sure and buckle up!"

"Hi, guys," Matt said. "Have a good day?"

Without thinking what she was saying, Brandi exclaimed, "Wow! Daddy Matt! You bought this? For us?"

A huge lump welled up in Matt's throat. He swallowed then swallowed again. He nodded and finally, around the lump he was able to croak out, "Yeah."

"This is so cool! Look at all the room!" She stood on the little platform just inside the door and looked around. Finally, she slid onto the seat and all the way to the window then brushed her hand across the soft leather. "Wow! It's great! super! It's new, too, I can tell! Mommy, this is super cool!"

Karl scrambled in next and sat down beside Brandi, grabbing his seatbelt immediately, but leaving room for his sister. However, Karin didn't sit down immediately; she went around Karl's legs and rushed up to the back of Matt's bucket seat. She laid her head on his shoulder and put her tiny hand on his chest, but as Matt turned she was smiling, her brown eyes sparkling. She didn't need to say a word everything was there in her eyes, as she looked up at him.

The lump in his throat didn't go away as he turned farther and put his arm around her. Into his ear, she whispered, "Cool, Daddy, cool."

Again, he had to swallow, he felt his eyes burning, but he wouldn't let any tears fall. He hauled her onto his lap then hugged the little girl, putting his mouth very close to her ear and finally whispered back, "Oh, Li'l Bit."

Faith closed the door behind Karin then moved to the front passenger door, she hadn't heard what Brandi called Matt, or the exchange between Matt and Karin. However, she saw him holding the little girl against his chest. The look on his face was priceless. After he spoke to her, he raised his head and laid his cheek on her hair. The look and the pose were of a daddy tenderly dealing with his little child. Faith's heart twisted in her chest, she already loved him, could she love him any more? Her head barely moved back and forth, but she admitted at least to herself, she loved Matt with all her heart.

To keep anyone, including Matt, from seeing the tears in her eyes, which she couldn't keep from falling, she turned, pulled the door closed and pushed the door lock that locked all the doors, then reached for the seatbelt hanging beside the door. She brought it across and studiously looked at the catch where she was to fasten the belt. She swallowed, hoping that would keep any more tears from falling. When she looked up, Karin was wiggling away and climbed onto the back seat beside her brother. Matt looked at her, so she gave him a watery smile, it was the best she could do.

Before he started up, but while the kids were occupied in the back seat, she reached over and squeezed his arm. He took her hand from his arm and gently raised it to his lips. After a brief kiss on her knuckle, she murmured, "Oh, Matt."

Karin's seatbelt snapping broke the spell and Faith pulled her hand from Matt's, but Brandi said, "Can we go for ice cream? Mommy, we could sit under the trees in the shade like we did before. Matt's never been to our favorite ice cream place. That would be way cool!"

Matt still looked at Faith, but with a wink, he said, "Sure! Why not? We have something here to celebrate, don't we?"

Brandi began bouncing on the seat, so of course, Karl and Karin started. "Yes!" Brandi exclaimed. "Yes! We got a new car!"

"A new car!" Karl crowed.

Even though that wasn't what he meant, Matt said, "Sure! Ice cream sounds great!"

Matt started the car and Faith gave directions, so soon Matt drove onto the parking lot of the ice cream shop. The place had a drive-up window, but there were lots of tables scattered under the trees. Matt barely shut off the car, when three seatbelts snapped. Brandi was on the move, and since she was the farthest from the door, that meant Karin and Karl had to move, too.

"Mommy, I see our table! We'll run and grab it before anybody else can. Karin and Karl want a cone just like me."

As the back door slammed, Matt turned to Faith and asked, "How did she know that? I never heard her ask even Karl."

Faith's eyes were dancing. "I guess it's that big sister thing. Come on! We gotta get in line and another car pulled in from school. We don't want to lose our place!"

Matt chuckled, as he opened his door. "No, wouldn't want that! No, not at all, of course!" However, he turned back, as Faith picked up her purse. "Uh uh, none of that! I said we'd come, I'm paying."

Faith smiled, left her purse on the floor; closed the door and the car beeped as Matt hit the fob. Faith walked around the front of the vehicle to him. Matt took her hand immediately and squeezed her fingers. They walked to the end of the line and stopped, but before they looked up to see the menu, she whispered, "What are you, Daddywarbucks?"

He chuckled. "Not really," he said, and hugged her to his side, but he felt a strong desire to give her anything her heart desired. He knew that in a few days he could easily do that, but so far, she had no idea that he could. At least until the money was in his bank that was the way he wanted it to stay.

Railene sat in her car. She forgot to put down the windows before she turned off her engine and the smoke from her cigarette filled up the enclosed space. First she opened the door and stuck her foot out onto the ground, but the warm breeze rustled her skirt and whispered across her pantyhose, making her uncomfortable. She pulled her foot back in, but left the door open, but the breeze turned into a stronger gust of wind and blew some of her papers off the dash. With some force, she yanked the door closed and gathered up the papers, stuffing them with greater force than necessary, back on the dash.

Momentarily, she sat back up and glared out the rearview mirror, waiting for some vehicle to come over the rise. She still couldn't reconcile how a vehicle could be sitting in the driveway and everybody could be gone from the house. What single mom would have more than one vehicle? For some reason it never occurred to her that someone could have come by for her. She fussed with her papers then slammed them on the passenger seat.

The sun shone down on the roof of the car, but Railene saw the tree branches moving in the steady breeze and was sure her papers would blow all over her car if she opened the door again. Finally, after she found a tissue in her purse and wiped the perspiration from her forehead, she turned the key to accessories and lowered the back windows so some air would circulate. While the accessories were on, she looked at the dash clock, it was nearly four thirty.

"Where could that … confounded woman and those kids be?" she muttered. "They should have been home from school long ago!"

Before they left the stand Faith grabbed a fist full of napkins. The thought crossed Matt's mind what a great mom Faith was. He carried two ice cream sundaes and Faith carried three cones in a carrier to the table where the children were. Matt set his two down side by side on the side with the empty bench, while Faith slid behind the bench, but leaned over so the children could each take a cone, then gave them each several napkins. After she set the empty carrier on the table, she set the rest of the napkins in the center so everyone could reach them.

She was about to open her mouth, but as she looked at each child, she realized she didn't need to remind them that it was a warm day and they should hurry with their cones, most of the ice cream had disappeared either into or around three mouths almost the instant the children took the cones. She smiled as she sat down and dug into her own ice cream. Hers was in greater jeopardy of melting away than any of theirs. Matt didn't say anything, but he was looking at her when she put the spoon into her mouth and glanced at him. His spoon was in his ice cream, but he hadn't brought it to his mouth.

Before she looked away, he mouthed the words, "You're beautiful." Her eyes widened and she slowly shook her head incredulously. She had no words to say. However, Matt watched her so closely he saw her head movement, so he nodded emphatically.

When all the ice cream was gone and all the trash was in the can, Brandi led the way back to the car. She pulled the back door open and herded the twins in ahead of her. Matt followed Faith and opened the door for her, then helped her in. He closed both doors before he headed around to the driver's seat.

"So, is it home now?" he asked, looking into the rearview mirror.

"Yes! We still got some time to swing before Mommy has supper ready," Brandi said. "We love to swing, especially with the wind blowing like this."

"Sounds good to me!" he exclaimed and turned the key.

Matt started up and turned toward Faith's house. Karl and Brandi both talked about their day at school and Faith encouraged them with some questions. Karin hardly ever stuck her thumb in her mouth any more, she was smiling. Matt marveled at how Faith was able to draw out things he never would have thought to ask. He loved this family, he loved being with them and helping with the kids in any way he could.

He turned into Faith's drive and crested the rise. The tree with the swing was right beside them when Matt looked ahead and saw the unknown car pulled up right behind Faith's car. Immediately, a bad feeling spread through him. Faith was turned in her seat, still talking with the children. No one else saw the car. He wondered what he should do, since Brandi already suggested they swing, but he didn't want to let the twins out of his sight, not now.

However, Brandi had her mouth open. "Matt, can you...." Instantly her face went from a happy smile to a frown. "Whose car is that? It's not a car we know and it's so close to Mommy's car she couldn't get it out if she wanted to."

Faith whirled around and stared then she looked at Matt with fear in her eyes. "Who could that be?" she whispered.

Matt shook his head, but drove up right beside Faith's car. The new vehicle was so much bigger that it blocked both cars, which was what he wanted. "Sit tight, kids, I'm about to find out who our visitor is."

He unlocked only his door and stepped out, but immediately Faith closed her eyes and sent up a silent prayer, even though she wasn't sure who the woman was. Rather than walking around either vehicle, Matt put his hand on the hood of the strange car and vaulted across. Railene had closed her eyes, so she was startled when the noise of another vehicle registered. Her eyes turned to saucers when she looked out her windshield and saw a man put his hand on her hood and jump across between the two.

With a smile, he bent down and asked, "Have you been waiting long?"

Railene was so taken back she had to swallow, but then she snapped, "Long enough."

"I'm sorry. What is it you need?" He recognized the smoker's voice instantly.

"I'm Railene Rolans. I've come to talk to Mrs. Lankaster about a set of twins she's housing illegally here."

Even though Railene was so snarky, Matt kept a smile on his face, as he asked, "Ahhh, and what agency are you with?" although he remembered the name from the woman's call earlier that afternoon.

She fumbled through her briefcase and pulled out a business card. Snapping it into his face, she said, "I'm with the Department of Children's Services of Thomaston. Who are you?"

His eyes drilling into her, Matt said, "I'm Matt Barns. We met with Maranda Fulton this morning. Anyone she sent a report to was to contact our pastor, Jim Harding, before contacting Mrs. Lankaster. Did you do that, Ms Rolans?"

Swallowing some of her frustration, she said, "I called that church, he wasn't in. He left a message on my voicemail that he would be out of his office until Monday. This issue needs to be taken care of today, not left until Monday!" she said, angrily.

Not letting her annoyance or frustration cloud how he acted, Matt said, "And why is that, Ms Rolans? Everything was taken care of through the foundling ministry of our church. What more needs to be done?" Looking at the house, which was obviously quite nice, Matt continued, "Do you think the children will be deprived here?"

"That's not the problem!" she snapped, pounding her fist on the steering wheel and accidentally hit the horn. The loud noise cornered in the small space made her jump. She swallowed, hoping to get control. Even so her frustration rose and so did her voice, "They came from Manhattan, that's where they should be housed. Here, they were placed in a single parent home. That's illegal. Who made an inspection? Who is supplying funding for these children?"

What he saw in person didn't make him like her any more. If she was a man, he'd have taken him by the collar and thrown him out. Instead, he said, "Ms Rolans, since these children were placed through a *private* organization, I don't think any of those questions have any bearing on this situation. I haven't parked you in, would you please leave this private property before I'm forced to call the police and request that they escort you away?"

She raised right off the car seat, put her hand on the armrest and glared at Matt through her window. Their exchanges were made with their voices carrying through the open back windows. "What!! I will do no such thing! Those children are here illegally! As I understand it, they could be in some danger!"

Acting overly polite, Matt said, "Really. So you have talked to Ms Fulton and she also passed on her erroneous information to you. I guess that's understandable. Ms Rolans, they are in no danger here. I will say this only once more. They were placed here through a private agency, never having gone into the city's foster care system or into the children's agency system last Friday. Therefore, let me remind you, they are not your concern. I would advise you to start you car, back away from this car and head your car toward town. I will give you five minutes to do that. If you don't leave within that time, I will be forced to call the police and have them escort you from this property. Good day, Ms Rolans."

Matt straightened up, but took a step back from the woman's car so he could watch to see the woman's actions. Her key was in the ignition, but instead of turning it, she fumbled with her briefcase, trying to stuff some papers into it. It was easy to see her hands shaking. Matt glanced at his watch, then bent down and looked at the woman.

"You have four minutes, Ms Rolans."

Just about to scream, Railene grabbed the steering wheel. She was in no shape to drive a car and she knew it. She was on edge ever since she talked with Maranda around lunch time. Also, she hadn't eaten lunch. She took her hands from the wheel and wiped them on her skirt, then pulled in a deep breath, but it made her chest hurt. She needed a cigarette. Her stomach growled, loudly. She looked out the window again and saw the man glance at his watch again then look back at her. Just before he spoke again, she yelled, "Give me a minute!"

Calmly, he said, "I have been, you're down to two."

With her hands still shaking so badly, she could hardly curl her fingers around the key in the ignition, she muttered, "Okay, okay, I'm going!"

"That would be appreciated," he said, calmly. "Since you're down to only a minute and the clock is ticking."

Finally, the car growled to life. Railene yanked the stick down a notch and gunned the car with much more force than she needed to. Fortunately, her wheels were straight, so she didn't touch the new car. However, before she could slam on the brakes, her rear bumper struck the cement of the second step leading to Faith's porch. There was so much force that the rear fender crumpled and cut into the tire. Not only was there a loud crunch, but almost immediately a loud bang as the tire deflated. The driver's backend fell with a bounce.

As Railene put her car into gear, Matt motioned to Faith to take the children in the house. Their doors were opening as Railene hit the step. Matt immediately moved up beside the car, just as Railene opened the door. She opened it with such force that the top corner of the door caught Matt's arm, instantly slicing into the muscle of his upper left arm. Only seconds later, Railene saw the gash and froze.

She had no idea how to handle such a situation. Railene couldn't remember ever being so out of control. Still sitting in the driver's seat, the car running, but going nowhere, because of the step and the flat tire, she looked at Matt, still standing between the edge of the porch and her car door. She couldn't tell if he was in shock, but he stood perfectly still looking at her.

"Say something!" she screamed. "You're hurt! Say something!"

He glanced at his arm, then back at her and asked, "What is there to say, Ms Rolans?"

The woman's face was beet red, as she screamed, "I don't know!" However, she grabbed the steering wheel, as if that would help.

Neither of them noticed, but the four from the SUV hurried inside and stood at the living room window looking at what was going on. Railene's words were loud enough to hear through the closed windows, but Matt's weren't. Of course, no one inside knew that Matt was hurt, but they could see the damage to the car.

Faith said, "Kids, keep watching, I forgot to get the phone from the kitchen."

"Mommy, you better watch, I'll get the phone for you," Brandi said.

"Thanks, Brandi, yes, hurry!" Brandi's feet were already moving. In only minutes she was back with the cordless phone in her hand.

Faith dialed 9-1-1. Soon a voice came on and asked, "State your emergency!"

"Yes, there's been an accident at my home. Could you send an officer, please?" She gave the address. "Oh, and a wrecker, too."

"We'll have someone there in a few minutes. Will an ambulance be needed?"

"No, ma'am, it's only a vehicle. We only need the police and... and the wrecker."

Matt pulled his handkerchief from his pocket and pressed it on the gash on his arm. The area felt a bit strange, but that didn't penetrate his thoughts. However, neither he nor Railene moved for several minutes. Tears sparkled in Railene's eyes, it made her angry, she never cried, not even over a very emotional situation in someone's home. However, she didn't want this man to see weakness or tears, so she bit down on her bottom lip. They were still looking at each other suspiciously when they heard a siren in the distance.

"Oh, no!" Railene cried.

"It seems someone called the police," Matt said, at the same time.

As the car with flashing lights crested the hill, Faith couldn't keep the children still any longer. Brandi exclaimed, "Look! The policeman's here! Can we go see?"

"Well, I..." Faith started to say, but Brandi was the only one who wanted to go outside. Without permission from Faith, she ran for the front door. The twins also moved from the window, but before Faith could comprehend that they weren't going with Brandi, they vanished. Only seconds later, she heard their running footsteps on the stairs. Brandi ran out the front screen door, letting it slam behind her.

Faith wanted to be with Matt, but since the twins ran so fast to hide, she felt she needed to go to them instead. Besides this whole business was because of them and she needed to be with them to make sure nothing happened that shouldn't. She turned from the window and ran for the stairs, too.

What she saw when she reached the second floor was Karin's little feet disappearing into Karl's room. She followed a little more slowly, pushing against the door he was trying to close. She would not let them be by themselves when they were so scared. "Karl, it's okay," she said, "I'm coming to be with you." When she talked so calmly to him, he stopped pushing the door, but both he and Karin hurried toward the bed.

She followed him in and closed the door behind her. Gathering both children in her arms, she took them to the bed and sat down, but they stood on either side of her. His eyes wide, Karl whispered, "Are they gonna take Matt away?"

"No, nothing like that, Karl. Something must be done with that woman's car."

"Oh, a policeman had to come do that?"

"Yes. Nothing's going to hurt you, either of you. Suppose we go back down and start supper? You can both help me."

Karl looked at Karin, who had big tears hanging in the corners of her eyes. "You're sure nothin' gonna happen to Matt?"

"I'm sure, Karl. He didn't do anything wrong. I'm not sure who that woman is, but I don't think she's supposed to be here. When Matt asked her to leave, she was the one who ran her car into the steps."

"Oh. Okay, Karin and me'll come help you."

Faith smiled. "Okay, come on!"

Outside, Brandi took two steps through the door, but screeched to a stop, just looking at the grownups. Matt stood closest to her, but he didn't even turn. Railene still sat in her car with one hand on the armrest of the open door. The engine was still running, Railene didn't have the presence of mind to shut it off. The officer's car stopped, the lights still flashing, two men opened the front doors and quickly stepped out.

As they approached, the driver asked, "What's the problem?"

Railene thought she'd be the one to speak first, since Matt hadn't moved except to pull his handkerchief from his pocket. However, as she opened her mouth, Matt said, "Officer, this woman drove on Mrs. Lankaster's property and waited for us to come home." He looked at his arm and repositioned the hanky on the gash. "She was not invited she was here without authorization, so I asked her to leave. She pressed too hard on the accelerator and ran into the porch steps. As the fender crumpled, a sharp edge punctured her tire. As she opened her door, she clipped me with the corner of the door here on my arm."

The younger officer had accompanied Railene several times on home visits when children were placed by her agency and problems had developed.

He turned to her, but had to speak across the car, because Matt stood behind the open driver's door. "Is that so, Railene?"

Dropping her head, the woman nodded. "I'm afraid so, officer. I…" she murmured, but she couldn't think of what else she wanted to add.

The lieutenant looked at Matt holding his handkerchief on his arm. "Is it bad?"

"It's bleeding a bit, but it's not life-threatening, I'm sure."

Brandi hadn't seen the handkerchief or the gash, but when she heard the question and Matt's answer, she ran to the edge of the porch right beside him, an anguished look on her face. Putting her hands around his other arm, she leaned over and said, "Matt, you're hurt! Did that awful woman do something to hurt you?"

Not able to take his hand away from holding the handkerchief in place, he turned to her and smiled. "It's okay, Brandi, it's nothing your mommy can't clean up and put a Band-Aid on I'm sure. It'll be fine."

Big tears pooled in her eyes. She hiccoughed as two tears slid down her cheeks, she murmured, "Oh, Daddy Matt…." She said those words so softly no one else heard them.

However, Matt's injury was much worse than anyone imagined. When Brandi put her hands on Matt's arm, he stepped back a little to be closer to her. He took his hand away from the gash, the bleeding had stopped, but when he tried to move his arm, nothing happened. He looked down at the gash and tried harder to move his arm again, but then he heard a grating noise and realized by the unnatural feeling he had in his arm that the bone was fractured and the pieces were probably pressing on some nerves.

The officer right behind him, heard the grating sound, realized what had happened and said, "Your arm's broken! It was from this door?"

"It appears so. It was fine when I moved up beside her car until she opened the door. I thought it was only a break in the skin at first."

Brandi was now really crying, with big tears chasing down her cheeks. She took her hands from his good arm and threw them around his neck. Belatedly feeling the strange sensations in his arm caused his knees to go weak and he felt himself sway, so he sat on the edge of the porch. Railene saw the exchange between the man and the child and fell back against the seat of her car, closed her eyes for a second and let out a long breath. Could anything else go wrong? Things had really gone south since lunch. It was now after five and she hadn't eaten, her hands were shaking very noticeably. She was libel to have a diabetic incident very soon. Besides, this was not a five year old child – part of a pair of twins.

Faith heard Brandi crying. She never cried, so Faith opened the screen door and with the twins holding a pant leg, they came out on the porch. "What is it, Brandi?" she asked, anxiously.

"Mommy, Daddy Matt's hurt real bad!" she cried, still holding him around the neck. "That awful woman hurt him!"

Faith rushed to his left side and fell to her knees beside him. The twins crouched behind Matt, between Brandi and Faith. Tears welled in Faith's eyes, but the twins immediately began whimpering. Karl put his hand on Matt's shoulder, but Karin put both arms around his neck. Railene opened her eyes as she heard the door open and watched the three join the little girl. She looked at the perfect family setting and swallowed, wishing she could melt into the ground. Her mind didn't even process that the twins were in plain sight, on the porch with the woman.

"Honey," Faith murmured, "what's happened?"

"My arm's fractured. It happened when she opened her door," he said. Even though he was in pain, he decided immediately never to take his eyes from the woman – especially now that the twins and Faith were in plain sight.

THIRTEEN

FAITH BRUSHED MATT'S BLOND HAIR FROM HIS FOREHEAD AND REALIZED THAT HE was sweating quite profusely. She avoided looking at Railene, she knew she couldn't stand her, but looked up at the officer standing close by and asked, "I already called for a wrecker, should I call an ambulance? I have the phone right here." She held up her cordless.

Before the officers could answer, Matt said, "No, you can drive me to the emergency room, the wrecker should be here. Also, these officers should be removing this woman from your property." Briefly, Matt took his eyes from the woman and looked at the officer closest to the police car. "Isn't that right, Lieutenant?"

Until Matt spoke to them, neither of the officers had moved. The officer nodded, as the other officer closest to the squad car turned toward his car. The lieutenant spoke over his shoulder, "I'll give a shout to find out where the wrecker is right away. Sir, don't you think you should be transported?"

"Yes, but Mrs. Lankaster can take me," Matt said, firmly. "As soon as you get this woman off this property we will go."

The lieutenant shrugged from the driver's side of the cruiser before putting his head inside his car and said, "As you wish."

The other officer looked at Railene and asked, "Are you hurt, Railene?"

"Oh, no! Just sick at the damage I've done." Looking at the family unit huddled around Matt and intent on learning about the situation she had fumbled, she asked, "Who are you?"

Matt looked at her, the pain was building now that he tried to move his arm, but he looked at her, his eyes narrowed and asked quite pointedly, "Is that something you need to know, Ms. Rolans? You do recall you are not authorized to be here, correct? Why would you have the right to know who I am? Or anyone else here for that matter."

She cleared her throat, glanced at the officer, then back at Matt and said, "Umm, no, I guess it's not my place."

"I didn't think so." Holding himself together by a thread of will power, he said, "It will be a good thing when you are removed from the property."

Faith put her hand on Matt's arm and whispered, "Are you sure about an ambulance?"

Shaking his head quite emphatically, he said, "No, of course not! When all this mess is out of here, we can go ourselves. I'm sure all I'll need is a cast. An ambulance would disrupt everything too much."

"Okay," she agreed, dubiously.

No one said anything. What was there to say? Railene had caused all the damage and came without authorization of any kind. The officers paced back and forth from the cruiser to the porch where Matt, Faith and the children were gathered. The wrecker came about fifteen minutes later; Faith had to move the vehicles so he could get to the damaged car, so she moved her car forward as much as possible. There still wasn't room to park the SUV in the garage.

It took nearly twenty minutes for the wrecker to load Railene's car, since it was bashed into the porch and too close to the house, but Matt and his family stayed on the porch and watched. The wrecker left first with the car and before the officer opened the back door of the cruiser for her, Railene turned to Matt and said, "Here's my card, send your hospital bill to the agency and I'll see that your bill is paid."

Matt, unwilling that the woman should get away with anything, snatched the card and answered, "Yes, I'll do just that. It's too bad about your car."

As she climbed into the backseat behind the wire in the cruiser, she said, "I'm sure you're really sorry." Matt knew what he would say before he had Christ in his life, he said nothing.

Before he entered the cruiser, the lieutenant said, "Sir, get to the hospital immediately!"

"Yes, I intend to."

As the cruiser followed the wrecker and disappeared over the rise, Faith jumped to her feet and said, "Kids, while I get my purse, go get in the SUV, we need to get Matt to the hospital. We need to get his arm taken care of right away!" She looked at him and asked, "Can you walk that far or should I bring the car over?" Looking at him more closely, seeing an unhealthy color around his eyes, she answered her own question. "No! You sit there, I'll bring the SUV over."

The pain was settling in, causing Matt to feel very light-headed and as Faith finished speaking, he looked up at her and gave her a weak smile. "I'd be grateful, Love."

None of the children moved, but Faith said, "Go on, kids. You can be buckled in by the time I get there with my purse."

Only a few minutes later, they were on their way to the hospital which was about five miles away. Faith was sure none of the children had ever been in a hospital, she knew Brandi hadn't, so she glanced in the rearview mirror and said, "Okay, kids, listen up." They were all very quiet, so Faith knew she had their attention. "When we get to the hospital, I want you all to stay in your seats until I get some help to get Matt inside, then you find a seat and sit. Matt will have to go in a little room for the doctor to examine his arm and he'll probably have to have X-rays, so they'll take him away for a while, but you may not get in the way. I'll probably be able to stay with you, at least some of the time. Do you all understand?"

The twins nodded and Brandi said, solemnly, "Yes, Mommy, we understand. We'll find seats right away and stay there."

"Thanks, guys, I appreciate that a lot," Faith said. She looked in the mirror and smiled.

Railene's officer friend turned so he could speak to the woman and asked, "What happened, Railene? How did you car end up backed into that step?"

Her hands still shaking, she wrapped them around her briefcase handle and swallowed. She knew some of her agitation was from her lack of food, but she couldn't stop her hands from shaking. She said, "I got a call from a friend at Child Protection about that household. It's a single mother who's housing twins. I was led to believe there was some problem in their being there. When I called, she wouldn't speak to me and referred me to her preacher. I think he was in cahoots, because when he called on my voicemail, he said he'd be out until Monday."

The officer scowled. "A preacher?"

She sighed and shrugged. "Yeah, something about a private placement through a church. I never heard of such a thing." After a few seconds, she swallowed and continued, "I decided to check it out and go to the house myself. I got there, there's a car parked by the house, but nobody's there. It all seemed really fishy! I cooled my heels there for over an hour waiting. Then when they came back, that man came to my car door, wouldn't answer any questions, but worked really hard to intimidate me. He got me all stirred up and then gave me five minutes to get off the property, then began counting."

Sweating profusely, Railene pulled a tissue from her purse to wipe her forehead and said, "I was so nervous, I floored the gas pedal and backed into the step. He moved up beside the car, but I didn't see him when I heard the bang, so I opened the door into his arm."

She raised her hands helplessly. "I really botched this one."

The lieutenant glanced over his shoulder and spoke for the first time, "Are those kids not supposed to be there? Why should you contact a church, anyway? It's a bit fishy, isn't it?"

Feeling light-headed, Railene cleared her throat and said, "Someone brought those twins from NYC to this church. At least that's what my contact said. No one contacted our department, so I tried to find some answers. You saw the results."

The other officer put his arm on the back of his seat and said, "Should we go back and get them, or go to the hospital and pick them up?"

Pulling in a long breath then letting it out, Railene said, "No, I'll try to contact that church on Monday and see what I can find out. It was obvious that man was very important in that family. Maybe there is a live-in…."

"If that's true, you know the agency authorities won't allow children to be in that environment!" Brian exclaimed.

Shaking her head, Railene said, "I've had it for today, I'm sure there'll be nothing that can't wait until Monday, not by the looks of it."

"Okay, Railene," Brian said, "but if you need help, let us know. We'll be glad to go with you on it. Just say the word."

"Thanks, Brian. I'll keep that in mind," she sighed and leaned her head back on the seat as the lieutenant drove down the street. She could only wish she hadn't thrown her lunch away, she wouldn't be this close to a diabetic incident.

Faith drove as carefully as she could, she knew that every bump hurt Matt. She was glad she brought the new vehicle it had a much smoother ride than her car. The children were silent in the back set. Karin especially had silent tears running down her face and her thumb was securely in her mouth. At the hospital, Faith parked at the emergency entrance, rushed through the doors and grabbed the first man she saw in scrubs. "Please, could you bring a wheelchair out to my car I have a very big man who's been hurt. He's kind of weak."

"Yes, Ma'am! I'll grab a chair!"

The man asked no questions, grabbed a wheelchair and followed Faith through the doors to the passenger side of the car. Matt had the door open and released his seatbelt. The children were unbuckled, but had their faces pressed against the window, staring, watching every move the man made as he brought the chair up beside the car. Faith stepped close to the back door, but didn't open it. She didn't try to help the attendant he obviously knew what to do.

"Sir, do you need help getting into the chair?"

Slowly moving in the seat and bringing his feet outside, Matt shook his head and said, "I think if I move sort of slow, I can make it. It's just my arm...." He very carefully picked up his hand and held it with his right hand. He realized as he turned that his whole arm was numb. Unless he held it with his right hand, his arm wouldn't do anything. He was becoming alarmed, but he realized that sitting in the car rather than on the edge of the porch floor had helped stabilize him. He didn't feel so light-headed.

The man put on the brakes, then held the chair as Matt slowly stood, then turned and sat in the chair. As soon as he was in the chair and the man backed it away, Faith opened the back door and the children piled out. Faith locked the car and was very glad the children were quiet. Karin immediately took Faith's hand and Karl crowded between her and Matt's chair. Brandi ran around to Matt's other side, but it was his left side, so she couldn't take his hand. The little crowd moved to the doors and soon was inside.

Inside there was lots of activity. Nurses and men in white coats bustled between several rooms. On the way to an empty examining room, the man pushing the chair grabbed a clipboard. Faith looked at Brandi, as they saw some chairs. "Brandi," she said, softly, "take Karl and Karin over to those chairs, please. I'll be out in a few minutes."

"Yes, Mommy." The children did as they were told, but sat straight in the chairs watching everything that happened around them.

The man left Matt in the chair, but came around in front and asked, "What happened?"

He held up his good hand and said, "Just a minute, please." then he turned to Faith and took her hand. When she bent over, he whispered, "Since that woman was from the Children's Agency and she left with those officers, I think you better keep a close eye on the kids. I wouldn't put it passed her to give them some cock and bull story and they come to pick them up. They have no right, call Jim if you must."

Nodding, she pulled in a long breath and remembered what they went through all day. Just hearing what Matt said about the woman scared her, so she said, "Oh, yes! I never thought of that! I will, right now! Don't you worry about anything."

"That's good, Love," Matt whispered.

As Matt finished giving his history, a doctor came in the room. He took the clipboard, read the notes and said, "Take him to X-ray." He looked at Matt, his arm rested across his lap. "The feeling's distorted in your fingers?" Matt nodded, so he said to the attendant, "Be sure they take every care of that arm and move it as little as possible, but get as many angles as possible."

"Yes, I'll be sure."

Only moments later, the man pushed Matt's chair down the hall passed the children. He smiled, at them and said, "I'll be back, guys. Be good for Mommy."

Faith pulled in a breath. The concern for Matt had her heart rate off the charts, but when she heard what he called her as he spoke to the children, it went into overdrive. As he disappeared through the doors marked 'X-ray,' she said to the children, "I must go find a phone and call Pastor Harding. You can stay here by yourselves for a few minutes, can't you?"

The twins nodded and Brandi said, "Of course, Mommy. We'll be right here when you come back." Faith could only hope that was true. Remembering that awful woman, she sent up a quick prayer that it would be true.

On her way to the desk, Faith looked at the clock over the main desk, it was supper time. It surprised her it was only that time, it seemed like so much had happened since they had the happy ice cream time, then arrived back home to find that awful woman. By now, Jim had left the church, and probably he and Marcia were sitting down for their supper. She sighed, she hated to call him at home, but this was so important and he needed to know. Her heart was pounding, what Matt said really scared her more than anything. Fortunately, the woman at the receiving desk said she could use her phone and she could still see the children. Momentarily she glanced at the woman and the phone then back to the children.

At the desk, she followed the woman's instructions and dialed Pastor Jim's home. He answered, "Hardings."

"Pastor, it's Faith. Matt's been hurt, could you come to the ER? I'll tell you about everything when you get here."

Without hesitation, he exclaimed, "I'll be right there, Faith!"

Not wanting to leave the children for long, Faith rushed back through the large waiting room and fell onto the seat, gathering the children around her. Wishing she could hold all of them tightly, but knowing she couldn't, she smiled at them. Hoping they couldn't feel her anxiety, she pulled Karin up on her lap and let Karl snuggle up on one side, while Brandi sat on the other side and wrapped her arms around Faith's arm.

"Did they take Matt to have pictures, Mommy?" Brandi asked. "Is that what it's talking about on that door that says 'X-ray'?"

"Yes, it's special pictures that show the bone and where it's broken. They're called X-rays. The doctor'll know then how to fix his arm and put a cast on it."

She barely finished her explanation when Jim Harding rushed through the doors. "Faith! Is everything all right?"

Only moments later, Marcia ran in also. "Faith! What's happened?"

Before Faith could answer, Jim turned to Faith, "Have the kids eaten? It is suppertime."

"No, this only happened about an hour ago. We didn't have time."

"Could Marcia take them to get a hamburger?"

Looking gratefully at Jim, then at the twins and hearing their tummies grumbling softly, she nodded. "This all happened so suddenly, but I think that would be much appreciated. We had ice cream after school, but you know little tummies don't keep too long and I've heard some rumbling just now."

"Of course, that's for sure!"

Brandi took on her big sister mode and held out both hands to the twins. "Come on, guys, we're hungry. Matt's getting his picture taken. We'll probably be back by the time he gets back." She kept her hands out towards the twins and reluctantly, Karin and Karl took them, Karin moving slowly from Faith's lap and Karl sliding from the bench.

Faith was in the car during Matt's exchange with Railene, so she didn't know all the details of what was said in the driveway at her house, but Matt told her who the woman was, and since she talked with the woman on the phone, she told Jim everything she knew. She finished by saying, "Pastor, Matt seemed to think she could come here with one or both of those officers and try to pick them up."

Jim whipped the cellphone from his belt and called Marcia on hers. When she answered, he told her to be sure and keep them close to her and bring them back as soon as they finished eating. When he hung up, he pushed the phone back onto his belt, smiled and said, "Faith, this has been some day, hasn't it?"

She sighed and shook her head, "Pastor, it started so early this morning and it's still going on! It's been something I'd rather not live through again. Can they really take the kids away? That woman we met with had to contact that other woman after we left her office!"

"Faith, they have no grounds, none what-so-ever. These children never were in the system, but we both know that doesn't mean someone like this woman or that one we met this morning won't try something. I think you used the word this morning; bureaucrats love to throw their weight around. Also, if it can be done, I'm sure they'll try anything to bend the truth as far as they can to get more money out of government coffers."

Faith could only shake her head.

Jim sat down beside her and put his arm around her shoulders. "Faith, you are one remarkable woman. You'll make it just fine."

Not believing him for a minute, she asked, "Jim, do you think it was Maryann who called that Fulton woman?"

Jim folded his arms across his chest and took several minutes before he said, "I have a hard time believing the woman is that malicious, but who else would have called that child protection agency? Of all things, Maryann should know those kids wouldn't need protecting, not in your house! What an absurd idea!"

"Yes, I hope so!"

About a half hour later, the man pushing Matt wheeled the chair back through the doors. Matt didn't look happy, but he gave Faith his crooked smile, as she rushed to his side. "What happens now, Honey?" she murmured.

"He's taking me to the cast room. I'll be there for a while. Hi, Pastor." He looked around and asked, "Where are the kids?"

"Marcia took them for some hamburgers. He'll put a cast on, then you can go?"

Matt made a face, and then said, "He thinks the nerve's involved, it's not going to be just applying a cast."

Faith's face turned white. "Oh, what'll happen?"

"He must stretch my arm under local anesthesia. He thinks the sharp bone edge is resting on a nerve, but if he can get it back in the right position, he can cast it."

With tears sliding down her cheeks, she bent over and put her arms around him. "Oh, Matt," she whispered, "I hope he can, really, I do!" Following a hiccough, she murmured, "Oh, Matt, I love you!" Even with others in the waiting room, she bent over and kissed his cheek.

The young man wanted to walk on water just then. If only he could take this lovely lady in his arms and hug her the way he wanted to… Even though he was in pain, a smile spread across his face. He slid his good arm out from between them and put it around her. "Darling, you can't know how that makes me feel! I love you, too, Sweetheart." He grinned at her and said, "Hold that thought, I'll be back after a bit." He kissed her, then said to Jim. "Pastor, can I ask a favor of you and your wife. Another one?"

"What is it, Matt?"

Matt sighed and shook his head before he said, "The doctor said this'll probably take at least an hour, to get my arm set properly. Would your wife be willing to take the kids to Faith's place? I don't think there's any danger of them being taken now, but I'm sure they'd be more comfortable if they were at home."

Nodding, he whipped his cellphone from his belt again. "I'll call her right now and she can take them without even coming back here. I'm glad you thought of that, Matt, they will be much more comfortable at home. I'll ride over there with you and Faith when you're finished. We'll have things in order in a minute."

Matt nodded as the assistant began to wheel him away. "Thanks, Pastor. I think we owe you one or two."

Jim chuckled. "Think nothing of it, Matt."

He called then sat down with Faith to wait, as Matt disappeared through another door and the assistant closed it behind them. "All taken care of. Marcia's got it covered. You know she's in her element with kids, usually, the more the merrier." He chuckled a bit. "Although I doubt she can get them in bed if it comes to that."

Faith sighed, as she watched Matt go, "God, don't let there be permanent damage. It's so important that he have the use of both arms."

Jim heard her murmured request and said, "Yes, I agree. Let's pray right now." He took Faith's hand and they both bowed their heads. "Father in heaven, work with the doctor on this. Help him get Matt's arm in proper alignment so that it will heal properly. Thanks, amen."

Faith let go of Jim's hands and fell back against the chair. "Wow! What a day!"

"Absolutely!"

The cruiser pulled up to the building where Railene worked. As Brian stepped out to open her door, he said, "Be sure and call if you still feel you want to go after those kids. I'll grab a car and take you." He looked more closely at Railene and asked, "Are you okay, Railene? You don't look so good!"

Wishing she had eaten her lunch rather than throwing it away or maybe that she had some crackers at her desk she shook her head and said, "Thanks, Brian. I think I need to evaluate this at my quiet desk. Perhaps it's not what I think it is." She shook her head. "Actually, I didn't eat my lunch and I'm a bit shaky right now."

Giving her a cocky salute, Brian turned back and sat down in the car, he wasn't into knowing how diabetes worked, and since Railene didn't elaborate, he didn't notice how she acted. Brian sat in the shotgun seat of the patrol car and pulled the door closed. As the lieutenant pulled away, Brian asked, "You think it's okay what Railene's doing, leaving that situation until Monday, Lieutenant? Could something really come of it?"

"She's kind of shook up." The man looked at the dash clock. "I guess we'll go with what she decides, we don't have all the details. We don't want to do anything against the law."

Brian also looked at the clock on the dash. "True, but why would she be involved if some law hadn't been broken?"

"Brian," the lieutenant looked sharply at the younger man. "Give it a rest. She'll call if she needs assistance with this. You know Railene, she's a by the book woman."

"You're right. That woman had a nice house. Who was that man, did you ever find out?" Brian shrugged. "I guess he could have been a live-in."

The lieutenant also shrugged. "You heard what he said to Railene. He never gave his name, not to us. It's possible he's a live-in, but let her deal with that, it's not our department. It was a nice house. If all the houses where kids are placed in the system were like that, we'd have nothing to worry about."

"Yeah, that's for sure!" Thinking about his own small apartment, Brian said, "I wouldn't mind myself to live in a house like that."

The lieutenant grinned. "So go invite yourself to live in!"

"Sure! I'll just do that! With three kids? Uh uh!"

"Oh, come on! You know you love kids. I know you'd just eat it up, that older one hanging around your neck and those two…"

"Mmm, not so much!"

The lieutenant breathed out a sigh. "I guess we need to head back to precinct and make a report. After all, emergency dispatch did call us out."

"Yeah, there was personal damage and also vehicle damage. Did you hear her? Railene told that man to send the bill for his arm to her!"

"Yeah, I heard and he was pretty emphatic that we get her off the property."

"Yup, wonder what that was all about anyway."

The lieutenant shrugged. "We may never know."

Railene sighed as she positioned her purse and gripped her briefcase then walked the few steps to the building. There were few lights on in the building, it was Friday and well after five. All the offices were officially closed and only a few dedicated individuals still stayed to finish up paperwork in their offices, expecting no disturbances from callers.

Railene had to use her key to enter the front door of her department. Although she knew any adrenalin had drained out long ago, her hand still shook so much she had a hard time inserting the key in the lock. There was no one in the office. She flipped on a light in the dark suite and walked down the hall to her office. She used her other office key and let herself into her private office. As she flipped the switch, she noticed another paper on top of the folder she had started about the twins who were with Faith Lankaster.

It was then she realized she didn't even know the twins names. This whole situation was one she wanted to sweep under the rug.

She set her briefcase down beside the desk and sank into her chair. In the quietness she realized her body still shook, and knew it wasn't from the stress of the day. She needed quickly to put food into her body or have a diabetic incident. She had no food in her office. It was Friday, if she had an episode who would find her? Putting both elbows on the desk, she closed her eyes and took a deep breath. After a few minutes she let her eyes roam over the paper.

Railene, Georgiana had me call that church for a copy of their 'Foundling Ministry' policy. Here's what they faxed over to us. Since those kids were never in the public system, and the church has this as part of their policy, I guess they are out of our hands. Maranda

Below the note was a fax on the church's stationery with the paragraph highlighted. Even without her permission, her eyes scanned the paragraph. Whoever the man was at that home was totally right, she had no right to be there. Railene sighed, as she crumpled the paper and dropped it dramatically in her wastebasket.

She put her head on her desk. "All that wasted energy, time and money," she grumbled. "I'll have a major repair job on my car and now with this, the boss'll have me pay for that man's arm. I don't believe any day I've spent for this department has ever gone so badly," she looked at the page that was still left in the folder. It was blank.

She pulled in a deep sigh. Much more slowly, she dug the paper from the trash and spread it out as best she could. She laid it on top of the blank page, read the highlighted paragraph through, then sighed again and slowly closed the folder. Monday would definitely be soon enough to deal with this.

Her stomach growled and she remembered throwing her sandwich away, in fact she could smell it. She swallowed a curse and muttered, "My diabetes is about to kick. I must get home."

Only ten minutes after she walked into her office, she turned off the light, locked the door and left. When she reached the receptionist's desk, she realized she had no way to get home and it was much too far to walk, so from the phone on the desk, Railene called a cab. In fact, that was the last thing she remembered doing. However, she moved to the main door of the suite, shut off the light, locked that door and walked back outside to wait on the sidewalk for the cab they promised in only minutes.

When the cab driver drove up to the curb a few minutes later, he found a woman sprawled on the sidewalk in front of the office building. Not seeing anything wrong, no bruising or fowl-play, he reached for her wrist and felt her pulse. It didn't feel right to him, so nearly frantic, he dialed 9-1-1 and soon an ambulance arrived. The medics quickly put her on their gurney and transported her to the hospital. They wheeled the unconscious woman in the ER as the doctor applied Matt's cast.

Maryann Swain called her friend Mel Sample after supper Friday evening. Maryann's husband was gone to play a softball game in the church league, so she was alone in the house. She really wanted to know what had become of their conversation on Sunday night. "Mel," she said, when the lady answered. "Did you find anything out?"

Hearing who was on the line, Mel pulled the phone cord as far as it would go and sat comfortably in a chair to talk. Mel and Maryann were good friends for years and they had many good conversations together. Mel wasn't a church goer, but she and Maryann had lots of things in common. "Only a few minutes ago, Maryann. Maranda called me after she got home. I guess she never got that Faith to answer until late Wednesday and she didn't come in until today. Guess what else?" she said, conspiratorially.

"What?" Maryann asked, expecting a juicy tidbit.

"When she went in today, she had some fireman and her pastor with her. I guess Maranda didn't get much out of them, but that fireman was all over Faith!" Mel swallowed. "I mean, Maryann, all over her!"

Licking her lips, Maryann said, "Wow! She's been a widow for three years, you know. But a fireman...?"

"Yeah, I know! An FDNY man, too. She's in a Bible study you're in, right? That's kind of hard to believe, isn't it?"

"Yes! That hussy was there on Wednesday, too. She monopolized the whole meeting, too, and then ran out! I'll keep an eye on this, don't think I won't!"

Mel had a satisfied smirk on her face, as she said, "Yeah, that's my recommendation! I'll talk to you again, Maryann."

Maryann disconnected, angry that things hadn't gone the way she thought they should. She immediately dialed another number, but the answering machine came on. With an evil smirk she said, "Pastor, Maryann. I think you need to have a talk with Faith Lankaster! I think something's going on you should be aware of. Call me when you get in, I'll be glad to explain." As she hung up, she muttered, "Would I ever!" This monkey business had to stop! She would make sure that it would; just as soon as Pastor called her back! She went to the TV in the living room to watch her favorite Friday evening show.

Behind the doors in the cast room, the doctor and the assistant helped Matt from the wheelchair up onto a table. They carefully supported his arm as he lay down on his back. The assistant pulled a rolling table with an adjustable top along side. First the assistant adjusted the top to hold Matt's arm straight out from his body, then both men carefully laid Matt's left arm onto the table. Immediately, the doctor drew up a syringe full of liquid and began to inject the fluid into several places around Matt's upper arm.

When the syringe was empty, he said, "I realize you couldn't feel too much before, but hopefully, you can't feel anything now."

"You're right on that score, Doc! I do feel like a pin cushion, though."

The doctor chuckled. "Yeah, I guess you would."

The doctor waited several minutes, wanting the full benefit of the anesthetic to work. Finally, he moved Matt's arm. They all heard the bones grate against each other and Matt made a face, not from the feeling, but from the sound. The doctor stopped moving his upper arm, but moved his lower arm until it was at the angle he wanted it.

With Matt's arm bent at the elbow, the doctor had his assistant, who was a much bigger man, pull on Matt's elbow. It was quiet in the room and all three of them heard a scraping noise, but as the doctor put his hands tightly around the arm at the place where the gash was, he felt the bone ends slide into place.

Immediately, the doctor said, "Abe, hold it right there! I'll get some plaster and wrap it around this."

"Will, do, Doc."

Matt was very glad he couldn't feel anything. The sound of the bone fragments sliding back against each other was bad enough he could imagine what it would feel like. He saw the man's bulging muscles as he held his arm, but then he watched as the doctor went to a glass fronted cabinet and take out several large rolls of what looked like white cloth. He went to the sink and filled a basin with warm water, then brought everything back to the table beside the table where Matt lay. Matt watched, but didn't say anything.

The doctor didn't waste any time, after all the assistant was using muscle power to keep Matt's arm in alignment. He dipped the cloth in the water, then pulled the end away and as it dripped, began to wrap Matt's arm with the sticky cloth. He started right under his shoulder joint. "What is it you do, Matt?" He needed to know, but he also wanted to distract Matt.

"I'm a fireman for FDNY for mid-Manhattan."

The doctor shook his head and exclaimed, "Not for a good while, you're not! We'll immobilize this arm with a sling that you may only take off to bathe or dress for several weeks."

Matt scowled at him then looked at his arm. "Hey, Doc, take pity on me! If my arm's immobile, I can't really do much for myself! I'm a bachelor! You're asking the impossible!"

The doctor continued to wrap the wet gauze around Matt's arm, from his shoulder to below his elbow, but he smirked and winked at the man whose arm he was efficiently wrapping. "Tell me, Mr. Barns, who's that beautiful woman out there who was crying over you? I think you're underestimating who you are, my man."

Matt watched the soggy material being wrapped around his arm. It was cold and wet enough that water dripped from his arm onto the table. In the air conditioned room Matt shivered. "Doc! Give me a break! I only met her last week! We've gotten pretty close, but she's got three kids who live with her, she doesn't need me as an extra burden. Besides, I couldn't live at her house. It wouldn't be right!"

The man shrugged, still wrapping the cloth around his arm. So far, he used three of the rolls. "I'll take this plaster up to your underarm and down below your elbow. We'll put it in a sling, but I want that as part of your daily wear for three weeks. If you feel any strange sensations any place on your arm or hand in the next few days, you come back in immediately. I have an office here in the ER, tell the clerk out there at the desk that you want to see me and she'll have me paged. I'm here all the time except in the dead of night. We'll X-ray this in three weeks and go from there." Matt only shook his head and sighed.

After he had the arm immobilized with the plaster, the assistant was able to release his hold, but the doctor cut out a window only where the gash was on Matt's arm. It was quite deep and needed several stitches. The stitches needed to be removed before the cast came off. As the doctor stood looking at his work, he asked, "How did this happen?"

"A woman in a foul mood pushed her car door open with a lot of force and unfortunately, I was on the other side. The edge of the door thumped my arm a pretty good wallop."

The doctor whistled and said, "I'd say, that's the truth! So you'll need a medical leave from the FDNY, won't you?"

"I suspect Colin can see the results of my mishap, but he'll need to know how long I must be out. So yes, I'll need something in writing."

Dr. Hindson shrugged. "Easily remedied, I'm on it right now."

The assistant helped Matt to a sitting position and brought a sling to his side as the doctor went to a desk, sat down and began writing. As he stood up, holding out the small slip of paper to him, he said to Matt, "Take some pain killers; Abe's got that prescription there on the clipboard. Over night, I think you'll feel better if you can elevate this on a pillow, so, yes, you can take the sling off as long as there's support under it. However, you really need to watch for any discoloration of your fingers. If that happens come right in and see whoever's here. I'm still concerned about nerve involvement." He smiled at the big man and patted him on the back. "No firefighting for a good while, my man."

"Thanks, I was up for promotion in five weeks," Matt grumbled.

The doctor shrugged. "Maybe your supervisor'll take pity and give it to you anyway."

"Mmm, maybe. You do know how strapped the department is after what happened last week, right?"

"Of course, I know! However, life goes on and you can't be part of fighting fires, Matt. Go on home and let that pretty lady take care of you."

"Sure!" As Matt turned to sit in the wheelchair again, he said, "The woman who did this said to send the bills to her department for them to pay. How do I do that?"

"At the front desk give them the info."

"Okay, Doc, I'll do that. I can't seem to make the words thanks come out too well, but I guess you did get things back the way they should be."

The man chuckled. "Yeah, a fireman brought down by a woman. That's bad."

"Mmm, you could say that again," Matt groused.

It was close to an hour later when the assistant wheeled Matt through the double doors into the waiting room. Faith was on her feet and by his side only a few steps from the doors, Jim was not far behind her. She looked at the cast and grinned. "I'd say you're out of commission for a few days, Honey."

Looking down at the big, unwieldy thing, then back at her, he said, "Mmm, you could say that. Doc said X-rays in three weeks."

"It's Friday, just think of the two little nurses you'll have for two days."

Matt rolled his eyes. "You'll bring them over to the B and B?"

"Nope! We'll take you home, two little girls are expecting you."

Time stood still.

Did this lady realize what she was saying? All day today they were put through the wringer because she was a single mom and the government authorities didn't like a single woman having custody of someone's orphaned children. They looked even harder and with less favor on unmarried couples living together having children of that nature. They had to deal with two women from two different agencies today and all because of a gossip from the church. He couldn't let that happen to her!

He grabbed her hand and exclaimed, "Faith! Do you know what you're saying?"

She squeezed his hand and answered immediately, "Of course I do! Yes, Pastor Jim and I've talked and he agrees you shouldn't be alone tonight."

"That's exactly right, Matt!" Jim added.

She was walking beside the wheelchair as the assistant pushed it. Playfully, she patted his head, "Besides, those kids may be in bed with you."

If I had my way, you'd *be the one in bed with me.* Not saying those words out loud, he said, "You think so?"

"It's a possibility."

Matt pulled in a deep breath, let it out and muttered. "We'll see."

Jim waited for a quiet moment and said, "I talked to Marcia. She has the kids all ready for bed, but they won't go, of course until they see you at the house. She's fixed some supper from what you had there at the house. We didn't get to eat, either, so we'll join you. A big man like you can always eat, I'm sure."

With just the mention of food, Matt's stomach growled. He grinned. "Yeah, I think it's a given, Pastor. We ate lunch a long time ago. We had ice cream after school, but that's long gone, too, I'm afraid."

"Oh, Pastor, I'm so glad Marcia's done that! I'll be sure to thank her," Faith said. "You folks have been so special today!"

Matt found who to give Railene's business card to and it went with his ER paperwork. Only moments later, they headed to the outside door. The car was still parked outside, so the assistant wheeled Matt out through the double doors. Faith used the key fob then quickly opened the door. Jim helped Matt from the chair, but he turned himself and sat on the seat. As soon as the wheelchair was out of the way, Jim closed the door, then opened the rear door and got in, while Faith went around to drive.

"So who did this?" Jim asked. "Faith said it was the woman from the children's agency."

"Railene Rolans from the Department of Children's Services here in Thomaston. She was sitting at Faith's house when we got home with the kids. I would assume that Fulton woman got her on the case the minute we walked out of her door this morning. Did she even call you to confirm anything with you?"

"Yes, when I came in off the playground I had something from that woman on my answering machine. I returned her call, but it went to her voicemail. I'd say it's a good possibility about that Fulton woman. I'd like to think we've seen the last of them all, but with these agencies always trying to get more money, it'll be a wonder if that's so. With women like we dealt with this morning one can never know."

Matt nodded and said, "I agree with you."

"So you're off work for a while?"

"Doc said no work until X-rays in three weeks. I'll need to go in tomorrow and take my medical leave slip, but I'd say that's it for a while."

After a moment of silence, Matt continued, "Pastor, something's been troubling me about all this. I thought about it that day Faith called to tell me about that Fulton woman's call. It had to be that woman who talked with Faith last Sunday night who got all this started. Can't something be done about that?" He looked at Jim, then at Faith and added, "I'm sure you know who we're talking about."

Wow! Matt's a new Christian! This is such a bad testimony! Jim let out a sigh and said, "I think I need to have a talk with her, Matt. I'm still not sure talking with her will remedy the problem, but I'll give it my best, believe me. That woman has many friends who think she's the straightest arrow in the quiver."

"It's hard to change a gossip," Faith murmured. "Especially, that woman, she has so many friends who think what she says is gospel." Faith shook her head. "I've often wondered why that is. Don't people know? Don't they recognize gossip for what it is?"

Jim nodded. "Yes, that's a fact." One good thought came to him, *At least Matt's first dealings with Christians were Brandi and Faith, thank You, God!*

Faith was glad to be going home - a long day and much of it very stressful. As Faith pulled over the rise in her driveway, they noticed all the lights were on downstairs, but not one in the bedrooms. Faith shook her head. "I'd say those kids are in rare form. Poor Marcia!"

Jim laughed. "Don't worry about her! Remember we had three. Doing kids is her thing. She's looking for that first grandchild with anticipation. Still, she's not holding her breath." Jim sighed, "We must get those kids and their spouses off dead center first. Careers are good, but waiting until you're almost past child-bearing age to think about having a family is a bit much."

Faith laughed, knowing where all three of those children were. "That's good. I'm real glad she's not holding her breath." She pulled as close as possible to the back door. "I would say, just off the cuff, that we can expect an onslaught of kids in about a minute."

FOURTEEN

"Uh huh, I agree with you," Matt sighed.

The adults still sat in the SUV, but all the doors were open when the back door of the house flew open and three little people streamed out with an adult trailing along behind them. "Daddy Matt! Are you all better?"

Chuckling, Matt held out his right arm from the passenger seat and Brandi ran to him, her arms spread. "No, Squirt, I got this lovely cast for a while. The doctor said I can't ride that big truck for at least three weeks."

Faith's face turned red. She hadn't heard Brandi call Matt 'Daddy' before, but the words came through loud and clear now. Jim heard them just as loudly and Marcia even from several feet away. Faith wondered what to do, if anything. They were out and Brandi had promised her she wouldn't give anyone, not Matt, not the twins, any idea about what she was telling her mom ever since the day they met Matt. Besides, what did Matt think? However, there was too much going on to worry about it now. She swallowed a sigh, just glad to be back home, finally.

Matt turned carefully in the seat. The cast was still damp and the doctor warned him not to be too active for twenty-four hours so that it could dry completely. The twins both looked at the big plaster cast on Matt's arm and their eyes grew huge. Karin broke away from everyone and ran to Matt and threw her arms around his legs. "Daddy!" Karin wailed. "Oh, Daddy!"

Time stood still.

Karin cried noisily and big tears slid down her cheeks. Faith stopped dead at the front of the vehicle and stared at the little girl. The child had finally broken her silence. Jim stood on the ground, but hadn't closed his door, he stared and his mouth dropped open. Brandi stood beside Matt, but she stared at the little girl and Karl was so surprised he sat down hard on the ground by the back steps. Marcia stood on the top step, but her mouth fell open.

Matt reached over and with his right arm, scooped up the little girl. After he planted a kiss on her cheek, he set her on his right knee. With her spoken words a huge wad of cotton filled his mouth he had to swallow hard. A non-verbal child had said her first words to him! Finally he could say, "It's okay, Li'l Bit. It's getting better starting right now."

The child flung her arms around him. "Daddy, good!"

Karl walked over and had to touch the wet cast. He made a face as he pulled his wet, sticky fingers away. "You can't go be a firemans, can you, Daddy Matt?"

Having all three of the children call him daddy completely stole his breath. He looked down at the little boy and with tears burning behind his eyes, he swallowed, before he could finally croak out, "You're right, Son. I have a paper getting me excused from working for three weeks. We'll see what happens then."

"Good, okay," he said, with finality.

Brandi looked around the back door to see Pastor Harding then she looked around Matt and saw her mommy. "Come on, guys, Ms Marcia fixed you some supper, it's gonna be all cold if you don't come in and eat it." She reached out both hands toward the twins, wanting to herd them back into the house.

"Okay, Brandi," Jim said, "I am kind of hungry and I heard Matt's stomach growl a while ago. We'll be right along."

"Well, come on! Get inside right now!" she exclaimed, exasperated, when the adults didn't move with quite as much speed as she thought they should.

"We're coming, Brandi," Faith said. "Matt's not moving quite as fast as you usually do. He's been hurt and the doctor gave him some medicine for it. He had to do some work on his arm, too before he put that big cast on, so he's not up to moving quite so fast."

Jim walked beside Matt up the back steps then Faith came to his other side. Marcia pulled out his chair at the table, but Jim helped get it close. Matt ate supper with the others; knowing he had to eat to keep up his strength. Bones healed best with proper nutrition; even so, he didn't feel much like eating. The ordeal, starting this afternoon when the door slammed into his arm, made him want to cover up in bed and sleep, then wake up from a bad dream in the morning.

As the numbness from the anesthetic wore off, his arm hurt worse than any burn he ever had and his body felt like it was about to shut down. He didn't know Marcia well enough to refuse her meal, but the pain in his arm took any enjoyment out of the experience. It was good, he had to admit, but he would have enjoyed Faith's cooking much more. A quiet evening with her and the kids was more what he felt like.

However, the children were another story. They ate at the fast food restaurant Marcia took them to, then came home and played for some time. Minute after minute until Matt came home they asked Marcia if she knew anything. All the time that the adults ate all three sat around the table; they didn't want to let Matt out of their sight.

Seeing how uncomfortable Matt was, the Harding's finished the meal. Marcia and Jim cleaned up the kitchen then they both said goodnight. Marcia hugged Faith, while Jim shook Matt's hand. Moments later Matt heard the car engine start up and he let out a sigh of relief. He new he needed someone to watch him through the night, but surely he could go find a bed now?

Shortly after the Harding's left, Faith and the children escorted Matt, who was glad for the clean clothes Faith handed him, upstairs to the empty bedroom. It was the room that Karl said was too big for him, but it was a lovely room, nearly as big as his at the B&B. He went in and sat on the bed, the kids each kissed him, then went to the girl's room, because Faith promised them a story and that was part of their nighttime routine since the twins came.

While Faith read them a short story, Matt pulled off the sling and his shirt, then went to the bathroom and took some of the pain killer the doctor prescribed. As he swallowed the pills, he hoped he'd soon be asleep. He went back to the room, closed the door, took off his slacks and sighed; glad to stretch out on the soft mattress, but pulling up the sheet was almost too much effort. As his eyelids drooped he pulled the extra pillow under his arm and clicked off the light. His strength was gone. He hoped the pain killer kicked in soon.

When Faith finished reading the story, the children asked many questions and she tried to answer them as best she could. He heard her say, "Shh, you need to settle down now. It's way past bedtime and Matt's probably exhausted, so it's time you all settled down."

"Yes, Mommy," Brandi said. The noise level went down a few decibels.

Matt heard the children's voices coming closer and all three came back to Matt's closed door. However, since the door was closed, Faith wouldn't let anyone open it. From the bed, he listened to the soft sounds outside the door, as Faith got the three wound-up kids into their rooms. Matt listened as Brandi's door closed. He hoped she would come back once she had their lights turned off.

Faith spent a little extra time in Karl's room because he was by himself, but soon she whispered to him, "Karl, I'll kiss you goodnight, then you must close your eyes and get to sleep, okay? I'll see you in the morning."

Sleepily, Karl said, "Okay, Mommy. I'm glad Matt's here."

"Yes, so am I, sweet boy." She pulled the door almost closed, then stood in the hall and debated whether she should knock on Matt's door. It was a long, very stressful day. It was hard to believe it was still the same day as when they went to the Child Protection Agency office. Too many things had happened. Finally, she made up her mind, not knowing if he was asleep already or not. "Are you still awake?" she whispered against the door.

"Yes, I'm still waiting for the pain killer to kick in. Come on in."

While she opened the door, Matt reached for the bedside lamp and turned it on. Faith looked at the huge cast resting on the pillow. Shaking her head, she said, "I'm so sorry you were hurt, Honey. I hope you can sleep."

"I'm hoping the same thing, Love." He let a sigh escape and said, "This bed feels great! I'm sure I'll rest well in it."

After a long kiss, she realized his eyes were drifting shut. She stood and smiled down at him, turned out the light and tiptoed from the room. She went to her own room, then on into her bathroom and started water running into her tub. Stressful things had marked the day, and she needed to relax. As she lay in the warm water with the bubbles covering her up to her chin, she thought about the man lying in the fourth bedroom down the hall. She loved that man and he never left her side today. She swished her hand leisurely through the water and thanked God for Matt who was hurt because he fought one of her battles.

As Faith lay in the warm water, she thought again about the long day. Matt was her support in the first meeting this morning, he coached her on what to say to the woman on the phone from the children's agency and he was the one to show that woman that she had no right to be on her property.

If he hadn't been there for her, she was sure that the twins would now be somewhere else. Where, she could only imagine!

Even in the warm water a shudder went down her back as she thought about it. It was unconscionable what government agencies would stoop to do! Now he was suffering pain and inconvenience and loss of employment because of that confrontation. She wondered if the woman would come back or contact the police to come. She stopped that thought before it took root; both Matt and Jim assured her it wouldn't happen. She had to believe them. Yes, God was in control! They had bathed the whole situation with prayer, both alone and together.

Finally, she let out the water, dried herself, slipped into her nightie and climbed into bed. She took her Bible from the nightstand and began to read, but her thoughts strayed to the man in the other room. He was so close. When they met, he lived on Manhattan. Only a few days ago he moved here to Thomaston, but quite a few blocks away from her. Because of circumstances beyond anyone's control, tonight he slept in a room only a few steps from hers. Oh, that she could keep him here!

In fact, she knew in her heart of hearts that he still wasn't close enough. When could they share this bed that she lay in alone? He told her he loved her, after she blurted out that she loved him. Did he really? Would he ask her to marry him? If he did, would it be soon? How long should you know a man before you married him when it was the second time around? Had he really thought about it? She knew if she met a man with three children and she had never been married, it would be daunting at best and totally scary at worst. She'd be on the next train out of town! Would he? But he was so good with the children!

Her sleep wasn't restful, several times she woke from a dream wrapped in her sheet like a mummy, sweating so her nightie was soaked and she was breathing hard. She was glad that each time there was no light in the room or that there was no one else sharing her bed. She was especially glad no childish eyes were trained on her, because the scenes had her blushing like a teenager in the throws of her first crush. Her life with Max had been good, exceptional, really, but if her dreams were any indication.... Well, so would life be with Matt. Even as she mulled over her feelings she remembered that stellar moment at Ground Zero on September eleventh.

The night was very long for Matt. The pain pills he took at bedtime took the edge off the constant pain and when the house was quiet, he fell asleep, but by midnight he was awake again. The bed was really very comfortable, but every time he tried to turn over in his sleep his arm woke him up, because the pillow came out from under it and usually, his arm slid down onto the bed. Every little thud jarred his arm. The first time he woke up it was too early to take another pain killer, but the next time his arm felt like a ton weight and he couldn't bring himself to move. He jammed the pillow back under the cast and closed his eyes.

The only thing good about the night was that as the anesthesia wore off, and feeling came back to his arm, his fingers were normal color and had normal feeling in them. After the strange sensations yesterday he was concerned that there might be permanent damage. Obviously 'muscle man' doctor's assistant had pulled his arm back to the right alignment. Several times before morning he thanked God nothing worse had happened and the twins were where they belonged – at Faith's. Now it was Saturday, maybe nothing more would come of the agencies.

Matt didn't know the woman and he was glad he didn't, but he was really angry at the woman who started the gossip and he sincerely wished that Jim could get a silencer onto her. From what Faith said about the woman it wasn't the first time she did such dirty work. He was glad and truly thanked God he met Brandi and Faith before this ever happened.

For a change, Faith was wide awake when Brandi and Karin started making noise. She listened to their whispers in the hall. They went in the bathroom briefly and the toilet flushed once, but instead of coming to her door, she heard the squeak of Karl's door and more whispers. The girls never left Karl out of their conspiracies. Fully expecting them to come to her room, she pulled the sheet up to her chin, but her door stayed closed, so she quickly sat up. She had no idea how Matt slept, but probably not well, she needed to intercept the children.

However, she wasn't fast enough because only minutes later, she heard Brandi say in a stage whisper, "Daddy Matt, are you awake? Can we come in?"

Faith groaned as she heard him say, "Yes, Brandi, I'm awake, you can come in." Instantly, she heard the particular sound that door made. His wide-awake response made her wonder how well and how much he slept during the night.

Had the children wakened him or like her, was he already awake? She wondered what went through his mind when he heard her daughter call him daddy. When all three of them had called him daddy last night, he hadn't reacted with shock or seemed angry about it, but the Hardings were there, he might not have wanted to make a scene. Three years ago was the last time she had any real dealings with men. How should she know?

Even though all three of the children called Matt either Daddy Matt or just plain Daddy when they came from the hospital, there was no time to have a talk with them last evening about it. Saying something to them in front of the Hardings didn't seem like the thing to do. Matt seemed to take it well, perhaps even getting a bit choked up.

Faith knew Brandi remembered her daddy; she was five and a half when his final illness took him to the hospital for the last time. They mourned him together for nearly a year, even with counseling. She was sure the twins remembered their dad; it was only weeks since they were with him. Some how, all three of them had hearts so filled with love for Matt that they all called him 'Daddy'. She caught her breath even tiny Karin broke her silence and called him 'Daddy'. That was such progress in only a week.

How could she know if it would send him away? She felt embarrassed that the children did that, after she told Brandi in the hearing of both Karl and Karin that they shouldn't call him daddy, at least not yet. She wondered what Jim and Marcia thought about it. She shook her head. This was in the realm of the unknown. Of course, they were all stunned when Karin spoke out loud and that took everyone's mind off the words she said.

She must find the time today to talk to them. It wouldn't happen right away, but hopefully sometime soon. She wondered if Karin's words would be the end of her silence or if she was so emotionally charged that they blurted out. She hadn't spoken since last October, was she now going to start speaking normally? Faith could hardly think that was so. However, she'd be glad. If that was so, the child wouldn't need that kind of counseling.

Faith had no time to contemplate. Only minutes later, Brandi opened her door without knocking and said, "Mommy, Matt doesn't have a toothbrush. Is it okay if I give him one of our extras so he can brush his teeth?"

Faith sat on her bed with her back to the door, working her feet into her slippers. "Of course, Brandi, you know that's fine."

"Okay, I'll get him one. He said he wants to take a shower and wondered if we have a big plastic bag he can put over his cast so it won't get wet. We have some somewhere don't we, Mommy? Would what we have be big enough?"

By now, Faith was up and had her terrycloth robe on. She pulled the belt tight and walked into the hall behind Brandi. There stood Matt, a twin on either side, in a pair of sweat pants that she washed the other day after they went to the shore and he hadn't had a chance to take back to the B&B. She felt her throat go dry as she looked at the magnificent man. His hair was messed up, not only from sleep, but he had dragged his fingers through it. Was that from pain or frustration? She didn't really want either to be the case.

She swallowed and tried to remember Brandi's question. A scowl moved across her face as she tried to remember. Just looking at the man had wiped every sensible thought right out of her mind. She looked back at Brandi and said, "Oh, we have some black plastic garbage bags under the kitchen sink, why don't you run and get him one. In the den, in the desk are some rubber bands, bring some of the big ones, too." Faith had to raise her voice, because Brandi was already on the move down the stairs.

"Yes, Mommy," she called back.

Faith looked back at Matt. He was blond, but his face was tanned and the blond stubble stood out on his cheeks. It gave him an air of adventure, and mystery. She hadn't seen his bare chest before, his blond chest hair made a perfect 'V' that ended somewhere below his low-slung sweats. His muscles were well defined, he was a very well made man and looking at him sent her heart rate off the charts. She had to swallow again, even as her cheeks burned. Fortunately it was a bit dark in the hallway, perhaps he didn't notice her blush. The only thing that didn't look right at all was the starkly white cast that covered his left arm. He hadn't put the sling on, since he wanted to take a shower.

Not knowing what to say, but feeling like she needed to fill the minutes until Brandi came back, she swallowed hard and asked, "Did you sleep well? Did the kids wake you up?"

Making a face and glancing at his arm, Matt said, "I've slept better at the station. I never realized how much I turn. Every time I did, the pillow moved and my arm fell onto the bed. Don't worry, the kids didn't wake me. It wasn't the bed's fault, either, it was very comfortable."

"I'm sorry. You need your rest!"

"The pain's not near as bad now that I'm up. I can take a pain killer now. One thing I'm really glad about, there isn't any numbness or tingling in my hand or arm. That was the biggest concern the doctor had, but everything feels normal." The twins stood on either side of him, but he held out his right arm and she stepped up in front of him. As his arm closed around her, he pushed her hair away from her ear with his nose and whispered, "I missed calling you after you were in bed. I've done it each night now." He chuckled a bit and added, "Of course, you did come in for a minute or two."

The blush moved up her neck and she felt it burning her cheeks. "Yes, that's true."

Brandi came back, her feet pounding on the stairs. Holding the bag in one hand, it was so big it trailed behind her and the rubber bands in her other hand, she said, "Here, Matt. Mommy, how does this work? This bag is so huge!" She held it up and the end trailed on the floor, even though her arm was stretched over her head.

Faith reached for the rubber bands first. "Yes, it is pretty big, but so's that cast. First, we slide a rubber band on his arm and take it all the way up past the cast, then stick his arm in the bag, gather it around the top, and pull the band down to hold it closed. We'll need to wad the rest of the bag up and put the other rubber band around the bottom so it won't get in his way, see, like this." She demonstrated, as if she did it before.

"Oh, I get it!" Brandi exclaimed. "Yeah, there won't be any water get in that."

"Nope," Matt said, "It sure won't."

Karl stood beside Matt and looked up at him. "Daddy, can I come help you get dressed when you're done in the shower?" he asked importantly. "I can get stuff for you if you want."

Matt looked down at the small boy and nodded. "You know, I think that would work real well. Why don't you meet me in that room when you hear the water go off?"

"Okay," he said, with a big grin. It was some time later when he and Matt came downstairs to join the girls of the family.

Matt pulled out his chair at the table and slumped into it. He looked at the clock and said, "I think I better call in to work now and tell them I can't work. After nine eleven there aren't many subs, but if one's available, they should have a chance to call him in. I will need to go in this afternoon when Colin comes on duty to turn in my medical leave slip, but that should be all."

"I wish I could take you, but I guess the train and the subway are best."

Brandi set her orange juice glass down and clapped her hands. "Goody! You can be home with us again tonight!"

The twins entered into the happiness and clapped their hands, but Matt waited until the noise settled. When they were quiet, he said, "Brandi, I think it's better if I go to my room at the B&B tonight." Brandi opened her mouth, but Matt raised his hand. "No, that's the way it'll be so don't argue."

For once, Brandi didn't argue or say anything, she didn't even pout, as she did sometimes. At first, Faith was astonished, but then she realized it was a very long time since that had happened. Usually, Brandi had the last word, but with love and kind words Matt stopped the discussion. Faith's heart constricted, the last time something like this happened was when Max was alive. Brandi needed a daddy actually; she needed Matt as her daddy. Would that happen? Would it be soon if it did?

She looked at the handsome man and her heart expanded with love for him. He was a big man, but he was utterly tender and loving with her and with them. As far as she was concerned, he could be theirs starting this weekend, today, this afternoon. She knew her own heart and the children were very clear, but she didn't know Matt's. He told her he loved her he called her some wonderful names, but was that enough to take them to the altar? She guessed that was a question to be answered in its own time.

Not long after lunch, Matt took the keys to Faith's car and put them in his pocket. He felt exhausted, but there were some things that must be done today. He took some time and said goodbye to the twins and Brandi; then waited until the children ran off to put his right arm around Faith. He squeezed her shoulder and she laid her head on his chest. He grumbled, "Believe me, this is not how I want to hold you! When you put your arms around me, this thing is between us and I can only put one arm around you." He sighed, "Three weeks is forever!"

She pulled back from his cast deeper into his arm, turned her head and kissed him. "It'll do, not very satisfactorily, but you aren't in the hospital because of it. I'm so glad you only have pain and there's no numbness. That can be long term or permanent."

He sought her lips again and after another kiss, he said, "Yes, I'm glad of that, hospitals are not my favorite place, believe me. I must go to the B&B then I'll go to the station. I should be home for supper." He pulled in another deep breath and said, "You do understand why I'm so adamant about not sleeping here tonight, don't you?"

"I think so, but maybe you better say."

"I know no one can see your house, but with that gossip and what we've gone through with those women from those agencies, I want everything totally above board, Love."

Faith let out another sigh. "Yes, that's probably a good thing. I have no idea why Maryann has it in for me! We've never been friends; that's for sure."

"Kind of what I figured. So, I'll see you for supper, Sweetheart."

She gave him her megawatt smile. "That's good, we'll be expecting you! Believe me, it won't be chicken nuggets either!"

He grinned his cocky fireman grin and said, "I was hoping you'd say that!"

The children went with Faith and stood on the back steps as Matt slid behind the wheel of the small car. As he backed around, he grinned, but he couldn't wave, not and steer. They watched the car until it disappeared over the rise by the big tree. He would be gone for at least three hours, probably longer. He had a long trip downtown, it could be tiring on a good day and this was not Matt's best.

As Faith felt her heart going out the driveway with him, she realized this was her opportunity to speak with the children about calling Matt their daddy, so she said, "Come on, kids, we have something important to talk about before there's any play time."

They went back inside and found their places at the table. Faith pulled out her chair. "What is it, Mommy?" Brandi asked. Her heart beat a little fast she thought maybe she knew what Mommy was going to talk about. She hadn't kept her promise because she called Matt 'Daddy' a couple of times.

Each child's eyes were focused on Faith as she looked around the table. She took a deep breath, clasped her hands together on the table and looked at the three faces looking back at her. This would be harder than she first thought. She took another deep breath and plunged ahead. "Do you remember what we talked about several days ago about calling Matt your daddy?"

Brandi lowered her head. In a little voice, she said, "Yes, we promised not to call him that until... um...."

"Umm..." Karl grunted.

Impatient to say what she needed to, Faith interrupted, "Kids, he isn't your daddy, not any one of you. You all know that. If we get married, he'll be Brandi's stepdaddy and then I think should be the first time any of you call him daddy. I know that's hard for of you, but..."

She saw the stricken look in Karin's eyes and the tears sparkling in them, so she held out her arms and Karin scrambled onto Faith's lap. Karl's face looked like a storm brewing and Brandi was biting her lower lip. "Kids," she said, much more softly, "I know you love Matt and I love him, too, very much, but he hasn't asked me to marry him. All three of you called him Daddy or Daddy Matt last night. We haven't known each other very long...." She sighed, "I really don't know what to say, kids. Believe me, I've never been so confused like this ever before. It's all new and I sure don't know how Matt feels."

"He never said not to!" Karl grumbled. "And... and all of us called him that last night. He didn't get mad!"

"I know, Karl." What else could she say?

Hopefully, Brandi looked up at her mommy and asked, "Mommy, could we ask him? Would that be okay?"

For quite a few seconds Faith sat and looked out the windows behind Brandi, before she finally said, "Yes, I think we should do that. He may be alright with it since he heard you call him that last night."

"Okay. Can we go play now?" Brandi asked, as if everything was settled. "We really want to go swing in the breeze."

After another long sigh, Faith said, "Yes, I guess so. Make sure I can see you, you know not to go over the hill."

"Yes, Mommy," there was a chorus of three. Karin wasn't saying much, but her answer was audible and that pleased Faith.

She hugged the little girl on her lap and said, "Thank you, sweethearts. It's a pretty day, go have some fun while Matt's gone." Of course, she didn't know and wouldn't ever know, but she wondered how much love the twins had gotten in their short lives. They were certainly gobbling up every bit here.

She was happy she could love them, but of course, they were such loveable children, it wasn't hard.

Matt went to the B&B and his landlady opened the door and greeted him. "Oh, my! What happened to you?"

Matt had decided not to say that a woman had done the damage, so he said, "A car door decided to take a chunk out of my arm and broke the bone. I think I'll live, though." He gave her his cocky smile.

"I should hope! You got some mail I had to sign for." She reached over the counter and pulled out a legal sized envelop. "Here, it came yesterday."

Matt held out his hand. "Thanks." He noticed the postmark as he headed up the stairs.

After closing the door, he put the envelope on the desk and looked at the nicely made bed. He hadn't made it yesterday morning, obviously the lady of the house kept the rooms clean and the linens changed as part of the price she asked. That was a welcome change from where he lived before; he had to do all of that himself. At the rooming house the laundry was in the dark, damp and dismal basement. He hated to go down there. Looked like things had changed drastically! He wouldn't complain.

He also realized as he looked at the bed that it looked much too inviting to ignore. He went to the bathroom first, but came back and fell on the bed. It didn't really matter when he arrived at the fire station, a nap couldn't hurt and after his restless night, a nap could do wonders. He jammed a pillow under his arm then even without a pain pill he fell asleep almost instantly.

He slept for a while, but then he dreamed or maybe he was in that nether region between asleep and awake. He lived every minute from the time they picked up the kids from school – from ice cream to the hospital - until he fell asleep last night. When they finally arrived back at the house, Brandi called him Daddy Matt several times, Karl called him Daddy Matt once or twice, but precious Karin had finally spoken out loud and called him Daddy. Each one of those times turned his heart over. Another scene came in clearly; there at the hospital, Faith told him she loved him. Did she really or did the circumstances force her to say the words? Well…she called him Honey, too…. a couple of times. That seemed natural enough.

He sighed, every action pointed to the fact that she loved him. She was anxious for his kisses, to have him hold her she stepped into his arms readily.

She called him 'honey,' she called him that quite a few times since she said it the first time. Of course, he called her similar names and that was because he loved her. The looks she gave him gave him a view into her soul at least that was what he thought.

How long should he wait to ask her to marry him? Had it only been eight days since they officially met? It was her second time, she had children she was responsible for.... Who knew? Even so, he wanted to ask her, to make his intentions known soon, even today. His eyes came open and he looked out the window at the sparkling, beautiful day. He felt refreshed, he realized the pain had nearly vanished and he was glad. He thought back, trying to remember when he last took a pain pill. It was before lunch. It was long enough ago that he hadn't felt the least bit impaired when he drove over. He was very glad of that.

Finally, he rolled over and sat up. He wasn't dizzy, his arm didn't hurt. He went in the bathroom and looked more closely at his face and immediately pulled out his electric razor. After a shave and combing his hair, he went back to the desk and picked up the large envelop. Carefully, he held it in his left hand and slid his finger under the flap to open it. A note and some cards fell out onto the desk.

He picked up the note which read:

> "Dear Mr. Barns;
> When I went to one of the banks to hand in the cards I was told that another two CDs were found in Miss Germain's name. You can let these mature at that bank, if you wish the date is only six weeks away, or you can cash them out. You can deal directly with the bank, their address is on the cards.
> All the rest of the cards for redemption have been delivered and your money should be in your account within ten days.
> Yours truly, Arnold B. Cochran"

Matt sighed, he was on salary with the FDNY and he had sick leave coming, but these two new CDs were even larger than any of the other single CDs. He must decide what he wanted to do with his life. He enjoyed being a fireman after he left college, but now his focus had changed, he would much rather be near this family that had adopted him, and that he loved with all his heart. At the head of the list stood a lovely lady who fit into his arms perfectly, who mothered those children just as perfectly. Would she have him? Did she care if he was a fireman or could he be something else?

A thought whirled into his mind, perhaps he should turn in his resignation today while he was there. Colin could look for his replacement. If he could get a sub, perhaps that person would work out to fill his position. He pulled his chair up to the desk, found a piece of paper in his things, clunked the cast down on the desk so his hand could hold the paper and began to write. He would hand it in along with his medical leave which the doctor gave him yesterday. He might as well get everything that was coming to him.

He knew it didn't need to be fancy, just the words saying he wanted to resign. It was not a good time, but he shrugged, was there ever a good time to leave a fire department? He folded the paper and put it in his shirt pocket, picked up his clean uniforms and the dirty one and left for the train station, then sat down on a bench on the platform and waited for the train to make the hour ride to the city. He was glad for the nap he took.

He walked in the fire station with several from his shift, but he was in jeans and a polo shirt, carrying his uniforms. Mario looked at him and asked, "What happened to you, old man?"

As they walked together, they passed the bin for dirty uniforms, so Matt tossed his in. "Hey, watch that! Call me an old man, would you? A car door bit a chunk out of my arm and broke the bone."

"Oh, man, that's bad! Colin will not like you."

"He knows already. I'm hoping he'll have you guys a sub."

"Mmm, well, look up ahead of you," he grumbled.

As a matter of fact, a person in an FDNY uniform that he didn't know, who had to be the sub was coming toward him as he spoke. She was a very shapely redhead, who also had a very striking face. The FDNY uniform she wore fit her tall frame well. Matt had to swallow, as far as he knew, she would be the first woman firefighter at this station; he hoped the men didn't razz her too much. Of course, they had dealings with women firefighters when they answered multiple alarm fires. They all knew how easy it was to be slapped with a charge of sexual harassment. It wasn't a pleasant happening, ever.

"Afternoon," he said, as he passed her on the way to the commander's office. There was no reason not to be friendly.

"Yeah," she said, hardly turning to look at him.

It occurred to him that she wouldn't know him from anybody. He wasn't in uniform, although he carried three. However, to her he was another man walking around the fire station on a Saturday afternoon. At one time he might have tried to make her acquaintance, but as he looked at her, even with red hair and a good looking face, he felt no interest. His heart was at a house beyond a big tree with a swing gently moving in the breeze or maybe it was swinging frantically with three children milling around. Either way, he would be happy to be there now, but there was business to take care of first. Possibly something Colin wouldn't like too well.

Colin was coming from his office and opened the door even before Matt could knock, so Matt didn't have to juggle his uniforms while he tried to open the door. Colin stepped back to let him in the room, then turned and closed the door. He looked significantly at the large cast and the sling on Matt's left arm, then went behind his desk and said, "You are not a sight for sore eyes, Matt Barns! What do you mean getting hurt off the job?"

Matt chuckled. "It wasn't my intent, believe me." Looking around the room for a hook to hang his uniforms on, he went to the door and hung the three hangers on the door knob. He turned back and pulled the papers from his pocket. "I brought in the medical slip, but Colin, I also brought in my resignation."

Sitting down heavily, the man said, "What was that?"

Matt came back to the desk and laid the two papers he pulled from his pocket on the desk in front of the man. "I think you heard me."

He grabbed the papers and pulled them in front of him, but before he looked at them, he said, "I do not like this, Matthew Barns, not at all! You have been one of the best men I've ever had and now you have the nerve to do this!" He cleared his throat and added, "Did you see who the powers-that-be sent as your sub for today?" He glanced down and started slowly to unfold the papers Matt placed in front of him.

"Yeah, I passed her on my way in here." He grinned at the uncomfortable man. "You will survive, Colin?"

Automatically pressing out the creases, he said, "Mmmm. I was told she will take your place until you come back and now you tell me you aren't?

I've never had a woman under me; these men have never had to deal with a woman. We may all get slapped with a sexual harassment suit and now you've sealed off the light at the end of the tunnel!"

"That's the way it goes, Sir."

"MMMMM," he growled.

After reading both papers through, he slapped one hand down on them and ran his other hand through his hair. He pulled in a breath and said, "I heard you moved out to the island, have you found work out there?"

All at once, Matt felt his knees become weak and watery, so he collapsed into the chair in front of Colin's desk. "No, not as yet, but that's a possibility. No, I've found a lady actually; she and her daughter are the ones who have the twins."

Holding up three fingers, Colin scowled as he looked at him and said, "Set me straight if I'm wrong, Friend. You are talking about a woman with, not one, not two, but three kids? and how old are these children?"

Matt chuckled. "You have it straight, Colin, a nine year old girl and five year old twins, a boy and a girl."

Shaking his head, Colin said, "You, Matt Barns, have my sympathies! You, a bachelor, are willingly taking on not one, not two, but three children under ten years of age?"

"Hey, I think it's great! The lady is my cup of tea."

Colin shook his head. "Better you than me.

"So..." Colin turned to his computer, "I suspect you want this resignation to take effect after you've used up any vacation time and any sick time you have coming, is that right?"

"You're a mind reader, Colin."

Working his fingers on the keys, Colin chuckled. "No, I don't think so, but I do have some business sense about me." He turned the monitor so Matt could see the screen. "You healthy horse! It looks like you have thirty days of sick time and nearly three weeks of vacation time. It's been ages since you took vacation!" he exclaimed. "Well, I suppose that's to be expected, you're from where is it?"

Matt shrugged, and said, "I'm single, remember? No sibs, my parents live in Montana, what's the attraction?"

Colin shrugged. "None, I guess. So you want the pay in a lump sum to be issued on the next payday or stretched out?"

Matt shrugged. "Doesn't matter, I guess a lump sum will be okay, it all goes into my account anyway. It'll be taken care of in one shot." Matt grinned at his boss. "It'll all go in with the hundreds of other dollars I've made over the years." He determined as he wrote out his resignation he wouldn't tell Colin and certainly none of the other fire fighters what he was now worth. When he learned the approximate worth of the estate, he decided to keep that knowledge close to his chest. So far, only the lawyer knew for sure. And to Matt's great satisfaction, he was a long ways off.

As an aside, but loud enough Matt heard, Colin shook his head and said, "Man, you lived through the most horrendous happening this city has known in recent years and never flinched. You worked well over thirty hours that day, came back the next day to work some more, but you break your arm off duty and you're out of here. Tell me, sir, what's wrong with this picture?"

Matt stood up and held out his hand. "Colin, that's not really the reason, but it'll do. Give my best to all the guys... oh, and gal, too."

"Mmmm. Get out of here and break a leg, too."

"Thanks. Shall I send you an invitation?"

Colin looked up, surprised, at the man at the door. "Wedding invitation?"

"Yeah, as I see it, if she agrees, it'll be before winter."

Colin moved from behind his desk and slapped his friend on the back. "Why, you old son of a gun! Of course! Send one. I'll post it in the lounge. I'll bet there'll be a delegation that'll come to see this jock tied up in knots!"

Matt's eyes twinkled as he looked at his friend. "I'll put you on the list. Hey, I think she's much too pretty to be a spider to tie me up in knots."

Colin chuckled. "We'll be looking for that lovely piece of mail any day. Best of luck."

"Thanks, Colin."

The children were outside playing. Faith looked out her kitchen window and all three were having fun in the sandbox. It was such a beautiful day, she decided to hurry and finish her work and join them outside. The phone rang, so she dried her hands and went to answer. It never occurred to her to let the machine pick up, since the woman from the children's agency called and then come by yesterday. She was a friendly person, so she hurried from the sink to the portable phone on the wall.

When she answered, the voice didn't identify itself, but said, angrily, "Do you still have those twins, Faith?"

Taken back by the bluntness and harshness of the words, Faith's heart began thumping hard as she recognized the woman's voice. Of course, she had nothing to hide and after licking her lips, she said, "Why yes, Maryann, of course, why would I not have them? They came to me through the foundling ministry of the church."

Hardly letting Faith finish speaking, her words exploded into the phone, "It's illegal! I've checked into it and it's illegal!"

"It is? Who did you check with, Maryann? We saw several people from two different agencies yesterday and none of them told us that."

Maliciously, she asked, "Who's we?"

"Pastor Jim went with me...." She thought about it for a minute and decided she didn't want to say any more, besides Maryann would only use anything she said against her, so instead, she asked, "Who did you check with, Maryann?"

It seemed Faith had taken a little wind out of Maryann's sails. "Well... well, a friend of mine knows a woman in one of those agencies...."

"That wouldn't be Maranda Fulton with child *protection*, would it?"

Clearing her throat, Maryann said reluctantly, "It could be."

Trying for that saccharin sweet tone that was very foreign to her, Faith said, "You know, we met with her for a short meeting, but nothing she said led us to believe the foundling ministry of the church is illegal, after all, Pastor wouldn't do anything illegal. You have a good day, Maryann!" Faith hung up knowing that the woman was taking a breath, planning to say more. As Faith's thumb covered the disconnect button she heard her blustering, so Faith pushed the button quickly and hurried out the front door. She was sure the phone would ring again soon. The woman wouldn't give up that easily, she knew, but she would not be available to answer!

The door was closing behind her as the phone rang again. Faith pulled in a deep breath. "Can that woman truly be a Christian?" she whispered.

FIFTEEN

WANTING TO BE ALONE FOR A FEW MINUTES, AND CERTAINLY NOT WANTING TO have to endure another tongue-lashing from the same woman after that conversation, Faith was glad she made it outside before she even had to listen to the answering machine. She took a deep breath and let it out slowly so her heart-rate would slow down to normal and hurried down the drive. It was Saturday and the mail usually came earlier than on the weekdays. She opened the box and pulled out the few pieces that were there.

All but one was junk mail, but the other piece was her phone bill. She turned back from the road and went to the swing. If the children went looking for her, they could see her sitting on the swing. She hadn't had a swing in a very long time, so she pushed off. She pumped her feet and legs; it felt good to be moving in the warm, sunny air. It was such a long time since she was on a swing she forgot how good it felt. She probably shouldn't let it go that long again. Pumping her legs like this was probably good exercise, too. She sighed, totally enjoying herself. Why let the kids have all the fun?

Fifteen minutes later, that was where the children found her, as she sailed back and forth through the breeze, her hair blowing. Giggling, Brandi said, "Mommy! You're swinging!"

Making her legs go and pumping hard, Faith said, "Yes, so I am!"

"How come?" Karl asked. "You're too big!"

"Uh uh," Karin said immediately, "She's Mommy, she's not too big. She can swing on our swing any time she wants!" she continued fiercely.

Finally, even though she didn't really want to stop, Faith dragged her feet and the swing stopped. "Did you guys want something?"

Now that she was stopped, the three crowded around her. "Yeah,

Mommy," Brandi said, "we were thinking. If we gotta wait until you and Matt get married, why don't you ask him at supper to marry you and then we can call him daddy right away." She nodded to both Karl and Karin. "We all think that's the way to do it."

Trying not to let her face show anything, even though her neck felt scorched, she said, "I see. You think that's the way to do it, is that it?"

"Yup!" Karl answered solemnly, nodding and slapping his fists on his hips. "You're our mommy and we want Matt for our daddy. And... and you gotta tell him! It's real 'portant." He said the words as if it was life and death. From his body language, yesterday was when she should have spoken those words.

Faith's heart constricted at the little boy's words. She knew he wanted a real daddy, any boy, aged five or fifteen needed a daddy. She wondered how hard it would be to adopt these orphaned children. However, she didn't want to make too much of Karl's words, so she said, "But it's the man who's supposed to ask the lady to marry him!" Faith looked from one solemn face to another. She sighed, "That's how my mom raised me. She said, it's the man's place."

Karin came close, then flopped on the ground and let out a big sigh. Faith looked at her, concerned. "What's the matter, Karin? What was that big sigh about? Are you all tired out?"

Brandi had her mouth open, but Faith shook her head slightly, so she closed it. Finally, Karin stood up and came over right beside Faith and put her hand on Faith's leg. With those big solemn brown eyes looking straight at Faith, she said, "Mommy, you gotta do it, 'cause Matt's a man and he don't know too much about this kind of stuff."

Faith managed to keep a straight face until now, but she threw her arms around the little girl and laughed. She picked her up and hugged her and kissed her cheek before she said, "Karin, you're precious! It was only a week ago yesterday that you guys came to me and Brandi introduced Matt to me. Let's wait for a couple more days and see if Matt can figure it out. Will that be okay?"

Nodding, without any hint of a smile, Karin's big eyes looked at her solemnly and she said, "Yeah, I guess. He is pretty smart for a man."

Faith jumped off the swing and looked at the children, wanting to change the subject. "Okay, I've had my swing, who wants me to push them? It's such a perfect day; we can't let this swing go to waste!"

"Me!" Karin squealed and grabbed the rope closest to her.

Faith's eyes were twinkling, she couldn't remember having this much fun in a very long time. "Okay, I'll give Karin a push!"

She pushed Karin one time and Karl barged ahead of Brandi and said, "I'm next!"

Matt decided there was no reason to stay around the fire station once his business with Colin was finished. His money would be deposited on the appropriate day, so why stick around? Besides, with the shift change everyone had their chores; they wouldn't stand around to talk to someone who didn't need to be there. He did salute Mario as he went by, but the man was on a mission and only nodded.

Matt hurried out into the sunshine and made his way to the entrance to the subway. In only a few minutes he was headed back to Thomaston. He decided once his last pay hit the Manhattan bank to open an account in his new hometown and close out the one here in the up-town bank. He couldn't think of any good reason why he should keep that account open. As of right now he had no ties to the over populated borough of Manhattan. He had no great affection for the borough either.

When he left the train in Thomaston, he went inside and found a newspaper holder. There was one paper left, so he put in his money and bought it. He took it to the car, opened the door and sat down, leaving the door open until it cooled down a little. He shuffled the pages until he found the classifieds. He knew he couldn't do anything for several weeks. The cast on his arm was too gigantic to do much. However, maybe he'd get an inspiration into something he could do when he was able. Just because he was now financially independent, he would not sit around and let life pass him by. His dad had taught him a fine work ethic, from today on, it would be something other than firefighting. Besides, he'd go bonkers or at the very least, drive Faith bonkers, if he didn't occupy himself in some way.

On the second page of the section there was a huge ad:

PUBLIC REAL ESTATE AUCTION
SEPTEMBER 29 AT 10:00 A.M.
THOMASTON COURTHOUSE
APARTMENT BUILDINGS, LAND, HOUSES.

Matt's imagination went wild. He had money to spend, he could buy some buildings and when his arm was back to normal, he could hire some help and get started working on whatever needed to be done to make them livable. If he wanted to sell them, fine, if not, he could rent them. Whatever, it would give him something to do. He folded the paper and laid it on the seat, closed the door and headed for home.

Matt's heart was light as he made the turn onto the street where Faith's driveway turned off. He made the turn onto the driveway and almost immediately caught his breath. There on the slight rise were the four people he loved the most. Karin sat on the swing, her head thrown back, her hair streaming out and a grin on her lips was a mile wide. Her feet were stretched out in front of her and Faith was pushing her. Karl and Brandi both leaned against the tree, but when they heard the car, they turned and raced down the bank.

Matt pulled up beside the tree and stopped. He didn't need to worry about rolling down the window, as soon as he stopped, his door flew open and two children were both talking at once. Their excitement bubbled over and they nearly clambered into the car onto his lap. The only thing that kept them outside the car was the cast and the steering wheel.

With a grin that stretched from ear to ear, Brandi said, "You missed it! We found Mommy swinging a few minutes ago."

"Mommy?"

"Uh huh. She was going as high as Karin! She was funny!"

Still more solemn than any boy his age should be, Karl said, "She's too big to swing on our swing!"

Matt stepped out and tussled his hair. "Come on, Karl, big people can do kid stuff. You think Mommy shouldn't have fun?"

Brandi was a few steps ahead of them, going back to the swing. Karl looked up at Matt and reached for his hand before he said, "Yeah, but she should have fun with you."

Matt swallowed. *My thought exactly.* He cleared his throat and said out loud, "Mommy and I had fun the other day when we walked down on the beach."

"How come we didn't get to go?"

"It was while you were in school."

"Can we go sometime?"

"Maybe, but it's late September, it's going to get cold pretty soon."

"Not before we go to the beach!" he said, stoutly.

"We'll see, Son."

"We never been to the beach," he informed Matt.

"Then," Matt declared, "we must do it soon."

"Good!"

The opportunity never came up, perhaps the kids forgot, but they never asked Matt if they could call him daddy. It was a regular night; the kids took their baths Matt took Karl and a storybook into his room, while Faith gathered the girls for their story. Matt loved this time when he read to Karl, he was learning about the Bible right along with him. God had done so much for him on September eleven. His heart was full. How could he thank Him for it all?

Soon, the lights were out in the two bedrooms without any protests. The children had a happy, full play day. After closing the doors, Matt took Faith's hand as they went downstairs for a few hugs and kisses. Faith went to the kitchen and brought back two mugs full of hot chocolate with a marshmallow on top. She handed one to Matt, then sat down close to his right side. After a few sips, he set his mug on the coffee table.

Putting his arm around her, he said, "Love, I made some changes today in the time I was gone. I hope you don't mind."

"What changes?"

"I'm no longer a fireman."

She sat up and looked at him. "Why not?"

"My heart's not in it. I want to be here." He pulled her more tightly against him and looked into her eyes. The love he felt for her overwhelmed him. After a kiss, he asked, "Remember that express mail envelope?" When she nodded, he said, "I received an inheritance from a great aunt. I hardly knew her, but it was quite significant, so I'll do something else, something here in Thomaston."

Sliding her arms around his waist, she laid her head on his chest. "Oh, Matt, oh, that's great! I'm excited for you!"

After a long kiss, he took his hand away from around her and fumbled in the pocket on his shirt for something that didn't take up much space. When he had it in his right hand, he looked up at Faith and grinned. He obviously felt he triumphed even with the cast on his arm.

"Sweetheart," he said, softly and waited for her to look at him, "could I ask you to marry me? I love you with all my heart and all my being."

Happy tears glistened in her eyes, but didn't fall. "Oh, Matt, oh, Honey, yes! Yes! As soon as possible! I love you, so much!"

He moved his fingers so that he held a beautiful, sparkling diamond up for her to see, but he asked, "Is there anyone I should ask?"

Her tongue in her cheek, she said, "The children?"

He saw the twinkling in her eyes and grinned. "You know, I really don't think that'll be a problem, do you?"

"No, not at all, Honey."

EPILOGUE

IT WAS THE THIRD SATURDAY IN OCTOBER. MATT'S CAST WAS GONE AND INDIAN summer was upon them. Many of the church ladies got together to make this celebration an exceptionally happy one. There were white chairs set up on the lawn and some of the church men had to set more up as more and more cars came. People wondered who would sit on Matt's side of the aisle besides his parents who made a special trip from the ranch in Montana, but there were dozens of uniformed firemen who came. Colin lead the delegation. He made sure Matt and Faith had chosen their wedding date when his former colleagues would be off duty. Matt's one stipulation was that he not bring them all on a fire engine.

Marcia brought her keyboard and she sat under the big tree. As she started to play, Pastor Jim led Matt and Matt's best man, Karl soon-to-be-Barns and Colin, his groomsman across the driveway. When the music started, Karin sprinkled petals from the garden flowers that still bloomed in the back yard all the way from the house, down the aisle, to in front of Pastor Jim. Brandi, a cherubic smile on her face, led her mommy to the place in front of all the people, as her maid of honor.

Marcia had to play one handed for several bars of music as she wiped two tears from her face. Faith was a beautiful bride, her face radiant, as she slipped her hand around Matt's elbow. Matt's eyes saw nothing, no one, except the lady who came to stand beside him. He was a big man, but he had a big heart and those he loved were close around him. He was content. He had been alone, but he found what he sought amid tragedy on nine eleven, now he was happy, his arms and heart full.

Time no longer stood still.